RATNER'S STAR

Don DeLillo received the Award in Literature from the American Academy and Institute of Arts and Letters in 1984. He has won the American Book Award, and the 1989 *Irish Times*, Aer Lingus International Fiction Prize for his novel, *Libra*. His latest novel, *Mao II* is published by Jonathan Cape.

BY THE SAME AUTHOR

Americana
End Zone
Great Jones Street
Players
Running Dog
The Names
White Noise
Libra
Mao II

Don DeLillo

RATNER'S STAR

VINTAGE

TO MARC AND CLAUDIA

VINTAGE

20 Vauxhall Bridge Road, London SW1V 2SA

London Melbourne Sydney Auckland Johannesburg
and agencies throughout the world

First published by Alfred A. Knopf, Inc., 1976
Vintage edition 1991

Copyright © 1976 by Don DeLillo

A portion of this book was first published in *Esquire*

Printed and bound in Great Britain by
Cox & Wyman Ltd, Reading

ISBN 0 09 992840 X

ADVENTURES
Field Experiment Number One

1

SUBSTRATUM

Little Billy Twillig stepped aboard a Sony 747 bound for a distant land. This much is known for certain. He boarded the plane. The plane was a Sony 747, labeled as such, and it was scheduled to arrive at a designated point exactly so many hours after takeoff. This much is subject to verification, pebble-rubbed (*khalix, calculus*), real as the number one. But ahead was the somnolent horizon, pulsing in the dust and fumes, a fiction whose limits were determined by one's perspective, not unlike those imaginary quantities (the square root of minus-one, for instance) that lead to fresh dimensions.

3

The plane taxied to a remote runway. Billy was strapped into a window seat. Next to him in the aircraft's five-two-three-two-five seating pattern was a man reading a boating magazine and next to the man were one, two, three little girls. This was as much nextness as Billy cared to explore for the moment. He was fourteen years old, smaller than most people that age. Examined at close range he might be said to feature an uncanny sense of concentration, a fixed intensity that countervailed his noncommittal brown eyes and generally listless manner. Viewed from a distance he gave the impression that he wasn't entirely at peace with his present surroundings, cagily slouched in his seat, someone newly arrived in this pocket of technology and stale light. The sound of the miniaturized propulsion system grew louder and soon the plane was in the air. Its angle of ascent was severe enough to frighten the boy, who had never been on an airplane before. With Sweden at war, he had received his Nobel Prize in a brief ceremony on a lawn in Pennyfellow, Connecticut, traveling to and from that locale in the back seat of his father's little Ford.

It was the first Nobel Prize ever given in mathematics. The work that led to the award was understood by only three or four people, all mathematicians, of course, and it was at their confidential urging that the Nobel committee, traditionally at a total loss in this field, finally settled on Twillig, born Terwilliger, William Denis Jr., premature every inch of him, a snug fit in a quart mug.

His father (to backtrack briefly) was a third-rail inspector in the New York subway system. When the boy was seven the elder Terwilliger (known to most as Babe) took him into the subways for the sheer scary fun of it, a sort of Theban initiation. This was, after all, the place where Babe spent nearly half his conscious life. It seemed to him perfectly natural that a father should introduce his lone son to the idea that existence tends to be nourished from below, from the fear level, the plane of obsession, the starkest tract of awareness. In Babe's mind there was also a notion that the boy would show him increased respect, having seen the region where he toiled, smelled the dankness and felt the steel. They rode the local for a while, standing at the very front of the first car to get the motorman's viewpoint. Then they got off and went along a

4

platform in a deserted station in the South Bronx and into a small tool room and down some steps and along a passageway and through a door and onto the tracks, where they walked in silence toward the next station. It was a Sunday and therefore reasonably safe; these were express tracks and no such trains ran on Sunday along this particular line. A local went by, however, one track over, shooting slow blue sparks. In this incandescent shower Billy thought he saw a rat. Wide bend ahead. For comic shock effect, Babe made a series of crazy people's faces—tongue hanging out, eyes bulging, neck twisted and stiff. Within ten yards of the next station he singled out a key from the ring of many keys he carried and then opened a small door in the blackened wall and led his son into another tool room and then onto the platform. And that was all or almost all. A walk down a stretch of dark track. On the way home they sat in the next-to-last car. A tripping device failed to work and their train, braking late, ran into the rear of a stalled work train. Billy found himself on the floor of the car. Ahead was stunned metal, a buckled frame for bodies intersecting in thick smoke. Then there was a moment of superlunar calm. In this interval, just before he started crying, he realized there is at least one prime between a given number and its double.

The stewardess arrived, driving a motorized food cart. Billy preferred looking out the window to eating. There was nothing to see, just faded space, but the sense of an environment somewhere beyond this pressurized chunk of tubing, a distant whisper of the biosphere, made him feel less constricted. He tried to think in a context of Sumerian *gesh*-time, hoping to convince himself this would make the journey seem one fourth as long as it really was. That wedge system they used. Powers of sixty. Sixty a vertical wedge. Sixty shekels to a mina. Sixty minas to a talent. Gods numbered one to sixty. He'd recently read (handwriting cunning and urgent) that the sixty-system was about four thousand years old, obviously far from extinct. More clever than most, those Mesopotamians. Natural algebraic capacity. Beady-eyed men in ziggurats predicting eclipse.

He squeezed past the man and his little girl tribe and went back to find the toilet. There were eleven, all in use. As he waited in the passageway between doors he was approached by a large rosy man nearly palpitating with the kind of relentless affability that the experience of travel never fails to induce in some people.

"My mouth says hello."

"H'o."

"I'm Eberhard Fearing," the man said. "Haven't I seen you in the media?"

"I was on television a couple of times."

"I was duly impressed. You demonstrated an absolute mastery as I recall. 'Brilliant' doesn't begin to say it. Loved your technical phraseology in particular. Mathematicians are a weird breed. I know because I use them in my work. Planning and procedures. Let's hear you say a thing or two."

"I'm not brilliant in person."

"I want to assure you that I admire your kind of intellect. Hard, cold and cutting, sir. What's your destination?"

"Not allowed to say."

"Flying right on through or deplaning along the way?"

"I do not comment."

"Where's your spirit of adventure?"

"First time in the air."

"Nervous, is it? Let's hear some mathematics then. Seriously, what say?"

"I don't think so for the time being."

"No room for cunctation in any line of work. But yours especially. Gifts can vanish without warning. Reach sixteen and it's all gone. Nothing ahead but a completely normative life. Shouldn't you be smiling?"

"Why?"

"We're strangers on a plane," Fearing said. "We're having a friendly talk about this and that. Calls for smiles, don't you think? That's what travel's all about. Supposed to release all that pent-up friendliness."

A door opened and from one of the toilets limped an elderly woman with a plum-colored growth behind her left ear. He hesitated before entering the same toilet, afraid she had left behind some unnamable

6

horror, the result of a runaway gland. Old people's shitpiss. Diseased in this case. Discolored beyond recognition. Possibly unflushed. Finally he stepped in, determined to escape Eberhard Fearing, bolting himself into the stainless-steel compartment and noting in the mirror how unlike himself he looked, neat enough in sport coat and tie but unusually pale and somehow tired, as though this manufactured air were threatening his very flesh, drawing out needed chemicals and replacing them with evil solvents made in New Jersey. Around him at varying heights were slots, nozzles, vents and cantilevered receptacles; issuing from some of these was a lubricated hum that suggested elaborate recycling and a stingy purity, this local sound merely part of a more pervasive vibration, the remote systaltic throb of the aircraft itself.

Cunctation.

Something about that word implied a threat. It wasn't like a foreign word as much as an extraterrestrial linguistic unit or a vibratory disturbance just over the line that ends this life. Some words frightened him slightly in their intimations of compressed menace. "Gout." "Ohm." "Ergot." "Pulp." These seemed organic sounds having little to do with language, meaning or the ordered contours of simple letters of the alphabet. Other words had a soothing effect. Long after he'd acquainted himself with curves of the seventh degree he came across a dictionary definition of the word "cosine," discovering there a beauty no less formal than he'd found in the garment-folds of graphed equations (although there were grounds for questioning the absolute correctness of the definition):

The abscissa of the endpoint of an arc of a unit circle centered at the origin of a two-dimensional coordinate system, the arc being of length x *and measured counterclockwise from the point* (1, 0) *if* x *is positive; or clockwise if* x *is negative.*

He undid his zipper, bent his knees to rearrange a snarled section of underwear and then slipped his dangle (as he'd been taught to call it) out of his pants. Words and numbers. Writing and calculating. Tablethouses between two rivers. *Dubshar nished.* Scribe of counting. How did it go? *Aš min eš limmu ia aš imin ussu ilimmu u.* Ever one more number, individual and distinct, fixed in place, absolutely whole. He tapped

7

the underside of his dangle in an effort to influence whatever membranous sac was storing his urine. Oldest known numerals. What had he read in the manuscript? Pre-cuneiform. Marked with tapered stylus on clay slabs. Number as primitive intuition. Number self-generated. Number developing in the child's mind spontaneously and nonverbally. Whole numbers viewed as the spark of all ancient mathematical ideas. How did it go? "The fact that such ideas consistently outlive the civilizations that give rise to them and the languages in which they are expressed might prompt a speculation or two concerning prehistoric man and *his* mathematics. What predated the base of sixty? Calendric notations on bone tools? Toes and fingers? Or something far too grand for the modern mind to imagine. Although the true excavation is just beginning, it's not too early to prepare ourselves for some startling reversals." Clockwise positive. Counterclockwise negative.

Eventually he managed to dispatch a few feeble drops of urine into what appeared to be a bottomless cistern. Then he washed his hands and combed his hair, using the large teeth of the comb because he believed wide furrows made him look older. A bandage covered a small cut on his thumb and he peeled it off now, sucking briefly at the crude wound and then flushing the bandage down the germless well, imagining for a moment an identical plastic strip floating to the surface of the water that filled a stainless-steel wash basin in a toilet on an airliner above an antipodal point. He double-checked his zipper. For the mirror he poured forth a stereotyped Oriental smile, an antismile really, one he'd learned from old movies on TV. He added a few formal nods and then unlocked the door and eased out of the tiny silver cubicle.

In his seat he rolled his tie carefully all the way up to the knotted part and then watched it drop down again, doing this over and over, using both hands to furl and then timing the release precisely, left and right hand opening at the same instant. After a long time the plane landed for a refueling stop. When they were in the air again he went sideways up the aisle past the toilets and into the rock garden. The area was crowded. He sat in a little sling, trying hard not to stare at this or that woman arranged in the odd deltoid chairs that were scattered about, ladies poised for worldly conversation, and he wondered what there was about high-altitude travel that made them seem so mysterious and avail-

ADVENTURES

able, two stages to contemplate, knees high and tight, bodies partly
reclined and set back from the radiant legs. All around him people were
solemnly embalmed in their own attitudes of conviviality. They drank
and gestured, filling the paths of the rock garden. Occasionally a particular face would collapse toward a kind of wild intelligence so that
within the larger block of features a shrunken head appeared, aflame
with revelation. Inner levels. Subsets. Underlying layers. In a chair
nearby was a woman in her fifties, wide-eyed and petite. She wore a
bright frock and her hair was cut straight across the forehead at eyebrow level. For her age she was the *cutest* woman he'd ever seen.
Glancing at the travel folder she was reading, he was able to make out
the large type on the front cover.

ANCIENT TREASURES / MODERN PLEASURES

A LIFETIME OF NEW RELATIONSHIPS IN TWELVE FROLICSOME DAYS
AND ONE DANGEROUSLY SENSUAL NIGHT

She looked up, smiled and pointed to a plaid shoulder bag that sat
drooping between her feet. He tried to respond with an expression that
would make her think he had misinterpreted her gesture as a simple
greeting that required no further communication.

"Basenji," she said.

"Translate please."

"I smuggled him aboard in my bag. Such a good puppy. I'm sure
he'd like to say hello to you. 'Hi, pally. Where ya headed?' "

"I make no reply."

"You're not an Amerasian, are you?"

"What's that?"

"What they used to call war kids," she said. "GI papa, native mama.
They sold for five hundred dollars in Bangkok. 'And that's no phony
baloney, bub.' You're about the right age for an Amerasian. My name's
Mrs. Roger Laporte. 'Hi, I'm Barnaby Laporte. Whereabouts you go to
school, good buddy?' "

She listened to every word of his reply with the eager obedience of
someone about to undergo major surgery. When he finished telling her
about the Center, she leaned toward the shoulder bag and patted it. In

9

addition to being cute, Mrs. Laporte had a distinct shimmer of kindness about her. It was amazing how often kind-looking people turned out to be crazy. He wondered gravely whether things had reached such a bad state that only crazy people attempted commonplace acts of kindness, that the crazy and the kind were one and the same. When she spoke on behalf of the dog, she tucked her head into her body and squeaked. It was the cutest thing about her.

"You must be very lonely," she said. "Spending all your time with grownups and doing all that research behind closed doors without the sunshine and exercise your body needs for someone your age. Mr. Laporte went to night school."

He hadn't clipped his toenails in a while and he realized that when he moved the toes of his right foot up and down, one particularly long nail scratched against the inside of his Orlon-acrylic sock. He passed the time allowing his toenail to catch and scrape, making a tiny growl. He wanted to sit somewhere else but was sure Mrs. Laporte would say something the moment he got to his feet. A man fell out of a hammock, his cocktail glass shattering on one of the rocks in the garden. If the dog's called Barnaby, did she name her kids Fido and Spot? Her large eyes blinked twice and then she hugged herself and shrugged, smiling in his direction—a series of gestures he readily interpreted as perkiness for its own sake. Of course that left him the problem of figuring out what to do in return.

"So that's a dog in there you sneaked aboard," he said. "What happens if it barks?"

"Basenji," she said.

He found a dark lounge and went inside. Two men sat at a table playing an Egyptian board game. Squares of equal size. Penalties levied. Element of chance. Billy recognized the game; he'd seen it played at the Center by colleagues of his. Numerous geometric pieces. Single bird-shaped piece. He thought of the "number beasts" of that time—animals used to symbolize various quantities. Tadpole equaled one hundred thousand because of the huge swarms that populated the mud when the waters of the Nile retreated after seasonal flooding. Men called rope-stretchers had surveyed the unplotted land, using knots to measure equal units. Taxation and geometry. In the dimness Eberhard Fearing gradually assumed effective form. Legs walking left.

"Good to see you."

"Right."

"Absolutely correct."

"Good."

He had a passing knowledge of the mathematical texts of the period. Problem of seven people who each have seven cats which each consume seven mice which each had nibbled seven ears of barley from each of which would have grown seven measures of corn. Legs walking left were a plus sign on a papyrus scroll.

"How was the bathroom?" Fearing said.

"I liked it."

"Mine was first-rate."

"Pretty nice."

"Some plane."

"The size."

"Exactly," Fearing said. "You've hit on it. I was telling a gal back there all about you. She'd really like to hear you hold forth. What say I get her and make a threesome out of it."

"I may not be here later."

"Where will you be?"

"I may have to meet some people."

"Just tell me where. We'll have a get-together."

"I'm not sure they're aboard," he said. "See, the thing of it is I'm not sure they're aboard."

"In other words you made an appointment beforehand to see these people. Before you even got on the plane."

"Right."

"Certain section of the aircraft at a certain time."

"Near the toilets."

"And now you're not even sure they're aboard."

"Right."

"These people of yours."

"That's the thing."

11

"How many of them?" Fearing said.

"Could be four, could be more."

"What are they—mathematicians?"

"Some yes, some other."

"Near the toilets."

"I just inspected," Billy said. "They're not there yet."

"I admire your intellect, sir. Admire it mightily."

"I heard that. Good to hear."

"Because there is no commodity we're shorter of than intellectual know-how. A man like me understands that. Nice talking to you. Ever find yourself nearby, why, drop on in. I'm near everything. Great churches. A lot of parking. Bring your associates if they ever turn up."

"They'll like to come."

"I use you people in my work."

The men at the board appeared to be on the verge of sleep. No theoretical reasoning or basic theorems. The practical science of physical arrangement. Sense of mass. Scientists still probing limestone blocks with radar to discover what's buried in those pyramids. He thought of the obelisk in Central Park and wondered if he'd ever get to examine an actual fragment of sacred writing.

Directions for knowing all dark things.

The plane flew above the weather. He went to sit alone in a rear area behind equipment racks and anticrash icons. A stressless hour passed. Or maybe four such hours. He'd forgotten which motion he was using to stroke through time, minute or *gesh*. This part of the airplane had apparently not been used for a while. It was dusty and cramped, its true dimensions concealed by an intricate series of partitions. Real plastic here as opposed to the synthetic updated variations in the forward areas. A sort of Old Quarter. He put both feet up on the front of the seat and hunkered, noting the array of digits molded into the chair, a set of individual polymerized bumps located between his shoes—0ᄂᄅᄃᄐᄐ—such that, rightsided and divided by a scrambled set of its own first three digits, yields a result just one number away from the divisor; such that digits of divisor and result match digits of original array (save one); such that each consecutive number (divisor and result) is the sum of the cubes of its digits. In fact nothing bored him

12

more than playful calculations. Yet his capacity to fathom the properties of the integers was such that he sometimes found himself watching a number unfold to reveal the reproductive structure within. Eberhard Fearing. It was only a partial lie he'd told that travel-happy man. A meeting *was* scheduled to take place (person or persons unknown), although not at this altitude. He closed his eyes. Jetliner passing through the sphere of vapor, through the blank amalgam of gases, moisture and particulate matter. Bloated metal ritually marked. A loud buzzer sounded.

He calculated with the ease of a coastal bird haunting an updraft. But beauty was mere scenery unless it was severe, adhering strictly to a set of consistent inner codes, and this he clearly perceived, the arch-reality of pure mathematics, its austere disposition, its links to simplicity and permanence; the formal balances it maintains, inevitability adjacent to surprise, exactitude to generality; the endless disdain of mathematics for what is slack in the character of its practitioners and what is trivial and needlessly repetitive in their work; its precision as a language; its claim to necessary conclusions; its pursuit of connective patterns and significant form; the manifold freedom it offers in the very strictures it persistently upholds.

Mathematics made sense.

He lowered his feet to the floor, eyes still closed, a circumstance that gave anyone watching enough time to determine what it was that made the boy appear an adept of concentration—simply his physical stillness, the seeming compression of his frame into a more comprehensive object. It was a stillness unaffected by the shifting of his feet and yet completely obliterated the second his eyes came open. This latter act served to release upon the world a presence essentially seriocomic in nature, that of early adolescence trying to conceal itself in a fold of apathy.

The buzzer sounded once more and a light flashed on and off. He returned to his seat. The plane landed to refuel again and this time he was one of the passengers getting off. He made his way through a dense crowd of people, none of whom seemed to be going anywhere or meeting anyone. He wondered if they lived at the airport. Maybe there was no room for them in the city and they came out here to settle, sleeping

13

in oil drums in unused hangars, getting up at sunrise and heading indoors to loiter. He reached his destination, a special boarding gate in an isolated part of the airport. Two men were there to meet him. They'd already collected his suitcase and now led him aboard another plane, much smaller than the first, no other passengers, some space to yawn and sprawl. His escorts were named Ottum and Hof. The flight was relatively short and after the aircraft set down on a deserted landing strip the boy and two men walked to a waiting limousine. Billy had the enormous back seat to himself. As Ottum started the car, his partner turned and pointed to a small sign taped to the folded-over underside of one of the jumpseats.

Please refrain from smoking out of consideration for
the driver of this vehicle, who suffers from:

☐ Hypertension	☐ Walking pneumonia
☐ Tuberculosis	☐ Smoke-related allergies
☑ Asthma	☐ Labored breathing
☐ Bronchial asthma	☑ Other

"We'll be there in twenty some odd minutes," Ottum said.

"This a Cadillac, this car?"

"None other."

"It came almost as a shock to see it. That's why I ask. Way in the middle of nowhere."

"No mistaking one of these vehicles," Hof said. "Custom job from top to bottom. What we call a meticulously customized motor vehicle. It's a Cadillac all right."

"The Rolls-Royce of automobiles," Ottum said.

Billy had been instructed not to tell anyone where he was going. There wasn't much he could have said, to Eberhard Fearing or anyone else, even if he'd wanted to. He knew the name of the place but very little about it. Apparently the people in charge were still defining their objectives and therefore did not release information except in minimum trickles. As to the reason his specific presence was considered essential, not a word had been spoken.

"Is this thing bulletproof?"

14

"Absolutely, top to bottom."

"I never thought so. I just asked the question because you think of a limousine this big as might as well having all the extras."

"It's for the top people," Hof said.

"Did it ever get shot at?"

"Course not."

"It's not a bubbletop, I notice."

"He notices," Hof said.

"I heard," Ottum said.

"Not a bubbletop, he notices."

"Two terrific sense of humors."

"Be a kid."

"I was only talking back."

"Just be a kid," Hof said.

He tried to revel in the expensive pleasures of the back seat, toying with gadgets and scraping the soles of his shoes on the edges of the collapsed jumpseats, freeing himself of whatever foreign matter had accumulated there recently.

"I didn't go through customs."

"We took care of that," Hof said. "You're a special case. It's a courtesy they extend to special cases."

They traveled over bad roads on a gray plain. He saw one sign of life, an old man with a counting stalk. Must be for tourists, he thought. In time a sequined point appeared on the seam of land and air.

"Maybe you don't know it," Hof said, "but you're more or less a legend in your own time."

They were coming to something. He knew immediately it was something remarkable. Rising over the land and extending far across its breadth was a vast geometric structure, not at first recognizable as something designed to house or contain or harbor, simply a formulation, an expression in systematic terms of a fifty-story machine or educational toy or two-dimensional decorative object. The dominating shape seemed to be a cycloid, that elegant curve traced by a fixed point on the circumference of a circle rolling along a straight line, the line in this case being the land itself. His attention was diverted for a moment as

15

the car passed through a field of dish antennas, hundreds of them, surprisingly small every one. Closer now he was able to see that the cycloid was not complete, having no summit or topmost arc, and that wedged inside the figure by a massive V-form steel support was the central element of the entire structure, a slowly rotating series of intersecting rings that suggested a medieval instrument of astronomy.

In all, the structure was about sixteen hundred feet wide, six hundred feet high. Welded steel. Reinforced concrete. Translucent polyethylene. Aluminum, glass, mylar, sunstone. He noticed that particular surfaces seemed to deflect natural light, causing perspectives to disappear and making it necessary to look away from time to time. Point line surface solid. Feeling of solar mirage. And still a building. A thing full of people.

Field Experiment Number One.

The car stopped next to some construction equipment. He got out, fascinated most of all by the slowly moving focal component, the structure's medieval element. Blinding silver on both sides. Streaks and textures elusive in their liquid iridescence. But the huge central sphere, propped by the V-steel, which itself was lodged inside the discontinuous cycloid, was filled with bronze-colored rings and was distinctly three-dimensional, spinning bountifully above him.

"What happens next?" Hof said.

"He goes to his quarters."

"Sure he doesn't see Dyne?"

"We take him to his quarters," Ottum said.

There was no sense of movement on the elevator. Absolutely no vibration. Not the slightest linear ripple across the bottoms of his feet. He might have been at rest or going sideways or diagonally. Not fond of this idea of stationary motion. He wanted to know he was moving and in which direction. He felt he'd been given a restraining medication and then placed in a block of coagulated foam, deprived of the natural language of the continuous.

The two men led him through a series of subcorridors that ended at the mouth of a masonite labyrinth. The reason for this, Ottum said, was "play value." After going through the maze they reached Billy's quarters, which Hof referred to as a "canister." There were no windows. The lighting was indirect, coming from a small carbon-arc spotlight focused on a reflecting plate above it. The walls were slightly concave and paneled in a shimmering material decorated with squares and similar figures, all in shades of the same muted blue and all distorted by the concave topography. The optical effect was such that the room seemed at first to be largely devoid of vertical and horizontal reference points. It was also soundproof, equipped with a "twofold" (or bed-chair unit) and an imposing wall assembly. Ottum explained this last element. It was called a "limited input module" and it consisted of a desk unit, tape recorder, videophone and monitor, temperature controls, calculator, "teleboard screen." This screen was part of a transmission system that included lasers, self-developing film, location indicators, a piece of chalk, a blackboard and ordinary phone lines; and it recorded and displayed anything written on the blackboard in Space Brain Complex, more than fifty stories straight up. Billy took off his jacket but couldn't find a closet for it until Hof released a lever in the module.

"See that grill down on the wall there?" Ottum said.

In one corner of the room was a metal grating about two feet square. It was set into the wall, down low, its base side an inch off the floor. Through the network of thin metal bars Billy saw nothing but darkness. He nodded to Ottum, who took a card out of his pocket and read slowly in an official voice.

"The exit point to which your attention has been directed is the sole emergency exit point for this sector and is not to be used for any purpose except that contingent upon fire, man-made flooding, natural trauma or catastrophe, and international crisis situations of the type characterized by nuclear spasms or terminal-class subnuclear events. If you have understood this prepared statement, indicate by word or gesture."

"I have understood."

"Most people just nod," Ottum said. "It's more universal."

Billy added a nod to his verbal affirmation.

"How long has all this been here?" he said. "The whole big building."

"Relatively brand new," Hof said. "Another few days of touching

17

up and that's it. People are already hard at work. So far everything's operating as per planned."

"Except the toilet bowls flush backwards," Ottum said. "I happened to notice earlier today. The eddy is right to left. Exact opposite of what we're used to."

As Billy opened his suitcase, the two men paused at the door.

"He's supposed to rest now," Hof said. "First he rests. Then he gets cleaned up. Then he eats and sleeps. Then he sees Dyne."

"When do I unpack?"

"Does he know he's supposed to stay away from the construction equipment?" Ottum said. "Maybe he should be told that officially. Does he know it can be dangerous for a kid to get too close to a giant crane?"

"This place has a lot of rules, it's beginning to look like."

"Be yourself," Hof said. "Only don't go too far."

He wrote a postcard to his parents in the Bronx, telling them about the bulletproof Cadillac. Then he lay on the twofold, supposedly to rest. Rest, clean, eat, sleep. If he slept now, it would throw everything off. He considered Ottum's remark about the giant crane. Why did he say "giant"? Why not just "crane"? Weren't all construction cranes pretty gigantic? He curled into the barely yielding pad of heavy cloth-like material. Was it possible Ottum meant a bird? No, not possible. But not *im*possible either. Okay, if a bird, what kind of bird? A stick-legged silent bird with giant wings that closed over the heads of small sleeping people.

Keep believing it, shit-for-brains.

He felt a cramp in his right foot. The toes bent down and in, locked in that position. Whenever he had this feeling he assumed he'd be lucky ever to walk again. Wondering what he'd do if the cramp began to spread he realized for the first time how truly soundproof the canister was. In his experience all rooms possessed a tone of some kind and he tried now to pick something out of the air, to isolate a measured breath or two, a warp in the monumental calm. Always a danger linked to the science of probing the substratum. In time he forgot he was supposed to be listening intently. He rested along an even line, ending at last this long day's descent to the surface of fixed things.

2

FLOW

To bear a name is both terrible and necessary. The child, emerging from the space-filling chaos of names, comes eventually to see that an escape from verbal designation is never complete, never more than a delay in meeting one's substitute, that alphabetic shadow abstracted from its physical source.

"Knowledge," Byron Dyne said. "The state or fact of knowing. That which is known. The human sum of known things."

He was a slight man, neatly dressed, his ears, lips and nose giving the impression they had been taken from a much larger person and

19

grafted on to this random face as part of a surgical jest. He sat alongside the main thalamic panel in Gnomonics Complex, an area occupied
by rows of consoles. Billy in an ovoid chair tried to pay attention.
There was no one else in sight. Photographs of great and near great
scientists covered the wall behind Dyne's head. He smiled experimentally, apparently a habit of his.

"In any case we're trying to create a sense of planetary community.
One people et cetera. Aside from maintenance personnel, everyone here
is either a scientist or a scientist-administrator. But we try to look
beyond science. A world view. The UN is in New York. The Copen-
hagen Zoo is in Denmark. We're right here. The largest solar-heated
building in the world."

"Curve of quickest descent."

"What's that?"

"The cycloid."

"I'm a scientist-administrator myself," Dyne said. "As such, it's my
pleasure to welcome you. We have in the neighborhood of thirty Nobel
laureates here. But none of such unique dimensions. What a vivid little
man. World's foremost radical accelerate. What exactly is your work
composed of?"

"Zorgs."

A dark spot appeared on the floor a few inches from Byron Dyne's
right foot. It seemed to be expanding, a stain of some kind. There was
no evidence of wetness, however. Just a shaded area redoubling itself.

"Can you tell me what a zorg is without being technical and boring?"

"It's pretty impossible to understand unless you know the language.
A zorg is a kind of number. You can't use zorgs for anything except
in mathematics. Zorgs are useless. In other words they don't apply."

"Microminiaturization."

"Is that your field?"

"We condense raw data. Those consoles behind you perform the
bulk of the job. Five disciplines make up Gnomonics Comp. Micromini's the biggest."

"Can you tell me what's my assignment now?"

"You've been sent to me for prebriefing. That's what this is. This
is prebriefing."

"When is briefing?"

"Right now it's enough for you to know the general reason for Field Experiment Number One. This is the fulfillment of mankind's oldest dream."

"What dream?"

"Knowledge," Dyne said. "Study the planet. Observe the solar system. Listen to the universe. Know thyself."

"Space."

"Outer and inner space. Each bends into the other. There are well over two thousand people living and working here right now. More on the way. One hundred nations are sharing the cost. Single planetary consciousness. Rational approach. World view. How many nations are sharing the cost?"

"One hundred nations."

"Good," he said.

A woman in tweeds entered. Another tentative smile half-inched its way across Byron Dyne's face. Encouraged, the woman approached.

"I'm Mrs. Laudabur of the World Expeditionary Bible Co-Op. They told me to see a Mr. Dyne."

"What do you want?"

"Our Bibles are hand-glued and hand-stitched by refugees. They told me a Mr. Dyne might want to order in bulk."

"Go away," he said matter-of-factly.

"Both testaments," the woman said. "Translated directly from the original tongues. Proofread by captured troops. Persian grain leather."

"We don't need Bibles. We have movies. Anytime we want, we can see Charlton Heston in chains."

"Bulk orders get steak knives thrown in."

"Totemist," he said. "Prayer harpy."

The foreshadowing stain had moved across the floor and started up the wall behind Dyne's head and was now in fact within several inches of a large photograph just to the right of the thalamic panel. Billy recognized the man in the picture. It was Henrik Endor, a celebrated mathematician and astrophysicist. He was bearded, in his sixties, and wore a star pentagram on a chain around his neck. Billy had met him once, briefly, at Rockefeller University, where Endor had described

21

himself as the wizened child of Thales and Heraclitus. His breath had smelled of peanuts.

A workman came in now and told Byron Dyne that the fire-safety system had developed a malfunction. Although there was no immediate danger, many of the walls and floors were filling up with "liquid preventative." The very thickness of the walls was a safeguard, keeping actual moisture from seeping through even if a silhouette effect was evident. As the workman's report neared an end, Mrs. Laudabur started waving a hand in his face.

"Can you direct me to a Mr. Dyne," she said, "because I've got it in my mind that the person I've been speaking to is not the target person and does not have authorization to order in bulk."

During the ensuing remarks Billy strolled through the area, noting that the consoles, sixteen of them, were arranged in such a way that seven were separated from the other nine by an L-shaped partition. This meant that the square of three was derived from the square of four by the presence of this border or carpenter's rule and that if the number of consoles reached twenty-five and if a new partition were erected, isolating nine consoles this time, the result would be the square of four deriving from the square of five, an odd number in every case (seven, nine, so on) determining the split relationship between succeeding square numbers. Never really seized by the need to calculate, he was more apt to be aware of pattern than of brute numeration. Seeing he was alone once more with the scientist-administrator, he made his way back to the chair. Dyad of great and small. In the city of the elect they had passed across the porticos and outer gardens, white-veiled men, initiates in numbers, Dorian dancers, led to cells equipped with slates and ordained to decode the symbol of the twelve-faced universe.

"I'll tell you a secret," Dyne said. "I was never any good in arithmetic."

They'd had to confront the terror of the irrational, this everlasting slit in the divinity of whole numbers. Subdivide the continuous motion of a point. No common measure this side of madness. Ratio of diagonal to side of square. Three segments of a line on Endor's five-rayed star. Nothing corresponds. Something eludes. Screech and claw of the inexpressible.

"To this day it's a mystery to me. The simple common ordinary whole numbers. How they work, how they interconnect, what they imply, what they're made of. The tininess of mathematics, that's another mystery. Micromini's a giant science in comparison."

"I don't think we can talk about it being a mystery. There's no mystery. When you talk about difficulty, that's one thing, the difficulty of simple arithmetic. But mystery, forget about, because that's another subject."

Dyne's smile cut off further discussion on the subject. He coughed into the sleeve of his suit jacket. Billy kind of liked that. It was both regal and sloppy, the sort of thing you'd expect from a serenely detached crackpot aristocrat. The man scanned the area now, eventually centering his attention on some theoretical point in the middle distance.

"Designed by a woman," he said finally.

"Good work."

"The entire concept. The execution."

"Nice job."

"Start to finish."

"What designed by a woman?"

"This entire structure."

"Big."

"Inside and out."

"I like the roominess."

"Do you know what kind of sphere that is that's set into the main structure? Armillary sphere, that's an armillary sphere. Used a lot in the Moslem renaissance. Of course ours is a supermodel. Much larger than anything they dreamed of in those days."

"Do people work in there?"

"Motion's so gradual and thing's so big they have no sense of movement. Sure, it's a working sphere. Tells time of day and year. Measures tilt of earth's axis. Measures height of sun. Measures coordinates of a star. Also houses four or five complexes and about six hundred people. This whole operation is self-supporting. Fume sewers and recycling units all over the place. Synthetic food machine-treated on the premises. Not to mention solar heating."

"You said."

23

"Did you see the antenna array on your way in?"

"Telescopes."

"Each dish contains a reflecting mesh. The entire array comprises what we call a synthesis radio telescope. Were you surprised at the size of each unit?"

"Small in size."

"It's the mesh," Dyne said. "We've used unimaginably tiny components in the mesh. Makes gross scanning easier than ever."

"Where did she put the bathroom?"

"So the combined operation is a sort of clock-radio if you want to look at it that way. Perfectly legitimate way to look at it. Between the armillary sphere and the synthesis telescope, what we have here is a gigantic microminiaturized clock-radio."

"Is Endor here?"

"Endor is living in a hole in the ground about ten miles east of here."

"A hole?"

"He refuses to come out," Dyne said.

The wall continued to darken in all directions. Billy turned and saw the same thing happening behind him and on both sides. Floor and ceiling as well. No immediate danger, the maintenance man had said. Just this tension. This gradual plastic deformation of a solid object into overflowing droves of motion.

"Which way's the bathroom?" he said.

"The prebriefing is not over."

"I won't be long."

"How long is not long?"

"When I'm finished."

"Tee-tee or big business?"

"Say again."

"Number one or number two?" Dyne said.

His mother often called him mommy. It was a case of double imitation. As a small child he naturally mimicked many of the things Faye said and often she responded with loving impersonations of his original facsimile. There was not the slightest mockery intended; she

24

might have been saying junior or bud or skip. It happened, however, to be mommy—an endearment located beyond the southernmost border of messy affection. It wasn't until he was nearly twelve that he was able to get her out of the habit.

His mother was also responsible for the second of his unwelcome names. The obsessive moviegoing of Faye's childhood and adolescence had been interrupted only by childhood itself, adolescence itself. Her extravagant attraction to movies was almost an act of violence. She had seen everything made in that period and was content to spend the mellowing years of her motherhood in front of the TV set, viewing the same movies again and again. Constant reader of trade publications and fan magazines, she was familiar with modern theories of promotion and packaging; the star system; mystique, charisma and product appeal; *and so*, when her own small son early demonstrated that he was no ordinary Bronx boy devoted to street-fighting and venereal entertainment, *she instantly* began to think in terms of mass audience awareness. This meant a surname less humdrum than Terwilliger. Simply by removing *e-r* twice, she arrived at Twillig, which had a distinct twinkle to it, perfect for a superstar.

Before his work earned enough money to enable the family to move to a neighborhood just south of Yonkers (*laundry rooms, terrace apartments, air conditioning, kids on bikes!*), they lived in an old building on Crotona Avenue, Billy, Babe and Faye, wedged between room dividers and other debris, on the fourth floor, overlooking a split-level playground, scene of ritual mutilations. His after-school tutor was Mr. Morphy, a small black man with a likable mustache. He wore the same suit every day for nearly five months, then changed to another for the rest of the academic year.

"I should have listened in school," Faye said. "I never paid attention. I had IQ to burn but I never listened to what the teachers told me. Realistically I should have paid attention. But I always sat so far back."

Babe was both rangy and overweight, carrying his excess pounds with daring grandness, an easygoing and somehow apt profusion, his body conveying some of the earned fluency of a former athlete, which he wasn't in particular, his active involvement in the playing of games being restricted to an occasional round of ace-nine ball with the sub-mafiosi who still clung to these polyglot surroundings, men with excess phlegm in their throats, rueful mortals of the poolroom, finger-biters, masters of deliberate spitting. Babe owned a sawed-off poolstick (for nonsporting purposes) and a large black attack dog. Poolstick in hand he sometimes stood by the window looking down at the boys and girls in the playground across the street. The dancers. The nodders. The actors. The self-styled playboy assassins. He took his hand-weapon with him when he walked the dog. Faye pointed out that if he didn't have the dog he wouldn't have to walk it and therefore wouldn't need a pool-stick to protect the walked dog or a dog for the poolstick or either one of them for himself because without the dog he wouldn't be out there. Billy didn't like the dog. He had never liked it and did not assign a gender to it. The dog used to push him out of the way and chew on his books. Late one night it appeared at his bedside and seemed about to speak to him. He knew by its expression that it was not likely to produce mere animal babble. If it opened its mouth it would speak. Words, not sounds. Fleshed meaning to replace those familiar growls.

"Go back to bed," he told the dog.

What he liked most about Mr. Morphy's visits were the new books the tutor brought along. The sweet clean shock of number theory. The natural undamped resonance of the symbols. Never more nor less than what was meant. Mr. Morphy soft-voiced and utterly dull pointed out one unchallengeable truth after another. Eventually these would lead to Pennyfellow, Connecticut. The Center for the Refinement of Idea-tional Structures. Twelve-wintered then he was, already nearly peerless.

When Babe came home from work he opened a bottle of Champale and drank it immediately. The next several took a little longer. Later he'd sometimes grip the poolstick like a baseball bat and assume the batting stances of famous ballplayers of the past. Faye and Billy would be asked to identify the man whose stance he was imitating but neither ever knew and this annoyed Babe to the point where he'd pick up the phone and call his friend from the subways, Izzy Seltzer. He then reas-sumed his stance, which Faye would have to describe to Izzy over the phone.

"Okay, legs wide apart, bat up in the air, hips wiggling, a lot of rear end."

Billy spent a year and a half at Bronx High School of Science. The daily journey wasn't easy, two long bus rides each way, and most of the ground covered was part of a landscape renowned for incidental violence. Gangs often made raids on the bus. In the afternoon they came out of the sun like Kiowa braves, nine or ten teenage boys, riding the rear bumper, pounding on windows, forcing the back door and improvising scenes of flash-terror. He liked Bronx Science but was glad when the Center offered him a place.

"This isn't an ordinary dog," Babe said. "It's an attack dog. I say the word, this dog lunges. I say the word, everybody better beware. This is a highly trained attack guard dog. With this dog at my side I can go into any neighborhood in the city."

"K.b.i.s.f.b.," Faye said.

"What's that mean?"

"Keep believing it, shit-for-brains."

"Nice talk in front of the kid," he said. "Where'd you hear that?"

"The kid brought it back from Connecticut."

Many times Faye and Billy stayed up until two or three in the morning, drinking coffee and watching old movies on TV. Across the airshaft a crazy old woman screamed and cursed. He could never make out what she was saying. Some nights he came close to understanding the sense of a particular shriek or the last several words in a long medley of invective. But it always eluded him. Although at times she seemed to be arguing with someone, there was never any voice besides her own. Most of the time she simply screamed a lot of fabricated words. People called her the scream lady. He was afraid of her but wanted to know what she was saying.

Faye took him to a department store on Fordham Road for a new suit to wear when he entered the School of Mathematics at the Center for the Refinement of Ideational Structures. The University of Chicago wanted him. Caltech wanted him. Princeton was eager to get him. He was even offered a research post in Akademgorodok in the Soviet Union. The final bid came from the Institut für mathematische Logik und Grundlagenforschung in Münster. The name of the place scared him so much he never even replied. In the end he decided in favor of the Center, one of the best places in the world to do work in pure mathematics.

One night, when the attack dog was still a puppy, Billy overheard a conversation between his mother and father. He was in bed at the time, consciousness slowly dissolving, and their voices brought him back from the sheerest drop.

"He doesn't do anything right."

"He's young, he'll learn."

"He does everything wrong."

"He's little yet, Babe."

"He doesn't listen when I talk. I talk, nothing happens. Best thing is put him to sleep. I'd sell him if I thought I could find somebody dumb enough to buy. We put him in the box and let them turn on the gas."

"No, Babe. N-o, no."

"We put him to sleep, Faye. He's not worth worrying about. They have a box they put them in. It's over in minutes, or maybe longer, depending on how much he weighs."

All children know their parents plot to dispose of them. Black box. Big room. Mad and Dag fitted with other people's faces. This is place without interruption, pinpointless time, motion extending beyond its own surrender to the Outside, and whether an isolated childhood encompasses the whole of "life and death," this converse density, is itself a question too compact to be intelligible, dimension n, containing the total unbroken distance over which a thing extends and the presiding energy that informs it, no "part" separate from any other, continuous being, hole to hole, nourished from below. Baggy gray faces saying *aga aga*. Mad and Dag with a reel and rhyme. Count to ten to ten. Box with Chinese insides. Gas pumped from exsanguine stomachs. Continued din of popping optic disks. Big T, little w, little i, little l, little l, little i, little g. Nourished from below, from below. Hopping Mad and gadabout Dag plotting to dispose. Count to ten to ten to ten to ten.

In the topiary garden about a dozen people driven outside by the shadow-flow drowsily swung in hammocks, sat on swings and lounged in wicker rockers. Hedges and shrubs were trimmed in animal shapes, such as those of baboons, mandrills and spider monkeys, but in a manner so stylized as to be nearly geometric. There were several large trees at the edges of the garden. Sunlight warmed Billy's face and fashioned precise shadows on the grass. He sat across a picnic quilt from Cyril Kyriakos and Una Braun, both dressed informally, the woman in a wide skirt, her legs stretched evenly across the grass, the man leaning back, body twisted a bit, left leg bent at the knee, a certain austerity in evidence, as though he advocated disciplined picnics. Una was a consulting hydrologist. Cyril had taught transitional logic at universities on four continents. Several other people reclined nearby and one of them soon disengaged herself to take a position just behind Billy and to his right, well placed (he suspected) to study his ear and neck. This was Mimsy Mope Grimmer, an expert on infantile sexuality.

"You're new here," Cyril said.

It seemed he was always new. Newness was his personal curse. He was forever being told that he was new here or there or somewhere. It was an injunction to explain himself, to give his listeners a brief summary of his existence thus far. To be new among adults, however, was not nearly the problem it was when he was with people his own age. The challenge was not as direct here. It could be met with an oblique remark which those assembled would be content to ascribe to shyness.

"All I knew about coming here was I was coming to a place with this name."

"They haven't given you any clues as to what sort of project you'll be involved in?" Una said.

"I find out tomorrow, let's hope."

"I'm not sure any of us knows why we're here," Cyril said. "I have a suspicion we're a bunch of technocrats pretending to be Earthlings or grown-up planetary children. Maybe we shouldn't be here at all. Maybe it's all a great big toy designed for significant play. Enjoy the pork analogue last night?"

"I'm a picky eater, everybody's always saying, so the type of food doesn't make too much difference."

"I think the food's good," Una said. "Everybody thinks it's good. We love the food here. We all really love it."

"I hate overcooked analogue."

"Cyril alone has looked on pork chops rare."

Una mentioned the fact that Cyril's wife Myriad was in the maternity ward at the top of the armillary sphere, many hours overdue. As though to change the subject, Cyril explained his assignment at Field Experiment Number One. He was part of a committee formed to define the word "science." The committee had begun meeting regularly long before a site had even been chosen for the structure itself. It was thought a definition would be agreed upon about the time ground was being broken. But the debate continued to drag on and the definition at present ran some five hundred pages. In addition to his work on the substance of the definition, Cyril headed a subcommittee devoted solely to phrasing.

"Just that one word?" Billy said.

Una was softer than moon daisies, blessed with erotic madonna's eyes, hair of vandyke brown. There was a sundial behind her. Embedded in the grass, it was carved from a limestone block the size of a funeral marker for a pet, its wrought-iron indicator casting an arrow-streak across the calibrated surface of the dial.

"There's never been a satisfactory definition of science," Cyril said. "I'm trying to apply rules of valid argument to the defining procedure. A noteworthy boondoggle thus far. I'll tell you our current problem. Our current problem seems to be whether or not the definition of science should include such manifestations as herb concoctions, venerated emblems, sand-painting, legend-telling, ceremonial chants and so on. There's a distinct methodology to each of these pursuits. Experimentation, observation, identification. Nature is systematically investigated, its data analyzed and applied."

"What is scientific about sand-painting?" Una said.

"A sand-painting represents the journey of a sacred being on behalf of a sick person. The medicine man has to learn to combine sands of many different colors so they'll trickle out of his hands in such precise mixtures that they'll form exactly the right kind of painting on the floor."

"Legend-telling and ceremonial chanting?"

"If a medicine man chants over your body all night and you wake up cured, that's science. At least some of my colleagues so maintain. You have to learn every nuance of hundreds of healing legends and chants. You need thorough knowledge of a great many medicinal herbs. Not only that but you have to be a good dancer."

They were joined by a man with ashes thumb-smudged on his forehead. To Billy's left he sat, white-shoed and affectedly sedate, introduced by Una as J. Graham Hummer, "widely known as the instigator of the MIT language riots" and a member of Cyril's subcommittee on phrasing. Telling time by the sun's shadow. More or less scientific than clock-recorded mean time? A group of people carrying garden chairs advanced across the lawn.

"There are rumors," Hummer said. "Something big's about to be announced. Seriously, the air is rife. Could involve our mathematical friend here."

"The only thing I anticipate right now is more shadow-flooding," Una said.

"No, something's happening. I know rife air when I see it. Something big and not necessarily water-borne."

Cyril: " 'All things are water,' said the Greek."

Una: " 'All things flow,' said the Greeker of the two."

Mimsy Mope Grimmer chose this moment to approach the picnic quilt. She sat very close to Billy, even tapping his wrist with lovely brooding intimacy, as though affirming a solemn connection between her knowledge of infantile sexuality and his particular state of affairs. Despite the melancholy blessedness of the gesture, he continued sneaking looks at Una Braun, whose gentle heat he found enveloping.

"Four to a blanket," Cyril said.

"We want to know about your beautiful wife," Mimsy said. "Tell us when the baby's coming."

"I don't know when but I know how many and what. Siamese quintuplets. Joined at the top of the head. We'll have to roll them to school like a hoop."

"You beast, Cyril. Don't. Awful man."

"The truth is I'd rather she gave birth to a wisteria tree or pair of mittens. Children make me uneasy. They seem the only ones able to escape their set places. They're continuous, you see, and mock us in secret ways. I have a recurring daydream about an afternoon game show on television. 'Abort that Fetus,' it's called. The studio audience is composed of obviously pregnant women, far too far gone for any corrective measures to be taken but a great studio audience nonetheless, keying the theme of the show and rooting very hard for the contestants. The applause light flashes and the master of ceremonies comes suaving out, all hair spray and teeth. He looks at the audience, points a jaded finger and says: *'How would you like to play'*—slight pause—*'ab-orrrt that feetusss!'* The women scream and cry and moan and then the first contestant is brought on."

"Enough," Una said. "More, more than enough."

"All through marriage I thought to avoid childmaking not by the usual means but by trying to separate myself mentally from the implied sublevel process of biological reproduction. My reasoning was that nothing significant happens without a psychic link. A test, then. An attempt to deny a localized point to those transient energies that guide the reproductive cells. Superstitious self-delusion perhaps. But who's to say for sure? In any case I remained a distinct and unconnected entity. Myriad, however, has immanence enough for two. At least that's how I interpret her present condition."

"We await the result," Una said.

She drifted off to sit in a basket swing attached to the lowest branch of a dawn redwood. Hummer went on about rumors and events, wondering aloud how different kinds of significant announcements might affect phrasing in the finished definition of the word "science." Perhaps someone here had discovered a new form of matter. Evidence of a buried continent. Signs of a tenth planet in the solar system. Hands curled, he allowed the ends of his fingers to meet and part perhaps twice every second.

"Tell us about the MIT business," Mimsy said. "I've never heard the details."

"There were no details."

"Did people really throw stones at each other and overturn cars and the like? I mean was there actual killing in the streets?"

"I was simply trying to assert that what there is in common between a particular fact and the sentence that asserts this fact can itself be put into a sentence."

"And this led to rioting?"

"It was simply a question of constructing models and then evaluating the structures. Shallow diagrams and deep diagrams."

"What was the final toll?" Mimsy said.

"There wouldn't have been any problem if I'd been able to arrange total computer access. But somebody named Troxl had leased overlapping time segments on all the area's computers. Elux Troxl. There wouldn't have been a problem if I'd been granted access. A Central American, I believe."

"Where is he now?"

"Hiding."

"In Central America?"

"In Germany," Hummer said. "They're all in Germany, hiding, lots of them."

"When did all this actually happen?" Mimsy said. "I mean the actual killing in the streets."

"It was the year everyone was using the words 'parameter' and 'interface.' But there wouldn't have been any problem if that fellow hadn't monopolized computer time."

Billy was not interested in plotting the orbits of Jovian moons. If Hummer's supposition was correct—that they'd brought him here to calculate a planetary path or the mass of a neo-electron—it was a waste of everybody's time. His kind of mathematics was undertaken solely to advance the art. In time to come, of course, what had been pure might finally be applied. He saw how the virginal circles of Eudoxus had led to a more coherent astronomy, how the conic sections of Apollonius had prefigured the spirit of universal gravitation. The world had its

33

uses, yes; ideas could be rotated to expedient planes. It wasn't his method to test the disposition of the physical universe but this didn't mean he reacted skeptically to those who drove hooks into nature. He considered the case of Archimedes, son of astronomer, floating body, lever adept, nude runner, catapulter, weigher of parabolas, tactician of solar power, sketcher of equations in sand and with fingernail on own body anointed in after-bath olive oil, killed by dreamless Romans.

"Do you ride?" Mimsy said.

"Ride what?"

"Well, see, I was wondering about recreation. What sort of active things you do."

"The usual."

"Golf, watercolors, growing pretty things?"

"That's not usual. Is that usual?"

"I guess it depends," she said.

"In handball there's a thing called a Chinese killer. That's an active thing I do, hit Chinese killers. It's when the ball hits right where the wall meets the ground so that there's no bounce. It's impossible to return a Chinese killer. The ball just skids along the ground, impossible to return. They have courts here? I could show you."

His voice seemed too big for his body. It was rough-edged and fairly deep, delivering every kind of statement with equally sneak bluntness, a dull abrupt impersonal voice that might have belonged to someone who called out names for a living.

"The ball just skids, does it?"

"What kind of sex goes on in a place like this?"

"All sorts, I'd imagine," Mimsy said.

"In universities it gets pretty oral, going by what I hear. I was thinking about this place if it's the same or similar."

"Maybe I should poll the staff."

"Nice bit of imagery," Cyril said.

"I suppose I should have said canvass the members."

"In my case, a good idea, however belated. My luck to cast my lot with a hyperfertile woman. Internal contradictions are at the very center of my life. Hooray for transitional logic. Helps expose the counter-examples that haunt our arguments."

34

"Wind chimes," Hummer said.

More people came into the garden, indicating the shadow-presence was spreading through the building. Mimsy leaned toward the boy, speaking in a mock whisper.

"How's your genital organization?"

"Remind me to check."

"You're already past your prime, sexually speaking. The golden age is early infancy. Soon after this the corruption of the erotic instinct takes place. In a very short time everything falls apart. The solidarity of opposites is completely shattered. Before you've learned to put two words together, you are mired in an existence full of essential dichotomies. I feel free to speak, since you raised the subject yourself a moment ago."

"For the body to become unafraid," Cyril said, "we need to live beyond the brain and with less talkative genitals."

"Someone's installed wind chimes."

Only the ashes on his forehead marred Hummer's antiseptic manner. Cyril looked toward the eighty-foot redwood, calling to Una Braun.

"Hydromancer, divine us a drink."

"Mere hydrologist," she said. "More's the pity."

"We can't escape our places, don't you see? Our sole hope is silver liquid wishboned from the earth. Otherwise forever fixed, our places in the series. That species of tree was once extinct, you know. Stayed that way for millions of years. Then an intrepid man traveled from a distant land with a handful of living seeds. Now the tree bears cones at opposite ends of the earth. Nourishment comes from unexpected places, doesn't it then, at times?"

"What's that mean?" Hummer said.

"I hope it doesn't mean Eastern mysticism and Western science," Una called.

Mimsy Mope Grimmer bypassed the primroses, stopping to pick a buttercup from a speckled bed. Her place on the grass was taken by Una, legs disappearing under wide skirt, redwood needles clinging here and there.

"Question of perspective," Cyril said. "If we're ever going to reach a definition of the word 'science,' we've got to admit the possibility that what we think of as obscure ritual and superstition may be perfectly legitimate scientific enterprises. Our own view of the very distant past may be the only thing that needs adjusting. This past, after all, continues to live not only in remote cultural pockets but more and more in the midst of our supercivilized urban centers. Simply admit the possibility. That's all I say. Primitive kinship systems are not necessarily antiscientific."

"Phrasing is the element that makes or breaks the definition," Hummer said. "The phrasing *is* the definition. An analysis of how we say what we are saying is itself a statement of the precise meaning of the word we are defining."

"No definition of science is complete without a reference to terror," Cyril said.

"Explain," Una said.

Billy tried to imagine the birth of Cyril's wife's baby. It would happen in grim lights violently. A dripping thing trying to clutch to its hole. Dredged up and beaten. Blood and drool and womb mud. How cute, this neon shrieker made to plunge upward, odd-headed blob, this marginal electric glow-thing. Dressed and powdered now. Engineered to abstract design. Cling, suck and cry. Follow with the eye. Gloom and drought of unprotected sleep. Had there been a light in her belly, dim briny light in that pillowing womb, dusk enough to light a page, bacterial smear of light, an amniotic gleam that I could taste, old, deep, wet and warm? Return, return to negative unity.

"Mysticism's point of departure is awareness of death, a phenomenon that doesn't occur to science except as the ultimate horrifying vision of objective inquiry. Every back door is filled with the terror of death. Mysticism, because it started at that very point, tends to become progressively rational."

"Gabble, hiss, gabble," Hummer said.

For the first time since the "picnic" began, Cyril Kyriakos changed position. He sat upright, legs crossed, and took off his shirt. Then, beginning to speak, he unbuckled a figure-eight harness and proceeded to adjust some locks, rings, cables and joints before removing his left arm from his body. Automatically, Billy looked away even as he continued to stare. Cyril put his shirt back on. He placed the arm and its suspension system across his lap, where the sunlight accentuated the high shine of the plastic laminate material. A small emblem set just below the triceps pad carried the words: A PRODUCT OF OMCO RESEARCH.

"It's been suggested that the logic I espouse isn't rigorous enough to do justice to the sheer dispersion of modern thought. But wasn't Aristotle too lax and Russell too insistent on being all-devouring? Sometimes I think I'd like to relocate, as they say in the business community. Give me algebraic invariants to play around with. Or too, too solid geometry."

Some people in one of the lower gardens were seated in the kind of triangular pattern studied in depth by early believers in the selfhood of numbers. What was ten was also four, triangle and password, *tetraktys*, holy fourfoldness. Hummer got up and left. Una got up, smiling, and shook out her skirt. Cyril nodded, rising, making ready to go, the woman lifting the quilt, smiling once more at the boy on the grass, while the man, Cyril, headed off now, side by side with Una, the plastic arm in his right hand and held parallel to the ground, glinting a bit, still, as they moved into the distance. Billy heard the wind chimes now, tone surprisingly precise, a sequence of whole-numbered harmonies, music as mathematics whistled into.

Hours later he stood naked in his room looking around for his pajamas, a moldy sock still in his hand. He felt something of himself in the material, a corporeal dampness, the faintest sense of coating, of his own rubbed-off yeast. His fear of the body's fundamental reality had not yet fully disclosed itself. In fact he often occupied himself with thoughts of rot. His own death, wake and burial were recurring themes. Of secondary interest was the putrefaction of his immediate family and then of close relatives and then more distant and then of friends in descending order of importance and finally mere acquaintances, broken down to compost. This was formal rot to be enjoyed on a theoretical level. Equally marvelous were the jams and scabs of his own living body. Excrement worried him a bit. Shitpiss. He did not have reveries about excrement. Not his own and certainly not anyone else's.

37

There was something about waste material that defied systematic naming. It was as though the many infantile names for fecal matter and urine were concessions to the fact that the real names (whichever these were) possessed a secret power that inhibited all but the most ceremonial utterance. He saw a segment of pajama leg sticking out of a stack of pillowcases and other linen that sat in a basket near the bathroom door. The sock in his hand reminded him of something he'd known for a long time in the vaguest of ways, a sort of accumulated fact; namely, he'd developed a personal stink.

Among the things beyond expression in various cultures have been the names of deities, infernal beings, totemic animals and plants; the names of an individual's blood relatives of the opposite sex (a ban related to incest restrictions); the new name given a boy at his initiation; the names of certain organs of the body; the names of the recently dead; the names of sacred objects, profane acts, leaders of cults, the cults themselves. Double substitutes must be used. Carefully devised code words. Taboo variants. Oaths are duly taken. An entire bureaucracy of curse, scourge and punishment is set up to discourage utterance of the unspeakable. Copyists of manuscripts are prevailed upon to resort to the strictest kind of transliteral deviousness. No writing that touches on the life of a secret subject can itself escape secrecy and in time culthood is conferred on document as well as primary figure. Often more than one person is concealed in the cult leader's generative shadow and the names of none of those who follow can be revealed except as provided by the contextural pattern itself, however primitive its design or childlike its claim to a scientific principle of arrangement.

He dropped the sock and got his pajamas. Before stepping into them he briefly juggled his testicles. This was a bedtime routine he'd lately developed not only for the common monkey sport of fingering those boiled orbs (dimeric witness to virility) but also in earnest celebration of the fact that his left testicle had fully emerged at last, making him not only whole but reassuringly asymmetrical as well, the left drooping a bit lower than the right, as decreed by nature.

Slowly he was getting accustomed to the canister's tenuous perspectives. In his pajamas he examined the components of the limited input module. He knew this was standard equipment for the sector he was in but he had no interest in learning how to work the thing. For whatever it was they wanted he'd need pencil and paper at most.

Someone was outside the door and now a knocking sound was evident, *bap bap*, a sort of cartoon noise, *bap*, as of an oval stone dropping on a bald infant's head. He opened the door to see a figure in oversized work clothes. The man listed slightly, giving the impression of being burdened beyond the reach of deepest fatigue, someone who sleeps in subways.

"They know me as Howie in this sector. The fume sewer man. Heard you were worth seeing. Maybe you want me to show you what's what down there, two or three levels down, what they got down where I work down there, fume sewers, evaporators, recyclers, backup spewing filters. You think this is far down. That there is a lot farer. I could take you eight levels down. Nobody goes eight levels down without a red pass."

"I'm supposed to go to bed."

"You're the only kid in this whole place."

"There's another one being born."

"Eight levels down in noise is some racket. Accelerators, storage rings, proton impactors, collision machines, Howie Weeden, always glad to meet a kid."

"They want me to get up early."

"Let's shake hands. People shake hands when they meet. You don't just say nice to meet you, one person, and the other person do nothing. People shake hands."

"I still have wet."

"What's that?"

"I still have wet on my hands from just washing up for the night."

"They told me to come look," Howie said. "They said there's a kid over there worth looking at for the way he adds numbers in his head."

"That's not what I do."

"I have a python in my room. Don't tell anybody. It's my best pet ever. Want to come watch it digest?"

"They have me on a schedule."

39

"There's a woman takes a bath every night at this time and you can see her in a ceiling reflector if you look through a hole in the wall standing on a bench in the workroom over near the next sector up one level. I'm the only one that knows. I call her the water woman."

"Let's go," Billy said.

He put on his robe and slippers and followed Howie Weeden through the play maze to a red elevator reserved for maintenance personnel. They got off and headed down a long empty corridor. Signs of the shadow-flow were everywhere. Howie moved quickly despite a double shuffle of his right foot.

"If anything happens, grab my tongue," he said.

"I don't understand."

"Just be ready to grab my tongue."

"I want to know why."

"I never had to tell anybody before. They always knew. You tell somebody to grab your tongue, you don't have to say why. Just if I slam out, go for the tongue, that's all I'm saying."

"How often does this happen?"

"More often than not," Howie said.

In the workroom he stood on a bench and put his head to a metal bracket at the juncture of two cement walls. After several minutes he looked at Billy, pointed to a specific perforation in the bracket and then stepped down to the floor. Billy wasn't nearly tall enough to put his eye to the spot in question, so Howie set himself on the bench once more, bunched up on all fours, as the boy climbed up his arched back and found a foot-grip alongside each shoulder blade. His hands were flat against the wall, head twisted, right eye almost in contact with the small vertical slit. There was a hole in the wall, perhaps half an inch in diameter, directly behind this particular level of the bracket and so he found himself peering through two openings, one punched by machine into the metal bracket and the other most likely resulting from crude workmanship or premature erosion of the wall, the sector, the level, the entire structure. Beyond both holes was a ceiling reflector.

"Just remember the tongue," Howie said. "This weight on my back isn't doing my skull trauma any good."

In the tilted mirror he saw Una Braun. Wearing a loosely knotted robe patterned in mellow colors she stood barefoot on pentagonal tile, her body a bit foreshortened by the angle of reflection, combing, combing her hair. Bottles of perfume and baby oil stood on a glass shelf. His knees went weak and he thought he would fall. Both hands were dug into cement, not finger-gripping (he feared she'd hear the scratching) but pressed desperately, palm and heel, into the wall. It was she, Una, about to bathe, undress and bathe, water woman soon to drop her robe and step into that clear and distorting, dense and uncolored element. Varieties of light glanced off the surface borders of air and water, water and glass, glass and oil, the whole room a medium of nonuniform density, these propagating waves graining her body, soon to be rubbed and soaped and misted, transformed in displaceable mass, passing through itself, beauty bare, an unfalsifiable and self-blinding essence, not subject to the judgments of mirrors, what Euclid might have danced to in the summer dusk. Oooo naaa. She stood combing her hair, the big toe of one foot digging idly at the inmost pentacle on a cool blue unit of tile. Now she smiled at a stray thought, a memory of home or long buried song lyric, one hand dropping to the whimsical knot on the robe's sagging belt, perhaps loosening it further, the other hand placing the comb on a shelf.

Do they comb their hair *before* they take a bath?

She lowered her head for a moment, moving partly out of his line of vision, returning seconds later. When she looked up, she saw him. That very section of wall, mirrored twice in the complex placement of the bathroom's reflecting surfaces, was spread across the ceiling. There was his right eye, magnified.

"Who is that?"

He kicked Howie's shoulder to indicate trouble.

"We're caught," he whispered.

"I heard," Howie said.

"What do we do?"

"Ask for tits and let me know what happens."

She hadn't moved.

"Show me your tits."

The sound of his voice surprised him in its unreal evenness and degree of clarity.

"Billy, is that you? Do I know that voice? It's you, isn't it?"

"Show me your tits please."

"Repulsive person. Wretched little boy."

He kicked Howie again, more urgently this time.

"I tried asking but nothing got shown."

"Ask for thigh."

"You ask."

"Who's up there?"

"You didn't tell me there'd be conversation. I expected to see things without this talk. She knows me by voice."

"Ask for hair," Howie whispered.

"Which area?"

"Below, below."

"You ask this time."

"Maybe, your age, you better stick with titties."

She was still there, evidently defiant.

"Let's have some boobs," he said.

"How very sad. Yes, more than anything, sad. Tragic individual. Sad, sad boy."

"Cheer me up with a quick tit."

He gave Howie a very light kick, as if requesting some confirmation of the brilliance of this wit under pressure.

"Undeniably wretched person."

"Left breast," he said.

"Demean yourself, that's all you do."

"While I'm up here. Some nipple. How can it hurt?"

Howie pushed up.

"Cheeks," he whispered.

"Nothing's getting shown."

"Ask for cheeks and report back."

"She's not showing."

Una left the bathroom in her own time, setting things in order, re-placing caps and closing lids; clearly she had no intention of scuttling away like a maiden outraged. There was nothing for him to do but climb down Howie Weeden's back to the bench and floor. The maintenance man studied him crookedly.

"What happened?"

"Gone."

"No bath?"

"Nothing."

"I played a trick," Howie said. "She already finished her bath. When I got up there I heard the water getting sucked out of the tub. I think it's here."

"What's here?"

"I can feel it. It's here. I'm getting ready to slam. The tongue. Prepare to go for the tongue. I'm slamming out."

The boy hurried out of the workroom and got on the nearest elevator. For a long time, in robe and slippers, he walked in and out of arcades, suede sitting rooms, meditation suites, past miniature waterfalls, around ornamental fountains, under arched gardens, through reference libraries, lush saunas, empty game rooms, totally lost, thinking wistfully of his crisp little bed. An unmanned cart marked EMERGENCY LINEN SERVICE went speeding by. All was quiet until he reached a transparent bridge leading to one of the upper sectors of the armillary sphere. The enormous motion of the sphere was audible, a continual muffled utterance less of machinery at work than of overwhelming mass in friction with surrounding air. He entered the sphere and stood just above one of the elliptic bronze rings. Arciform spaces. Flowing motion. To be up so high, turning, contained in material receptive to visible light, was a liquid thrill, the night sky so clear and near and living. As he was swept gradually past the edge of a steel support he saw something pierce the sky, an incandescent object dragging vapor-light behind it and needling in and out of darkness. Aloft too long to be a shooting star, it might have been a snow-maned comet, come sunward to orbit, or a supernova's argon shriek. In other places the sky was tranquil, although nowhere completely still, and he wondered whether the flash he'd seen was part of the process of a star being formed, point of light set within the fiery trigon, that name given to the first, fifth and ninth signs of the ancient zodiac. Twelve equal parts. Thirty-degree arcs. Earth, air, fire, water. Triplicity of fire. Fire's pre-eminence. Equilateral triangle of fire. Men born under new stars are destined to lead revolutions.

Eventually he reached the correct sector. Workmen were placing huge acetylene devices along the walls of the corridor, presumably to keep the shadow-flow from "spilling over." He went to his quarters, sat at the module and began looking through the manuscript he'd had in his possession since leaving the Center to make the journey here. It was a handwritten document given to him by his friend and mentor, Robert Hopper Softly—a work-in-progress detailing Softly's observations on any number of mathematical topics. As he browsed he heard a tiny sound, *ibd*, and eventually noticed, to his left and just above eye level, that a message was appearing on the teleboard screen, a chalk-scrawl beamed by laser:

See me
Earliest a.m.
Space Brain Complex
U.F.O. Schwarz

"The teacher of the secret book died between the fire-pillars at Tarentum. Those of his disciples not burned to death were killed by mobs. The mathematical brotherhood was dispersed. What, we ask, did it leave behind? A sense of order in nature. The notion of mathematical proof. The word 'mathematics' itself. But the teaching didn't end, spreading through the Mediterranean, maintained in formal order for over two hundred years. Numbers as the basis of creation. The religious instinct arithmetized to regrettable effect. A dream of water put out by flames."

He went inside to brush his teeth, mis-squirting a strip of toothpaste into the wash basin, where it formed a line and curve resembling a crumpled number four. Directing the tube at the figure he proceeded to close the curve, making line and zero, or ten from four. But sooner or later he would have to stop fooling around and brush his teeth. So he spoke a password to his mouth, *tetraktys*, and it opened.

44

3

SHAPE

Remarks from Softly's work-in-progress:

"The unattested cadence of the heavens had been based on the circles of Ptolemaic calculations, a format supported by the Polish monk Copernicus. All work on celestial events was superimposed on the mirages of animism, prophecy and the Christian occult. Motive soul drove the planets and it was held that every orbit described a musical scale. The problem of course and solution as well were distinctly mathematical, although not without some hearsay of the empyrean."

When Billy stepped off the elevator he was in Space Brain Complex.

This was a vast computer area, quiet at the moment, no one in sight. In the middle of an open space stood a small office of frosted glass, a cubicle really, and he headed toward it. Sitting inside on a swivel chair was U.F.O. Schwarz, a densely packed individual weighing well over three hundred pounds. Attempting a jaunty sort of greeting he tried to pivot in the chair. Nothing moved, however. Concentrated flesh. Eye slits. Bubblelike hands. The chair was equipped with a footstool, which Schwarz managed to nudge toward the boy, kicking it soccer-style.

"Is that all one computer out there?"

"Space Brain."

"Whose office?"

"Kind of cramped."

"I have the feeling you carry it around with you."

"That's about as funny as a dead kid's toy," Schwarz said. "We're waiting for Nyquist but I guess I can bring you up to date in the meantime. We chose this time and place because we knew we'd have complete privacy. I'm the person who arranged with Professor Softly to bring you out here. Spoke to him in person. Reported certain recent events. He talked at length of your extraordinary abilities."

Schwarz had a glass of orange juice in his right hand. He tilted the glass slightly now, the surface of the liquid assuming an elongate outline. Billy began guessing the large man's weight, keeping the figures to himself.

"What do you know about space?"

"Not much. Maybe even nothing."

"Stars and planets."

"Last night I saw a comet or something. I don't even know what it was. That shows how much I know."

"Doubt it was a major comet," Schwarz said. "One's long gone and the other's not due for a while."

"Pure mathematics is my field."

"We've been contacted by someone or something in outer space."

"I do pure work. A lot of it is so abstract it can't be put on paper or even talked about. I deal with proof and nonproof."

"Beings in outer space. Someone or something. An extraterrestrial civilization."

46

"What about it?"

"They've contacted us. We picked them up on the synthesis telescope. They transmitted and we received. Pulses. Signals were transmitted in irregular pulses. We happened to be tuned to the right frequency. Space Brain has printed out a tape covered with zeros and ones. Mostly ones. The message was not repeated. This is unfortunate but not disheartening. One hundred and one pulses and gaps. The pulses we interpret as ones. The gaps or pauses as zeros. There are only two gaps. The transmission was fourteen pulses, a gap; twenty-eight pulses, a gap; fifty-seven pulses. Total of one hundred and one information units. One zero one is binary five, which may or may not mean something. One hundred and one is also the lowest three-digit prime. Then we have the arrangement of pulses—fourteen, twenty-eight, fifty-seven. Plenty to work with, don't you think? At any rate we are not alone. Something is out there and it is talking to us."

"What is it saying?"

Schwarz paused here, locked into the framework of his petrified baby fat. What was odd about his way of speaking was the fact that nothing moved but his lips. Independent animation. Now, however, he raised the glass to his pouched face and nibbled at its rim. Billy heard a faint metallic tapping coming from well beyond the perimeter of the small office, less faint a moment later, then less again.

"That's our problem. We don't know what the transmission means. Space Brain has printed out hundreds of interpretations without coming up with anything we can call definitive. Dozens of men and women have also failed. Radio astronomers, chemists, exobiologists, mathematicians, physicists, cryptanalysts, paleographers, linguists, computer linguists, cosmic linguists. I'm sure you know Endor. We got Endor here to decode the message. Endor seemed the one man who couldn't fail. Famous the world over. Well versed in all aspects of extraterrestrial communication. A first-rate mathematician. A brilliant astrophysicist. Science prizes hand over fist. He worked at the message for a great many weeks. Then he worked some more. He kept saying it's probably so simple we can't see it. One day he stopped working and just sat in a chair in his room for about seventy-two hours. Finally he went to live in a hole in the ground. That's where he is at latest report. He's living in the ground. He eats plants and worms and refuses to talk to anyone. You're our last hope, it looks like. When Field Experiment Number One became a functioning entity we never in our wildest dreams thought we'd be lucky enough to receive signals from a supercivilization so early in the game and then unlucky enough to be unable to unravel them. We feel certain it's a mathematical code of some kind. Probably a number code. Mathematics is the one language we might conceivably have in common with other forms of intelligent life in the universe. As I understand it, there is no reality more independent of our perception and more true to itself than mathematical reality."

"Did you just fart?"

"This is serious," Schwarz said. "Try to pay attention."

"We're in a little room here without any air blowing through."

"This may be the most important day of your life."

"Have some mercy."

"Numerically the transmission is very suggestive. Everyone who's worked on it got off to a great start. But they all fizzled out. After Endor left for the hole, your name came up. All you have to do is tell us what they're saying. We have the capacity to transmit an answer. Pretend you're the imperial mathematician. The emperor and his cousin the bishop want to know the meaning of a new star in the heavens. In the town square the witch-hunters are gathering twigs."

Olin Nyquist tapped on the door frame with the point of his silver cane. He was evidently blind, an angular man with a high forehead and well-honed jutting chin. Small crisp flakes adhered to the inner edge of each eye.

"It's all a question of shape," he said.

He moved to a corner of the office and stood motionless, shoulders wedged between adjoining walls.

"Shape, design, emblematic pattern."

U.F.O. Schwarz explained that Nyquist was an astral engineer in charge of simulation programs for the synthesis radio telescope here. One such program was based on the fact that the dish antennas not only picked up radio emissions but also took galactic photographs as clear and detailed as those taken by optical telescopes. These pictures, already somewhat "artificial," being the result of radio data received, mixed and computer-converted to electrical impulses, were then broken down and stylized even further by Space Brain, which was able to simulate gas outflows, explosions, the expansion of molecular clouds and other observed and probable phenomena. The result was known as the "computer universe."

"In some shape or other we try to find the pictorial link between the universe and our own senses of perception," Nyquist said. "What does the universe look like? A balloon that's expanding? A funnel full of ball bearings? A double helix? A strip of paper twisted and connected in a one-sided ring? Where are we in the universe? We can't see enough of it to say. Some of us think the universe is closed. We think it has positive curvature. We think it pulsates in cycles of expansion and contraction, every beginning and end defined in fire. Of course it wasn't very long ago that the universe was regarded solely in geometric terms. Circles, squares, equilateral triangles. Back far enough, I suppose, people used animal shapes or parts of animals' bodies to explain what sort of design they were part of. A whale's tail perhaps. I never thought I'd see in braille/A cosmos structured like a tail."

"Cracks," Schwarz said.

"Tiny cracks in the model are becoming evident, it seems. There is the problem of absolute velocity. There is the suspicion of matter crossing over to us from elsewhere. There is the lack of cause and effect in the behavior of elementary particles. Certain basic components of our physical system defy precise measurement and definition. Are we dealing with physics or metaphysics? Maybe we need a fundamental reconstruction of our ideas of space and time, or space-time, or space-time sylphed, if the latest theory is to be taken seriously. I plan to introduce sylphing compounds into the computer universe. That may tell us something. What we need at this stage of our perceptual development is an overarching symmetry. Something that constitutes what appears to be—even if it isn't—a totally harmonious picture of the world system. Our naïveté, if nothing else, demands it. Our childlike trust in structural balance."

"The common snowflake," Schwarz said.

"Think of the fundamental order of atomic structure as seen in the periodic table. Think of the laws of planetary motion. Consider the fact that, relative to their respective diameters, the average distance between stars is roughly the same as the average distance between atomic particles in interstellar space. Is this mere 'coincidence'? From the Medieval Latin. To happen together. Something and its shadow. Think of the secretion patterns of red ants. The shell of a chambered nautilus. The cubic crystals in ordinary table salt. The honeycomb, the starfish, the common snowflake—all so stunningly reasoned in surface configuration. But not nearly final enough to soothe our disquiet. However, there's always the view that an ultimate symmetry is to be avoided rather than sought, the reason being that this structural balance represents not victory over chaos and death but death itself or what follows upon death. A logarithmic spiral. The polyhedral cohesion of virus crystals."

"The wiggle," Schwarz said.

"The star is a common G dwarf. It's called Ratner's star. It lies away from us a bit toward the galactic center. We've analyzed the variation or wiggle in its path and we believe the object in question is a low-mass planet that occupies the star's habitable zone. If you can decipher what the residents of this planet are saying, it may mark the beginning of an exchange of information that could eventually tell us where we are and what the universe looks like. It's safe to assume the Ratnerians are superior to us. They may help us draw a picture. A seamless figure no less perfect than its referent. I'd personally rejoice, although it's hardly likely I'd still be here for the receipt of such information. I think I'm finally tired of being made to journey from speculation to accepted fact and from there to sudden doubt, denial and contention. Does the red shift, for example, really mean what it seems to? I visualize an eight-column headline in the newspaper. UNIVERSE SAID TO CEASE EXPANDING; BEGINS TO FALL BACK ON ITSELF; MILLIONS FLEE CITIES. Of course if evidence of universal blueshifting is ever found, it will merit the smallest note. This is documentary void. Not void whose essence is terror. Not the human sensorium streaked with darkness."

Nyquist put his free hand to his mouth, quickly, as though to stifle a giggle. All along he had seemed to be staring at the tilted glass in

Schwarz's hand but now he turned his head toward the boy. His eyes appeared to be surmising the existence of an optical path along which might travel any number of topics neither generated nor perceived in the usual manner. Billy couldn't recall ever having seen a blind man laugh and wondered whether there was usually an element of grotesquerie involved—the salivating laughter of someone who has forgotten how it's done or what it's supposed to look like to others. He waited for Nyquist's next remark, hoping it would include something humorous, an epic quip or two that would make Nyquist himself flash his fizzing teeth and gums in the sort of uncontrollable expectorating glee that Billy associated with the handicapped. What Nyquist did in fact was to extend his long cane and begin to tap it gently on the metal leg of the vinyl chair that held his colleague.

"Fortunate, aren't we, to be alive in enlightened times," he said. "It was often the case" *tap* "that enemies of science" *tap tap* "could only be circumvented through allegory and indirection. Now there are no enemies for us to circumvent. When I was a boy in the old country I heard stories of a woman who used her father's skull as a drinking cup. The man was long dead, needless to say, but whether this qualifies as a mitigating circumstance is open to question. She was said to have witch's grip, one of the lesser manifestations of the forbidden arts. Or should I say sciences? In any event I was obsessed with such stories for many years, imagining the smoke rising from crisscrossed sticks, the first ultraviolet tick of pain. Today our science is such that the only thing we need to fear is the substance in the drinking cup. And now I think it's time" *tap* "I went away."

With that, Nyquist moved sideways out of the small room and headed across the open area, apparently laughing in suppressed spurts as he approached the elevator. It occurred to Billy that U.F.O. Schwarz seemed to be sitting in his own lap.

"That was a little background there."

"Nobody's seen the planet. Is that what I understand was being said?"

"We know there's an orbiting body because of perturbation in the star's path."

"How much do you weigh?"

"It's a condition I have."

"I'd like to be able to see the figure on a scale."

"If I felt I could trust you, I'd ask you to guess," Schwarz said. "Most people underestimate when they guess. To try to make me feel good. Knowing I have a starch bloat condition. But I don't think I can trust you to do that."

"Three forty-eight."

"I'm suggesting you adjust downward."

"One guess is all I give myself. Figured I might as well lead with my best punch."

"A strategist in our midst," the man finally said, his tongue scratching at that opaque glaze in which it was adrift.

Billy had agreed to a tour of Zoolog Comp and when he got off the elevator he followed an arrow to the pisciculture lab. He went inside, pausing before a formula-fed baby dolphin. The area was blue and silent. Everywhere were tanks of newly born fish and marine mammals. In the eyes of the dolphin was a dreamy sense of dislocation, its dimension of remembrance perhaps, the chemical arrest of transient land-history. Billy watched a sari-clad woman approach. She was Rahda Hamadryad, a dimpled Hindi. Her smile fluttered down to him. As he admired the way the sari was draped over one shoulder, she told him that Zoolog's director was eager to meet him. Before they left the area he looked back in the general direction of the dolphin, seeing instead an octopus in quadruple squat.

Rahda led him to a smelly room where they sat at a table covered with lunchtime debris. Around them were tiers of reptiles and long slender egg-sucking mammals. It was clear that news of the special nature of his mission had already begun to spread. Rahda didn't seem to know exactly what was involved but she gave the impression that his body was outlined in luminous smog. She told him most of the people in this sector were doing research in animalalia.

"Our rats have a synthetic vocabulary of nearly fifty words."

"Who'd want to talk to a rat?"

"They have remarkable conceptual abilities," she said. "We communicate with them through a series of color-coded shock mechanisms."

"With me and rats, it's stay out of each other's way."

"They sort items. They subdivide different classes of the same item. They choose correctly from among several linguistic shock alternatives. Perhaps our toads may be more to your liking. Our toads count dead flies all day long. It was Aristotle who maintained that man's rationality is based on his ability to count. The toads no doubt use the same prelinguistic thinking we used eons ago. Wordless flash-thinking. Of course they have yet to utter a single human word, rat or toad. We've used color, rote learning, computer syntax, shock, prolonged shock, sign language, many kinds of stimulus response gadgetry."

"What about apes?" he said. "Maybe apes would make some talk with the right training."

He was watching her bend the edges of a paper plate someone had left on the table. Again and again she folded the plate so that a different point on the circumference of the circle touched the same ketchup speck every time, a small stain located well off-center. She kept studying the resulting creases. Her eyes were large and deep. She had relaxed flesh, he could tell, trying to catch her eye in order to reassure himself of her continued willingness to smile at him. He rarely expected smiles, even from people he liked. But there were times when being smiled at seemed important.

"Apes don't have the anatomical structure for our kind of talking," she said. "However, we are even now in the process of restructuring. We are looking forward to a new kind of phonetic performance from our apes. Something much more significant than tapping out symbols on a console."

A man walking by advised Rahda that the director was now ready to see the visitor. She led Billy through a series of laboratories and "postscrutiny habitats." These latter areas were set up for the benefit of research animals recuperating from arduous projects, each habitat quite small and easily convertible from desert to marshland to jungle surroundings, depending on the need.

"I would like to hear more about your work," she said. "Research with animals is very satisfying. But sometimes I wish for a more abstract pursuit. Something lonely and distant. Perhaps you could tell me what you do at this remarkable institute I've heard so much about."

"I'd like to, sincerely would, seriously, but it's the kind of work nobody can talk about unless they know the language."

"You know the language surely."

"But you don't," he said.

"You talk. I will listen."

"I'll talk if you let me do one small thing. I just want to touch your leg behind the knee. Nothing personal. The soft place behind the knee. In return for talk."

"You want to touch me."

"If we could do it without anyone taking it personally."

"I am *harijan*," she said.

"What's that?"

"Untouchable."

"What happens if you're touched?"

"I am an outcast. There are millions and millions of us. We are considered unclean. I could not use the public well in my village. In university I could not live with upper-caste students. But I think you're a very special individual. I would not object if you touched me."

"Does something happen to a toucher of the unclean?"

"Nonsense," she said. "Just behind the knee. We will slow down to make it easy. I lift the garment."

"Why do untouchables have that name?"

"I have halted and am waiting."

"Is something supposed to happen if you're touched?"

"You cannot think that, surely."

"They wouldn't give you that name without a reason, would they? I'm not saying it's a good reason. They're probably too sensitive to dirt on others. I just want to know in my own mind what I'm doing."

"There is the office," she said.

Peregrine FitzRoy-Tapps pointed out an enormous armchair beneath a photograph of a pair of elephant tusks. All the pictures in the room were of tusks, horns, stuffed heads and rifles in trophy cases. FitzRoy-Tapps was vaguely diagonal in shape. Those visible parts of him that came in twos, like eyes, ears, shoulders and hands, seemed to be arranged at slightly varying elevations, each to each.

"The animals are here to learn but no less than to teach. Animalalia in particular is a learn-and-teach operation. It wasn't this way in Croaking-on-Pidgett, I can tell you. That's spelled, incidentally, as if it were pronounced Crutchly-on-Podge. But it's pronounced Croaking-on-Pidgett. A lovely old village and even older river. But the animals tended to be uncooperative. We let them mix in a large enclosure not far from the local vicarage. What went on was often ambiguous. How nearly like sex, I found myself thinking. Mornings were a revelation, however. Most mornings I walked past the vicarage and through the formal garden over to Muttons Cobb, which is spelled as if it were pronounced Maternity St. Colbert. But it's pronounced Muttons Cobb, as those not privy to the idiosyncrasies of the region learn to their eternal discomfiture. Afternoons I strolled through the arboretum and then carried a picnic basket full of cakes and ale out past the snuff mill to the embankment along the Pidgett. I took my evening meals in the refectory at the manor house. Afterward I sometimes took port with the others in the common room. I liked to smoke my pipe in the deanery garden before retiring. The night creatures were just beginning to scream then."

The armchair was so large that Billy's feet didn't even come close to touching the floor. He felt helpless and wished he could think of a good excuse for leaving.

"Life was so much simpler there and then. When someone did something well, I simply said: 'Well done.' When things came apart, I said: 'Bad luck, bad luck.' When someone's work fell markedly short of that individual's abilities, I felt compelled to say: 'Get cracking.' And so in the normal course of events there was little else one had to say. 'Well done.' 'Bad luck.' 'Get cracking.' To this day I find it difficult to imagine a situation that couldn't be fully resolved with one of these phrases. Of course, times have changed and so have words. People expect more these days. It's not enough to utter the suitable phrase. But it was enough in Croaking-on-Pidgett; yes, more than sufficient, I believe. It was enough in Little Whiffing as well, now I think of it. It made no

difference how bleak a particular situation appeared to be. The ap
phrase tended to settle matters. No action is more suitable than the ap
phrase. Of course, one addresses such a phrase only to suitable people
'Well done, sir.' 'Bad luck, bad luck.' 'Get cracking now.' Surprisin
how well these sufficed."

He spent all afternoon in the solarium near the top of the armillar
sphere. It was a cloudy day and there was only one other person or
hand, an extremely old woman reading a book that seemed no les
venerable a specimen than she was. He closed his eyes for a while
thinking and turning, dulled by the prospect of the work ahead. Bore
dom was summer pavement on a Sunday, the broad empty glare o
regimented concrete. He decided to give the message a couple of days
of his time. If he found no evidence that the transmission was a genuine
mathematical statement, he would go back to the Center and resume
work on zorgal theory.

"I know who you are," the woman said.

He opened his eyes, not bothering to force a polite smile. She gestured
him forward. He went to sit next to her among tall plants and scattered
magazines. He had never been so close to anyone this old. It occurred
to him that when he was a child he wouldn't have thought twice about
this episode, having viewed old people as static forms of theater, even
less changeable than he was. But now the simple act of sharing a sofa
with this woman filled him with distant suspicions. He was alert to sour
odors or the possible grossness of the inside of her mouth. He didn't like
the idea that she was striking in appearance, feeling that people her
age should travel in groups in order to melt into each other's presence
Rouge seemed to be baked into her hands, face and arms. A black silk
scarf was wound tightly around her head, making him think she might
be bald. She wore a full cape with fur collar.

"Do you say *yes* to life?"

"I guess so," he said. "Sure, why not."

"In the science of subjective mind-healing, both cause and effec
exist in the full and perfect idea that the mind is Mind. Everything de
pends on mental typography. This is why we use capital letters so often
Not only in the pamphlets in our reading rooms but in the way we pic

56

ture our thoughts. Fear-Chains of Asthma. Dominant Drift. Ether of Timeless Being. My name is Viverrine Gentian. Who are you?"

"You said you knew."

"And so I do," she said. "I was simply wondering if we agreed."

"What's that book?"

"It's a story called *Somnium*. A beautiful and extremely rare book. Written in Latin with a smidgen of Hebrew and Greek."

"What's it about?"

"It's an experimental novel, an allegory, a lunar geography, an artful autobiography, a cryptic scientific tract, a work of science fiction. A man goes to sleep and dreams he is reading a book. In the book is a boy whose mother makes a living by selling goatskin pouches to sailors as charms. When the boy is fourteen she sells him to a sea captain who leaves him on an island. Here he learns astronomy from the famous Tycho Brahe. In five years he returns to his mother, who announces her intention of calling forth, or stating as a proposition, her demon-teacher, the spirit of knowledge. Mother and son sit with robes over their heads and hear a voice. It delivers a veiled narrative of the moon. Only certain people are fit to undertake a journey to the moon, says the voice, and here I quote verbatim: *'Especially suited are dried-up old crones who since childhood have ridden over great stretches of the earth at night in tattered cloaks on goats or pitchforks.'* The voyager must make his journey during a lunar eclipse, traveling along the axis of the cone of the shadow cast by the earth on the moon."

"So far I like it."

"The year of the dream was sixteen aught eight and the dreamer's sleep was dissolved in wind and rain, as was the book he was reading. Perhaps you'd like to feel it in your hands."

Her smile was a ghastly pressed rose. Carefully he turned the shaky pages, all so old they appeared on the verge of self-granulation. His respect for the antiquity of the volume was secondary to a swarming fear of the woman's reaction if the book should in fact crumble in his hands. She might lash out or spit. (K.b.i.s.f.b.) Speak a phrase so devastatingly apt he would never be able to forget it. Taunt him with logical paradox.

"Here."

Viverrine Gentian took back the book. Sunlight was everywhere now, a late-afternoon profusion, the air bursting with musical dust. She appeared to withdraw slightly, sinking further into the cape.

"When must the voyager make his journey?"

"During a lunar eclipse," he said.

"What was the year of the dream?"

"Sixteen aught eight."

"True prayer is scientific," she said. "The answer to a prayer is in the prayer when it is prayed. This is called Mind Science Unity. Cap M, cap S, cap U. When you touch yourself in the male or female region, you dementalize the secular prayer. This is important for someone your age."

"What about washing?"

"When did you last wash?"

"This morning."

"How do you know those were your parts you washed?"

"Who else's would they be?"

"Can you be absolutely certain those weren't female privates you were washing?"

"I ought to know my own by now."

"The genitals are famous for the tricks they play on the brain. It's merely a question of genus, isn't it? Shape-changing, I mean. A question of numbering one's holes. Did you look carefully at the items you washed?"

"I know my own."

"When you touch yourself too often, you change the shape."

"What shape?"

"It's no longer pleasant here," she said. "I much prefer the solarium when the sun's not shining."

He sat with feet well apart and arms not only extended but lifted slightly above the arms of the chair. He was fairly sure nothing would happen to him if his arms touched the arms of the chair but what worried him slightly was the fact that the arms of the chair were called "arms" and that his arms were also called "arms" and it was just barely possible that this business of self-touching applied not only to parts of the body but to parts of the body and parts of other objects that happened to have the same names. Arms of chairs, legs of tables, hands of clocks, eyes of needles. He knew that what the old woman said would not have permanent effect but for the time being he was determined to be alert, particularly careful of where he sat and how he conducted himself in the bathroom. He took comfort in the properties of sunlight and in sunlight's negative print—the shadow cast by the armillary sphere. He couldn't see the shadow from his chair in the solarium but he knew the figure it made on the earth below could be one shape and only one, that of a pristine ellipse.

4

EXPANSION

Slowly he pivoted, careful to note every square foot of floor space. It was definite. Someone had dismantled and removed the cubicle in which U.F.O. Schwarz had told him about the radio message from outer space. Nothing in particular had replaced it. Around him, everywhere he looked, were the component parts of Space Brain itself, far from dormant now. The computer extended to the ends of the complex, coded along the way by various colors, lights, bells and strange arrays of symbols. Technicians were at work, perhaps a hundred of them, tending the huge machine. There were several levels of noise, people in shifting groups, rotary units turning, a sense of hypertrophia, something growing outward toward a limit. A small industrial vehicle came to a stop alongside him. It was equipped with a sidecar and carried a sticker on its front bumper that read BEEP BEEP. Behind the wheel was Shirl Trumpy, a woman who often laughed right through her own words (he was soon to learn), making it hard at times to understand what she was saying and therefore why she was laughing.

"You're late," she said. "I'm on my third lap of the day."

"I forgot the appointed time."

He climbed into the sidecar and they moved off. As she steered around objects and people, Trumpy explained that Space Brain was beginning to spread beyond its own hardware. Originally they'd used the smallest crystals in existence and the result was a stored-program sequential machine—of unprecedented sophistication—weighing only fifty pounds. But it was too successful. It began to solve problems that couldn't be posed without new components and new housing. The problem board had to be expanded. This led to additions elsewhere. Space Brain helped with the additions and was therefore self-designed, at least in part.

"Ridiculous, of course, to refer to it as a brain," she said. "But we had a contest to name the machine and 'Space Brain' was the winning entry. So we're stuck with it. Tremendous excitement over your presence. Word's been getting around. We all feel this is finally it."

"Where are we driving?"

"Code analysis checkpoint."

"What for?"

"To show you what we've come up with so far in the way of statistical analysis. One notion everybody agrees on. We're the only ones who picked up the signal from the planet that's orbiting Ratner's star because we're the only ones in the world who are tuned to the secret frequency. It's our frequency and it's secret. Obviously they're a super-technical civilization. It's up to you to tell us what they're saying."

"Other telescopes have picked up signals. This has been taking place for years. They all claim it's outer space making contact. Everybody thinks they're hearing from some superior beings. What makes these beings so superior?"

"Relax, Mr. T."

"Have they proved Fermat's Last Theorem?"

Speaking and laughing simultaneously, Shirl Trumpy headed the vehicle to a remote part of the complex, stopping finally behind a series of blank display screens that were part of the computer's graphics unit. He had a little trouble getting out of the sidecar and she annoyed him by offering to help. She was a lanky woman with prominent bones and when she laughed he had the feeling her skeletal structure would crack in a dozen places. It irritated him when people enjoyed themselves with such intensity. They looked ugly laughing. If they could see what they looked like, they'd probably learn how to restrict themselves to a smile. She led him to a lone console near the display screens and asked him to press a button. A card dropped from a slot and he took it in his hand to study. It was about eight inches long and six wide, covered with vertical and horizontal lines forming small squares of equal size, most of them blacked in, the demarcating lines being pale blue in color. This was a sequence grid, Trumpy explained. The pulses from Ratner's star were represented as black squares, the gaps or intervals as white squares. Many such grids had been devised, both by Space Brain and by the people who had tried to decipher the message. These diagrams were meant to help the searchers ascertain whether or not the message had been intended as a two-dimensional picture. Using such a picture, she pointed out, the extraterrestrials might convey an enormous amount of information even though they'd transmitted nothing more than ninety-nine pulses interrupted twice—a total of one hundred and one units of binary information. She pressed the button a dozen times, getting that many sequence grids from the slot and explaining why a statistical analysis had failed in each case to confirm that the pattern was indeed an attempt to convey an intelligible picture or a series of coded symbols that might tell us something about the senders' physical characteristics, the chemical composition of life on their planet and so forth. The fact that there were only two gaps (or white spaces) led most people to conclude that the message was numeric in character rather than pictorial.

The small squares made him think of graph paper. Early days of compass and straight-edge. Thin blue lines intersecting to the ends of the page. Horizontal x and vertical y. Numbers as points, as positions on a surface, and equations as sequences of points, as geometric shapes, and shapes as sequences of numbers sifted through the intersecting lines and represented as equations. He remembered exploring those other-worldly curves from one degree to the next, lemniscate and folium, pro-gressing eventually to an ungraphable class of curve, no precise slope at any point, tangent-defying mind marvel.

Trumpy described how Space Brain had investigated the possibilities of explaining the message in terms of wavefront reconstruction, contour mapping, a simulation response program that was part of *their* (the Ratnerians') computer universe. None of these inquiries yielded the slightest evidence that the message was of intelligent origin.

"So you think it's pure numbers or nothing," he said.

"Exactly."

"I think it's nothing."

"True, the signals weren't repeated. But we're confident this is gen-uine contact."

"What happens next?"

"You talk to LoQuadro," she said. "He used to do your kind of mathematics before he had the first of his attacks, so maybe the two of you between you can figure out the star code and then I can go back to programming a search for what's true after the computer has declared everything false."

"What's this about attacks?"

"Sleep attacks," she said. "Attacks of deep sleep."

"What happens, he falls down?"

"Sleep spells. Recurring and uncontrollable."

"And you really think we're in contact."

"Is Ratner's star an illusion? Of course not. It's out there and every-one knows it. Is the planet's existence a hoax? Ridiculous. There's clear evidence of a planet in orbit around the star. Is someone transmitting signals? Absolutely. Is our synthesis telescope receiving on the secret frequency? Nods of affirmation."

"But isn't it possible to give instructions to the computer to make it print out a wrong series of zeros and ones?"

"A child could do it."

"Then maybe that's why Endor or nobody else could find a pattern. There is no pattern. Everything got jumbled up between the telescope and the computer."

"Theoretically it's possible. I don't deny it. But it would take an awfully clever child."

"That almost makes sense."

"An awfully clever child or a very psychotic adult."

"So it's possible this whole thing might be a waste of time is what you're saying."

"Many things are a waste of time," she said. "How can we learn from the past unless we repeat it? Time for me to go, Mr. T. Stay at code analysis checkpoint."

She laughed, said something, got into the little vehicle and drove off. He dragged a chair to the console and sat down. His mind blunted by the cybernating drone in the distance, he leaned toward the console and put his head on his arms just as he'd done so many times in first grade during the ten-minute rest period every afternoon, nicks in the wood desk, sleep pulling, chalk trails in the air. From a series of three dreams had evolved a life fulfilled in mathematics and philosophy. The dreams occurred within a single night. The first two concerned the terror of nature not understood and the last of them harbored a poem that pointed a way to the tasks of science. The world was comprehensible, a plane of equations, all knowledge able to be welded, all nature controllable. These were dreams generated by the motion of a straight line, a penciled breath of linear tension between day and night, the limit that separates numbers, positive from negative, real from imaginary, the dream-edge of discrete and continuous, history and prehistory, matter and its mirror image. The dreamer, a soldier in repose, applied the methods of algebra to the structure of geometry, bone-setting the measured land, expressing his system in terms of constants, variables and position coordinates, all arranged in due time on the scheme of crossed lines forming squares of equal size. Compass and straight-edge. His periodic segregation from the other children. Private time to plot coordinates on pale blue lines. Then rest at last. Head settled on well-notched wood. Fingers identifying every penknifed name and date. He loved a girl who squinted, Billy did, but this was just the first grade and he knew he'd love again.

When LoQuadro touched the back of his neck, he nearly leaped from the console. With his foot the man moved a chair across the floor and sat next to the boy, who wasn't sure how long LoQuadro had been standing behind him. The latter wore steel-rimmed spectacles and a gray suit and tie. He was nervously alert, seeming to be engaged in self-espionage, ever attentive to the fluctuations of electric potential in his brain.

"We can discover the truth or falsehood of our own final designs only if we teach ourselves to think as a single planetary mind. This is the purpose of Field Experiment Number One."

"So I hear."

"True or false. Yes or no. Zero or one. Data is processed in. Current travels through the core magnets in the memory unit. The problem is transistorized and solved. The answer is processed out on cards, tapes or sheets of paper. Computers are like children. Yes-no, yes-no, yes-no. Space Brain is a superhybrid. A little bit of yin in yang. A microdot of yang in yin. This machine is a science in itself. Bi-Levelism, I call it. I'd like very much to take you into void core storage. It may help you see the message in a new perspective."

"What do you mean by take me into?"

"Physically."

"The woman before said it's stretching out past its own hardware. That doesn't sound like something I want to get taken into physically."

"The problem concerns the true nature of expansion," the man said: "Consider science itself. It used to be thought that the work of science would be completed in the very near future. This was, oh, the seventeenth century. It was just a matter of time before all knowledge was integrated and made available, all the inmost secrets pried open. This notion persisted for well over two hundred years. But the thing continues to expand. It grows and grows. It curls into itself and bends back and then thrusts outward in a new direction. It refuses to be contained. Every time we make a breakthrough we think this is it: the breakthrough. But the thing keeps pushing out. It breaks through the break-through."

"What thing?"

"Our knowledge of the world. The world itself. Each, the other and both. They're one and the same, after all. It's been said that philosophy teaches us to talk with an appearance of truth about all things and to make ourselves admired by the less learned. There's one branch of philosophy this definition doesn't cover. Bi-Levelism. Bi-Levelism teaches us to talk with an appearance of truth *and falsity* about all things and to make ourselves admired by the *more* learned. True-false. Zero-one. Yes-no. On-off. Come, we'll visit the void core."

"How about holding it for later?"

"Let me allay your fears."

"The woman said to tell you I should stay at code analysis check-point."

"Trumpy writes programs. That's all she does and all she knows. The void core isn't part of the computer's reasoning assembly. Trumpy is concerned with routes of language and logic. She hasn't been to the void core and in fact has no direct knowledge of its existence. Space Brain contains a deeper electronic route than Trumpy ever dreamed of. The void core is at the hypothetical center of this route. I think you should spend some time here. It will help you understand the implications of bi-level coding in its latest form."

"You want to take me to the actual place."

"Yes."

"I wouldn't be good at it."

"It's not a question of skill," LoQuadro said. "The only thing you're doing is coming with me to another part of the area."

"It's a physical event. I wouldn't be good at it. Physical things are something I'm not used to doing in my work, being a pure mathematician."

"So was I."

"She told me."

"I was a mathematician."

"She said."

"I missed the world," LoQuadro said. "The seas and beaches."

"Is that why you switched?"

"I was, oh, better than some. But no hope of true greatness. Mathematics is the wrong discipline for people doomed to nongreatness. However, that's not why I switched. I didn't switch to computers because I missed the world or because I was haunted by my own inadequacy per se. It was all too occult for me. I'm the type of person who's willing to confront moderately awesome phenomena. Beyond that I lose my bearings. Chipping away at gigantic unproved postulates. Investigating the properties of common whole numbers and ending up in the wilds of analysis. Intoxicating theorems. Nagging little symmetries. The secrets hidden deep inside the great big primes. The way one formula or number or expression keeps turning up in the most unexpected places. The infinite. The infinitesimal. Glimpsing something, then losing it. The way it slides off the eyeball. The unfinished nature of the thing."

"There may be a lot of crazy things in the world that scare you and me but mathematics is the one thing where there's nothing to be afraid of or stupid about or think it's a big mystery."

"Did you find that carved on a temple wall somewhere?"

"I'm just saying."

"Because it has a ring of lyrical antiquity."

"Make remarks."

"And I am stirred beyond all imagining."

"Go ahead, say things, I don't care."

After giving Billy a long searching steel-rimmed look, LoQuadro explained that a visit to the void core would provide the boy with a chance to observe bi-level coding procedures firsthand (enabling him perhaps to adapt such methods to his own attempts to decipher the transmission from Ratner's star) and might also furnish an insight into the glitch problem. Glitches, he said, were irritating little kinks in a computer, often difficult to locate and straighten out. He went to one of the display screens nearby and with the index finger of his left hand tapped several times at the keyboard that occupied the bottom third of the unit. The screen went white. Then a series of alphanumeric characters appeared, shimmering a bit before going still.

```
010011              COxxxx
100110              COGxxx
010111              xxxxxx
011001        xxGx  xxGx
110011              xxGx
100110              xxx
                xUx
010101              xUx
101001              ITx
010111              Oxxxx
100110              Ex
              xRxxxxxx
110010              5xx
110100              xxATbxxxxxxxxxx
100100              xxxxxxxxxxxxx

                         OGRE OGRE OGRE
```

LoQuadro returned to the padded chair next to the console. He continued to give the impression that he was a clandestine witness to his own thoughts.

"Every so often it turns up while we're scanning some graphics material," he said. "It just turns up. It's just there. I can't find it in the routing system. It's too well integrated. Trumpy claims she can't find it either. But I suspect she's the one who put it there. It's her glitch. What's more, it seems to be a double glitch. First it interrupts other visual data. Then it interrupts itself. It's a six-bit hollerith double glitch. Do you know what I just realized about you?"

"No."

"You never say anything clever."

"Why should I?"

"Kids are always saying clever things. They're famous for it. People are always quoting their kids' clever remarks."

"I'll write home. Maybe they keep a scrapbook."

"Not now," LoQuadro said. "I have to leave for a while. Important appointment. Wait for me here. I'm meeting with representatives of a Honduran cartel. They're flying in from Germany. They want to lease computer time."

·

"That must be Elux Troxl."

"You know?"

"Just his name."

"How do you know?"

"This person Hummer who's on a committee to define the word 'science' said something about a person with that name being from Central America who rents computer time and is hiding out in Germany."

"Except that's not his name. Nobody knows his name. It could be anything. I don't even know if they're Hondurans. The cartel is Honduran but the agents, I suppose, could be something else."

"What's your part in this?"

"I market excess time," LoQuadro said. "Don't tell anyone I told you. Not a soul knows this. The cartel wants to take advantage of Space Brain's tremendous versatility. Computer time-sharing usually benefits everyone in the long run. If time is available, someone might as well market it and that someone might as well be me. Computers are like children."

"What happens if I'm not here when you get back?"

"Day-night, play-sleep, on-off."

Within the series one, two, four, seven, eleven, he was quick to discover the buried series one, two, three, four. He could walk but not talk. He didn't talk until he was past the age of three. His mother used to look directly into his mouth and urge him to say something. She would speak to his mouth and beg it to answer. It was his father's opinion that the boy knew words but simply didn't want to say them. His mind knew words. He spoke with his mind and to his mind. To and with his mind. In time he will speak to his mouth with his mind and then from his mouth to the room and the people in the room.

"Soon as he talks I'm taking him into the subways," Babe said. "I'm taking him down into the tunnels. I'm anxious to show him what the tunnels are like. But not until he talks. I want to hear his reaction."

The attack dog was given no name at first. It was simply called "puppy." As the dog grew bigger and blacker, this means of identification became by default the animal's official name, at least as far as Faye and Babe were concerned. Billy didn't call the dog anything and never had. He tried to stay out of its way and remembered most of the time to keep his books at a level that the dog-up-on-hind-legs could not reach. This meant he had to stand on a chair to put his books away and then again to get them down. This was part of the normal course of events on Crotona Avenue. Faye, defrosting the refrigerator, would hurl potfuls of hot water into the freezer compartment. A cooking mitt on each hand, she would hold the large pot well away from her body and then slowly ease back, dipping like a discus thrower, before uncoiling in a grimacing vortex to splash water all over the icebound walls of the freezer. Babe sometimes walked through the apartment with the TV set in his arms. Whenever the rabbit ears failed to deliver a clear picture he would pick up the unwieldy set and take it to another room. On hot summer nights, during the three-hour span of a ballgame, he sometimes touched down twice at each room in the apartment, getting a better picture with every maneuver but then losing it a short time later. The set was heavy enough to force his legs into an occasional stagger-spasm. On the set, as he carried it, were several empty bottles of Champale, a pack of Camels, an ashtray, an enormous cigarette lighter and ten or twelve of Faye's movie magazines. On many such nights, as Babe made his silent bulky passage through the rooms and as Faye sat by the window commenting on events below, Billy and his friend Ralphie Buber stood in the kitchen spitting in each other's face. Whoever ran out of saliva first was declared the loser. However, the game was not discontinued at this point. The winner went on spitting until dry, at which time both boys, not ready to end the contest, were reduced to mere simulation, their lips and tongues going through the motions with nothing of consequence being expelled besides the recurring sound: *two two two two.*

"That's about the dumb-assest thing I've ever seen," Babe said.

The car he owned was an officially defunct Ford model called the Urban Eco-Pak. It was an extremely bland automobile, too lacking in distinction to be called homely, and it had recently become infested, as though to compensate for its utter dullness, with several forms of insect life, roaches predominating. During the winter months Babe

rarely used the car, being content to look it over every time he walked
the dog. Any vandalism short of flagrant didn't bother him and on most
nights he circled the small lump of metal just once and continued on
his way. In the summer he took family and friends to the beach.
Leaving the car to bake in the huge crowded parking lot he accompanied Faye, Billy and the two Seltzers (Izzy, from the subways, and
his small daughter Natasha) past rows of automobiles and through the
handball courts and onto the boardwalk and across the tract of hot
sandy stone to the rail above the beach itself, the teeming strand, that
long radiant curve endlessly submissive to the bleak waters of the
Sound. Midsummer Sundays at Orchard Beach were like troop maneuvers on desert terrain with every man using live ammunition.

"They have a religious problem," Faye said of a married couple in
the building. "They're both Irish Catholic."

Often it ended incoherently. There were stabbings, riots, thunder-
storms. Faye would wrap Billy in a large towel and he would take off
his bathing suit and then sit down to squirm into his pants. On the
boardwalk they'd watch the police come sweeping across the beach in
full uniform, nightsticks held at chest level, legs pumping high. In distant tidal flats male swimmers wearing religious medals did gymnastic
exercises. Lightning tore across the dark sky and the boy felt an overwhelming sense of urgency, of odd tense giddiness, an emotional voltage
in the air, something coming, more than storm or violence, something to
run from laughing, fear and expectation together, and he was soaked
through with rain now but feeling lighter, more *sentient*, brushing away
his matted hair to see a group of men and women attacking a few individuals and then a second group charging into the first, slash and
batter, a lone enormous woman sitting in the sand trying to get her
shoes on and being rocked back by her own shifting weight, foot
eluding hand, the high-stepping cops beginning to knock people down,
everywhere this ever sweetening tension, people bleeding, thunder going
whomp, a squad car bouncing over the sand, gunfire in section seven,
wind and rain, a raw sundering in the impetus of bodies, people fleeing
into the water, death and sheepish laughter, *whomp*, dark sky and life.

Billy had been told Natasha squinted because her mother ran away

71

from home. She was extremely frail, her body quivering as though suspended from the end of an eyedropper. Her father often took the kids to the botanical gardens. Together Izzy and Natasha expressed the unfocused sadness of love divided. On notably sad days Billy sometimes felt obliged to whisper in their presence as a way of deferring to their mutual loss. Natasha squinted at many different speeds, depending on the situation.

"Girls have three armpits," Ralphie Buber said. "The extra one's between their legs."

Across the airshaft the scream lady cursed the universe. During movie nights, as Faye and Billy sat laughing in the cave-glow of the TV set, the woman shrieked and rattled, none of her words seeming to belong to any known language. One day Billy and two friends were being chased by the janitor through a series of passageways and alleys that ran under and between several adjacent buildings. With the route to his own building sealed off, he climbed the first set of stairs he found. It took him eventually to the fourth floor of the building behind his own. A door was partly open and there the woman stood. Although he had never seen her before, he knew it couldn't be anyone but her. The scream lady. She was standing about five feet away from him in the dark doorway of her apartment. A white paper napkin was pinned to her hair. She wore two or more bathrobes. The outer robe was opened, revealing another beneath it, and judging by the unwarranted mounds and ridges in this second and tightly belted robe, there may have been one or more beneath that. The woman's feet were bare and this more than her curious way of dressing, this even more than the fact that she was the scream lady, this really worried him. Old people's bare feet had always caused him some concern. It was not in the order of things for old men and women to go around barefoot and it made him want to throw lighted matches at their feet to teach them a lesson. He stood watching her now, ready to dash away, already leaning, one second from all-out flight. She took something from the pocket of her outer robe, a piece of paper with writing on it. He kept his eyes on her pitted face, abysmally collapsed, looking as though it had been blown in by some natural force. She rubbed the paper against her fore-

72

head in a circular motion over and over. Then she bit it fiercely and extended it in his direction, producing sounds all the while, acoustic interference so random it seemed to come not from her jawless sucking mouth but from a small hole in her throat. He leaned toward the staircase, all his weight on one leg, and then suddenly and without forewarning even to himself he propelled his body in the opposite direction, snatching the paper from the scream lady's hand. He read it on the roof five minutes later, teethmarks still indenting its surface, tinges of pearly spittle evident in these jagged spaces, while a few feet away a man with a long stick guided a flock of pigeons in training arcs of gradually increasing length.

> Stockmark ave/rage 549.74 (29/1929) grim pill
> of pilgrim welfare (fare/well) scumsuckers inc.
> & brownshirt king/pres. (press/king) of U.S. of
> S/hit/ler & secret (seek/credit) dung of U.S.
> Cong/Viet Cong & Christ/of/fear Columbus discovered
> syph/ill/U.S. 1492 + 1929 = 3421/1234/4321 astro/bones buried
> under ever/grin tree in Rock/fooler Center 50 St. +
> 5 Ave. = 55 St/Ave/Stave (Cane Abe/L/incoln 1865 +
> 1492 +1929 = 5286/PANCA DVI ASTA SAS

Settled in front of the TV set with a lapful of muscatel grapes, Faye pointed out to Billy why certain performers were considered classic. "I like to watch him work," she'd say of a particular actor. "Watch the way he does this bit with the water glass. Watch this now. See it, see it, the way he rubs the edge of the glass against his lower lip before he drinks. Nobody else could get away with that. It's a classic bit. I like to watch him work." Other times she spoke of growing. Certain performers were interested in growing as artists. Others were not, either because they were too dumb to grow or because they were classic and not only had no use for growth but would be diminished by it.

Sitting on the blanket at the beach he studied his father's belongings. The sawed-off poolstick was there, brought along for riot protection. The stainless-steel cigarette lighter was there, nearly the size of a deck of cards. The flame it made was immense. Every time his father put his thumb to the rickety wheel, Billy moved away. With the huge bluish flame would come a surge of furious air, an effect he associated with something being put out rather than something kindled, the last breath of a body hardly formed, heat and light sucking at an ultimate moment. Walking through slush outside the supermarket he asked his mother why they'd named him William Jr.

"We didn't think you'd live."

"What do you mean?"

"You were born early, mommy. They rushed you into an incubator. You were so itty-bitty we didn't expect you to last the weekend."

"What's that got to do with being named after my father?"

"We didn't want to waste a new name."

"Big joke."

"We thought we'd save the new names for a healthier kid."

"Fun-nee."

His father's shoes were also there, scuffed and monumental, located between the cigarette lighter and the newspaper. It was hard to believe that creatures with feet large enough to be suitable for these containers actually walked the earth and that one of these creatures was his own pop, his flesh and blood, Babe of the subway tunnels. Are we really of the same race of people? Did I really come from him and her or is it all some kind of story they tell to kids? Ovulation, intercourse, fertilization, pregnancy, labor, delivery. It can't be that simple. There must be more they aren't telling us. A circling bird, a dream, a number whispered in the night. At his side Natasha seemed to look directly into the sun. Izzy Seltzer cautioned her, semitragic in his faded swimming trunks, hair everywhere on his body, white-tipped clusters curling from his nose and ears.

Billy at four still thought of himself as something that would never be altered. "Small boy." He did not yet perceive the special kinship between humans of different sizes and failed to realize he was destined for other categories. This part of childhood then was a brief chapter of immortality that would be recognized in due time as having been set between biological states reeking of deathly transformation. Some years later, sitting in the bathtub, he would bounce in prepubescent rage on the smooth porcelain as his mother's head appeared in the doorway.

"Is you is or is you ain't my baby?"

"Drop dead please."

At four, however, completely in accord with the notion of forever being this thing called "small boy," he lived in a deep sunny silence unthreatened by a sense of his own capacity for change. There was no doubting the fact he was exactly what he was meant to be. He was sure he met the requirements. It was all so totally fitting. He was native to a permanent inner environment just as certain fish as a species never stray from coastal waters. His shape was carved in the very air, body and mind forever.

LoQuadro led him back across the complex, seeming to take the same route and make the same small detours that Shirl Trumpy had taken and made when earlier she'd driven him in the opposite direction. Shadows were cast on the walls and floors by hulking computer units.

"Did they lease?"

"They leased."

"What do they need Space Brain for?"

"Didn't say."

"I guess if someone's in hiding, it figures he won't tell you what he wants your computer for."

"Quite the modern master of sarcasm, aren't you?" LoQuadro said. "Anyway he wasn't in hiding. He was in isolation. There's a big difference."

"I heard hiding."

"We're going to the outer void core. From there we can work our way down between the augment interrupt mechanism. In theory there isn't the slightest obstacle in our path."

"Wait."

"That's where the dream originates."

"Wait please."

"In an unnamed sector at the center of the void core."

LoQuadro made a sudden turn and led the boy past a group of workmen installing tape drive units at a frenzied pace. He didn't remember passing this area with the woman in the funny truck. He wanted to heed his own words ("Wait please") but he kept right on moving as if he were being drawn into LoQuadro's wake through natural enforcement of some low-lying aerodynamic law. They walked through a blinking corridor and into a semicircular storeroom full of folding chairs partially folded. LoQuadro approached a small door at the far end of the curved wall. The door was no more than three feet high, leading Billy to think it was some kind of emergency escape panel similar to the metal grating in his canister. There was no doorknob in evidence but he noticed a small white circular device set into the door. Maybe a bell or buzzer. Sliding door leading to an elevator maybe. There were no printed warnings or coded symbols. Only the small inscription: OMCO RESEARCH. Looming above the door LoQuadro turned to face him.

"Forgot the goggles," he said. "Have to go back for them. Can't go in there without goggles. You'll have to wait here. You're not authorized to draw equipment or even to enter the area where equipment is drawn. Am I correct? You have limited access."

"Nobody told me one way or the other."

"Your canister has what kind of module?"

"Limited input."

"Then you have limited access. The two go together. Promise me you'll be here when I get back with the goggles."

"I definitely promise."

"But will you definitely be here?"

"I didn't go away last time you left."

"I'd like some further assurance. All my life people have been making promises to me and consistently breaking them. What further assurance can you give me?"

"I give you my word."

"Not nearly enough," LoQuadro said.

"I'll swear on a stack of Bibles."

"Forget Bibles."

"Any stack."

"What about a stack of books of my choosing?"

"What will you put in there?" Billy said. "Give me some titles."

"First say you'll swear."

"First tell me what you meant when you said that thing about the dream."

"What did I say?"

"It originates in the void core."

"Actual fact."

"Because if you're saying the computer has dreams, I saw that movie on 'Hollywood Ghoul School' a long time ago."

"D-r-e-a-m."

"Which is what?"

"Discrete retrieved entry-assembled memory," LoQuadro said. "A series of data flashes in mnemonic code form tend to occur in certain nonoperational phases and are later retrieved."

"The guy ends up going crazy after his father and the girl take apart the computer and they find little pieces of baby human brain tissue grafted onto the circuits, which explains why the hospital was missing all those kids."

LoQuadro's right foot was tapping uncontrollably. Its movements did not seem related to any other part of him. Tapping in this manner he resembled a wildly impractical household robot designed to step on passing insects. Seconds later he toppled into a cluster of partly folded chairs. Billy thought the fall would wake him but it didn't. Neither did the noise of crashing chairs. Nevertheless the boy backed quietly out of the room. He didn't try to imagine what was on the other side of the little door. It didn't occur to him to peek inside or even knock. Void core. The name was enough to send him in the other direction.

In his canister he thought about the message from Ratner's star. One hundred and one total characters. As U.F.O. Schwarz had pointed out, one hundred and one was the first three-digit prime—indivisible except by itself and the number one. Possibly important. He thought for a moment about the pulses or ones. Fourteen. Twenty-eight. Fifty-seven. This, in digits, was a recurring decimal. One four two eight five seven. Worth thinking about.

The answer, assuming there was a question, had to be simple. He tried to think along the lines of the simplest arithmetic. One zero one. Ninety-nine ones and two zeros. One four two eight five seven. Fourteen *gap* twenty-eight *gap* fifty-seven. He knew the others who'd worked at decoding the message had started out the same way but there was always a chance they'd overlooked something obvious. He thought of Softly wobbling in a rocker on his front porch in Pennyfellow. What would Softly do? Crack a joke and whistle through his pinky fingers. Which is about what this whole thing deserves.

There was a light knock on the door, a sort of loose-knuckled frolicsome blow. He found a woman standing outside and remembered to move back so she could enter. Her clothes were of the freely swirling type that might be classified either as terribly dramatic evening wear or out-and-out pajamas. She was tall and silvery, her expression one of painstaking animation, as if she didn't realize it was no longer necessary to be vivacious. A ribbon was awry in her hair and there were specks of confetti on her shirt and pants.

"I'm Soma Tobias."

"H'o."

"Were you at my party?"

"I don't think so. Be seated anywhere. What party?"

"My going-away party."

"When was it?"

"It started last night and it's still going on. I just wandered away for a while. Saw the light under your door and knew you were up."

"It's only afternoon," he said. "Sure I'm up."

"But don't you love to languish in bed all day long? To grow more feeble by the hour like so many French geniuses of the arts and sciences. Don't you think there's a wistful tenderness attached to those brilliantly apathetic periods of time we tend to spend in bed during the day? I fully expected to find you a-dawdle in your twofold."

"Are you drunk?"

"It's my going-away party," she said. "I'm going away."

"What were you here for in the first place?"

"Checking the structural soundness. Making sure they did justice to my concept."

"Are you the woman architect?"

"Some years ago I abandoned myself to the rhythms of the cycloid. Most gorgeous curve in nature. A figure of magical properties. It was then I resolved to apply that shape to a building, a city, a giant tombstone if need be—whatever kind of commission I could wangle."

"Tombstone?"

"Pascal became seriously ill the same year he did important work on the cycloid. They found a lesion on his brain."

"I just read something about that."

"What do you think of my design?"

"It's good from a distance."

"What about close up or inside?"

"I'm nodding."

"The Jesuits oppose the cycloid form. Did you know that? There's an old man named Verbene who's been after me ever since I got here."

"How could anybody be against a geometric shape?"

"The Jesuits oppose anything that can be turned upside down and still give pleasure. The cycloid of course is one such thing. Stunning gravitational wedding bowl. Marvelous pendulum properties. This priest Verbene has been at me hammer and tongs."

"What do you call that outfit you're wearing?"

"His red ants give me a pain," Soma said.

"What do you mean, red ants?"

"He studies red ants. He's founded a whole system of learning based on red ants. It's called red ant metaphysics. Met him yet?"

"He studies red ants?"

"Red ants and their secretions."

"And you think he's after you because things upside down shouldn't give pleasure?"

"The cycloid is geometry. I don't know why they have to get sex mixed up in it. Really I can't get over my surprise at not finding you in bed. Mathematics and pain. Bed-rest and meditation. Growing feebler by the hour. Puling and moaning in the iridescent fatigue of your genius."

He listened to her talk about the going-away party. It was like a monologue on insomnia. Or insomnia itself. Not that he minded. He had no special desire to resume work on the code. And it was nice having a woman around, even if she was all partied out, too weary to make dissolute history on his behalf. Beyond Soma Tobias's presence, however; beyond her voice; beyond the objects in the room, the room itself; beyond all these was the picture of a pale blue line, the locus of a point having one degree of freedom. Blue on white. Figures and movements. Pulses humming through the anesthesia of coordinate four-space. Was he meant to seek an equation and stretch its variable frame across an interstellar graph? Might be worth exploring. Axiomatic method. One fleeting motion true of another. The coordinate system had made calculus imaginable and this study of fluid nature's non-sequential sum had fueled the growth of modern mathematics. He saw it crowding its boundaries. Coordinates numbering n. Nature's space and his. To increase in size by the addition of material through assimilation. To become extended or intensified. What did mathematics grow *against*? Not nature but imagination. Yet when it poured through the borders, did it return to the physical world? Fundamental laws. Pebbles racing in vain down the slopes of an inverted cycloid. All minds meet in equal time at the bottom of the geometric hole.

"There he was," Soma mumbled. "Fourteen years old. Spending entire mornings in bed. Thinking how utterly useless were all those demonstrations of the authoritarian mind. All those sophistries and subtle equivocations. Frail of body, fond of bed."

"Who, Pascal?"

"You weren't listening."

"I was thinking," he said.

She rose and moved toward the door, so tired she sagged, defeated cheer still painted on her face. He followed along urbanely, managing to dodge her elbow when she opened the door.

"You're very spry for your age," she said.

"I almost understand that remark."

In seconds she was gone. He noticed the emblem sketched on the teleboard screen, a star pentagram drawn with the unbroken motion of the hand, and he knew Endor wanted to see him.

80

5

DICHOTOMY

Through the night there had been a competition in the topiary garden, people flying box kites adorned with paper lanterns. Prizes for design, color, maneuverability, speed of ascent, time in the air. Several kites had fluttered into soft flame, every such event accompanied by sounds of pleasurable regret from below. The burning frameworks remained briefly aloft, no longer parts of flying toys but in the lazy breezes of that perfect night resembling a class of mythical invertebrates determined to burn themselves away rather than return to the porous earth, where they'd earlier shed the silk of transfiguration.

In the morning the bulletproof Cadillac headed due east. Billy once again had the back seat to himself. The driver was a man named Kidder. The road was very straight and he barely had to move his hands on the wheel. He was so motionless in fact that Billy was reminded of LoQuadro's body disrupted by the human glitch. Reverse dissociation.

"We're not too far from the silos."

"What silos?"

"You must be a city boy," Kidder said.

"That's right."

"You never find silos in cities. That's true no matter where you travel in the world. You never find a silo in or near a city."

"How far is it, where we're going?"

"Ten miles hole to hole. That's supposed to be a joke. Door to door. Hole to hole. Get it?"

"I only get half of it."

"I'll settle for that," Kidder said.

"Door to hole. That's the part I get."

"Let's not talk for a while. I'm concentrating on the road. I can't drive on straightaways unless I really bear down. Even as I talk, I'm paying no attention to what I say for fear of losing my concentration. I have no idea whether I'm making sense or not. For all I know I'm speaking in a foreign language. Or even crazier than that. If I lose my concentration, I veer. It's like something's grasping at the car."

"The last time I was in this car there were two other people where you're sitting."

"Then you weren't in this car," the man said. "You were with different people in a different car."

"How fast does it say you're going?"

"A jack rabbit could keep up with this car the way I'm driving right now."

"Never."

"Do you know how fast our friend the rabbit travels at top speed?"

"No."

"Seventy-four feet."

"Per second?"

"Per second per second."

"I don't even get half of that one."

"Maybe there's nothing to get," Kidder said.

"I thought we weren't talking."

"Cute as a tack, aren't you?"

The driver gradually eased off on the accelerator. There wasn't much scenery in the area. The morning was clear and mild. Billy had made double knots with the long laces of his low-cut sneakers. He wore jeans and a pullover shirt. Something hit the windshield now, leaving a melancholy gob on the tinted glass. Endor. What does he want? Why is he behaving this way? A famous person for thirty years and he's living in the ground. One failure and he gives up everything? Maybe it's not even genuine contact. Just some radio waves traveling through space. Coming from a hydrogen cloud or all somebody's idea of a joke. Playing tunes on the computer. Endor had married three times, suffered injuries in two wars, flown jet aircraft to nearly record-breaking altitudes to do photographic research in astronomy. He had written several books of a speculative nature, best-sellers every one. He was an accomplished cellist and founder of an all-mathematician chamber group. Heads of state had honored him in marble halls.

"We're there," Kidder said.

"Why don't you stop?"

"What do you think I'm doing? It takes time to stop. You don't just stop. I have no idea what I'm saying to you at the present time because I'm engaged in bringing this car to a complete stop and my attention is so focused that I'm not aware of my own conversation. So you'll excuse me if I make a foolish remark or two. Even now, with the car almost totally brought to a stop, I couldn't tell you what words I'm in the process of saying."

Billy walked thirty yards to the edge of the hole. Endor was standing at the bottom of the hole, exactly where everyone had said he'd be. The hole was about fifteen feet long, eight wide and twelve deep. There seemed to be another hole inside the first, a tunnel gouged out of the dirt at one corner of the original hole, the hole proper. Endor's shirt and trousers were well shredded. The five-rayed star he'd always worn on a chain around his neck was no longer there. His sage face was sunburned and muddy. Several small crawling things moved about in his white beard. Hands on hips he looked up at the boy, who was reluctant to sit at the edge of the hole (with legs dangling in suitably youthful fashion) for reasons he did not care to articulate to himself.

"You're the only one I'll talk to, lad."

"I'm ready for anything you have to say."

"I sneaked up to the computer area yesterday to get one last look at all the sequence grids and radio maps and print-outs and other crapola. The whole stinking computer universe. Hoping it would all come together in this one last look. But it stayed apart. It definitely did not come together. Back to your hole, Endor. Get back before they see you and start moving their lips. Expecting you to react to their idiot phonemes. Talk to the boy. The boy's done pure work in the pure field. Am I right, Big Bill? You'll find the answer. It's yours for the asking. You're the right mind in the right body. Wouldn't surprise me if you've found it already. Am I right? You've deciphered the ·message?"

Without waiting for a reply he lowered himself to his knees and crawled across the floor of the hole into the second hole. Billy didn't try to see what he was doing in there. Couldn't possibly result in anything beneficial. He turned to make sure the Cadillac was still in the area. Kidder leaned on the front door, flipping a coin. About ten minutes passed. Endor crawled out of the lateral hole. He appeared to be chewing on something. He looked up at the boy but didn't bother standing.

"If all matter possesses one nature and seeks to unite with all other matter, why are things flying apart?" he said. "Answer me that."

He crawled back into the second hole and remained concealed there for several more minutes. When he emerged this time he got to his feet.

"Our galactic center is leaking gas like crazy. What does it mean?"

"I don't know."

"Colossal explosion, methinks. It's so dense in there. A million times denser than where we are. Planets get torn out of orbit in that kind of density. Too many stars. Too much force and counterforce. In just our galaxy alone, do you know how many stars there are?"

"No."

"That's just our galaxy alone. It's just too much, too big. There's no need for everything to be so spread out. Why is the universe so big? And why despite the billions and billions of stars and hundreds of millions of galaxies is there so much space left over? They say things are still fleeing from the original explosion. Things flee, eventually to come together again, blue instead of red. What do they say about me, Big Bill? Do they say I eat worms?"

Endor crawled into the second hole again. He was gone for about half an hour this time. The boy sat crosslegged on the grass, flicking his index finger at the tips of his shoelaces. The famous scientist returned and got slowly to his feet. Strips of clothing hung loosely from his lean body. Everywhere on his face was a sense of the wailing contradiction that lives along the edges of science and time. He scratched at his beard and spat some rusty stuff into the mud.

"Mathematics is the only avant-garde remaining in the whole province of art. It's pure art, lad. Art and science. Art, science and language. Art as much as the art we once called art. It lost its wings after the Babylonians fizzled out. But emerged again with the Greeks. Went down in the Dark Ages. Moslems and Hindus kept it going. But now it's back bright as ever. I got too careless for mathematics. Forgot how swift and deadly it can be. I turned in my panic to empty-field sources and black-body radiation. It was fascinating for a time. You could peer and count and measure and sigh. You could ponder the heavens. You could say: 'Ahhhhh, there it is, look and see.' But the size of the universe began to depress me. I thought the Ratnerians might be offering us a simple declarative sentence or a neat cluster of numbers that would tell us why the universe is so big. When I failed to interpret the message, there was no recourse but the hole. You're lucky, Big B. Right mind in right body. Insect larvae. That's what I eat. Tell them when you get back. Endor eats insect larvae. He doesn't eat worms as such. Larvae. Quasi-worms. Worms pro tem. Furry little items fresh from the earth."

He crawled back into the second hole. The sun was directly overhead. Billy stretched out on the grass, being sure to keep his feet away from the edge of the hole and yet unable to explain to himself why he'd taken this curious precaution. He conjectured from one to three:

1) Endor would grab his ankles, drag him into the hole and eat him.

This made no sense, of course. It was stupid. Endor was respected throughout the world. On the other hand he was a man who had chosen to live in a hole. No, it made no sense. People didn't do things like that. It was stupid. But people under stress did do things like that. Endor was under severe stress. Endor was a person. Yet this was logical thinking and the last thing he wanted to do was trap himself with words and propositions. He knew a logical trap was the worst kind. Numbers had two natures; they existed as themselves, abstractly, and as units for measuring distances and counting objects. Words could not be separated from their use. This fact made logical traps easy to fall into and hard to get out of.

2) Endor ate insect larvae and might pull him into the hole and force him to do the same. This was more frightening than number one because it was more likely. It was just as stupid but a lot more likely and therefore warranted fear. He had no objection to other people eating larvae as long as he could watch from a safe distance. Endor might not physically force him to eat baby insects but could possibly make the eating of these things seem an invigorating pastime. He had the ability and experience to set a language trap, using scientific persuasiveness and his knowledge of large words and the spaces between such words.

3) Endor had access to a second hole of unknown dimensions and might grab Billy's ankles and drag him across the first hole and into the second. This was worst of all. The second hole was a concealed entity, a truer than usual pit, a repository for all the disfigured outgrowths of the morbid imagination. People liked to arrange encounters for him with holes, tunnels, sightless eyes, artificial limbs, models of computerized maw. Of these forms of experimental terror he had directly experienced only one. This was the subway tunnel, a region less dreadful than it might have been only because of the word "subway," which was familiar and specific, evoking sound, color, scent and shape. Endor's second hole evoked none of these. It evoked only: *second hole*. Untraveled territory. Nothing to picture. No noise to imagine in anticipation of the real thing. It was only twenty feet away from him, the entrance to the hole's hole, but it wasn't the real thing, or the fake thing,

or the thing. Who knew what it was? The power of logic, so near to number and so distant, filled his body with warped vibrations, as of a harp string plucked by monkeys.

Endor reappeared. The boy, still frozen to the grass in a state of propositional dream-shock, heard the great man clawing against the sides of the hole proper. This, it turned out, was his way of getting to his feet. Billy knelt at the rim. Endor began to urinate into the second hole, adjusting his stance so that the long feeble arc terminated at the point where the second hole commenced. Although he redeposited his scaly old dangle, he didn't bother fastening his pants and so the zipper just sagged there, fatigued and silver in the sun.

"It tugs hard, lad. I feel it in the bottoms of my feet. There is *want* at the center of the earth. Never mind impressed force and inverse proportion. There is sheer *wanting* to contend with. Every day I feel it more. It reaches higher in my body. Everything is want. Everything wants. To be a scientist. Do you know what it's like to be a scientist? I am asking you and telling you these things because these are things you would otherwise have to ask and tell yourself in the years and decades to come. My books on science sold well. But I didn't know until recently what it means to be a scientist. It means the opposite of what people believe it to mean. We don't extend the senses to probe microbe and universe. We deny the senses. We deny the evidence of our senses. A lifetime of such denial is what sends people into larva-eating rages."

Endor crawled into the second hole, returning moments later.

"Science requires us to deny the evidence of the senses," he said. "We see the sun moving across the sky and we say no, no, no, the sun is not moving, it's we who move, we move, we. Science teaches us this. The earth moves around the sun, we say. Nevertheless every morning we open our eyes and there's the sun moving across the sky, east to west every single day. It moves. We see it. I'm tired of denying such evidence. The earth doesn't move. It's the sun that moves around the earth. It's maggots that are generated spontaneously in rotten meat. It's the wind that causes tides. If the earth moved we'd get dizzy and fall off. If the moon and sun cause tides in oceans, why don't they cause tides in swimming pools and glasses of water? There's no variation in the microwave background. Why is this? Because we're at the center of the universe, that's why this is. Don't forget maggots. Whenever you see rotten meat you see maggots. In the meat. In and of the meat. Born of meat. Meat-engendered. Maggots come spontaneously from meat. If not, from where?"

"Flies lay eggs," Billy said.

"Flies lay eggs."

"Flies land on the meat and lay eggs. Isn't the maggot just an early stage in the fly cycle or whatever it's called? Flies lay eggs."

"Flies lay eggs," Endor said.

He snatched at something and put it quickly in his mouth. Something from the hard mud at the side of the hole. Something soft-bodied, wingless, elongate and probably very much alive. Vivid slime dripped through his beard. Fresh green larval fluids. After half a minute he stopped chewing. Billy turned to check on the availability of the Cadillac.

Endor returned to the second hole, remaining there for fifteen minutes this time. Billy tried to ignore the fact that the elderly scientist had quite recently urinated into that very area. Was it before this visit or the previous one? Either way there was bound to be a chemical residue. When Endor returned, part of his shirt was sticking out of the crotch-opening in his pants.

"Men shrink in space," he said. "We have X-ray silhouettes and stereoscopic photographs to prove it. The heart of an astronaut actually shrinks. So do his limbs and torso. Nothing tugs at the man in space. There is no want. None of that universal suck and gulp. His muscles lose tone. His blood accumulates in the wrong places. Chemicals in his body become deranged. In short there is none of the poetry of falling matter. Want is everything. Everything wants. Without want, the bones lose calcium. Without want, potassium vanishes. It used to be thought that matter was falling. In the beginning matter fell. It fell uniformly. It was in the nature of matter to fall. The uniform motion of falling matter meant there was no interaction between particles. No force intervened to disrupt the uniform and utterly beautiful matter-fall of all things everywhere. But then there was a swerve, it was thought. Something, or everything, was nudged into the most imperceptible of swerves. Two particles lightly touched, adhering for the most imperceptible of seconds. This random interaction was the origin of the universe as we know it and fear it today. But nothing in this ancient poem of matter falling precludes the notion that matter continues to fall. Matter is now thought to be organized, interactive and guided by well-defined forces and yet nowhere in the scientific canon is there evidence to dispel the poetic impression that matter-now-organized is constantly falling, which is what I said in the previous sentence if you were listening. It's in the nature of objects to fall. The whole universe is falling. This is the meaning of dreams in which we plunge forever."

He crawled out of sight. When he returned this time he had difficulty getting to his feet. His face and arms were crusted with mud. Mud had accumulated under his fingernails. There was a chunk of dry mud in what remained of the breast pocket of his disintegrating shirt. He finally straightened up. Mudless things with segmented bodies moved through his hair.

"We begin to see how lawless everything is. Once we go beyond planar surfaces we see how mysterious a subject is the geometry of space and time. Who is turning the laws of the universe upside down and were they true laws to begin with? How to explain unexplained energy. Where to find the standard candle. The universe is falling. Yes or no. That's the single pre-emptive riddle. Mull it over and tell me what you think."

Before Billy could say anything, Endor crawled into his tunnel, if that's what it was. The boy didn't mind because he had nothing to say on the subject of falling matter as it pertained to the riddle of the universe. In sixty seconds Endor was back.

"Einstein and Kafka! They knew each other! They stood in the same room and talked! Kafka and Einstein!"

He crawled back into the hole's hole and remained there for a very long time. The hole proper was now in shadow. Billy wondered how Endor survived the nights. Never mind the nights, he then thought. The days. The diet. The boredom. Good weather and bad. Fear and despair. Outrage, loneliness, memory and death. When Endor returned this time, Billy was first to speak.

"What do you eat besides larvae?"

"When I'm feeling hale enough I claw my way up to the rim of the hole and eat the grass or whatever I find growing within arm's length. Some intense little plants in the vicinity."

"I guess there's nothing you can do about drinking except wait for it to rain and drink the rainwater."

"I drink the mud," Endor said. "There's rainwater and earthwater in the mud. I suck and gulp at the mud. Suck and gulp are the activating principles behind the abstract idea of want."

"What do you do in that other hole every time you go in there?"

"I dig, I claw."

"Just with your fingers?"

"There's a clothes hanger. I keep a clothes hanger in there. It's the only thing I brought with me to the hole. I thought I'd need something for my clothes. Something to hang my clothes on. But it turns out I use the clothes hanger to dig. That is, when I dig. Mostly I just claw. I use my fingers to claw."

"I don't see how you can get very far with a hanger. I could have brought you a spoon or fork."

"I never claw without uttering sounds. Otherwise what's it all for? Never underestimate the value of clawing. But never simply claw. As you claw, utter whatever sounds seem appropriate. Nonverbal sounds work best, I find. Otherwise why bother? This is a cruel brand of work."

"Why are you digging and clawing? Why do you claw?"

"Let me see if I'm up to answering that question. There are any number of ways I might reply. Could say the larvae are tastier the deeper I dig. Could answer naturalistically and say I am creating a shelter from the elements. Could, if I cared to, make a series of enigmatic remarks concerning man's need for metaphysical burrows that lead absolutely nowhere. But I believe I'll stick to the answer I gave before you asked the question."

He crawled away again. Billy wasn't on the verge of leaving but he was very close to thinking about leaving. Endor finally returned. This time he neither got to his feet nor remained on all fours. Instead he sat back against the side of the hole, forearms resting on raised knees.

"You're the only one I've talked to, lad. I've had a strong conviction for quite some time. Both before and since the hole. Better light out for a hole, Endor. Find yourself a hole and light out fast. That was my conviction. I still have it. Things here aren't what they seem, Big B. I don't think I'm any closer to dying than I was before the hole. Excluding pure chronology, of course. In other words I didn't come here to meet a quick end. Another thing. The sorrow of simply being is no greater here than it was in pre-hole environments. When you talk about simply being, you're talking about things like holes and rusty mud. My mind is the same, my eyesight, the way I dream, the way I smell to myself. It's surprisingly easy to adjust to living in a hole. Out there, in other words, there's just as much holeness and mudness. Almost time you were leaving, lad."

"Right away."

"Want to watch me eat some more larvae?"

"That's the best part of being here. The eating. I like the sound it makes."

"Keep down, Endor. Don't take any crapola from those mongers."

"What's a monger?"

"Someone who traffics in, peddles to and deals with."

"Am I going yet?"

"It's time now to tell you why I summoned you to this place, this hole."

"You already told me."

"What did I say?"

"You said you were telling me these things because they were things I'd have to tell myself in the years to come. So you're telling them to me now. I guess to get me ready."

"That's not it," Endor said. "This is it."

He crawled into the second hole and remained for about half an hour. Then came out talking.

"There's a dark side to Field Experiment Number One. Now listen. If you've ever heeded anything, heed this. This is it. An outright warning. There is a dark side to it. The importance of the message from Ratner's star, regardless of content, is that it will tell us something of importance about ourselves. That's it, you see. The importance. But there are people and things I want to warn you about. Nameless danger. Be alert for nameless danger. Pending developments, you're the big little man. That makes you important. You are pivotal to the schemes of the mongers. The importance of the code. The namelessness of the danger."

"Is that it for now? Because the car's been ready."

"Visit my room at Field Experiment Number One. It's not one of those shimmery canisters. I designed it myself. Had things shipped in special. It's a room that may comfort you in the time of your inevitable terror, much as I hate to use that kind of defeatist's terminology. It's a room in and of time. Nice place to sit and think. I am special blessed. You are blessed. This is our joint curse. Visit with my blessing."

"I'd like to be excused now."

"My books sold well," Endor said. "I popularized the secrets of the brotherhood all too obligingly. But never a nonverbal word passed my pen. Light out for the hole, Endor. Claw your way down through the silicates to the core iron. Rest in that darkness safe from larvicide. Then start to claw again."

A helicopter went beating past the hole. Billy watched it circle once and then touch down not far from the Cadillac, the blades stirring up dust and leveling tall grass, a state of disturbance created, the emotion that sweeps across the bow of a storm, more than natural agitation. It was as though the afternoon had been fine-sliced into altered rates of movement. A different kind of pace asserted itself, traced in frame-by-frame instants of urgency, expedience, stress, wind-whipped news carried from a very official location. It was an executive helicopter but the man who emerged wore a laboratory smock and red and white basketball sneakers. He gestured to Kidder, who immediately got into the Cadillac and drove off. Billy looked into the hole, hoping Endor would have an explanation for the appearance of the helicopter and departure of the limousine. But Endor had disappeared into the second hole. The man waved to Billy, who got to his feet and headed in the direction of the small aircraft. Since the blades still rotated loudly, the conversation that ensued was at a near shout.

"My name is Hoad. I work on the star project. Hoad. We were in the air when we got word about the star. They told us where you were. We came here to give you the word and get you back to headquarters at once."

"What word?"

"The star is part of a two-star system. Space Brain has just confirmed it. Two-star system. We've suspected this but weren't sure. Now we know. The star is binary."

"Ratner's star?"

"There are two of them," Hoad shouted. "Binary star. Two-star system."

"What does this mean? How does this affect things?"

"It doesn't affect things at all and in practical terms it means next to nothing."

"Does it mean there's less chance of life on any planet that's in orbit in that kind of system?"

"There's less chance, yes, but it's far from impossible. There can be one or more planets in a multiple stellar system capable of supporting life. It's a three-body problem. Suitable orbits, equal mass, temperature variations. But the chance of life as we know it or don't know it is certainly better if the planet in question orbits a single star."

"So it's bad news then."

"What?"

"It's bad news."

"It doesn't negate the message. The message exists. Someone or something sent the message from the neighborhood of Ratner's star."

"There's one thing I don't get."

"What's that?" Hoad shouted.

"Why bother telling me this kind of news? My job is supposed to be the code, break the code. What's the difference to me whether Ratner's star is one star or two stars? The message exists. That's all that matters to me."

"Exactly what I just said."

"I didn't hear."

"Exactly what I said. The message exists. Your job is the code, not the star. But we wanted to tell you about the star because we thought it might help you with the code. Now that you know there are two stars instead of one, you might want to alter your calculations. Or at least view the transmission in a different light. I don't know. We don't pretend to know. We hope you'll know. Come on—Poebbels is waiting in the chopper."

"I'm not sure I want to ride in that thing."

"I've logged I don't know how many hours in spiral-wing aircraft," Hoad yelled. "It's safer than your own two feet."

"Who is Poebbels?"

"Who?"

"Poebbels, who's waiting in the chopper."

"Poebbels," Hoad shouted. "Senior to me. Respected and feared. Supervises plausibility studies. The transmission. The telescope. The computer. The star system and planet. Othmar Poebbels. I hope he dies."

"You hope he dies?"

"You weren't supposed to hear that."

"Why are you wearing that outfit?"

"Poebbels insists we dress this way. Come on, let's get going. Whatever you do, don't act frightened. Even if you're terrifically scared of being aloft in a small aircraft, don't, whatever you do, show it. Poebbels hates to fly. If he knows you're scared, he'll be doubly scared. I don't think I could bear that."

The only good thing about the trip, from Billy's viewpoint, was the part where he approached the helicopter with ducked head and unnatural scuttling steps. Although he wasn't wearing a hat he put his right hand to his head as he proceeded importantly to the aircraft. Despite his bent-over shoulder-first approach, he didn't feel foolish. He liked getting on the helicopter; it was, after all, an executive helicopter and he felt as he imagined six-figure executives probably feel when they duck under the blades and fly off to lavish spas for rubdowns and hard bargaining.

He was seated behind the two men. Hoad at the controls manipulated switches. The noise inside the aircraft reached a punishing intensity, all conversation edging gradually toward the level of an outright scream. Poebbels was about twice Hoad's age, Hoad twice Billy's. The boy had noticed, as he climbed aboard, that Poebbels had very heavy eyes. They gleamed in his head like die-cut precision parts. Hard to imagine eyes like that ever slipping out of focus. Above the eyes was a single broadband eyebrow and above that was dark vigorous hair growing downward into Poebbels's forehead. The noise level brought about contorted looks on all three faces, an automatic shrinking inward.

"We agree the message exists," Hoad cried. "One star or two, the message is not negated. The kid agrees on this. We agree. The pulses and gaps exist. We have contact. There is transmission. Something intelligent lives in the vicinity of Ratner's star."

"Get this zombie ship in the air," Poebbels screamed.

As the helicopter abruptly rose, Poebbels's entire body became taut. Billy felt his own fear uncurl from his stomach (a slick veneer of freak tissue) and dissolve into artless vapors. Poebbels, unclenching a bit, turned slightly in his seat and, although his mouth was only inches from Hoad's right ear, began to direct to Billy a series of high-volume remarks.

"I have work-ed in many fields," he shouted. "I have done work with discrete things. I have done other work with continuous things. How do discrete things relate each to the other? I have wish-ed to answer this question. In the final resolve, all there is to do with discrete things is to count them. One two three four five. There is to count them and there is to use them in a universal logical language, which I hope one day to live to see. I am individually distinct. The individual Hoad is equally distinct. There is unbroken space between us. Of the continuous, I have also done good work. Flow and grow. This is my way to put this work in a short rhyming phrase. Flow and grow. To help me remember. This is what we do right now in this zombie ship. Rate of change every little instant. Move, movement, motion. All together in one smooth whoosh. We have broad wings and soar in untrammel-ed way through the sky of creatures of scant mass. If I give the order to suspend and float on air, then we are all of a sudden a discrete thing and good only to be counted. I make second order and we are continuous again. Flow and grow. I believe this is the meaning giv-ed by the star people. How to join together discrete with continuous. I have hope in your methods, smart fellow. To be sure, this is purely theoretical hope, since it is a fact that my studies in plausibility lead without escape to the conclusion that all events thus far pertaining to the star are lacking in verisimilitude, acceptability and likelihood."

In the distance, beyond the main structure, Billy could see the synthesis telescope—hundreds of tiny dish antennas. A fear bubble traveled upward through his respiratory system. The eye-narrowing mouth-tensing expressions remained unchanged on all three faces. The sun was low now in the western sky. Othmar Poebbels, resuming his address to the boy, once again began screaming in his assistant's ear.

"Simultaneous great men of history," he said. "Ideas bred in two scientific minds at one and the same time. Many examples. Two men thousands of miles away. Speak unsame languages. Differ in all respects. Twin theory phenomena. The dance of two radiant minds in the endless night. But always some conflict sneaks in. Dichotomy. Clash and counterclash. You have seen Endor. A sight to see. Digging in the ground. Endor and Poebbels. In the early days we did much good work together. I have progress-ed little by little to the belief that all thought can be put in scientific language which we then manipulate according to strict laws. Submit all reasoning to calculation. Throw in symbolic structure. In this way we end man-made error in the universe. The purest of pure science. This is my hope for the future of everything. Endor meanwhile is trapped in matter. I have talk-ed in this intimate way to show you my respect of your career, small American colleague."

The aircraft began its slow passage down. Immediately all tension vanished. The noise and screaming, the vibrations, the grimaces, the fear bubbles, the lack of sufficient space—all were forgotten at once. Billy watched the horizon correlate itself with the helicopter's flickering descent. Evening peace was settling over the land in patterns of startling visibility. It was a time of precise and unimpelled delight, plain lines of blue and gray, things taken in, men returning, all scattered creatures come together from their day of tumbling in the sun. Units glided into place, every level of descent opening to the fall of the toy-bright object. There seemed no force in nature. All motion was uniform motion occurring in a straight line. Shadows of departed figures themselves departed. To fall in this way, uniformly, equal to but never influenced by other falling things, seemed almost to dispel the sorrow of ponderous being. Free, unswerving and independent of friction, the plunge was like a childhood sigh, devoid of obedience and rote, never evolving, nowhere close to the boned-out howl of those voices departed to the edge of the pure word, evident in the sequence of related sounds only as a timeless sigh—not of this woman in murmurous bliss or that man half leaping in her arms in a spangled blaze of bird-fish symmetry and delicate brute creation, but of a child, only that, a child is all, his sigh a knowing contemplation of time and place and all those darker energies that constitute his peril.

"The craft is down," Hoad cried. "I've brought the craft to earth."

He flipped switches and then jumped out and circled the helicopter in an analytic manner, appearing in his smock and high sneakers to be a doctor of parked cars. As Billy began to rise from his seat, Poebbels put a hand to his forearm and looked carefully into his face.

"I will accompany you to the outskirts of the lobby," he said. "Yes, I will be honor-ed to walk at your side, mathematical phenomenon."

"Where's the lobby? I never saw any lobby."

"Fourteenth floor."

"What's it doing there?"

"Whatever lobbies do," Poebbels said. "Your face is notably clean. This is most important in one's overt conduct. In my group I insist that all subordinates devote themselves to being neat, clean and quick. In order to win their fear, I am often irrational on the subject. Plausibility studies demand the utmost in these areas. We discover this empirically time and again in our daily work. I see you wear sneakers. Very excellent boy-model. I am happy at this moment. I abound with joy. The zombie ship is down and still we live. I have many times remark-ed to my colleagues that the only miracle attach-ed to human flight is that the human heart does not cease to beat in midair. You are happily an exemplar of neatness despite your time in or near the hole and I am glad to accompany you, transcendent intellect, to a point within sight of the lobby. But beyond that I have no wish to go, for I must hurry down to the first floor or I fear I will miss the arrival of the vaunted black fanatic from Australia."

"Who's that?"

"He is said in words to be a dervish, fiend, deity and seer. On other occasions he is referr-ed to in purely scientific terms."

"As what?"

"Master of space and time," Poebbels said.

6

CONVERGENCE INWARD

The blandishments of Softly's hands, Billy recalled, had made the small animal seem to frown, lap-pampered though it was, whispered to and courted in the pedagogic manner children use with pets (although Softly, of course, had left childhood far behind), and it was afternoon and very green on Softly's porch, immersed in spiral vines and bordered by trees and uncut shrubs, and they'd been talking of this and that, Billy recalled, when Softly plucked from nowhere the speculation: "I wonder if an object too dense to release light is any *purer* for the experience. Does it rank as a sort of Everyobject? Are catatonic people setting a standard for the rest of us? Is the electro-magnetic spectrum a model for the perceptual limitations implicit in any nonblind species of life? And other related questions."

One zero one.

Not only the lowest three-digit prime but the smallest three-digit palindrome. Not only reads the same forward and back but rightside up and upside down. And not only when looked at directly but also when reflected in a mirror. Continues to yield palindromes not only when squared and cubed but when raised to even higher powers.

Thus he passed the time, in regressive play, feeling certain there was nothing to be found anyway, no code to break. He glanced from time to time at the manuscript just to his right. Something about eighteenth-century men working in the service of kings and dowager queens. Court mathematicians of Russia and Prussia. "Only a small fraction of the work that shaped their art was devoted to the dim practicalities of the day. Every new paper, memoir, volume broadened the scope of mathematics itself. Ironic that this amplitude of class should be accompanied by such grim individual funneling of effort, convergence toward an existential center. And curious to find two men doing inter-related work and suffering for it so differently. Both of them were productive well beyond the inner margins of old age. Genial cyclops with a weakness for children. Detached gentleman content to die." It was odd to sit at a desk called a module inside a room known as a canister and to read, under such conditions, of a man who had begun his work before the birth of Catherine the Great and who did not end it until nearly nine hundred books and articles had been published in his name. It was doubly odd to be engaged in trivial calculations based on a series of radio pulses believed to have been transmitted by living things in another part of the galaxy and to reflect, in such circum-stances, on a man whose genius had been acclaimed by Napoleon but who was drawn into star-ponds of such inertia that he left his greatest work unopened on his desk for two full years.

The videophone chimed.

"It was as though no experience could escape such minds. The neural center was intent on total concentration. At the bottom of it all dwelt a collapsed object, fallen into its own fundamental being, model of the mathematician himself, invisible except in madness and final pain."

The videophone chimed. He pressed a button and listened as a small male head, calling itself Simeon Goldfloss, announced the existence of a shortcut to the amphitheater in the armillary sphere. Billy didn't know why the man was giving him this information but he was grateful for the excuse it provided to shun further work on the code, at least for the time being, and so he followed Goldfloss's directions, although not with much enthusiasm. A few people were scattered around the amphitheater. Goldfloss stood, nodding, and Billy walked slowly over there, trailing his lack of interest like a baby sister. Then he sat, arms folded across his chest. In the narrow aisle the man maneuvered himself into semi-erect posture, facing the boy, one foot up on the seat adjacent to Billy's.

"A lot of people think this might finally be the answer to the secret of Ratner's star. But before the hall fills up and we get started, I'd like to summarize our findings up to now."

"What might finally be the answer?"

"The aborigine," Goldfloss said.

"Summarize what findings? I didn't know there were any findings. I thought that's what I was here for. To make the findings."

"There have been and will continue to be findings. In the next ten minutes about eighty people working on various aspects of the star project will fill this little theater. They've all made findings of one kind or another. That's why we have the computer universe. To simulate events in order to reach conclusions."

"Who's this aborigine?"

"We hope to answer that question here today."

"How can an aborigine help out on a scientific project?"

"It's not inconceivable that some things exist beyond the borders of rational inquiry. Most everyone will come here to gibe and twit. Fair enough. I may decide to join the fun. But it's important to remember that we haven't gone into this without first investigating every shred of evidence concerning the aborigine's totemic powers."

People were entering the amphitheater. The chatter began to spread in intersecting lines as men and women turned in their seats, moved from tier to tier, stage-whispered improbable rumors up and down the gallery. The sense of festivity, however, was never really total. Across the spaces between bodies a secondary communication seemed to be developing, a secret accompaniment to words and gestures, and it was simply the mass suspicion that through every level of hearsay and high delight there might eventually pass the shaft of a primitive spear.

"We're on the verge," Goldfloss said. "I've never sensed this kind of excitement. I have the feeling something sensational is going to come out of this operation in a matter of days. A new way of viewing ourselves in relation to the universe. A revolutionary human consciousness. And you're at the very center of events."

"Me and the aborigine."

Goldfloss sported dundreary whiskers and wore a silvery denim suit.

"Ratner's star is a main sequence star and its sister star is a black hole. We can't see it but we know it's there because of the pattern of X-ray emissions. So what we're dealing with is a planet in an orbital situation that involves a yellow dwarf, namely Ratner's star, and a supermassive invisible object, or gravitational singularity if you will, or black hole, to use the popular term. That concludes our summary."

A woman wearing an eyepatch entered the chamber. Billy had never seen a woman with an eyepatch. Wondering why, he decided men get in more fights. It was a black patch and covered the right eye. He watched her climb to the fourth or fifth row across the aisle, where she sat alone, a well-shaped woman in her forties, hair cut short, complexion pale, idle lilac scent humming in the air about her.

"Ratner's star is our future," Goldfloss said. "What we've received is most likely the key to their language and to every piece of knowledge they possess. Once you break the code we'll have no trouble reading future messages. We'll know everything they know. In that sense the star is our future. The message itself is probably boring. 'Eight squared is sixty-four.' 'We have twisted molecules.' Typical cosmic announcement. What follows, however, will alter the very core of our being."

A man appeared on the floor of the amphitheater. Silence was instantaneous. Goldfloss, still semi-erect in the aisle and with his back to

101

the man, reacted to the sudden hush by turning slowly and then easing into the seat next to Billy.

The man standing below them, although obviously accustomed to wilderness and excessive sun, was just as obviously white; that is, he was clearly Caucasian, pink-tinged in some spots, ruddy in others, merely freckled elsewhere. He wore old khaki shorts, bark sandals and a string headband ornamented with eucalyptus nuts. His bare sunken chest was scarred and pigmented—three linked circles in red and black. He gazed up one tier of seats and then across the top row and slowly down the second tier.

"Most of you know me, if at all, by the name Gerald Pence. However, I haven't used that name for a very long time. I am called Mutuka now. I arrived, you see, among the nomadic people of the outback in a motor car. Mu-tu-ka, you see. I've been given this name and use no other. Those of you who know me are probably aware of the extensive work I once did in futurology. This is no longer part of my dreamtime, or *tjukurpa*. I use stone tools now. I eat lizard and emu. I find peace in the contemplation of rock art. Since deciding to live among the foragers, I've learned the language, *wangka nintiri*, and have begun slowly to understand the higher reality of nonobjective truth. The secrets of the bush are extraordinary indeed. Hard to unravel, harder to explain. Yet with the passage of time, they become less and less extraordinary and soon appear to be nothing more than the natural schemeless flow of nonevents. I don't intend to reveal the secrets of the bush. My role here is a very limited one. The man, the extraordinary individual who grows less extraordinary by the day, the forager and seer whom, it is fitting to say, I am privileged to accompany to this point in geographical history—*his* role is to accomplish nothing less than the creation of an alternative to space and time."

This second silence was extremely fragile. The sense of something vast produced from something very small—an explosion of laughter, for instance, from a tiny bubble at the end of someone's tongue— seemed to threaten the carefully woven equilibrium in the hall. *An alternative to space and time.* The phrase was so neatly pre-emptive, so crisp in its implication that the coordinates of all human perception might be not only less reliable than had been thought but completely disposable as well; the sheer efficiency of the phrase, its self-assurance —these were probably enough to guarantee that any laughter of sufficient duration would eventually find its way to the hysterical end of the spectrum. But the silence held and tightened.

"The nomadic family I live with has no name even in its own language. Its language has no name. The secrets of the bush have no name. The man himself, the aborigine, has neither name nor descriptive title, even among his people, most especially among his people. The few white men, *walypala*, who know of his existence call him variously seer, demon, traveler, god. He doesn't wish to be given a name. He doesn't wish to be seen. Indeed there's been some question as to whether there is anything to see. It's not a simple matter to talk of someone who has no name or title and does not wish to be given any. One could try to get around it by referring to such a person as 'he who has no name.' But this description then becomes his name. The names of the various dialects spoken by the desert nomads are usually descriptive in precisely this way. Let me offer an example: 'the language having the words *foot* and *hand* but not *feet* and *hands*.' This is the actual name of a dialect. For obvious reasons those who speak the dialect don't refer to it this way. My own nomadic family are a noncounting people. They forage and make throwing spears. Some have blond hair. This is fairly common among desert aborigines. Our visitor's hair, so it's said, is completely white. My people can count only as far as one. They don't understand the multiple form at all. Beyond one, everything is considered a heap. What we call a boomerang has no name in their dialect except on its return trip to the person who hurled it. Stuck in the dust it is nameless. Held in hand, nameless. Released, it remains nameless. Returning, however, it acquires a name—a name so sacred that even if I knew what it was I could not speak it here. A colleague of mine in the early days in the bush was clever enough to ask what the boomerang was called as it pivoted in midair. This was Beveridge Kettle, as some of you may have guessed by the cleverness of the remark—dear man, never found. Happily, the foragers have adopted me. I drink from their billabongs. I see their ghosts—I see their *mamu*. When a boy was circumcised recently I was among those chosen to eat the foreskin. I hunt their kangaroo. I help care for their dingo dogs. I throw their barbed spear— I throw their *kulata*."

Billy shifted in his chair. He was tired of Mutuka and wanted to see the real aborigine, if there was one. If not, he wanted to go to his room and spend a few moments mentally dwelling on the ingestion of the foreskin. This was new to him. He'd heard about puberty rites and he knew about circumcision but the idea of concluding such antics by eating the kid's foreskin was completely new to him. Something that novel and disgusting deserved consideration in an atmosphere of total solitude. He looked across the aisle toward the eyepatched woman but someone had taken the seat to her left, effectively blocking his view.

"In the dreamtime there is no separation between man and land. The people act out events in the lives of the dreamtime beings. We become the dingo, the eagle, the bush turkey, the one-one-one-eyed man, the man of beating stick-stick, the man who forages in nameless space. People visit the places of their dreaming—a rockpile, for example, that contains the spirit of the lizard, snake or bandicoot from which they've descended. And they address the rockpile as 'my father, my father'— *ngayuku mama, ngayuku mama*. People wail at the places of their dreaming. The kangaroo novice performs his dance. Human and animal forms are considered as one. Time is pure and all place is birthplace, the dreamtime site. The bandicoot, incidentally, is a ratlike marsupial."

A man got wearily to his feet and left the amphitheater. Across the aisle another man leaned forward for a moment, giving Billy an unobstructed view of the woman with the eyepatch. She happened to be writing something in a notebook. He watched her tear out the page and pass it down to the man in front of her.

"The bush abounds with tektite," Mutuka said. "These glassy objects are found elsewhere in the world but only in our particular strewn field are they used so successfully in the conduct of magic. Tektite, as all of you must know, is possibly of meteoric origin. The white-haired aborigine, our visitor, uses an uncommonly smooth tektite object for magical purposes that transcend anything ever known in the bush and, I would venture to say, beyond the bush as well. This curious juxtaposition of the primitive and the extraterrestrial is hardly a recent development. Among the desert aborigines, sorcerers have been using tektite in their magic for unnumbered generations. It is almost certain that the white-haired aborigine's magic object, his tektite, his *mapanpa*, is what enabled him to travel to the radio star in the timeless time of the dream-time."

Mutuka scratched his forehead under the eucalyptus nuts. To Billy he no longer looked strange in his shorts and body paint. There was something almost noble in the unsuitability of his dress. Comedy and nobility were interchangeable among some people. Noble or not, what he said was pretty boring and Billy hoped the aborigine would soon appear. He noticed a piece of note paper being passed across the aisle. Three people got up and walked out. He didn't know whether they were leaving out of boredom or because Mutuka had claimed that the aborigine was capable of traveling into outer space. Both circumstances were equally believable. Monotony and nonsense. Comedy and nobility. Mutuka appeared not to notice the people leaving.

"The dream-being known as the one-one-one-eyed man is in fact a three-eyed man. Their difficulty with multiple forms is what leads the foragers into somewhat awkward terminology. Nevertheless there is reason to believe not only that some animals of the archaeological past on planet Earth had three eyes but also that man himself possessed a third eye and that the pineal gland is a vestige of such an eye in the middle of the forehead, the human forehead. Our visitor himself may or may not possess a third eye. Such are the secrets of the bush."

Ten people walked out.

"Extrasensory perception is the least of his gifts. With his tektite object he is able to sit in time and then whirl faster and faster until this very motion becomes a sort of nth dimension, as the mathematicians say. When word reached me in my brush hut of the apparent contact between Ratner's star and this installation, I went immediately to the revered totemic site where the white-haired one sits, as we say, in time. My informant, your own Dr. Glottle, had given me stellar notations, schematic diagrams, an evolutionary track profile and so on. With my own tektite object I asked the aborigine, who was hidden from my view

105

inside a shell-like rock formation—I asked by striking the object on the most sacred stone of his dreamtime site—I asked whether there was life as we know it in that part of the universe or great undulating desert-sea of light and dark, as it's often called. I do hope you'll bear with me as I try to recount what happened next and at the same time seek to avoid referring to him, *him*, by any name or designation. This is the most sacred part of the narrative. It must be free of naming. Circumlocution is absolutely essential. The narrative must be pure. Direct naming on my part from this point forward would surely cause me to be excluded from any further participation in whatever is destined to happen here today."

These last few sentences, which seemed sincere enough to Billy, led to a nearly general exodus. Mutuka simply paused in his recitation until the movement ceased. About twenty people remained of the original eighty or ninety. Next to Billy, Goldfloss sat nodding, his eyes totally blank, a picture of dignified fatigue.

"Augury is the least of his powers," Mutuka said. "The answer to me at the dreamsite indicated in ways I am not permitted to recount that yes, yes, yes, there may well be totemic dream creatures living on more than one of the more than one worlds that revolve around the star that sits in time in the part of the desert-sea that speaks by radio to the *walypala* at Field Experiment Number One. There then occurred the gyration that invariably follows the sitting in time. I heard but did not see the gyration. When it ended I was informed that yes, yes, there is without doubt a dreamtime of creature beings on that world. The journey taken during the gyration is what we have come here to repeat, although the word 'journey' is just as inadequate in this instance as it would be if we used it to describe the way electrons change positions in nuclear space without actually moving through this space. Time and space will be replaced by the nameless dimension of the whirl. They will be purified, if you will. Pure time. Pure space. There will be sitting in time. There will be tektite manipulation. There will be whirl. There will be journey, although that word is inadequate, to the area of the radio star. Then we'll have a question and answer period."

An attendant wheeled a miniature flatcar onto the floor of the little theater. It was about eight feet square, apparently a freight-loading device of some kind. In the middle of it was someone or something covered in white canvas. The shape of the canvas indicated that the person beneath it, if it was a person, was probably sitting with legs crossed and head slightly bowed. That's all there was, a white canvas mound in the middle of a little flatcar. The attendant left the hall. Billy waited for Mutuka to say something. But he simply stood there, waiting, apparently no more useful at this stage of the demonstration than the twenty spectators who remained in the hall. For a long time everyone waited. Then Mutuka left his spot at the side of the flatcar and took a seat in the first row of the section that Billy was in. In less than a minute twelve people left the chamber. The fact that Mutuka no longer had any influence on matters seemed to have no effect on those who remained. Maybe they had nowhere else to go. Goldfloss had degenerated to a splayed position, limbs extended, head flung back in a profound swoon. The others were sprawled in their seats and in several cases across two seats; all but Mutuka, who sat erect with legs formally crossed, hands resting on upper knee. Billy thought there were few things less appealing than the sight of a man's bare legs in a crossed position. Twenty minutes passed. The canvas mound sat on the flatcar. A man up front stood and yawned, turning as he did so, his arms spread like the wings of a banking plane. His face was empty of everything but the yawn itself. A tender grimace. A photograph of time-drams ingested by the human mouth.

Slowly the canvas began to move. Yes. There was movement in the specific area of the white canvas mound that sat in the middle of the loading device. The yawning man took his seat. Aside from that, response to the movement was slight. Mutuka's head may have gained several degrees of arc in a tiny rightward sweep. Billy nudged Simeon Goldfloss, who reacted slowly, as though unaligned with the landscape, expecting to find himself on a Mexican bus.

The canvas was clearly whirling now. In a matter of seconds it had picked up a good deal of speed. Billy couldn't believe that a man sitting with his legs crossed was capable of whirling that fast. His hands and arms would be doing all the work and it just wasn't possible for human hands to move that quickly or for human arms to take that much stress. If Mutuka had said that the whirler was a holy man from India, an expert in gyrational body-control, Billy would have had less trouble believing what he saw. But the person under the canvas, if it was a person, was supposedly an aborigine. The answer had to be a rotary mechanism that the person was sitting on. The person simply sat on a disk that turned when a button was pushed. Either that or it wasn't a person. The entire thing was mechanical, an oversized model of the agitator in an automatic washer. Those were the two best answers: 1) a large disk and someone sitting on it; 2) a large agitator and no person at all. He thought of two other possibilities. One ridiculous: a small individual running in very tight circles. The other intriguing: an aborigine with white hair and possibly three eyes who had recently finished sitting in time and was now in the process of whirling into the nth dimension, where he would come upon Ratner's star.

The white canvas no longer seemed to be turning. There was a distinct sense of motion but he now realized that the canvas itself was relatively still. Occasionally it would flutter a bit as though being influenced by the moving thing inside. The bottom edges of the canvas were now and then lifted off the flatcar, indicating that the thing beneath it was moving at speeds so tremendous that a hovering factor had been introduced into the relationship between canvas, flatcar and moving object. The canvas, which looked fairly heavy, was definitely being lifted into the air and at times dented by the centripetal action within. Even if he'd been able to time the little hops made by the canvas and to tilt his head accordingly, Billy was much too high in the gallery to get a good view of events taking place beneath the canvas.

For the first time since the whirling began, a sound became evident. The thing or person was apparently moving fast enough to cause sound to be emitted. The sound was faint and remained so, a distant whimper too stylized to be called childlike or animal but never less than terrible to hear, a process sustained at the edge of nonentity. He found it hard to believe that the friction or vibration produced by physical forces alone could bestow such emotion to sound.

A long time passed. The whirling beneath the canvas continued. The low moan delivered itself, neither rising nor dropping in volume. The canvas was lifted more frequently and showed further evidence of the incredible speeds attained by the thing beneath it in the suddenness and depth of the indentations that appeared on its surface. Nobody in the audience spoke. There was no movement aside from an occasional shifting of weight. A good show, he thought. A good performance and maybe more than good and maybe more than a performance. A man below him picked a sheet of paper off the floor, read it without interest and then handed it up to Billy, who assumed it was the note written earlier by the woman with the eyepatch. She had left long ago but the note paper had evidently been making the rounds.

Without warning the noise stopped. A long moment passed. He was in the midst of framing the thought: *something is about to happen.* Before he could finish, it happened. The canvas shroud leaped violently, not unlike a living thing responding to a terminal instinct. It was quickly sucked out of the air in a broken-back spasm, snapped inside out by some horrible inhaling natural trap.

Deep silence ensued. Nothing stirred. The canvas lay flat on the loading device. Whatever it had once covered was no longer there. It had vanished completely and only a canvas puddle remained. Sitting in time.. Tektite manipulation. Nameless dimension of the whirl. This latest development no doubt meant the aborigine was embarked on phase four, the "journey" to Ratner's star. Billy sat immobilized, pondering the vastness of what he'd seen and hadn't seen. No one else seemed very interested. After a while Mutuka rose from his seat, went to the flatcar and carefully lifted the shroud. There was nothing under it that could be seen by the unaided eye. It wasn't until this point that Billy realized he was holding the note in his hand. It took a conscious effort to raise the paper to his face and read it.

> *It's done with an isometric graviton axis.*
> *I saw it twice in a nightclub act in Perth.*
> **Pass it on.**

He was certain she had written the note before the flatcar had been wheeled in. How had she known what was going to happen? Had she guessed it from something Mutuka said? Or had Mutuka himself been part of the nightclub act? Maybe that was it. She'd not only witnessed this *kind* of trick; she'd seen it done by the very same man. Billy imagined this Gerald Pence guy, an ex-futurologist, going from town to town in the outback with his space-and-time disappearing act, fooling the half-breeds and superstitious miners. But what was an isometric graviton axis? And could he be sure that the note found on the floor was the same one written by the woman with the eyepatch?

He went down to the floor of the amphitheater. First he inspected the canvas and flatcar, finding nothing, certainly no trace of a large disk or agitator. Then he got on his knees and peered under the flatcar, even reaching in with his hand to feel for trap doors or soft spots. Nothing interesting. He stood up for a closer look at the canvas shroud, shaking it out and then fingering along the seams. Affixed to one corner was a small tag that read: PROPERTY OF OMCO RESEARCH. Nothing else anywhere. He turned toward the six or seven people in their seats, well spread through the gallery, and simply shrugged, palms up. Mutuka was sitting at the edge of the loading device, facing a blank wall. Billy decided to approach.

"So where's the aborigine?"

"I don't know," Mutuka said. "Who are you?"

"A mathematician who works on the star project and who wonders if the aborigine is now on his way to the star."

"No, no, no, no."

"Why no?"

"You see, he sits in time. Then he whirls, you see."

"Then he goes to the star."

"No, no," Mutuka said. "He's never done it that way. You see, the whirl is the journey. The journey takes place during the gyration. He's not supposed to disappear. He's never done it that way."

"Then the whirl itself is the nth dimension. He doesn't whirl and then become invisible and then come back. He just whirls."

"Yes, of course, absolutely."

"He makes the journey while he's whirling."

"Yes, yes, of course."

"He makes the journey while he's whirling," Billy said to the others. "This wasn't supposed to happen."

He shrugged again. The other people made their way out, dazed and

110

sated, a collection of volunteers roused from prolonged experimental sleep. Goldfloss was the last to depart. Billy walked with him to the elevator outside.

"It was very ambiguous. I feel ambivalent about it. All I really remember is somebody named Motor Car talking about boomerangs. I guess I dropped off once or twice."

Goldfloss patted his side whiskers. The elevator door opened and he stepped in, yawning. Billy headed back to the amphitheater, where Mutuka was still seated at the edge of the little flatcar.

"So then he hasn't come back yet."

"Who are you?"

"I was here for the demonstration. I was one of the ones who stayed for the whole thing."

"I believe he's still here," Mutuka said. "Somehow he's compressed himself. He hasn't actually gone away. He's here but we can't see him."

"What's a graviton isometric axis?"

"You've got it backwards."

"Maybe I reversed the words purposely to see if you'd let on to knowing."

"Odd if I didn't know," Mutuka said. "I spent twenty-three years in futurology before going into the bush. I was a futurologist before the word was even coined."

"How were things in Perth last time you were there?"

"Exactly who are you?"

"Just wondering about the nightlife in Perth."

"I spent two days there. Never been back. My home is the bush."

"Two days and two nights?"

"They usually go together," Mutuka said.

"So you think he's compressed himself."

They sat without speaking for a long time. This period of waiting began to take on the character of a vigil. The feeling between them grew nearly fraternal, drawing them to the subject of their ritual observation. Of course, there was also something comic about the watch they kept. They were watching over something that wasn't there. The aborigine wasn't there and neither was the tektite object. Nothing was there but the idea of an nth dimension. They watched over this idea until well past dinnertime.

"One last thing I'd like to ask," Billy said, "before one of us gets tired and goes. My question is why did you give up your whole career that you spent twenty-three years in to go live in the empty desert with these aborigines?"

"They're fun to watch."

An attendant entered the amphitheater. There was a hawser tied to a ring at one end of the flatcar and the attendant took the line and pulled the flatcar out the door with Mutuka still seated at one end, his legs held straight out to keep his feet from bumping on the floor.

On his way back Billy got lost in the play maze. He knew he was very close to his canister but there wasn't much he could do about it, since nobody was around to give directions. He kept walking between the Masonite panels, up one row and down another, wondering whether the array of zeros and ones might be the equivalent of a single number. It was easy to imagine a system in which every common whole number is composed of one hundred and one subnumbers, all of which have to be arranged in proper order and then counted before the person doing the counting is allowed to proceed to the next number. An extraterrestrial programming code maybe. Could be that what they've transmitted is really one unit of information—not one hundred and one. More to come maybe. The rabbit in the hat on Softly's lap.

He hadn't been through the maze since the day he'd arrived. He tried to recall the arrangement of panels, shifting his perspective so that he viewed the maze from above. His memory of events wasn't exceptional. Where he rarely failed was in a spatial framework. He was able to recall entire pages of complicated text by summoning the pages themselves—typography, space between lines, degree of airiness, the visual personality of words or numbers. Density of text discouraged him slightly. Breezy sort of pages were memory's wading place. What he saw were relationships, the design and arrangement of type-metal shapes. When he had trouble remembering something related to mathematics he usually turned off the lights. He'd tried simply closing his eyes but an unlighted room seemed to work better. He liked the feeling of being surrounded by dark objects and hazy shapes. It wasn't memory they contained but their own sprawling shadows, the only perfect death. Porcelain cats and glass figurines of little girls. Sitting in darkness seemed to him a totally natural act, a minimal process subject to the calculus of variations. It was the favored way of nature itself. States of equilibrium. Principle of least action. Point of minimum energy. Zero rate of change. He wasn't sure at what moment he first became aware that the woman with the eyepatch was walking with him stride for stride. She wore an armful of jade bangles. Black silk shirt and pants. Her name, she said, was Celeste Dessau.

"I've never seen you here before."

"I don't come here," he said.

"They change the panel arrangement every day. I find it renewing, I really do. Serious play usually is. Of course, there's a thin line between serious play and neurosis. The same famous thin line we find nearly everywhere. What were you thinking about?"

"Sitting in the dark."

"Charming," she said. "You've existed in my mind a long time, you know. Ever since I first read about you in the journals and technical digests."

"You keep yourself well."

"What do you mean?"

"I don't know," he said. "It just came out."

"Turn left here."

"A nervous remark, that's all."

"It must be a curious feeling to exist in someone's mind and not even know that person is alive."

"It's hard for me to say what it's like because I don't know who out there might be thinking about me."

"I expected a stark and haunted face."

"Why?"

"One hears things about pure mathematics. But you don't look especially driven."

"What did you think of the aborigine?" he said.

"It was just an excuse to gather together. We were all very lonely.

113

Loneliness among the overeducated is the saddest thing in the world. Your own work here is the only touch of romance in our lives. An idealized exploit at last. We want you to discover a beautiful sentiment in the message of the star people. We expect your announcement any day now. In fact we're depending on it."

"But what about the note you wrote? Do you really think it was all a trick?

"I didn't write that note. The note I wrote was about my horoscope. I was passing it to a friend down front. Some time later somebody passed me a note about a nightclub act. That's when I decided to leave."

"The whirl was pretty good. You should have stayed for the whirl."

At a junction in front of them, two men with books to their noses nearly bumped heads. They moved in silent glides, seeming to overstep themselves, to be walking beyond their physical limits. Objects in topological space, he fancied. "Isoperimetrical readers of Virgil." Human members of open sets in reciprocal orbit. Several more people were evident here and there, their bodies crossing the space at the end of matching panels.

"Science avers that for every black hole there's a white hole," she said. "All matter lost in black holes must inevitably reappear through white holes either in another part of the universe or in an alternate universe. My work here is interdisciplinary. This is the loneliest kind of work. I find it hard to make real friends."

He liked the way she'd said that: *science avers*. He also liked her close-cropped hair and the way the bangles clicked when she moved her arm. He'd never associated close-cropped hair with lonely people. In his experience that kind of hair went with firm, self-controlled and unflinching people. He was happy to learn that Celeste Dessau had a soft interior to counterbalance her somewhat hard-edged surface. Nevertheless he doubted that science averred the existence of white holes. It appeared too convenient an explanation. Maybe science supposed, conjectured, surmised and pulled its hair out by the roots, guessing. He didn't think it went beyond that. On the other hand maybe it did. How would he know? Maybe science did aver. One white for every black. Who knew? In a dumb kind of way maybe it made sense.

114

"Symmetry is a powerful analgesic," the woman said. "Tell me more about sitting in the dark. Maybe I can work up enough courage to do it myself."

"Sometimes I write in the dark. At first it would come as a shock to turn on the light and see how big all the writing looked on top of each other or falling off the page. But I'm a lot better at it now."

"Living defensively is the central theme of our age. How else can we live? Biologically we've instructed ourselves in the deepest way possible that living in a defensive manner is the only way we'll survive, both in theme and fact. Maybe your hunch is right. Sitting alone in a room isn't enough. We should turn out the lights as well. The only way to survive is to curtail one's perspective, to exist as close to one's center as possible."

"I just do it because it helps me concentrate."

"How old are you?"

"Fourteen."

"The worst age," she said. "Too old to be cute. Too young to be sexy. A haunted fourteen. That's the kind of face I thought you'd have."

He felt he should be getting back to work. He hadn't experienced this eager yielding to a sense of obligation since he'd left the Center. In a roundabout way the aborigine was responsible. Billy had been impressed by the gyration and disappearance. As the impact of these events began to manifest itself, he found he was more receptive to the idea that events in general merited his attention. If the aborigine could spin off into the nth dimension, maybe there was something to this star business after all. Plausibility by association. People were crowding into the play maze. This must be what they do instead of naps, he thought. Serious play. To enter an area in order to find your way out.

"We sit in our dark rooms," Celeste Dessau said. "Traffic in the area is being rerouted for reasons nobody is willing to discuss. Wild animals have been seen entering the city. All air-mail letters are returned to sender. We are determined not to turn on the lights. Manhole covers begin shooting into the air. It rains in triplicate."

Throughout the maze there was a general mood of well-being, most likely arising from the basic satisfactions of negotiating intricate pathways. It was necessary to move sideways now because of the mass of people.

"Now I exist in your consciousness as you've existed in mine. When you least expect it, I'll surface to share your life."

In his room he sat at the module and took a number two pencil in hand. He thought he heard a metallic click behind him. It was so slight he didn't even turn around. He started working and a second later heard a papery slither followed by another click. This time he turned, seeing an envelope propped against the emergency exit grating at the base of the wall. He went and got it. It was a manila envelope, roughly nine inches by twelve. He wasn't surprised to find nothing inside it. Two notes in one day were one too many. Nothing remarkable about an empty clasp-envelope coming through the exit hatch. Not in this place. Perfectly in keeping. When he sat down again he realized there was something drawn on the front of the envelope, its face, as it were. The envelope had come into the room backside—and blank surface—showing. He studied the labeled drawing with some interest.

He assumed this was Celeste Dessau's way of continuing to exist in his mind and he assumed furthermore that other reminders of her existence would be forthcoming, every new message designed to reaffirm her image. Already he could see her black-clad figure lurking among a mass of cells in his brain, passing softly through every synaptic cleft. He saw her crouched behind his eyes, co-opting his vision, opening the world to further mistranslation. He went to work now, looking into ring structure and fields, coming quite by accident upon a twillig nilpotent element. This was one of two mathematical entities named in his honor. The other was a stellated twilligon—a figure, coincidentally, that had more than a casual resemblance to the drawing on the manila envelope. He continued his present explorations almost to the notched dot of midnight, rearranging the surface of one zero one, looking for fresh connections in the texture. As always when he worked with this much concentration he began to feel a sense of introverting pressure. There was no way out once he was in, no genuine rest, no one to talk to who was capable of understanding the complexity (simplicity) of the problem or the approaches to a tentative solution. There came a time in

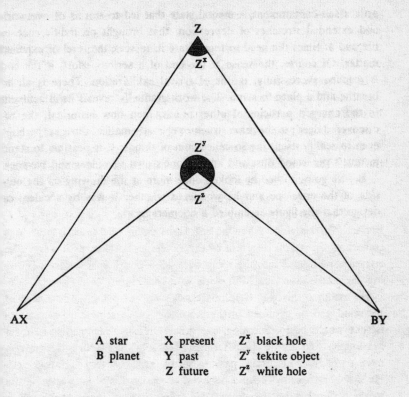

A star	X present	Z^x black hole
B planet	Y past	Z^y tektite object
	Z future	Z^z white hole

every prolonged effort when he had a moment of near panic, or "terror in a lonely place," the original semantic content of that word. The lonely place was his own mind. As a mathematician he was free from subjection to reality, free to impose his ideas and designs on his own test environment. The only valid standard for his work, its critical point (zero or infinity), was the beauty it possessed, the deft strength of his mathematical reasoning. The work's ultimate value was simply what it revealed about the nature of his intellect. What was at stake, in effect, was his own principle of intelligence or individual consciousness; his identity, in short. This was the infalling trap, the source of art's private involvement with obsession and despair, neither more nor less than the

117

artist's self-containment, a mental state that led to storms of overwork and extended stretches of depression, that brought on indifference to life and at times the need to regurgitate it, to seek the level of expelled matter. Of course, the sense at the end of a serious effort, if the end is reached successfully, is one of lyrical exhilaration. There is air to breathe and a place to stand. The work gradually reveals its attachment to the charged particles of other minds, men now historical, the rediscovered dead; to the main structure of mathematical thought; perhaps even to reality itself, the so-called sum of things. It is possible to stand in time's pinewood dust and admire one's own veronicas and pavanes.

Before going to bed he looked once more at the drawing on the outside of the envelope and he wondered whether it was by accident or design that the figure resembled a boomerang.

7

REARRANGEMENT

Synthetic figures on the glass slide moved at timed intervals in a bright clasping skater's blur of identity and division. As one microsphere parted from another, a third joined a fourth. This coincident symmetry did not astonish the lone brown eye that watched from above. Billy thought of the process as a simple one, that of artificial objects being rearranged on a limited surface. There was something wholly touching about these microspheres, these subcreatures of polypeptide origin. They possessed the innocence of small things viewed from a distant point.

119

"Shouldn't you be getting back to work?" the woman said. "I feel guilty about letting you linger. So much depends on you."

He raised his head from the eyepiece. Desilu Espy in her starched close-fitting tunic and high white socks resembled a puffy schoolgirl whose age had somehow doubled before she'd found time to don appropriate clothing. She and Billy stood in a glass booth in an area set aside for research in extramolecularism. Beyond the enclosure, in every direction, were all the elements of modern laboratory swamplife—electron microscopes, optical rotation instruments, rows of precision devices for measuring, photographing and synthesizing the unseeable, everywhere a sense of insomnious acids. He put his eye to the microscope once more.

"We're analyzing a giant molecule," she said. "It's more complex than anything ever found in the spectral lines in the Milky Way. Perfectly stable under heat and light. This is a good sign in terms of do we or do we not find the building blocks of life beyond the solar system. Don't you have work to do?"

"I'm not finished looking at this."

"Sometimes I wonder wouldn't it be simpler if the Ratnerians just turned up one day. Or wouldn't it be almost as simple if we used an enormous topographical marking to indicate to any visual monitoring device that there's intelligent life on Earth. Somebody thought of a huge pine forest planted in Siberia in the form of a right triangle. The monitoring device would see it and report back to its people. Ideas like that really appeal to me. They're such human ideas. Only humans could think of ideas like that. Radio emissions are impersonal. What can you learn about a civilization from pulses and gaps? We could plant a right triangle of pine trees with a square of blue spruce attached to each side. The extraterrestrials would be charmed by it. If not, we wouldn't want to know them anyway."

She stood five feet away, watching over him with a clear concern for the object entrusted to his secular pleasure. Without raising his head from the instrument he closed his scope eye and simultaneously opened his free eye. He shielded this action from Desilu Espy by putting left hand to forehead in a pretense of deep concentration. As she continued to talk, he stared at her knees, the only items discernible under the circumstances. Very clean. Clean knees. A clean-kneed woman.

"Are you sure you shouldn't be getting back to work?"

"I worked last night."

"Here comes whosis himself. What's-his-name. He's probably going your way. He can take you back."

"I didn't know I needed taking."

"I've put together a tiny discussion group for this evening," she said. "The gymnasium just around the corner. You have to come. They'll want to see you."

"Haven't they seen me yet?"

"Your wrong eye's open."

He raised his head and stepped down the small aluminum ladder he'd been using to position himself at microscope level. A man was standing outside the glass booth, smiling ironically. He was small and seedy-looking, dressed in a wrinkled ill-fitting suit that gave the impression it had just traveled thousands of miles, perhaps with him inside it, at the bottom of a steamer trunk. He was so close to the booth when he spoke that his words made small clouds on the glass.

"Tea more noot."

"Now I remember," the woman said.

"We meet at last."

"Who?" Billy said.

"Timur Nūt's his name."

"You in your area of mathematics. I in mine. The two colossi. You with your loyal supporters. I with my own fervent assemblage. We bestride the mathematical firmament like colossi. Each with his own following. Each able to refute the accepted formulations of the past with laughable ease, no? Keen sense of competition to be sure. But we are never less than gentlemen. Mutual respect. The true beneficiary is mathematics itself. You with your pure preoccupations. I with mine. Our combined genius beggars everything, including description."

Billy had never heard of Timur Nūt. He didn't know how to respond. Almost anything he said might be taken the wrong way. The man seemed very sure of his position. Someone this seedy and foreign, smiling ironically, couldn't be taken lightly. There were two possible ways to proceed. One was to say little or nothing. The second was to attempt a systematic destruction of the man's imagined stature. He felt two things could happen if he took the second approach. His devastating arguments would cause Nūt to break down completely, leading to one of two responses. Either an embarrassing plea for mercy or an episode of semiphysical retaliation. This latter possibility might include recriminating looks, one, and maybe abusive gestures, secondarily. But an attempt at systematic destruction could have an alternate effect, one much more likely than a breakdown and very terrible to contemplate. Timur Nūt by logical means would prove he was indeed a renowned mathematician, the equal of any. Using both inductive and deductive reasoning he would demonstrate an astounding verity, the kind of undislodgeable truth that would render absurd everything Billy had previously believed to be true. He had the seediness to do it.

"Okay, what's your specialty?"

"Nūtean surfaces."

"Never heard of them."

"They're pseudospherical."

"Zorgs."

"I know them well," Nūt said. "We'll be a match for each other. Two massive intellects. It's only natural we meet on the field of battle. I must warn you, however. I never take prisoners."

"How do we do this?"

"Two out of three," the small man said.

His face had disappeared behind the vapor made by his breath on the glass. With his index finger he drew an ironic smile on the shapeless second face formed in steam. Desilu Espy unlocked a panel in the glass booth and Nūt led the boy to the nearest corridor. The elevator door opened.

"Come in," a voice said.

There was a chubby man standing in a corner of the elevator. Billy and Timur Nūt got on. The passenger introduced himself as Hoy Hing Toy. The door closed.

"I ask three questions and then you ask three," Nūt said. "If there's

122

a tie, a neutral observer asks three more. Two series out of three is the winner. Don't answer too quickly. There are layers of meaning here."

"I'm ready."

"Question one. An equation of the nth degree may have how many solutions?"

"It may have n solutions."

"Don't be so quick to answer correctly. Tragic mistakes can result."

"It's pretty obvious. The answer is n."

"Question two. Remember, layers of meaning. Using no more than one hyphen, how would you characterize a geometry that is not Euclidean?"

"Non-Euclidean."

"Question three. You're answering too fast. How many dimensions am I talking about if I'm talking about umpteen dimensions?"

"Dimensions that are many in number but the exactness of said number being left unsaid."

"Syntax counts."

Hoy Hing Toy nodded his head slowly. Billy couldn't tell whether he was agreeing with the answers or paying silent tribute to the subtlety of the questions. There was nothing very distinctive about the questions, he felt, aside from their childishness. The questions strongly supported his conviction that Timur Nūt wasn't what he claimed to be. Of course, he'd twice said something about layers of meaning. This indicated a logical trap of some kind. Questions so simple they were all but un-answerable. He recalled the questions one by one and they were simple all right but in the dumbest of ways, especially the one about umpteen dimensions, although non-Euclidean with one hyphen wasn't far behind. He stopped wondering about the questions and turned his attention to the elevator. It should have arrived in his sector long ago. These were high-speed elevators. Soundless, free of vibration, extremely rapid.

"We're not there yet," he said to Hoy Hing Toy, asking a question in effect.

"I seem to agree."

"Is it because we haven't arrived, you think, or because we're stuck?"

"I know what you mean."

"If we're not there yet, it could be because we just had to slow down for some reason. But if we're stuck, we're not moving at all."

"It's impossible to tell," Hoy said. "You know how these elevators are. We must take them on faith. I have always suspected they never move at all. There is simply a new backdrop erected and then the door reopens."

"It's an interesting sensation," Nūt said. "Always we have stood in the elevators without seeming to move. Now we are really not moving and there is no change in sensation. It's absolutely the same whether we move or stand at rest. Something is being violated here. Some rule of motion or logic, no? Perhaps we're not stuck at all. We're moving with infinite slowness. There are three of us in an elevator that by law holds no more than twenty-one people. We are one seventh then. Zero point one four two eight five seven, one four two eight five seven, one four two eight five seven, on and on and on. Multiply decimal by number of people. One becomes four as four becomes two as two becomes eight as eight becomes five as five becomes seven as seven becomes one. Infinite place-changing. I don't like nonrepeating decimals. Pi makes me furious. To how many places have they calculated pi? And never any semblance of lawful progression. Over one million decimal places. A book-length whimper. Your turn now. Three questions. No more or less."

"I'm concentrating on getting out of this thing."

"I'm sure they've been alerted either above or below," Hoy said. "The alert mechanism is almost certainly automatic. Wouldn't you think? In a building like this? Even as I speak, they're probably working feverishly to repair the cables."

The fact that Nūt was aware of recurring decimals disturbed Billy almost as much as the stalled elevator did, assuming it was stalled. The monologue on decimals supported the haunting possibility that Nūt was exactly what he said he was. True, the support was slight but it was enough to be worrisome. And of course he'd chosen to discuss a decimal that had the same digits, in the same order, as the number array transmitted from Ratner's star. A person could do a fair amount of multiplying without changing these digits—merely their order. Nūt had already demonstrated what happens when the array is multiplied by three. Were the Ratnerians trying to indicate something about multiplication? About the fraction one seventh? About original digits rearranged? If so, why hadn't they put the first gap after pulse one instead of pulse fourteen? He slouched in his corner, arms crossed on his chest, each hand clutching the opposite shoulder.

"Two great savants," Timur Nūt said. "You in your rarefied specialty. I in mine. You have flung down the gauntlet and I have taken up same. Your turn to make the questions. Cluster of three."

"I'm in no mood right now with the way this elevator's been behaving."

"Very well, I ask again. Be prepared for hidden levels. Question one, second series. What word leaps to mind when I say that one hypercomplex number times a second hypercomplex number is always equal to the second such number times the first?"

" 'False.' The word 'false' leaps to mind."

"No extra credit for speed of reply."

"Come up with something tougher. Maybe that's the way to slow me down."

"Do your dreams exceed your grasp?"

"Wait a minute."

"Question two, second series. Do your dreams exceed your grasp? I am counting off the seconds."

Billy looked at Hoy Hing Toy. Hoy was tugging absently at his necktie as though the fiendish complexity of the question had reduced him to inane reverie. It would be interesting to see how Nūt justified the question on mathematical grounds.

"If dreams don't exceed grasp, all human life is futile. Science offers many basic differences between man and animal. We have symbolism, organized speech, self-awareness. We are more often than not repelled by our own vomit. But the most important difference is that man's dreams exceed his grasp. There is no future for mankind unless this is so. Think of a Dedekind. Or a Riemann. Think of a Riemann. These men fulfilled the dreams of an earlier mind. They were dreams in living form. That a Riemann was able to do original work on n-sheeted

Riemann surfaces was hardly accidental when we consider how very well the way had been prepared for him. That a Dedekind was able to formulate the Dedekind cut was due in part to a non-Dedekind influence. In their mentor's intellect was the first white flash of the mathematical existence of these men. They exceeded his grasp."

"I think we're moving," Hoy said. "Are we moving?"

"Inability to answer duly noted. Your dreams most certainly do exceed your grasp."

"We're moving."

"How do you know?" Billy said.

"Something has changed," Hoy said. "I seem to believe we're moving. I have a sixth sense in these matters. Any opinions anyone? The door will reslide open any second now. Do they expect us? Will the scene be set? Or will we walk out upon absolute void? I believe we seem to be moving. Feelings pro or con?"

They were silent for a time, listening for distant whispers or trying to apprehend whatever spectral information might be sealed into the elevator with them.

"Question three, second series," Nūt said. "Who invented Nūtean surfaces?"

"That one I can guess."

The trifling nature of this last question made Billy feel better. It was one of the sillier questions, almost as dumb as umpteen dimensions, and it tended to negate the effect of Nūt's discourse on Dedekind and Riemann. Billy didn't like the way he'd referred to them as "a Dedekind" and "a Riemann," as if he'd been talking about a peach and a pear. But it was true he knew their work to some extent. Doubly fortunate then his question about Nūtean surfaces.

"We've stopped moving," Hoy said. "What do you think? Are we still moving or did we just stop? Even as you hear the sound of my voice, I am sensing a stoppage."

"If that's good or bad, I think it's bad."

"Two men, both giants, each in his own field," Nūt said. "It now becomes the turn of the younger of the two to question the older thereof."

"Maybe later."

"No hidden levels."

"Why not?"

"All meaning restricted to one layer."

"You had extra layers."

"Zorgs excluded."

"They're my field."

"We're here," Hoy said. "The door is opening. The door has opened. We can step out. I knew it. I have a sixth sense. Who heard me say it? We're here. They fixed it just in time. We won't fall after all."

In his canister Billy showered and washed his hair. He put on his terrycloth robe and shadowboxed a while. Then he sat down to work in purposeful isolation, tracing whatever relationships he could find between the common whole numbers fourteen, twenty-eight and fifty-seven, soon extending his search to include fractions where there had been integers alone, negative quantities where positive had prevailed, imaginary numbers to replace the real, managing in a remote part of his mind to watch himself at work, an old man (cuter than most) in a small old cluttered study, wearing a robe and peeling slippers, sitting at an oak desk rough to the touch because it was layered with the sprinkled pink grains of his brush eraser, thriving on plain food, irregular sleep, constant work, finding himself pleased by this history of his future, a factually accurate illusion, electric heater on the floor, desk lamp with crooked shade, manuscripts stacked in four corners of the room. Systematic inquiry. Precise definitions. Complete proof. Every new dawn brings paeans to his universality. Number-theoretic insights to big-game theory to post-Nūtean surfaces to bi-level nonstandard analysis. Credited as the engineer of a vast shift in mid-twenty-first-century mathematical thinking. Age times six. Eight five seven one four two. He was distracted from this interlude of austere self-veneration by the awareness that the sheet of paper on which he was calculating was not perfectly flat, containing many distortions in the form of furrows and grooves, meager ravines, curvature rampant from point to point. He practiced his signature for a while and then got dressed and returned to the research area in which he'd spent part of the afternoon. In minutes he found the gymnasium where Desilu Espy, the clean-kneed woman, had gathered the members of her discussion group.

Here and there on the burnished floor men and women greeted each other with elusive half-kisses. This was something he had never seen in the Bronx, the way they darted at each other's cheeks and ears, the custom of puckered conversation at short range. He'd expected his hostess to come sweeping toward him in stylish evening attire, laughing in the silvery lilting manner that people employ at such gatherings, dressed (he'd expected) in nonfunctional satins and moody little shoes, coming across the gym haunch by haunch in a motorized feline glide of supple perfection. But she turned out to be wearing the same canvas shoes, knee-socks and bacteriologist's harness she'd had on earlier. Of course this wasn't a party, he reminded himself. It was just a discussion group. They were here to discuss something. However, the lights were low and there was that pigeon-kissing everywhere he looked. She took him past the swimming pool and introduced him to Commander and Mrs. Burris Shrub. The commander was large and broad-chested. He wore a gray business suit, double-breasted, with enormous sagging lapels. His wife was decrepit, a pink-white woman who kept striking herself in the face with a lacy handkerchief. Every dreamy swipe released a pinkish mist of face powder from the outermost stratum.

"I'm Calliope Shrub," she said. "Are you one of us?"

"Depends what you mean."

"She means outsiders," the commander said. "I'm here merely to observe. Possibly learn a thing or two about hypothetical weaponry. Mrs. Shrub is vague at times. Pay no mind. Happens to people married to dominant figures. I understand you're planning to do some tricks with matches and coins."

"She's hitting herself in the face."

"Historical inevitability has changed since my day," Shrub said. "There's no longer any grand sense of sweep to the affairs of men. Where are the complex historical forces, the tides, the currents? What happened to the wide canvas on which we were supposed to play out our roles? It was simpler in my day. We could talk about the surge, the tragic pageant."

"Does your wife know she's hitting herself with that hanky?"

"No and I don't want you telling her."

"I won't."

128

"She's better off not knowing."

"Why does she do it?"

"That's something I hope I never find out."

"Nervous habit maybe."

"I'd rather not know."

"I won't say a word."

People moved through the dimness, touching and murmuring. He took a walk around the gym, finally choosing the parallel bars as his vantage point and sitting in a folding chair that was set beneath them. Involuntarily he began thinking about the code. It had never really left his mind of late. It was part of him now. It was distinct from everything else but just as much a part of him, conditionally equal, the problem located in whatever neocortical region nurtures the intuition, that contrapuntal faculty his mathematics relied on. It was as though he had two existences, right and left terms in an equation, and was obliged to face the danger that one of them, the mathematical, might overwhelm the other, leaving him behind, name and shape. To consider invisibility as a skill. To forget your own existence in the will to persist. He'd always felt, Billy had, that thinking constantly about a problem was tantamount to solving it. A neatly dressed man with a thoughtful goatee squatted alongside his chair, whispering a name, Haroun Farad, knees creaking as he settled into his crouch. He wore a black armband. Risks in this system of fixed idea.

"In my dog-ravaged land they would rip each other apart to drink as we drink here."

"I was told discussion. Is it refreshments too?"

"My voice whispers," Farad said. "The book in the inside pocket of my suit coat is in very feverish demand here. Three-dimensional photos. Babies with tails. Antlered men. A woman with a pouch. Meet me at an arranged site and we'll discuss terms."

"Let's see some samples before I say."

"A duck-billed lady."

"Who died if you're wearing that black on your arm?"

"It's for the aborigine," Farad said. "A little joke we started up."

Desilu Espy approached the parallel bars with a glass of eggnog wobbling on a tiny saucer. Billy retreated into shallow darkness a few yards away. People stood in small groups, speaking quietly. He watched Haroun Farad get to his feet and accept the glass.

"Milk content?"

"Someone said you were thirsty."

"What is the milk content?" Farad said. "If the number of drops is more than there are letters in the world *Ilāh*, the drink must be re-purified. Take it out please. Remove the milk."

"And they told me you had no sense of humor."

"I'm serious when I say this thing to you. Take the milk out or I won't drink of it."

"Terrific, the richness and variety of native forms of humor."

Nonintersecting straight coplanar lines, he thought. Given a straight line and any point not on this line, it is possible to draw through this point only one line that is parallel to the given line. Once upon a time, he thought.

"In my dog-ravaged land we don't make cheap gestures in the direction of friendship. The dogs make such things impractical, shall we say. They roam the country in packs of ten thousand or more. At the smallest provocation they're at each other's throats, snarling and ripping. In this environment of large thirsty dogs there is not the time for gestures. We live, those few of us who still live, in a state of concurrent but separate existence vis-à-vis the dogs. The land is lean and bare. So is the conversation. Submission to the rightly guided one is the only accepted form of behavior. Milk is the subtlest of insults. These are the realities. The dogs have made it so. We don't expect others to understand. In our ability to coexist with the ravaging dogs, we have made the beginnings of something mysterious."

Billy moved slowly around the gym, keeping close to the walls. At the exit stood Calliope Shrub, casually slapping herself with the handkerchief. When his hostess was alone, finally, Billy approached her.

"What's under discussion here anyway? I thought this was supposed to be a discussion group. Everybody's standing around whispering. What's the topic under discussion? I came here expecting to hear something discussed."

"We're discussing you," Desilu said. "You're the topic under discussion. Not only that but you're scheduled to address the group in about two minutes flat."

"What's supposed to be my subject?"

"Matches and coins was my understanding. A combined demonstration-address."

"While I'm still here, what do you know about a book that's in very feverish demand, I hear, because of its pictured deformities."

"Deformities in what context?"

"Tails and pouches."

"The feather baby is my all-time favorite," she said.

They made a point of staying away from the kitchen. Faye reached in there once to get something from the refrigerator but was careful not to look toward the sink. Her arm came around the door frame and her right hand groped for the upturned handle on the old Crosley Shelvador. She quickly snatched what she needed and slipped back out, lizardlike as possible, keeping body to wall. At no time did she look toward the sink or toward whatever was growing in the sink, whatever boneless archesporial horror. Occasionally they heard a knife or fork slide off a stack of dirty dishes and fall into the wan lymphatic solution that had begun accumulating many meals ago and that apparently had spawned the thing itself, the horror, the overripe science-fiction vegetoid. Of course, they didn't really believe something was growing in there. It was an extended fantasy, a joke arising from the fact that the material remains of roughly twenty meals were packed into the sink, everything sitting in semiliquid matter due to a clogged drain. Occasionally they heard tiny gargling sounds, flatulent rondos, a plate (or something) sliding across the face of the plate beneath it. They laughed at these noises, continuing to avoid the kitchen.

It was Faye who first referred to the thing as a vegetoid. It was her theory that the vegetoid threatened something even deeper than their lives. It would not bite or sting. It would not emit a deadly stench. Instead the vegetoid would absorb them. It would continue to grow until it slopped over the rim of the sink and eventually filled the apartment.

They would be powerless to move. People in such situations were always powerless to move. This became Faye's theme. Absorption by the shapeless mass. Total assimilation. They would be incorporated, transformed and metabolized. They would become functions of the inner liquid maintenance of the vegetoid. More extreme than death, this was de-occurrence, the most radical of cancellations. It was funny, a funny theory. They shared a number of laughs over it. Occasionally they heard a stacked glass overtilt (somehow) and fall into the equatorial blend. Their speech began to deteriorate.

"Coming to get, get, get you."

They sent the dog in there several times but it always emerged unchanged, conveying no sense of traumatic creature-experience. They spoke to each other like very small children, making up scare words, using mimicry to ridicule. They heard more sounds from the kitchen. They joked some more. They talked of laying cinder blocks in the doorway and pouring cement. The vegetoid will ooze under, Faye said. It will seep through. We are powerless to move. That night Billy was awakened by the wordless cries of the scream lady who lived across the airshaft. It was the first time she'd ever screamed loud enough to interrupt his sleep and he listened for a time, failing as always to distinguish a word or two. Then he heard a second noise and it came from the opposite direction, the kitchen, and he sat up and concentrated, the sink maybe, the drain, a prolonged watery gasp, suction-whirl and a general settling of utensils, and he got out of bed and took the stunted poolstick with him into the kitchen, where he turned on the light and saw that the thick colorless fluid had drained from the sink, taking with it whatever hellish anomaly, if any, had been engendered there earlier and leaving behind nothing worse than the massive litter of dishes and pans, and so he turned off the light and went back to sleep and in the morning someone told him the scream lady was dead.

"She was no worse than some I could name," Faye said. "Naming no names but I've seen worse."

As a first-grader with his friend Natasha in what was left of the schoolyard at P.S. 32, he was confronted one day by Aniello Vaca, the eleven-year-old son of a man reputed to have tentacles—the metaphorical kind that reach into every area of legitimate business. Aniello himself had an operation going here and there and liked to use the relevant terminology, often describing the cash results of his extortion activities in and around the schoolyard as "a tremendous envelope." This particular day he approached the two first-graders, addressing his remarks to Billy.

"I want to see how smart you really are. Let's say I give you a job. You work for me thirty days. Running numbers, makes no difference, doing anything, I don't care. Now you can get paid two ways. Listen to this, because it's up to you which way. I give you ten thousand dollars right up front and you do thirty days' work. Or, listen to this, I give you a penny the first day, two cents the second day, four cents the third day and I keep doubling it for thirty days. You start with one measly cent. You work thirty days right through, Sadays and Sundies. I double each day. Or you get ten thousand big ones, straight up and down, I peel them right off, cash on the barrelhead. So which way is it? I want to see how smart everybody says you really are."

"Penny first day and keep doubling."

"Why is that, jerko?"

"I end up with lots more."

"I'm ready to peel off ten thousand chibonies and you stand there and look me in the face and tell me this penny-ante deal is a better envelope. Tell this girl to stop squinting, hey. This girl gets on my nerves, this girl."

"I end up with five million three hundred and sixty-eight thousand seven hundred and nine dollars and twelve cents. Penny the first day and keep doubling for thirty days."

"This girl squints one more time, I'll kick your ass."

"Why my ass? Kick hers. Or maybe you're afraid she'll kick back."

"That I'd like to see."

"Natasha, kick."

"I'm waiting and hoping," Aniello said.

"She won't kick today. But that doesn't mean you're safe forever. Let's see you come back tomorrow. Bring your friends. She'll kick every ass that gets in her way. That's the way she is. Some days she really feels like kicking ass."

On Mr. Morphy's first day as special tutor he asked the small boy to add all the numbers from one to twenty-four. Billy knew there was a key. The number one went with twenty-four, two with twenty-three, three with twenty-two and so on, each pair totaling twenty-five. The key was twenty-five, which was simply to be multiplied by the number of pairs, obviously twelve. It was like climbing a ladder. You went up to twelve and then from thirteen down the other side to twenty-four (a ladder, he'd one day reflect, or a stellated twilligon) and it was easy to see that every corresponding set of numerals added up to twenty-five. The number twenty-five also possessed a certain immovability, refusing to disappear or even change places when raised to the second, third, fourth or higher powers. While the resonant number twelve matched one-to-one the letters in his fictional name, the scrawl on his birth certificate (William Denis Terwilliger Jr.) represented a unit length that totaled a satisfying twenty-five.

Babe began to spend more time at the window, sipping Champale and looking across the street at the playground four stories down. The reason was Raymond (Nose Cone) Odle. Raymond was seven feet, two inches tall but his finesse on the basketball court contradicted this fact. Although Babe wasn't a basketball fan he couldn't help being impressed by Raymond Odle, a senior at DeWitt Clinton High whose moves were already legendary among the syndics of the tristate basketball underground, heralding the age of the little big man. When people witnessed his implausible wrist-dribble or his zero-gravity double-pump fadeaway jumper off a pick at the high post (a shot that often concluded with the metal-gripping drollery of backspin and dead-rimming), they knew they weren't seeing just another demonstration of giantism engaged in a parody of faunlike grace. Raymond was truly fluent and his moves were essentially those of a guard or small forward. His touch was light and deft, his movement toward the basket an uninterrupted medley of hip-swerves and epigrammatic deceptions. When he came off the boards with a rebound he seemed to drop more slowly than the other players, able to pause up there, a final ripple of his body, easily shaking people off in the course of his serene descent. The name NOSE CONE began to appear in headlines on the sports pages. Also spraypainted on the walls of buildings. Raymond's largesse as an athlete, his fullness of style, was most evident in the free and easy atmosphere of the playground games. Babe watched from the window. People stood outside the fence, nodding. In the playground the little kids chanted: "No'Co, No'Co, No'Co."

Billy was just starting at Bronx Science when Raymond Odle was a senior at Clinton and they rode the same bus. One day he found himself sitting next to the seven-foot-two-inch athlete. The length of Raymond's fingers almost made Billy faint. Dusty brown bones. Leathery sticks. So ancient and breakable. How could fingers that long and fierce seem delicate as well, seem *readable*, ten numbered documents made from the stems of aquatic sedges. He was sure one blow from Raymond's thumb would be enough to disfigure him for life. Yet he felt secure next to the long man, figuring no marauding gang was likely to attempt a raid on any bus that contained Raymond (Nose Cone) Odle. So whenever possible he shared a seat with the basketball player, squeezing nervously past Raymond, who got on a stop earlier and liked to sit in the aisle seat and stretch his legs. There was a lot of conversation on the bus, most of it from Raymond's schoolmates, directed Raymond's way, particularly before an important game.

"Lose their shoes, No'Co."

"No'Co, shoot the eyes, little-big."

"Throw the rock, No'Co."

"Put some hurt on their heads, No'Co pivotman."

Billy sat in the window seat, huddled in his mighty parka, a book or two opened in his lap. There was an intricate knowingness to the voices, the ever tensile quality of street experience, something old and secret, possibly dangerous to hear. He liked the fact that Raymond never replied to comments made by the other boys. Raymond was above it all. Raymond had the moves.

"Bring us a move, No'Co."

If in the right frame of mind, on the right day, he would oblige by doing a silent little sit-down version of one of his moves on the court. He did this by bouncing in his seat and simultaneously tapping out an abbreviated foot-routine without bothering to uncross his legs. He wrung out every such move in deadpan fashion while his schoolmates went wild, pounding the sides of the bus and uttering near sobs of joy. In all the months they shared the same seat Billy heard Raymond speak but one sentence and it was directed at him, Billy, in evident wonder at the disparity between his age and the involved titles of the mathematical texts he carried and gingerly read, sometimes two at a time.

"What I got sitting downside me here is getting to be nothing but two eyes and a head."

Babe made crazy faces to entertain the kids, among them Ralphie Buber, who was twice Billy's size but appeared to be sharing his brain, as Faye put it, with a silent partner. It wasn't unusual to see him coming along the street carrying a live crab taken from one of the fish markets on Arthur Avenue. He would hold the crab in his right hand and improvise a prehensile claw with the left. Then he would stand on a corner and leap out at passing cars, left hand and live crab extended, making as he leapt a strangulated glottal sound that may have been intended to represent what crabs say when trying to scare automobiles.

"Movies are the dreams I never had," Faye said. "They say everybody but everybody dreams. It's just a question of remembering is how they usually put it. I'd like to believe that, mommy, but it's no go. In my case it's not a question of remembering. It's a case in my case of sorry lady no dreams for sale. Movies take place in the dark. That's their magic for me. I saw them all, every one of them I could get to go see. At the Fairmont, the Deluxe, the RKO Fordham, the Paradise, the Valentine, the Ascot, the Fox. I went everywhere and saw every picture, the greats and the stiffs, great and stiff alike. What's great is that they were all great, even the stiffs. Because they took place in the dark. Because everybody wore costumes. Because it was like something you were remembering instead of seeing for the first time. We talked back to movies then. You could do that then. If somebody in the picture said something stupid, you said something back. If you wanted action, you told them to stop kissing behind the ear and get to the swordplay. The ushers went up and down the aisles with their flashlights, trying to shush people up and telling people to get their feet off the seats. Boys tried to pick up girls. People squeezed in and out of the aisles through the whole movie, going to the bathroom, going for candy and soda, going to the lobby to just hang around. Meanwhile the balcony is a

136

total zoo with smooching, arguments, heavy necking, candy wrappers flying around, feet up on the seats, talking back to the picture. Now if I want to go to a movie I have to go downtown. Around here they're either shut down, or supermarkets, or high crime areas with chandeliers. So it's TV for me. No great loss as long as they keep showing the classics. The movie industry perished in about the nineteen forties anyway. Artistically it just dropped dead. Maybe the war killed it. But they were great all the same, pictures then; I vouch for every one of them, swordplay or no swordplay. I was a little girl. Then I was a grown woman. It all happened in the movies."

There was a shooting on the second floor late one night. Babe went down to watch the police outline the body's position in chalk. People stood in the doorways clutching their own arms. Little kids slid out from the massed adults and played in the halls, running up and down the stairs in their underwear. A transistor radio played Latin soul. Babe was the last person to leave the scene, having observed the details with the same degree of attention he lavished on construction sites and people changing flat tires.

"Who was it?" Faye said.

"Alphonso Rackley."

"Do I know him?"

"Fishnet shirt."

"Wears a T-shirt underneath?"

"Him."

"Do they know who did it?" she said.

"There was talk his brother-in-law. I overheard a remark or two being passed. Common Saturday night occurrence."

"Overheard who—cops?"

"Ballistics team."

"Then what happened?"

"They marked the body," he said. "It was spread up and down four or five steps, so it took them a while to mark it."

"Then what?"

"Put him in a body bag and carried him down. Three patrolmen. Two front, one rear."

"Do they have the brother-in-law in custody?" she said.

137

"He fled the scene."

"What about the blood?" she said. "Do I have to walk through a pool of blood on my way downstairs tomorrow?"

"The super cleaned it."

"It must have left a gorgeous stain. I never talked to this Alphonso person in my life. Now I'll be avoiding his personal bloodstain for the next ten years."

"D.O.A.," he said. "That's the way they'll log it in their log books when they get him to the morgue."

"Dead upon arrival."

"I talked to a detective on the scene. He asked me any family. I said the only family's the guy that shot him. I told him I knew the deceased. I told him we talked in the hall once or twice. The deceased carried a small lead pipe in his back pocket everywhere he went. So with me and my poolstick, it gave us something to talk about whenever we saw each other in the hall. He was quiet and soft-spoken. Never had much to say. Everybody liked Alphonso. I told him that. I told him I couldn't think of any reason why anyone would want to do a thing like this to a person like the deceased."

Raymond Odle's grades were not good. Naturally this fact alone wouldn't have prevented most colleges from recruiting him. There was a worse problem. He had accepted a sum of money (four figures, it was said) in return for lending his name (or nickname) to a recently incorporated ice cream franchise operation that had outlets in all five boroughs. Double Dribble Nose Cones. It was Babe's opinion that the young man's amateur status should not be shattered by one minor mistake. Strict legality prevailed, however, mainly because the case received a great deal of attention at the height of a public outcry against pampered athletes and questionable recruiting practices. In the end the only school that would accept Raymond was an unaccredited junior college that specialized in maritime studies. The school was located on an old supply ship permanently at anchor near the Shackleton Ice Shelf. The basketball team played only four or five games a year. A pickup team of scientists from a research station near the Ross Ice Shelf flew in every six months, weather permitting, and the forty members of a New Zealand basketball club, the Christchurch New Celtics, took a chartered flight down to Antarctica whenever they found themselves with surplus funds. So Raymond Odle's moves on the court, those effortless serifs of his, were destined to be witnessed only by novices, fellow students and a few bearded meteorologists.

The playground games continued for a while. But Babe noticed that the players now wore combat boots. The games grew edgy. Glass from broken wine bottles littered the asphalt court. No one seemed to care about the score. The players wore combat boots and gave each other immoderate chops to the neck in lieu of strategic fouls. He stood by the window, the poolstick at arm's length, and on the lumbering blue bus his small son remembered the strange dangerous language spoken to the giant at his side by boys of an ageless race.

Hoy Hing Toy was waiting for him when he came sneaking out of the gym to avoid addressing the members of Desilu Espy's discussion group. They went to a remote sector well below ground level. Beyond the experimental accelerator they descended a flight of metal stairs and entered a ramp at the top corner of a spacious chamber. A gigantic balloon filled much of this space. Hoy led the way to a small glassed-in office set away from the ramp and located about fifteen stories above the floor of the chamber. Radio maps and pulse charts were scattered over the desk top. Billy looked down on the silver balloon.

"Important new development," Hoy said. "I seemed unable to reveal it earlier because of that fellow Nūt in the elevator with us. I must identify myself fully and forthrightly. I'm the Toy of the Toy-Molloy affair. It's only right you should know. I tell all my associates."

"What's the new development?"

"Star collapse," Hoy said. "I have always suspected that other people's opinions matter a great deal, considering the incident. Of course, this happened long before your time, meaning I may have to redelineate."

"First tell me why I'm here."

"The Toy-Molloy incident. In case you were wondering what incident."

"What about it?"

"I was senior consultant in obstetrics and gynecology in an ultra-modern hospital affiliated with a world-renowned university. In the delivery room one day, demonstrating advanced procedures to a distinguished panel of observers, I delivered a baby, clamped and cut the umbilical cord, handed the baby to a nurse, waited for the placenta to emerge, scooped it up and ate it in five huge gulps, then examined the woman's uterus to make sure everything was out, a fairly routine procedure, this last part."

"What made you want to eat that thing?"

"Something came over me."

"What happened after that?"

"There was a lot of commotion," Hoy said. "Then I was seen leaving hurriedly."

"So you figured you'd better change jobs."

"Naturally I wanted to put as much distance as possible between myself and childbirth. After a period of wandering and soul-searching, I ended up here. Expert on star collapse. Do tricks with matches and coins in my spare time."

"Who's Molloy?"

"Beg pardon?" Hoy said.

"The Toy-Molloy affair. Who's Molloy?"

"The mother and child," Hoy said. "It was their placenta, so their name got attached to the incident. I think I hear him. He's coming. Pretend we've been working. Look busy."

"You think who's coming? I don't hear anything."

"I thought I knew those steps."

"Whose steps?"

"Are you saying it was nothing? If so, I seem to agree, based on the fact that we're still alone."

"Clue me in."

"Ratner's star is on the verge of becoming a red giant," Hoy said. "Increase in luminosity. Startling increase in radius. According to the computer universe, we must go forward with all possible speed. Of less importance is the fact that the star is not binary after all. It is definitely one star. However, it seems to have two planets. So now we know, within reason, what we're dealing with. Even as I speak, we should be expediting accordingly."

"Expediting what?"

"The code," Hoy said. "Go forward on the code. The Ratnerians may be trying to tell us how to avoid the very disaster they're faced with. Expansion and subsequent collapse. They may well have the answer but not the time in which to implement it, even with their vastly superior technology. The time is now. Wouldn't you think? In a situation like this?"

"I don't see the hurry."

"We launch at dawn," Hoy said.

"Launch what?"

"The cosmic photo balloon—what else?"

Hoy Hing Toy took out a cigarette and lit it. With a fancy backhand maneuver he tossed the match into the air and walked away. Billy watched the match come down. It landed in the left cuff of Hoy's trousers. Hoy at the moment was looking out at the huge balloon. A burn mark appeared on his cuff. Then his pants were on fire. Billy wondered whether it was all right to tell him. He didn't understand his own hesitation. Why wouldn't it be all right? Of course it was all right. It was his duty to say something. Nevertheless he stood there watching the tiny fire. Sometimes it was hard to say things. Things were so complicated. People might resent what you said. They might use your remarks against you. They might be indifferent to your remarks. They might take you seriously and *act* upon your words, actually *do* something. They might not even hear you, which perhaps was the only thing worth hoping for. But it was more complicated than that. The sheer effort of speaking. Easier to stay apart, leave things as they are, avoid responsibility for reflecting the world and all its grave weight. Things that should be simple are always hard. But hard things are never easy.

"Pants on fire."

"My pants are on fire," Hoy said. "Fire burn burning."

"Who else should I tell?"

"Foot leg fire flame."

"Try rolling," Billy said. "Roll over on the floor. Smother. That's the word I want. Roll on the floor and smother the flames."

He followed Hoy around the desk as the chubby man hopped on one foot and tried to remove his pants in transit. Smoke gathered in the small office. Hoy lost his balance and skidded kicking across the top of the desk, spraying maps and papers. Eventually he regained a measure of equilibrium and sat on the desk, left leg bent in as he tried to get a smoldering shoe off in order to simplify removal of his pants.

"Things like this make me self-conscious," he said. "I feel a seeming urge to apologize, first for making demands on other people's attention and then for my own deep sense of embarrassment. I am too grown to inflict my public suffering on others. I appreciate your patience and fully hope you will accept my expression of genuine regret."

It was hard to distinguish the dwindling smoke from its own pale shadow shifting on the walls. Billy took a chair in the corner and browsed through an atlas of the heavens, wondering how a person might manage to hide inside a page-thin surface in order to measure curvature that varied drastically from point to point.

8

SEGMENTATION

The note said only that representatives of the Honduran cartel wanted to see him. Time and place were not given. The words were written in singular idiot script on the back of a manuscript page that he himself had misplaced earlier in the day when he'd taken Softly's work-in-progress to the dining unit to read while he picked at his shrimp analogue.

"The shadow of the modern age of mathematics began to rise on whitewashed walls about the time that the spirit of the guillotine made itself known, deranging the dreams of one slight child who later made

143

his mark through exactitude, ably dispelling much uncertainty from the fluid patterns of analysis."

He glanced again at the unsigned message, wondering why it was stamped with the seal of a notary public. Then he inserted the page in the manuscript and returned to the module to calculate. Before him was a printed tape of the one hundred and one units of information. He stuck a decimal point at the beginning of the array of zeros and ones, viewing the sequence as an infinite binary fraction that paraphrased the extraterrestrials' natural number system, the ones representing composite integers, the zeros designating primes. Although nothing he'd done had yielded specific evidence that the code was genuine, he felt increasingly confident that something positive would soon happen. The transmission was simply too suggestive to lead nowhere. He was even ready to believe he was getting close to an answer or at least half an answer, whatever that meant. There was fresh pleasure in his toil. (But did it enrich the discipline?) From the corridor he heard what sounded like someone gargling. When he opened the door he found two men on the other side of it, standing in single file. They walked into the canister. After a pause he followed.

"The best place to begin a story is as close to the end as possible," one said. "So let's by all means proceed with the placing of the bodies rearward first in sitdown locations. I have appropriated for myself the nom de nom Elux Troxl. This is not my nom. This is merely and simply the sound-identity I have assigned to my nom. That over there is Grbk. Beware of how you address remarks to him. He is mal y bizarro, officially rebuked many times for exposing his nipples to little children. A tragic person, very sadiensis. Of course, the law in such matters is far from clarid. A man's nipples, so to be, are not legal private parts, et so on. Just be sure to speak in tones gentivo and get not too close. He smells like a foot, that over there. His whole body is like one large nonshapen foot in terms of odoriferens."

"So what's the end of the story if you want to begin as close to the end as possible?"

"One slice at a time," Troxl said. "The way to arrive at a limit is to take segmentable things and make them littler, to snip and clip."

"I heard your name before from the lips of someone who said you go around renting computer time."

"You never heard my name—only my name's name. I as myself have citizenship and air rights in a dozen-half countries. That over there is my coadjutor. We are here under the single auspice of an international moñopoly with headquarters outside Tegucigalpa. Nothing trivionis about this operation."

He had noticed when the two men were standing in single file that Grbk was a full head shorter than Elux Troxl. Now that they were seated he could find nothing characteristic about Grbk. The man was nondescript. If he were asked then and there to describe Grbk, he wouldn't have known what to say. Grbk was nondescript. Of course Troxl had said he smelled like a foot and that was a distinguishing feature of sorts but Billy was seated across the room from Grbk, too distant to confirm the other's appraisal. Troxl himself was carrying an attaché case and wearing a white linen suit that was gray (in the strangest places) with perspiration stains. He had flesh-colored hair parted just over his left ear. His face was empty of any center of interest, badly needing a mustache or other unifying element, Billy felt, observing that there was nothing at present to hold things together. It was Hummer, a colleague of Cyril Kyriakos, who had first mentioned Troxl. Then LoQuadro in Space Brain Complex had said a thing or two. Few people here had any link to speak of with others in the structure. An occasional name was mentioned, a hint dropped, and that was the extent of it, a set of rapid sequential jumps, no suggestion that something continuous was taking place.

"A Sino-Chinese group tried to take us over," Troxl said. "But we had a leasing agreement with your computer and that made the differenz. Space Brain is a science in itself. Fascinating monolithic children, the computers of today. I love the whole cuckoo gestalt. We rent by the solar month, all fees payable in Nipponese new yen. Signed, sealed, sworn and notarized. Space Brain helps us stabilize the variables in money access curves on the graph economique. We manipulate abstract levels of all theoretical monies in the world today. Since no other group shares time on Space Brain, we are mathematically in a regulating position that others may not even dare to envy. These others have machines that are computers manqué compared to Space Brain. Perhaps you would like to be shown a glance at our leasing agreement, merely in the spirit of collaborundi. As a duly self-sworn notary public I'm granted the empower to use the raised seal of my profession. It's all perfectly llegalismo. That over there does the stamping. His hand is footsore. A furious blister of a man. I tell you watch him every momentito, that over there. Do nothing agitante. One fake move and out come the nipples."

"Yet I still don't know why you're here."

"First we confirm your identidad. First name first. Nilly. This is correct?"

"Billy, not Nilly."

"Meaningless slip—do forgive. Nada de nadiensis. Full begging of pardon."

"I hope that was an accident."

"Try to excuse my wordage. Half of it is my fault. But most of it is the fault of that over there. I find him distraxis at times. But enough funyaka and gameski. We're here to make an offer."

"What kind?"

"We want to lease you," Troxl said. "Your human mind added to Space Brain will help us manipulate the money curve with greater assurity than ever. What absolute glück in the subskirts of Tegucigalpa when I announce that you've undersigned with us, witnessed here this day and affidavitized by me in extenso. We admit to a lust for abstraction. The cartel has an undrinkable greed for the abstract. The concept-idée of money is more powerful than money itself. We would commit theoretical mass rapine to regulate the money curve of the world. Sign here please. That over there will stamp."

"Not interested."

"I doubt my ears," Troxl said.

"I don't know anything about money curves and I'm not interested in finding out. I'm not even sure what a cartel is. I just know you must be pretty shifty if you're sharing computer time in a scientific project where just getting into the place is supposed to be out of bounds for practically everybody."

"I'll describe our work modus so as not to confuse your expectment. We acquire air space. We make motion studies in and out. We lease and sublease multi kinds of time—makeshift, standby, conceptual et al forth. Then we either buy, sell, retain or incite revolution, all totally nonprofitless, done merely to flux the curve our way."

"Definitely forget it."

The expression on Troxl's face did not change. He did some excessive sweating in the area of his left knee. After a while he leaned over and blew in that direction several times, apparently trying to dry the moisture on his pants leg. Then he looked at Grbk.

"The childnik isn't very gemütful," he said.

Grbk neither replied nor indicated in any way that he'd even heard his superior's remark. A fretful prickling silence began to accumulate in the room. Billy didn't like the way the air felt. It was like subway air or tenement hallway air, aged and layered, moist with body poisons. Maybe Grbk (the man-shaped foot) was exuding his personal odor. Billy didn't want the silence to grow more important than it already was.

"Is Grbk's name Grbk or is that just the name he gives his name the way you do?"

"Grbk a nom de nom? Hilario!"

"I'm curious to hear how he spells it."

"Unspellable," Troxl said.

"If you can say something, you can spell it."

"There are things past spelling and far beyond counting. No word or number reaches there. You must live inside a schnitt not to know of this. I can only say tant pis, piccolissimo. I position you neither here nor elseplace. Oblivio obliviorum."

"Capital G-r-b-k."

"Prove it," Troxl said.

"Make sense for a change."

"Show me the vowelles at least."

"None."

"At variente with general usage, no be so? Fit for eye charts."

Grbk spoke for the first time. His voice was a near gargle, the proto-laryngeal reconstruction of the sound of a lost language. It seemed to be forcing itself through a medium more resistant than air.

"Gwo turd heil."

Billy looked at Elux Troxl.

"Go toward hell," Troxl interpreted.

Grbk took a deep breath before speaking again.

"Thing-cud, sea worts mor bett."

"Thing-kid, I say words more better than you."

"Gud yr lungo," Grbk said.

"Guard your language."

"Tlung mv utmo spd."

"His tongue moves with more utmost speed than your tongue," Troxl said.

"Hindlag bemost."

"You lag behind. You are hindmost."

Grbk took another great breath before exhaling the next remark. "Hins fins."

"His hands are finished," Troxl said.

"What does that mean?"

"It's the way he says the number ten."

"You mean counting fingers."

"Hins fins," Grbk said.

"He's guessing your age. He says you're ten."

"Thing-cud, he, it, sit, muck sud, betuk to wesperole wo nama ta bu sakro nix farbioten yooz, sud muck, he, it, sit."

"Thing-kid, he, it, sitting, maker of sums, is betaken to the night hole where names exceedingly marked as sacred will be no more forbidden of usage, sum-maker, him, it, sitting."

"I'm expecting his tonsils any second," Billy said.

He sat tensely in the twofold, ready for nearly anything. Compared to Grbk's dumb blunt semispeech, Troxl's locutions appeared in retrospect to be models of formal cultivated discourse. He tried to watch both men at once.

"Katzenjammer time," Troxl said. "I feel maldressed for the occasion. Sad to see how partitionage diseffectuates the young. Suffering and phanguish. But this is life as it is lived in the world of existenz. A nothingness full of pitfalls."

"Pitfallful," Grbk said.

"We're forced to conclude you extemporarily from our cartel. Nihil ex nihilo. A thing deprived of living existenz."

"Don't say that word any more. I don't like it."

"Beyond the final number you'll find nothing to cling to but existenzphilosophie. In your case the philosophie will have to suffice since you possess no existenz. Being bjorn isn't enough to give you claim to existenz; it must be merital. Nilly will be clingless beyond the ultimate number."

"There is no ultimate number. Mathematics depends on infinity. You can keep on counting forever. It never ends, the number series."

"The others grow fativi on bulk orders of goods and orderables. Real money is germed and clumsy of usage even if capable of spendfulness. We call it the negauchable currency in the transargot of cartel regulation. The curve, however, is pure. It is ours to control with the help of your precisionized brain. Think of yourself enwrapped by ladypeople. Such will be the fame of your power. A penthouse manned by women. All sizes dressed in filmed subgarments. Merely agree to follow the curve. Otherwise beyond the last number is the faceless chaos, which is just a gateway to the abysm itself. All limits twisted out of shapule. Impossible to converge thereon. Your existenz becomes unthinkable in this warped region. But this is just a warm-up, for beyond the big abysm is the voidal nicht y nacht. Metamathematik. Zed to the minus zed power. Much más than that I don't even dare to whisper."

"Máslessness," Grbk said.

"Beware of that over there. His hands are verging on the shirt. This means he dwells in the fixed idée of unbuttoning. Double conical protuberances. Nipples as nipples. This is something I as myself have no wish-inclination to look upon. As observer I remain but as myself I am very much repelled by the erotic corruption of children. He's done this to many boys and girls, the publication of nipples, but up to now I've yet to see it as myself."

149

"Tell him I'm fourteen. If he knows this, he may not want to expose to me. I'm a lot older than I look. He probably likes to expose to younger kids. Tell him he won't get anything out of it, my being older than he thinks. I'm getting up and leaving unless you start explaining fast. I know there's no reason to run. It's just a man's nipples and all he wants to do is show them to me. In my mind I know this. But I'm running anyway."

"Decommence," Troxl said to his assistant. "The boykid is determined not to join us. No point in depraving the air further. I say haltung and rebutton. You're contractually bound to obey me. Don't take that shirt ovsk. Decease at once, fetid mammal."

Billy was away, bumping out the door and hieing himself to the play maze. From here he staged his escape, coming eventually to a small and lavishly mirrored room, a barbershop in fact, all tile and ivory, smelling of coroner's tonics. There was no barber in sight and only one chair, occupied. The chair was angled in such a way that the occupant's head was about five feet off the floor. Since the head was wrapped in a towel and the body covered with the customary tonsorial bib, all he could see was the person's shoes. Slowly he circled the chair, halting immediately when he saw a hand emerging from the sheet, fingers extended. There was nothing repulsive about the hand—no warts or raised and rampant veins—and so he took it and shook it.

"Shlomo Glottle," the man said in a smothered voice. "I knew it was you from your footsteps. Where's the barber?"

"I don't know."

"I fell asleep and dreamed I was screaming. When I woke up, no barber. I've been hoping to meet you for a long time. When I heard you were coming here I couldn't believe it. Then word reached me that you were actually here. 'He's on the premises, he's in the building.' Imagine how excited I was, a person who's always wanted to chitchat with someone like you. Have you met the aborigine?"

"I'm having a little trouble hearing you."

"Let me rephrase the question. Nobody's actually met the aborigine. The aborigine seems to be unmeetable. If he exists at all, we'll have to depend on poor old Mutuka to act as spokesman and since Mutuka's gone back to the bush, that ends that. Were you at the demonstration? That's the question I should have asked in the first place."

"There's a towel on your face."

"Talk up. Don't be shy. Use some of the lung power you were born with. It's my understanding the aborigine visited more than one planet when he traveled to Ratner's star. I was the person who informed Mutuka at the outset that we were receiving signals from Ratner's star. Mutuka then consulted with the aborigine in the bush and eventually brought him here for the demonstration and it's my understanding and correct me if I'm wrong that at the demonstration the aborigine was quoted more or less parenthetically as having claimed there is life on more than one satellite of Ratner's star. Space Brain has now confirmed a two-satellite configuration. We have computer confirm on this. The white-haired one didn't just say life, life, there is life. He said more than one world, more than one planetary body, making your work here no less urgent more than ever. 'He's on the premises,' they said. 'He's actually in the building.' It is you, isn't it? Those are your footsteps, right? You're the math wizard, aren't you?"

Shlomo Glottle's right hand had been so free of imperfection that Billy, watching the same hand now unwrapping the face towel, unreasonably feared the effects of some awful law of reverse compensation, a counterbalancing deformity of the face perhaps, Glottle's face, a half-mouth maybe or exposed mucous membrane, the face that at this moment was coming out of the towel, and so, knowing it was stupid on several levels, he left the barbershop and hurried toward the source of the odd toneless music sounding along the corridor.

"I tell the truth about people."

In an antique chair sat a small wan woman playing a string instrument triangular in shape, its neck unbent and body obviously carved by hand from raw reluctant wood. The room was soft with dust and shadow, everywhere the ruck of clustered objects, most of them plainly put together and left to themselves to grow into the look of familiar things, every angle, plane and coloration recalling the hush of some mellow room where beaded dresses rest limply on the arms of rocking chairs. In a wide glance he saw old piano benches and cellos in repose; medieval wind instruments; puppets, toys and small statuary; ceremonial spears and halberds; a white tricycle; stoic bamboo bound in corners; two-string Oriental violins; and finally an enormous organ with neon tubing for pipes.

From her chair the woman, at eye level with the boy, seemed to smile him into the room, almost imperceptibly, her eyes measuring his hesitation in the melting desert light.

"People come to me to discuss their names, if interesting and strange. It's my avocation, my serious amusement, the study of names. Naturally I have other work here, crystal structure, but often I wonder which is more useful, silly hobby or vital science."

She continued playing the crude instrument. The sound it produced made him uncomfortable. It was stark and dry, lacking all resonance, a small voice howling through cork.

"I like literally to segment a name until nothing remains. Few names yield completely to this practice. I remove one letter at a time, retaining meaning, it is hoped, to the very end."

"What's your name?" he said.

"Siba Isten-Esru."

"Pretty good."

"Seven Eleven."

"Serious?"

"These are number words of a people who go back to the very dawn. The half-name Isten is of special consequence to me. *Isten* is the word for the number one in Assyro-Babylonian. We can ask ourselves what this particular number one contains. By removing the first letter, the *i*, we arrive at the root word *sten*, indicating narrowness, as in the Greek *stenos*, or narrow. This inclines us to be encouraged, this *stenos*, since what we are engaged in is the very process of contraction. What next then? We remove the *s* from *sten*. This yields 'ten,' our second number word, this one in English as you're well aware. But there is more to this particular ten, for it is contained within *isten*, giving us ten and one, or eleven, which is doubly curious because my full surname, Isten-Esru, means precisely that, eleven; or, expressed literally, one and ten, *isten* stroke *esru*. This eleven, which we've discovered not only in my full surname but in the English ten contained in the Assyro-

Babylonian one, is the loveliest of two-digit primes, an indivisible mirror image of itself. Remaining with ten a moment longer, we know that in Roman numerals it is written large X. When we shrink this monster, we are left with an unknown number, not to mention an illiterate kiss. So thus far we have severed twice, to *sten* and ten. We now remove the *t* of ten. Our segmentation would seem to weaken here but not if we gaze carefully into the artful enate process taking place. For here we have a reversal, a sudden shift from the narrowing trend to a new phenomenon, one of growing outward, of expanding. In English the fragment *e-n* is often used to make verbs out of adjectives, adjectives out of nouns, and is likewise added to nouns to make verbs—'lengthen' and 'heighten,' for instance. To grow, to increase, to gain. Reversing the letters *e-n* for a moment, we concentrate on the Greek *nu*, or *n*, and we see that it comes from the Phoenician word for 'fish,' which in turn developed from a Semitic root meaning 'to increase.' So there it turns up again—expansion. Now the Greek *e*, after some refinement, turned out to be the reverse, graphically, of the Phoenician *e*, which itself was somewhat Chinese-looking. In the parlance of my own field, crystallography, these *e*'s are enantiomorphic, unable to be superimposed because one mirrors the other. To conclude our stimulating discussion of the fragment *e-n*, I would like to refer to the ancient practice of gematria. In the Greek form, *epsilon* is assigned the number five, *nu* the number fifty. The resulting fifty-five, totaled in digits, equals ten, or *esru*, of which the digital root is one, or *isten*. Not uninteresting, eh? Now to the final contraction. We have removed the *i*, the *s*, the *t*, and now we take away the *e*, leaving us with lonely *n*, the well-known mathematical sign for an indefinite number. This suggestion that precise limits are lacking tends to reinforce the sense of expansion inherent in contraction. There is also large N to be considered. This is Sir Arthur Stanley Eddington's cosmical number, his symbol for the total number of particles in the universe. And little *n* is as well the abbreviation of the Latin *natus*, meaning 'born,' which returns us full-belly to the word 'enate,' growing outward, and to its fetal twin 'enatic,' related on the mother's side. So we begin with *isten*, or one, and through shrinkage, growth and reversal we have come finally to an indefinitely large quantity, giving birth to blank space and silence."

The wind-dry music cried from her hands. She wore several layers of pale yellow material and her feet were encased in monumental sandals.

"People ask about their names in an attempt to add to their self-knowledge. Anyone of woman born is by nature superstitious. We stand in awe over the unseen and half-known. Our work here helps us escape this tradition. We try to leave the dark behind. Positive numerical values. Bright shining stars."

He thought of a passage in an old textbook. Back of the chapter where review questions lurk. Acres of windswept italics.

When do we say that a variable quantity becomes infinitely small?

We say that a variable quantity becomes infinitely small when its numerical value decreases indefinitely in such a way as to converge toward the limit zero.

"Your name is a contraction, is it not?"

"Terwilliger was shortened by subtracting *e-r* at the beginning and *e-r* at the end."

"With your permission I'd like to examine the result."

"Twillig."

"Obviously a highly artificial name. This is good. I like this. It's a silly name, true, but it vibrates with felicitous little ripples. My first reaction is strictly a sense impression. Twinkle and twig. I see and touch star and stick. 'Twinkle' is cute, insufferably so, a verb put together solely for the nursery purpose of reiteration. I believe it derives from the Old English word for 'wink,' suitably enough, and it has some relevance, I suppose, to your work on the star code. It's a fact that centuries ago in my part of the world men studied mathematics in order to become astronomers, to ponder the heavens. Astronomy was not the ultimate goal, however, but merely a preparation for astrology. 'Twig' is perhaps more germane."

"So far I don't see myself at all."

"Undoubtedly twigs were employed as one of the earliest means of numeration and most likely evolved into the tally sticks and counting stalks used at the very dawn or soon thereafter by the most advanced peoples of the Near, Far and Middle East. But let's to more important matters get."

She moved her body as she spoke, side to side, and his eyes were on her hands at rest on the rough wood rocking in her lap.

"There are two distinct parts to your name and they comprise the essence of my analysis. *Twi*—two. *Lig*—to bind, as in 'ligate' and 'ligature.' Is it your destiny then to bind together two distinct entities? To join the unjoinable? We all wait for your answer."

"I don't know how I'm destined. Nobody knows that about him- or herself. I'm surprised somebody in crystal structure can expect an answer to a question like that."

"Considering your name, it's the obvious question to ask," she said. "It would surely be remiss of me not to ask it. We anticipate a reply at your earliest convenience."

"Is it possible to leave without feelings being hurt?"

"*Twi*, it's important to note, means not only 'two' but 'half,' while *lig* can mean 'constrict' as well as 'bind.' I think of half-light, or twilight, and further of twilight sleep, that self-erasing condition induced by drugs and designed to ease the constricting pain of childbirth. But who or what is being born?"

"You're the expert."

"It's your name," she said. "That means you're responsible for whatever pointed references I can shake out of it. You're the two-part toy and boy in a made-to-order carrying case. Names tell stories. Twinkle and twig. The first two bites of the suppertime story poem. Naturally names that go back to the very dawn have greater storied content than modern names, most of which are merely convenient denotations packed with noise value."

"I make no reply."

"We conclude," she said. "*Twalif*, Germanic compound, gives us two left over, two beyond ten. So both two and twelve figure in your story. We follow the root word through various twists and forks in the road until we spy the Old English *twigge*, or 'branch,' which justifies my original sense impression and returns us to 'twig,' 'stick,' 'stalk.' Enough, it's over, run."

"This room and these old things," he said. "What are these old things doing here? It's like a storeroom. What's all this stuff for?"

"These are Endor's effects. Henrik Endor had these things sent here soon after he arrived. This is all his. He was a collector. He used to collect things. This room wasn't being used, so he had everything put in here."

"Is this Endor's room?"

"Endor's room is padlocked. This is the hobby room. Nobody has been in Endor's room since he started living in the hole. They padlocked Endor's room and named this the hobby room. Those are the two changes we have witnessed since Endor departed for the hole."

"I'm leaving now," he said.

"Names tell stories and so do numbers. *Zahl* and tale. One coils continuously into the other. *Zahl, tal, talzian, tala,* tale. Number, speech, teach, narration, story. Not uninteresting, eh? Whorls of a fingerprint. Convolutions of tree-ring chronology."

"Here I go."

"Is that an idiomatic expression?" she said.

"Here I go?"

"Charming speech form. Very peculiar to itself. I must remember to use it at the first opportunity or soon thereafter. I wonder if you'd mind repeating it for me just once."

"Here I go."

"I think I have it," she said. "Thank you so much."

Her fingers returned to the strings of the singular instrument. The lost sound commenced, toneless and hollow. He decided to take a walk on one of the broad lawns that stretched nearly to the synthesis telescope. It was still light. Sweet mist was suspended in the air, making everything tremble. He saw someone in red kneeling at the base of a distant tree. Everything else was aquamarine, a sunken meadow, fresh scent of vespertine breezes, sounds he'd never heard before, how the wind made forests seem to verge on bursting and where a hidden stream failed in sand, all tempered within by vanishing light, the abundant sundown blush that made this oceanic hour whisper to the senses. The figure was that of a man wearing a cassock that was fire-engine red. At first he appeared to be meditating but as Billy drew closer he realized the man was looking at something as he knelt in the grass. A small hill. A nest of some kind. An ant hill. The man had silver-white hair with a perfectly round bald spot in the middle and he was studying the ants as they moved from one opening of the nest to another and then out again. Billy got down on one knee for a closer look.

"Armand Verbene."

"Say again please. What language is that?"

"It's my name."

"I thought you were telling me welcome in a foreign language."

"Armand Verbene, S.J. Forty years a priest. A condition wholly accidental to beatitude. These are my ants, my red ants. For years I've been trying to convince the scientific power structure that red ant metaphysics is a hard science."

"I hear you're opposed to the cycloid as a geometric figure because it has valuable properties even when it's upside down."

"My work deals with the proposition that the divine essence is imitable outside itself. There's nothing soft here. This isn't long-range weather forecasting. I study my ants rigorously. I use rigorous methods. Every creature possesses a divine likeness and therefore attains to the divine ideal through assimilation. This is in theory. For proof we cite the creatures of the physical world as evidence of the reflectability of selfward-tending teleological perfection, rightside up, red ants in particular."

"I draw a blank."

"What kind of ignorance am I dealing with here?"

"How many kinds are there?"

"As many as the mind of man can catalogue. Don't they teach ignorance in school anymore? In your case I believe I'm dealing either with antecedent causal ignorance or consequent causal ignorance. If antecedent causal, either compound antecedent causal or simple antecedent casual. Of course, consequent causal ignorance always follows upon culpable retention, which can be caused and spread by three subsidiary kinds of ignorance—affected, connatural and crass."

"What do you learn from the ants?"

"The ants and their semifluid secretions teach us that pattern, pattern, pattern is the foundational element by which the creatures of the physical

157

world reveal a perfect working model of the divine ideal. Now can you tell me what it is that serves as the foundational element?"

"Pattern, pattern, pattern."

"Correct," the elderly priest said. "Notice the uniform spacing maintained by the ants as each one emerges from the nest. Notice how interchangeable the ants seem to be. Try to observe secretion patterns with your untrained eyes. Everything they do for us here today is part of a plan. This is self-perfective activity, the patterned plan, and it is this evidence in nature that tends to be supportive of the notion of a divine essence imitable outside itself and that also tends to lead us implicitly to the conclusion that self-perfective free activity in this life leads to beatitude in the next."

"For ants?"

"For people."

"But why study ants?" Billy said. "Why not snow leopards or albatrosses?"

"Why not ants?"

"Why not snow leopards?"

"Why not ants?"

"Okay, but why red ants? Why not black ants?"

"Why not yellow ants?" Verbene said.

"Okay, why not?"

"Because red ants secrete uniformly. Their secretions are nonrandom. They can be classified and studied."

"What do you learn from these secretions?"

"Everything," the priest said. "A given ant will always secrete at a fixed number of centimeters from the secretion of the previous ant save one. Within this pattern we find secondary and tertiary patterns. It's all very measurable. There's nothing soft about it. I use strict empirical methods. What kind of methods do I use?"

"Strict and empirical."

"Correct," the priest said.

"I'm only answering because you're old. I know I don't have to answer."

"There are more terrifying questions than mine waiting just around

158

the corner. This is because you've reached the most terrifying of ages. Passion is the violent outward thrust of the sense appetite and it's always accompanied by extreme bodily changes. I know the operative appetitive urges you must be encountering. Urges and semiurges. Your little body is beginning to grow and to sprout and to want. It needs, it pleads, it desires. I think it's worthy of note that passions do not tend to be inflamed without the presence of concomitant phantasms. This is what you have to be on guard against. There are two kinds of concomitant phantasms, mild and erotomaniacal."

"Dirty thoughts, you mean."

"Correct."

"So far you haven't told me anything I really want to know."

"Many people die while having sexual coitus," the Jesuit said. "It puts a strain on the heart and causes cardiac arrest. Sex should never be furtive. This causes added strain. If it must be done, it should be done with a spouse in a bed in an atmosphere of mutual love and trust. Avoid technique. Technique causes many problems. Technique can kill. If heart palpitations occur during coition, interrupt at once and think about parasitic worms infesting your anal canal. This is called ideational analogous restraint. If, in interrupting, you cannot by strength of will or imagination dispel the urge to emit, then effect your emission in a clean drinking glass or sanitized specimen bottle left at your bedside for this purpose. Do not discard your emission. Take it at once to your spouse and assist in the immediate and direct uterine ingestation of your emission, using whatever nonmechanical means are necessary so as to effect nonimpediment of fertilization. It is not necessary to actively seek fertilization; it is sufficient not to impede it. These are fine but thrilling distinctions. If spillage of your emission is willed as end or means, you have committed the sin of sins."

"In the middle of a heart attack?"

"End or means," the priest said. "Sin of sins."

"What's the story on premature genuflection?"

"We dip to one knee just before we enter a pew and then in cadence with the word 'peace' every time the priest says: 'Peace, peace, peace, it's a long time a-coming.' Some people kneel on the steps outside the church and I suppose this sort of kneeling might be termed premature. Pilgrims still crawl on their knees from shrine to shrine. There's been more of that lately but there aren't many shrines left and so the distances they have to crawl are very great."

"I'm trying to understand this."

"Think upon it," Verbene said.

He picked up one of the ants and let it move across the palm of his hand. He studied it with what appeared to be total concentration. The ant traveled the length of Fr. Verbene's middle finger and disappeared beyond the tip. Verbene turned his hand palm down and watched the red ant move across his knuckle.

"He'll wound me with his mandible. Then he'll spray formic acid directly into the wound."

"Why?"

"Because he's an ant. Everything he does is based on patterns of self-perfective activity."

He returned the red ant to the earth. Billy realized the ants were going in and out of the nest without collecting food or carrying nest-building materials. He asked the priest about this.

"The workers have already gathered the food. What we've been observing all this time is a very special class of ant. They aren't workers, soldiers, queens or brood. They don't secure food. They don't perpetuate the species. They don't protect themselves from the elements. These ants simply crawl and secrete. These are the pattern ants. They enter, they exit, they secrete. These are the ants of red ant metaphysics."

"Do you ever expect red ant metaphysics to be called a hard science?"

"Not in our lifetime," the priest said.

"You mean not in your lifetime."

"We all die, boy."

"But my lifetime figures to be longer than yours."

"Here's the secondary pattern," Verbene said. "See, this one's about to secrete right now, zunk, lovely, and then he'll pick up the secretion of the previous ant and carry the sticky substance into the nest, whereupon he'll emerge and redischarge it exactly so many centimeters from his own previous secretion save two. We see here evidential proof of the divine ideal."

Billy continued to watch the ants emerge from the nest at fixed intervals. He wondered whether, beneath the nest, there was a huge tunnel in which a hundred million ants waited in line to come out and secrete in their well-ordered patterns. Or was he seeing the same five or six? The mist was thicker now, making the background fade. Light seeped into the trees and earth, into the nest and the bodies above it.

"I'm haunted by the thought that red ants don't need red ant metaphysics," Verbene said. "Just as stars don't need astronomy. Just as numbers don't need number theory. Red ant metaphysics is inherent in the colony. If anyone has formulated this study, credit the ants themselves. I'm in a state of personal anguish over this question because the scholar-priests of my order have been historically driven to adopt a pose of agonizing self-doubt. This done, I can tuck up my skirts and leave. Be it said first, however, that every colony of ants represents an extremely complex social organization. They have labor, they have self-defense, they have procreation, they have architecture. What of the pattern ants then? What of those that simply crawl out to secrete? Reflect and ponder. Deliberate a while. Theology? Logic? Mathematics? Art? Think upon it, boy."

On his knees the old priest hummed his evening prayers. Billy rose to leave, his pants moist and smudged at one knee, coming away with blades of grass smeared to the fabric. He walked across the lawn, enjoying the wet smells and dense underwater sensation, last light strained through haphazard gauze. In his canister he turned off the light and worked, making progress in several directions. There was often an element of suspense in his calculations and when he felt this heightened interest coming over him now he got up, as always, and began to pace, trying to order his thoughts, space them to the rhythm of his pacing. Because the canister was dark he immediately noticed a span of light under the bathroom door. He went to the door and opened it. The light was on, all right, and the tub was occupied. Someone was in his bathtub. It was a woman, fully reclined, immersed in suds up to her neck, expressionless, right there in front of him. She was blond and strong-featured, hair upswept in an aromatic bale, clinical blue eyes studying the figure of the boy, who had halted in midstride like a small forest creature downwind of some novel beast, some danger-laden presence sufficiently near to spike the wary nostrils with fabulous balm. Her clothing hung on a towel rack inches from his face. It was an outfit full of slits and apertures, dynamic evening wear, extremely high-powered, rich in fetish content, and he found himself wishing to see her dressed in this ultraseductive apparel, aware of the irony of his desire, backing into the totally serene confusion of it all, the inverted fundamentalism of maleness allowed its answered prayer. His body remained taut. He didn't think he could take a step forward or back to save his skin. He tried to keep his face blank, a level eye steadied on her chin just above the water line.

"Who are you?" he said. "Not that I mind."

"Thorkild."

"What about a first name?"

"What about it?"

"You do what kind of work here?"

"Decollation control."

Her arms were extended along the edges of the tub. He thought she must be pretty tall, judging by her name.

"So how come you're here?" he said. "Checking up on how close I am to working out the code? Somebody send you to check?"

"I'm here because the plumbing's run amuck in my sector."

"No water?"

"Too much water," she said. "It's in the walls and under the tiles."

"The wet shadow. The shadow-flow."

"Precisely."

"Come back when you're finished."

"You'll have to explain that."

"In other words, I'm saying use my tub anytime. Not just this once. Find it convenient to return."

"Yours was the first unoccupied canister, so I slipped right in."

"If you're interested, I think I'm almost close to getting somewhere. I can feel it beginning to happen. You're the only person who knows this of my work on the code up to now."

"I was never in favor of bringing you here. I'm telling you this because I believe in ruthless honesty even when using another person's facilities. For years it's been assumed that interstellar radio communication would have to be mathematical in nature. Mathematics, so the argument goes, is the universal language. A civilization initiating contact would surely attempt to establish an identifying link through the grammar of mathematics, which is a higher grammar than all others and the only conceivable bond between creatures who differ in every other respect. Numbers would be used. The concepts of addition and subtraction. The rudiments of logic. This is our programming, this is what we've agreed upon and this is precisely what I deny. Those aren't human beings out there. What we believe to be logical may have no bearing on the way they think, assuming they think at all in our sense of the word. The fact that they've apparently constructed an apparatus for transmitting signals doesn't mean they've used the same scientific means we would use. Perhaps there is no apparatus. There may be other ways to transmit radio signals, ways unimaginable to us. And perhaps there is no message. This is even more likely, that the signals were the result of errors in our receiving equipment or computer. You have no business here really. This is the cruel hurting truth, regardless of whose bathtub I happen to be occupying at the time."

"I can't get rid of this feeling that I'm close to half the answer."

"Remember, we're dealing with interstellar distances. Probability of misinterpretation is quite high. Even if the signal is genuinely artificial, cosmic noise could easily cause a slight error, perhaps one pulse too many, a misplaced gap. There's always the chance the signal hasn't been separated out properly. The decollation effect is even more of a problem. Blank intervals between pulses being cut off. Haven't you ever wondered why there were ninety-nine pulses and only two gaps? The decollation effect. Gaps shortened or eliminated completely. The message wasn't repeated, remember, and this makes error detection a hopeless task at best."

"Let's have some thigh."

"It was not only wrong of them to bring you here; it's wrong of them to allow you to do advanced mathematics at all. You shouldn't be allowed to touch a mathematical text until you're seventeen or eighteen. Rudiments, yes, all right, certainly. Advanced work, not until you're

older. You lack the broad-based education that produces a savage spark
of intellect. Yes, all right, it's easy to cite Abel and Galois. Epochal
work while still in their teens. But look how they ended. One destitute
and tubercular, dead at twenty-six. The other shot to death at twenty,
buried in a common grave. You're brilliant but not savagely brilliant.
I miss the killer instinct of the liberal arts major."

She put the soap in the soap dish. He had the impression, as he rarely
did with an adult female, that nothing he said or did was subject to those
special allowances made for his age and sex. Thorkild did not seem to
acknowledge modifying circumstances. It was like dealing with a female
his own age. He was not automatically regarded as an endearing specimen. There was none of that mock coquettishness he'd come to take for
granted. He was denied the skittish delight of being talked down to or
smiled upon or led along. She prepared to get out of the tub.

"Before the accident," she said, "I wouldn't have cared one way or
the other. But in my present condition I don't wish to be seen naked.
So leave please, for both our sakes."

"What accident?"

"I have no lap."

"That's hard to picture."

"Very little lap to speak of."

"How do you sit?"

"That's the question," she said. "No major difficulty as long as I extend myself. Seated, there's a problem, the lap being a factor in a person's seated state."

He waited outside, not even able to enjoy the sound of Thorkild
standing up in the tub, rising in a silver cascade that should have been
spectacular to listen to, trickle-tongue streams taking murmurous routes
over her body. He moved out of the small entranceway and into the
canister proper. The room was still dark. He smelled something unpleasant. Body mold. Debris lodged between toes. It was faint but clinging, a hard-core odor. He didn't turn on the light, afraid he'd see Grbk
in a chair. His mind couldn't produce a clear picture of Grbk sitting.
The chair was there, quite detailed, but the man in the chair was no
more than a latent shape. He thought of running for the door. He had
laplessness behind him and a latent man ahead. With luck he'd be able

o get to the door before Grbk could snatch at him and force him to watch the nipples being exposed. Suddenly the smell became a noise, easier to locate, coming from the wall to his right, down low, an ambiguous noise, maybe the sound of Grbk's zero-grade voice gargling out some stop consonants. The sound was definitely in the wall and he knew that if he tried to run past the sound to the door, the sound would hear him and lunge, becoming pure touch. But he was desperate enough to try it. He had confidence in his quickness, his ability to cut and veer. Being small he presented an imperfect surface to anyone prepared to grab. He heard the sound become another sound and then a voice in the dark.

"Open up."

He paused, not moving out of his runner's crouch.

"Open up what?" he said.

"The stupid dumb-ass grating."

"Are you Grbk?"

"What kind of Grbk? It's Harry Braniff. Open up, okay?"

"I'm not opening anything until I turn on the light."

"As a personal favor to me, I wish you wouldn't do that. My left eye is light-sensitive. It can take normal lighting in the outside world but the light the way it bounces off the shiny walls of these canisters it's too much for me, causing personal injury and mental aggravation. So do me that favor."

"No talk without lights."

"You insist, right?"

"Lights we talk."

"Okay, wait'll I close my left eye and put my hand over it for added protection. The eye's closed. Here comes the hand. Okay—now."

Billy turned on the light and went over to the grill set into the wall just above the floor line. Through the metal latticework he saw Harry Braniff's face, hand over left eye. Billy sat on the floor in front of the grating. He couldn't tell whether Braniff was standing on a ladder or on solid ground, some kind of access tunnel or interior walkway. Either way, Braniff's body was below the level of the grating, leaving only face and hand visible in the dimness beyond the barrier.

"I thought that smell was Grbk. What's that smell?"

"That's my breath. People notice it wherever I go. A matter of dietary preference. I eat a lot of Limburger on onion roll smothered in garlic."

"What was the first sound I heard?"

"That was my breath too. I was breathing pretty hard. It's not easy getting up here."

"What was the second sound?"

"That was me trying to get the grating opened up so I could deliver the object. I didn't know anyone was here. It was dark in here. I was told open the grill, put the object in the room, close the grill, make your departure. But I couldn't get the grill opened up. So do me that favor and open it up."

"First tell me what the object is you're supposed to be delivering."

"I was told a tape cartridge," Braniff said. "Judging by its look and feel, that's exactly what it is."

He helped the man remove the grating and then accepted the cartridge. To be on the safe side he reinstalled the barrier before going on with the conversation.

"You're not supposed to be in there," he said. "They read me a pre-pared statement the first day I was here. That's the exit point for this whole sector. We're not supposed to use it except in emergencies. I can get in trouble over this."

"I was told open the grill, put the object in the room, close the grill, make your departure."

"Who told you?"

"I was told if anyone asked I shouldn't vouchsafe a reply. But be-cause you're only a kid and you helped me open up the grating, I'll let you in on a piece of hard-earned wisdom gleaned from many years of delivering things to dumb-ass places. Are you prepared to remember this and learn from it?"

"Yes."

"There is always a higher authority than you think."

"Is that it?"

"Sometimes the person in charge isn't the person or persons who seem to be in charge. No matter how far up or down the line you go, there's always someone else. That's what Harry Braniff has gleaned."

"The person who gave you this tape to deliver to me was a one-eyed woman or at least a woman with an eyepatch. She said she wanted to exist in my mind, so one time she put an envelope with a drawing on it through the grating or probably you're the one that put it there and now she's sending me this tape with probably her voice on it just to keep me aware of her existence so she can keep on existing in my mind. I know it's her. The woman in the play maze. She had one bad eye and you have one bad eye and hers was the right and yours is the left and that's the way things have been happening around here. Celeste Dessau sent you. It all holds together. It makes sense. It fits right into the pattern."

Thorkild opened the bathroom door and appeared in the entrance-way, dressed in that hit-and-run outfit he'd seen hanging on the towel rack. When he looked back to the grating, Harry Braniff's head and hand were gone but the sound of his voice, barely audible, drifted up from the darkness below.

"Keep believing it, shit-for-brains."

9

COMPOSITE STRUCTURE

News of the conference spread rapidly, causing rumor to flourish, much of it humorous in nature, centering on the notion that ninety percent of the universe is missing. It was the second formal conference in the brief history of Field Experiment Number One. (The first, predating Billy's arrival, had been presided over by Endor and concerned the transmission from the area of Ratner's star.) It even had a name. Conference on Invisible Mass. As the hours passed, there was less jocularity in evidence and a greater degree of uneasiness, particularly among those who'd heard the latest rumor.

He walked into the conference room.

ADVENTURES

The latest rumor concerned the people who'd been selected to attend the conference. All (with one exception) were experts in alternate physics. Why did this cause uneasiness and tense speculation? Because many scientists questioned the utility and general merit of alternate physics, dealing as it did with the effects of suppositional laws on hypothetical environments.

Since he'd been invited merely to "sit in" on the meeting, Billy took a chair in the corner and tried to look like someone "sitting in." Three men and a woman sat at a large octagonal table. There were no pencils, note pads or glasses of water. He took this to mean that extremely serious matters were about to be discussed. No time for customs, rules, formalities or informalities. The woman's name was Masha Simjian. The men were Maidengut, Lepro and Bhang Pao.

"Who's chairing?" Simjian said.

She looked from face to face, sucking on hard candy all the while, cheeks indented and thin lips thrust sourly outward.

"Let's all chair," Maidengut said. "Except whoever's sitting in."

"All right then, who's participating and who's sitting in? Show of hands please."

"I'm sitting in," Billy said.

"Show of hands."

He raised his hand.

"It's my understanding," she said, "that persons invited to sit in on a formal conference aren't permitted to speak unless directly addressed."

"Why or because," Lepro said.

"What do you mean?"

Maidengut, a blocklike man, spoke out on Lepro's behalf.

"He has trouble distinguishing between 'why' and 'because.' In his language the same word is used for both. So in order to save time and avoid confusion he uses 'why' as well as 'because' and leaves it to the listener to match the right word to the context. In other words he says 'why or because' instead of 'why' individually or 'because' individually."

"Time to begin," Simjian said. "Who wants to get things moving?"

Bhang Pao shifted in his chair, drawing everyone's attention. He wore a dark suit and tie. His face was round and pleasant, shady manila in color, and on his head was a bowl-shaped toupee, incongruous not

169

only because it suggested an unprofessional haircut but also in view of its glossy look and poor fit, these factors combining to engulf any trace of authenticity.

"We've long known about invisible mass," Bhang Pao said. "Galaxies are no longer flying apart at previous rates of speed. We must presume they are being held together by gravity. However, the mass needed to generate this much gravity is not present in or between the galaxies themselves. There is unexplained mass. A great deal of unexplained mass. Really a whole lot. What is it? Where does it come from? Why can't we find it?"

"Succinctly put," Simjian said.

"Don't interrupt my train."

"Please go on."

"Visible matter cannot account for the failure of the galaxies to disperse at prior speeds. Therefore we frame a hypothesis based on missing matter and we estimate that this matter is many times greater than the sum of all detected matter in the universe. Of course not everyone accepts this model. Some years ago it was determined that interstellar deuterium abundance relative to hydrogen is lower than was thought. This means less density than suspected, which in turn means not as much invisible mass as previously conjectured. However, I regard these findings as tentative in the extreme."

"Bravo."

"Everything I've stated may prove to be total poppycock," Bhang Pao said. "Perhaps time will tell. Perhaps time will do nothing of the kind. All we can do as scientists is try to determine the nature of the invisible mass, assuming there is such mass and that it's invisible. Some say the laws of physics are different in remote parts of the universe. Others argue that hydrogen clouds invisible to our most sensitive devices account for the missing mass. But now a new theory has been put forth, one of vast implications."

"Do we ask questions as he goes along," Maidengut said, "or do we hold them in abeyance?"

"Let's let him finish, but when he does I've got some extremely incisive queries to make," Simjian said.

"But now a new theory has been put forth."

The telephone buzzed once.

"Vast implications."

Masha Simjian got up and answered the phone, which was part of a mounted array of devices set into the wall. She listened for a moment and then turned toward Billy.

"Contingency personnel," she said. "There's a loud party going on in your canister."

"Who, mine?"

"A very wild party, contingency says. He hasn't made a security check yet. Wanted to contact you first. I'm repeating what he says semi-verbatim. It sounds excessive. Drinking, shouting, raucous laughter. Someone singing in a very loud voice. Obviously intoxicated, he says. Your canister. A wild, wild party. I'm paraphrasing."

"That's not a wild party," he said. "That's just the tape of a wild party. I was listening to it when they told me to come up here and sit in. There's no wild party. Tell contingency it's just a recording."

"This is a one-way priority phone. I can't tell him anything. You'd better go down there and straighten it out. Unfortunately we can't delay Bhang's clarification of invisible mass. But that doesn't mean you don't have to come back. You have to come back immediately. Melcher-Speidell wants to see you."

"Who's that?" he said.

"Be serious."

"I never heard the name in my life."

"Security man's waiting," she said.

He took the elevator to his sector. Since he hadn't heard the entire tape, he intended to run it over from the beginning. The tape had surprised him to the degree that he now tended to believe what Harry Braniff had crudely implied after making the delivery, that the woman with the eyepatch had absolutely no part in this. First, there was no sign of her voice on that portion of the tape he'd already played. Second, no one on the tape had referred to her in any way—not in dialogue, moan, bellow or song. It was a party tape, all right, and a wild party at that. The focus of the recording was Cyril Kyriakos, the one-armed transitional logician and somewhat cynical father-to-be who had talked a while with Billy and others on the day of the shadow-flow.

On the tape, scattered among shouts, odd remarks, volleys of laughter, sounds of stunning insults and objects flung at walls, weaved freely into all this scat and roar, was an extended song delivered by Cyril in a dissonant tenor voice, altering the metrical flow as he went, talking the lines, then chanting ecclesiastically, sometimes wailing at the high-pitched edge of panic. Billy saw the contingency man waiting in the corridor. He stood there flexing his knees and slowly swinging his arms in front of him, right fist popping into the palm of his left hand, this contact made in synchronization with the bending knees—a characteristic stance of security personnel everywhere. The corridor was quiet, however. No hint of a party or the tape of a party.

"I'm contingency for this sector," the man said. "Kyzyl by name."

"There's no party in there. That's just a tape recording."

"I wondered why it stopped so suddenly."

"Tape."

"I wondered what kind of party would stop so suddenly," Kyzyl said. "Orgy parties sometimes do that out of sheer exhaustion."

"I'll put the volume way down this time."

"While I was here a personage came by and said he wants to receive you in his apartments at the top of the armillary sphere."

"Apartments plural?"

"This is acoustically what I heard."

"It must be Melcher-Speidell."

"He gave no name but said I should be sure to escort you to his quarters."

"Why do I need an escort all of a sudden?"

"An aborigine was seen in the building early this morning."

"What was he seen doing?"

"Lurking," Kyzyl said.

O the Swiss and the Swedes
Are at it all right
A bore of a war
And no end in sight

172

ADVENTURES

They're killing each other
With unlikely skill
Who'd have believed it
Neutral and Nil

It's a bore
What a bore
It's a bore of a war
Logically sound
But soft at the core

When Vienna surrenders
To Cambridge symbolic
The null class is Z
The peace terms a frolic

O bore
What a bore
It's a bore of a war
Deft but bereft
Of a Renaissance roar

VOICE 1: What's black and white, left or right, growing little and has no middle?

O bring on a genuine algebra war
Del Ferro, Fontana, Cardano, Fior
None of these formalist postulate sets
Less of this Either and Or

VOICE 2: This is horrible or words to that effect. Why must they break the furniture?

VOICE 3: End of the world. It's behavior suitable for the end of the world. This is an end-of-the-world party. First in a series. Alcoholic stupors befitting the end of the world. Oblivion as conscious art. That's all it is, reaction to the rumor that most of the universe is missing.

173

Fourth dimension Yorkshireman and versifying Jew
Pedagogic modern logic came too late for you
One is one, two is one, three is two anew

Theory of invariants
Turbulence serene
Higher space contains a trace
Of double umbral sheen

VOICE 4: Just realized. Cyril and lyric. Cyril's lyric. Just came to me. Lyric and Cyril.
VOICE 5: So what?
VOICE 4: Bit of insight, that's all.
VOICE 5: Insight into what?
VOICE 6: What's not composite. Can't be divided by insight. No divisors whatsoever except itself and one. What into what is one. What times one equals what. What times two equals two what. The square root of what is irrational.

Nature intrinsic reveals itself
Consistent as one, two, three pence
Point by point an event unravels
Invariant in its sequence

But physical significance
And theories vague and sure
And modern relativity and empirical proclivity
All yield the abstract field
To mathematics pure
To mathematics pure
All yield the abstract field
To mathematics pure

Shadow of a figure
Projected on a plane
Two is one, the one that was
Different and the same

VOICE 3: But it's not just what's missing. Not just the conference. Not just the name of the conference or the people at the conference. It's the rumor about the mohole.

VOICE 2: Sounds familiar, that name.

VOICE 3: It's the whole idea of a mohole that's got everyone so anxious and depressed.

VOICE 2: Where have I heard that word?

VOICE 6: Where plus when times the square root of minus-one equals point-event.

Matrix theory
Covariant junctions
Hyperelliptic theta functions
Umbral notations
Dimensional swarms
Wine-red canonical binary forms

Algebraic granite

Before the set of all sets
Not members of themselves
Before the class of all classes
Similar to a given class

O chant and pant a hymn ironic
To deductive demons fierce and chthonic

Axiom of reducibility
Rule of inverse probability
Fallacy of affirming the consequent
Fallacy of denying
Incremental confirmation
Who is dying

Play away the sense
Of the logical consequence
Of living
A is disconfirmed to some extent

B is bent
Beware, boy, the formal argument

Geometry shimmering on rose-stone columns

Before the set of all sets
Not members of themselves
Before the class of all classes
Similar to a given class

O recite a litany in extremis
To the peaceful end of logical premise

Our Lady of Inferred Entities
Prey on us

Wielder of Occam's Razor
Spare our multiplicities

Expounder of the Unthinkable
Have mercy on our system of signs

Elucidator of Logical Form
Guide our superstitions

Annihilator of Tautologies
Bless our refrains

Language Inviolate
Forgive us our stammer

VOICE 1: Two answers really. A book that's being read. The universe itself.

Toiled both on their compound discriminant scheme
Dividing the light on the half-shadowed shore
Induction, experiment, rapturous dream
That night we slept no more
That night we slept no more

Shadow of a figure
Projected on a plane
Two is one, the one that was
Different and the same

Kyzyl escorted the boy to the top of the armillary sphere. To get there they had to take two elevators, enter a fire exit and climb a flight of stairs.

"If you ever have to go to jail," Kyzyl said, "a designated autonomous area is one of the few good places left for that. UN trust territories I rate no better than fair. When we speak of torture, I recommend avoidance of canal zones. This is when we speak of physical torture. Stomping, flaying, bastinado, electric shock. The psychological variety, when we speak of that, you can do a lot worse than enclave republics or gulf protectorates. In protectorates, speaking from personal experience, they use only moderate hooding, they go easy on the monotonous noise, they deprive the body of sleep only in rare instances. Upon release from incarceration you find that you experience only the minimum symptoms. Startle-responses, yes, affirmative. Insomnia, to be expected, but not chronic. Sphincter-spasms, poco poco. Not much heightened anxiety. And very little dread. When we speak of the hooding experience, with or without monotonous noise, and when you've gone through this experience and you're able to function with very little dread, this is when you're entitled to regard yourself as fortune's favorite."

Kyzyl waited outside as the boy entered the large suite of rooms and sat in a laminated chair that smelled faintly of chemicals. The place looked like a mysterious bi-level motel. Colors were neutral and every surface was designed to be heat-resistant and scratchproof. Materials were clearly cheap and unembellished, stressing utility. At the same time there was something grand about the setting, a self-importance not associated with motel decor, and this is what accounted for the composite nature of the suite's appearance. The furniture was immense and the ceiling extremely high. Arched passageways connected the rooms. Enormous mirrors were everywhere, surprising him with his own image, which, as sometimes happens when a person faces a particular mirror for the first time, was not quite what he was accustomed to seeing. He heard heavy steps behind him.

"Yours is a name synonymous with genius."

Orang Mohole was a man of ambiguous pigmentation. He introduced himself and sat in one of the oversized synthetic chairs. He wore a gold mohair smoking jacket with padded shoulders, platinum lapels and a bit of drizzly silver saddle-stitching on each pocket.

"This used to be the maternity ward," he said. "Once the last baby was born, I had it converted. All very unofficial. Not hush-hush really. Just unofficial. No one knows who shouldn't know. I've longed for a setup like this ever since I saw the royal apartments in the summer palace on Guam."

"I thought you were Melcher-Speidell. That's who I was expecting to walk in. When I heard you walk in, I thought that's who it was."

"Melcher-Speidell is a mediocrity and a bore."

"How do you rate yourself?"

"Twice winner of the Cheops Feeley Medal."

"What else?"

"Acknowledged kingpin of alternate physics."

"How come you're not at the conference?"

"Small potatoes," Mohole said. "I sent Bhang in my place. Bhang will present my view of things."

"I thought it was pretty interesting, hearing about what's missing and why they can't find it."

"Who's chairing?"

"They'll all chairing," Billy said. "But there's a lady there who's more or less taken it over."

"We did research together years ago," Mohole said. "Heavy forms of hydrogen."

"What's the story on her?"

"Mediocre breasts."

"What about the leg department?"

"Fair to average."

"I'm supposed to go back there."

"First I want you to tell me the status of your calculations."

"I'm getting close to something."

"Too bad," Mohole said.

"Why bad?"

"First let me tell you what we've got out there. Ratner's star is not about to enter the red giant phase as previously believed. It's a white dwarf. It'll remain so unless it degenerates further to the pulsar stage. This is Space Brain's most painstaking analysis to date. There's one planet, not two. A planet so large it seems to be radiating in the visible end of the spectrum. Enough heat at its core to make it glow. So it's really not a planet at all but a dim star. A dwarf to be sure but a star nonetheless. A red dwarf star. So what we've got out there is a binary dwarf. One red star, one white star."

"That means there are no beings. It must be too hot for beings to exist on that kind of surface if it glows. So no message. Nobody to send."

"You're half right," Mohole said. "Two hot gaseous spheres, completely uninhabitable. No message-senders, true. But there *is* a message. It didn't come from Ratner's star, however. It only seems to have originated in that part of the galaxy. This is because Ratner's star probably lies within the value-dark dimension, or mohole totality, as I sometimes call it. So the emphasis has shifted from the message itself to the primary source of the message and the secondary nature of the message. We don't really mind if you keep working on decipherment. But the emphasis has shifted."

"Let me see if I have this straight."

"Of course you have it straight."

"But I'm getting near a solution."

"Whether you are or not is less important frankly than where the message came from and why it was reflected, if that's the word I want, toward our part of the galaxy. There's even a feeling among some of my colleagues that you should be prohibited from doing further work on the code. This is to avoid ambiguity. The feeling is that an answer at this point would only beg the question. This is an extreme position, however, and I don't expect it to prevail. Would you like a greenie?"

"What's that?"

"Sometimes my neurons misfire."

"Is it a pill?"

"You swallow it," Mohole said. "You don't stick pins in it or call it up on the telephone. It doesn't have children of its own and a two-car garage. Yes, it's a pill."

"What would it do for me?"

"Depends on what type brain you have."

"They come in types?"

Mohole got up and took a meditative stroll around the large room. His hands were plunged into the deep pockets of his smoking jacket. He wore two-toned shoes, silver and black, with tasseled laces. His trouser cuffs had been unstitched and extended full length, leaving shriveled indentations where the turned-up folds had been. He took a large green pill out of his pocket and put it on his tongue. His face seemed a hasty contrivance, making Billy think of a police sketch of a suspect as described by several witnesses. There was too much space between the eyes. His lips were very thin, seemingly at odds with the general heft of his body. He had a flat nose and high cheekbones and his electrified hair curled almost straight up. He closed his eyes now and threw back his head in a sudden convulsive motion, simultaneously gasping as he swallowed the pill.

"Except for the first one thousandth of a second, we can trace the evolution of the universe from the big bang to the present moment," he said. "In my early work on background radiation, which is detectable evidence of the fireball of the big bang, if there was a big bang, I developed a theory, listen to this, about a strange kind of mechanism at work in the universe. This is the value-dark dimension, or mohole totality, and it's the core idea of a unique system of relativity. This is Moholean relativity, just beginning to attract attention, very controversial, named by me after myself. What I theorize happens in a mohole is that X-rays, gamma rays, ultraviolet light, radio waves, gas, dust clouds and so forth are trapped and held by relativistic forces we don't fully understand as yet—forces created in the first one thousandth of a second after the universe began. Incidentally it's no good trying to visualize a mohole. I've already tried and it can't be done. Nobody knows what it looks like because it doesn't look like anything. And we can't pinpoint its location because it seems to have many locations— another way of saying there are moholes numbering n—and they all seem to shift, affecting different parts of the computer universe for varying amounts of time. The sum total of all moholes is what I call the value-dark dimension. All the key words in this explanation, by the way, are totally misleading due to the everyday quirks of language."

He returned to the chair and sat.

"A mohole traps electromagnetic information, among other things, and then either releases it or doesn't. It's as though the mohole were a surface that absorbs light and sound and then reflects either or both to another part of the universe. But it's not a surface and it doesn't absorb. It's a mohole. It's part of a theoretical dimension lacking spatial extent and devoid of time value. Value-dark in other words."

He rubbed his crotch briefly and then crossed his legs without remembering to unwedge his hand.

"The answer to what happened in the first one thousandth of a second after the universe began probably hinges on an investigation of exo-ionic sylphing compounds. This substance seems to be present, as far as I can tell, wherever there are moholes, although what I've just said indicates, more than anything else, the inadequacies of human language in the face of the mohole phenomenon, since 'wherever there are moholes' implies that a mohole occupies space, which it doesn't. I suppose it could be said that a mohole is space-time raised to a higher electrovalent power, or sylphed."

He leaned to one side, resting his head in his free hand and appearing to be on the verge of sleep.

"My model of the universe is open at the bottom, closed at the top. Imagine two triangles sharing the same base. With one abnormality: the base is invisible. This gives us two apexes, representing the closed top, while the lack of a base signifies the invisible mass. Can you visualize such a figure?"

"A stellated twilligon."

"I postulate eventual collapse in a sort of n-bottomed hole or terminal mohole. First let me describe the two paths of expansion in my model—

paths represented by the two left or ascending sides of the twilligon as you call it, both lines generated by the same point. One path is taken up by detectable matter, growing outward since the big bang. The other line is gravity, getting stronger as the universe becomes more dense with both detectable and missing matter. We are currently at the apex of matter, the halfway point of gravity. As expansion ceases we turn our attention to the right or descending sides of the figure. What was open begins to close. Matter begins its inward fall at the apex of the twilligon. Gravity becomes dominant at the sub-apex. The two right sides converge at the same terminal point. Gravity clutches matter in a terrific frenzy."

His hand had sunk even deeper into the pouch between his thighs and he spoke very slowly now, talking almost by rote.

"Nothing escapes the final collapse into an entity that nearly contradicts the word 'entity.' On second thought, let's not say 'nothing.' Let's say 'almost nothing.' I leave an opening, you see. I make an allowance for an indefinite number of bottoms. The average hole is either bottomless or uni-bottomed. An n-bottomed hole allows my model to qualify as an open universe. This is the privilege of a self-confessed maverick. A minor maneuver just short of cheating. All this gorgeous matter-crush shouldn't have to end in a totally hopeless situation. I give things a chance to drip through. The final mohole is not leakproof. I leave a little opening. We can't actually see this on paper or even in our minds because the two descending sides of the twilligon conclude in a single point and you can't have an opening in a point. But we can pretend a little, can't we? We're not so scientific that we can't have a little make-believe, right? Then, if something drips through, there's a continuation, another chance, the universe refreshed."

Seconds after he spoke the last word he closed his eyes and fell asleep. Billy thought of leaving but remembered that Kyzyl was waiting outside to escort him. He assumed Kyzyl wouldn't leave, or let him leave, without some word from Orang Mohole, who had put the escort rule into effect. After half an hour Mohole opened his eyes.

"If Moholean relativity is valid," he said, "we'll one day witness events that do not conform to the predispositions of science. We may be confronted, pay attention, with a totally unforeseen set of circumstances. This is implicit in Moholean relativity and explains why my theorizing hasn't won greater support."

"You said you got the Cheops Feeley Medal."

"Twice," he said. "But neither time for moholes. Just mention the value-dark dimension and people go glassy-eyed. All these fears about invisible mass. These morbid parties full of whimpering people. Missing matter is explained by Moholean relativity. The mass holding the galaxies together is trapped in moholes. This is why we can't find it. Some people accept this but many more don't. Thus the end-of-the-world parties. Oddly the people showing the greatest fear are often the same ones who support every step in my formulation, from the big bang to the n-bottomed hole. The explanation for the missing mass frightens them more than the fact that so much mass is missing. These are scientists so-called. What's your reaction?"

"If you deserve it, you should get it."

"It would be unprecedented, a third Cheops Feeley. The award secretly coveted by everyone in the sciences. The one they'd lie and cheat to get. It's the underground prize, given for work that has an element of madness to it. Of course, no one says this openly. But we all know that madness content is a determining factor."

"How much in cash?"

"When you talk about cash, stick to the Nobel Prize. I'll never get one of those, not for something with the high madness content of moholes."

"If it's so crazy, why blame the people afraid of it?"

"Theory, in theory, that's in theory. Everything we've discussed is pure theory. In theory it's soothing, it's lovely, it explains a great deal. If the theory is ever tested, however, and if they find evidence of real-life moholes, then it's every man for himself. The laws are different there, you see. Although some of my lesser colleagues would argue against this, I am convinced that alternate physics is not designed to cope with physical reality; that is, with the real world. As kingpin, I would probably react more drastically than anyone. This has always been part of my psychological value pattern. I have never been far from snapping. This is in confidence I'm telling you this."

"What do you think would happen if you snapped?"

"We won't talk about that," Mohole said.

"Anyway, about the Nobel Prize, aren't they holding up some of the awards this year?"

"You got yours."

"I think they're trying to decide some of the tricky ones."

"I'm completely self-taught," Mohole said. "I took correspondence courses. I went to the library. I practically lived in the library. A lot of people become deeply involved in their work but only self-taught people experience total murderous obsession. It took years but I finally beat them at their own game."

"What game?"

"Science."

"What's wrong with two medals with your kind of background?"

"I'm a snapper, that's what wrong. When things start getting unbearable I see myself getting a high-powered rifle out of the closet."

"Then what?"

"We won't discuss it further."

"They'll want me getting back there to sit in."

"I was fanatically determined to make my mark among the great figures of modern science and I've done it, I've succeeded, a two-time Cheops Feeley medalist, all the work and struggle rewarded with an entire theoretical system of relativity named in my honor. But plenty could still happen if it moves out of the realm of theory."

"Named in your honor by you yourself."

"Are you criticizing?"

"Not that I'm criticizing."

"Einstein wasn't *all* wrong, you know. I certainly don't think my efforts lead inescapably to that conclusion. He did some promising work in pure mathematics before regrettably abandoning that field at the age of sixteen, I believe it was."

"You mean Einstein wasn't all *right*. He made a little mistake here and there. That's what you mean."

"If I seem to be raising my voice," Mohole said in a calm tone, "it's only because I recognize your right to correct me. I wouldn't be yelling if I didn't respect you. Yelling is a bond between people who respect

184

each other despite invalid corrections. We yell and scold as a way of paying homage to each other's views. This is the burden of friendship between extremely high-strung individuals. If we didn't accept the burden, we'd be sworn enemies. Friendship is exasperating at best. But think of the alternative."

"I am."

"The essence of my brand of relativity—that in a mohole the laws of physics vary from one observer to another—is at odds with every notion of the universe that displays a faith in nature. In the value-dark dimension the laws are not equally binding in all frames of reference, whether accelerated or nonaccelerated, and if I get up and leave suddenly it's because I have to use the vomitorium."

He put another green pill in his mouth. Billy was certain that if he threw his head back as abruptly as he had the last time he swallowed, the head would smash against the back of the chair, perhaps causing a whiplash injury to Mohole's neck or spine. But this time he used an abbreviated head-jerk, beginning his gasp sooner and sustaining it until a scant trace of bilious secretion appeared on his lips. Billy thought this would be followed by stomach matter, the gush itself, but before it could happen Mohole rose from the chair, uttering hoarse dry sounds, and disappeared into one of the rear chambers. When he returned he was wearing a turquoise cravat.

"So the radio signals have the characteristics of an echo," he said. "Although a mohole has no surface and radiates no heat, the message gives every indication of having been reflected from a high-temperature object of very dense surface composition."

"But you don't want to know what it says."

"Now that Ratner's star has been ruled out as the source of the transmission, we don't want to presuppose a new conclusion. We want to pursue certain lines of argument without outside equivocation. In other words you needn't overexert yourself on cracking the code."

"You want to find out who sent it and from where but not what it says."

"It would only beg the question."

"An answer."

"Exactly," Mohole said.

"It's probably not a good idea to say who's going to stop me if I decide to keep working."

"Can you blow bubbles with spit?"

"Only little."

"I do big," Mohole said.

"Can you sneeze out of just one nostril?"

"Have a greenie."

"They're so big. I've never seen pills that big."

"Have one for your head."

"Look how big."

"Have a greenie."

"Even if I knew what they did to my type brain, I couldn't swallow it because of the size."

"Some people are swallowers, some aren't. I concede that. But have one anyway."

"Can you belch at will?"

"A greenie," Mohole said.

"Everybody knows about drugs and jumping off roofs."

"Do it to please me."

"How can it please you to give me something I don't want?"

"That's the way high-strung people are. We expect others to make small sacrifices for the sake of our emotional calm. Now that I've explained things, will you take the greenie?"

"No."

"I feel hurt when people refuse to accept what I offer. I can't tell you how hurt I feel. Hurt enough to snap. Granted, some people aren't known as swallowers. Still, I hurt all over. In fact I see myself with a high-powered rifle and a whole lot of ammunition. I'm standing in a window high above the street."

"What else?"

"That's all I'm saying."

"Make a deal."

"My psychological value pattern is what it is and there's nothing I can do about it."

186

"A deal," the boy said. "I'll take the greenie if I can keep it for later."

"Done," Mohole said. "Once it's out of my hands and in yours, I know you've accepted it and I feel less inclined to raise my voice, much less fill the streets with random gunfire."

"The lady told me to get back at once."

"That reminds me. I'm having some female companionship drop up later today. Maybe you'd like to stay around and meet it."

"What's it consist of?"

"There's only one but she might have a sister."

"They told me to get back at once and I didn't. If you could find out for sure about the sister thing, I could try to leave the meeting early again."

"Do you like it here?"

"What, here?"

"The whole big place."

"I don't see myself making a career out of it."

"Are you entering into things?"

"No."

"Enter into things," Mohole said.

"I don't see it."

"Make an effort. Are you making an effort?"

"No."

"Make an effort," he said. "That's what I failed to do at your stage of the game and even much later. I didn't enter into things, with the result that I felt left out, consistently on the verge of snapping. I didn't make the effort. So what would happen? I would see myself with a high-powered rifle and big boxes of ammo. I'm standing in a window high above the street. I'm firing wildly. I'm shooting anything that moves. Then I'm yelling at anyone left out there who'll listen. 'I'm a snapper! I snapped! It's not my fault!' Yelling and firing simultaneously."

"What then?"

"Maybe you'd better tell me your partner preference," Mohole said.

"Whatever's normal in my situation."

187

"Maybe you don't want someone's sister. There are different varieties of companionship dropping up to a place like this."

"Let's stay with the sister thing for now."

"Tell you what let's do," Mohole said. "You go on back to the conference and I'll contact you when I've made arrangements. It might turn into a very unique soiree. It just happens that I'm a paid consultant to a sex engineering outfit. Devices galore."

"I like the name."

"That's not their name. That's what they make. Remember not to tell anyone I've had this place converted. No one knows who shouldn't know. And don't worry if I seem to raise my voice. When I stop shouting at you, that's the time to worry."

He showed the boy around the rest of the suite. The furniture in every room had the same surly gleam, a waxless finish that seemed an indestructible trait rather than something adhering to the objects themselves. There were towel racks everywhere. Refrigerated air seeped from large vents in the wall. The sofas, drapes and lampshades had plastic covers labeled OMCO RESEARCH. There was no sign of the translucent inner surface of the sphere itself; partitions had been erected as part of the renovation. An ornamental footbath graced the vomitorium. Mohole opened a cabinet and displayed his collection of "specialty scents"—artificial fragrances packaged in aerosol cans. Billy noted a few of the labels. "CHEESE, CRACKERS AND DRINKS." "DINNER FOR TWO—SEAFOOD SERIES." "WOOD-BURNING FIRE." "COFFEE TABLE AURA —FRESH FLOWERS, CIGARETTES, AFTER-DINNER CORDIALS." "HEAPED GARMENTS." "BEDSHEETS AND HAND LOTION." "NUDE FEMALE BODY (MOIST)—SENSE OF URGENCY SERIES." One can was simply marked "YVONNE, YVONNE." The suite's seeming contradiction, that of functional objects contained in a space of baronial proportions, made the boy feel slightly dislocated. But the sight of so many TV sets, all with swivel mechanisms, revived him. It was like a nineteenth-century motel, magnificent and bland, the traveler desolate in this unnatural immensity, a painless estrangement for all.

"Poverty is exhausting," Kyzyl said. "I've seen it etched on many a face. We used to make early dawn sweeps across the urban centers, tagging indigents for further study. We'd proceed forth in unmarked half-tracks and commence tagging with coded markers. These were tired people. When we speak of poverty, this is co-synonymous with extreme fatigue. Migration patterns can't be studied without tagging. But the average migrant indigent, even when we talk of his fatigue and his flagged-out spirits, he sometimes posed a bodily threat to the funded personnel. He with his people resisted being tagged, resisted wearing the tag, resisted the idea of tagging, the whole concept enforcement. It was a study. There was funding. But the poverty mentality resists this. Migrant workers, as opposed to indigents, were too lethargic one way or the other. People who follow the sun are easy to tag and we had checkpoint activity throughout the warmer zones. But the indigents resisted. We utilized no force or prereaction sweeps except as they applied. Applied force is sanctioned by most confederations of the destitute. This is first-hand from personal experience that we utilized only optional weaponry and never inflicted as we say incommensurate pain. Pain inflicted had to be equal to the threat to our persons. There's a difference between exhaustion and lethargy. Exhausted people are known to be dangerous. They don't display the torpor and stupor of people who follow the sun by the truckload, making them easy to tag. So the question of fatigue is double-edged, commingled with the language problem, and many experts on dialect proceeded forth into the urban enclaves to explain to the indigents that this was all a study to learn more about their migratory patterns. A funded study. But they resisted the coded markers. They fought with their teeth and feet. In our lightly armored vehicles we conversed among ourselves. 'How tired they seem,' we said."

Billy realized that Kyzyl was escorting him back to his canister rather than to the large room with the bare octagonal table. This made sense, come to think of it, because Kyzyl didn't know he was supposed to return to the Conference on Invisible Mass. Once inside, with Kyzyl waiting beyond the door, he decided in a moment of minor defiance to do some further work on the star code. He turned off the light and began to calculate, his silky pencil forming giant numbers on the plain white sheet. The videophone chimed five times. He pushed a button on the panel and the screen filled with light. There was no one there, however. The only thing he could see was a tricycle in the background, dimly.

"Big B., can you hear me?"

"Where are you?"

"It's Endor."

"Talking from where?"

"On the floor," the voice said. "Don't want you to see me. But I want you to hear. Can you do that?"

"You're coming in weak."

"How about now?"

"Better."

"I'm down on the floor shouting up into the talk gadget. Don't try to see me. Do you know where I am?"

"Down on the floor."

"I mean where in what locale."

"The hobby room."

"Good guess."

"I recognized the tricycle."

"That's where I am, all right. Walked in early this morning. Came in from the hole. Came limping through the mud and grass. I've been digging, lad. Clawing my way down. But I wanted to take a break and come weaving in all mud-laden and scrawny for the express purpose of talking to you. You can't see me, can you?"

"No."

"They padlocked my room. You know that?"

"Yes."

"What are we going to do about that?"

"I don't know."

"Neither do I," Endor said. "With no room of my own, I had to come up here to the so-called hobby room. At least they haven't touched my things. My things are intact. Important to have things of your own. Untouched and intact. But there's still the other room to think about, the real room, padlocked. We'll have to figure something out, Big Bill, because eventually you're going to want to sit in my room a spell. Things are scheduled to get worse around here. That much I know. You can count on it, although you'll wish you hadn't."

"So what do I do?"

"Sit tight and listen. I want to tell you all I know. Admittedly it's not much but we have to assume it's better than nothing. Might help you forestall the mongers. I'm all skin and bone. You can't see me, can you?"

"You're coming in weak again."

"My hands are cupped to my mouth. I'm on my back with cupped hands to mouth to get my voice up to the talk mechanism."

"Hardly hear you."

"Skin, bone and whisper," Endor said. "Tell you what, Big Bill. Close your eyes and I'll get myself up on my feet and talk right into the thing. Tell me when you're ready."

"Now."

"Eyes closed?"

"Shut tight."

"I don't trust you," Endor said. "I'm going back down to the floor. On the count of three, you can open your eyes. I'll cup my hands tighter this time. That should funnel my words up to you in the loudest death-wheeze I can manage. One two three."

"All open."

"I love to count," the voice said. "Counting has given me special pleasure down through the years. I can think of innumerable occasions when I stopped what I was doing and did a little counting for the sheer intellectual pleasure of it. I admire the work of the Prussians in this regard. Kronecker, Jacobi et al. Those Prussians could count. Since getting settled in the hole I've gone back to finger counting. Usually I start with the thumb of the left hand. Sometimes the pinky finger just to vary the routine. I'm taking some pebbles back with me this trip. One thing the hole lacks is pebbles. That's what I'll do on the way back. Gather some pebbles. It'll break up the trip. Also give me something to count besides fingers. What's eighteen times eleven times twenty-three minus five hundred and one plus forty-three multiplied by two minus eight thousand one hundred and ninety-two?"

"Zero."

"Just testing your wits," Endor said.

"I don't like that kind of calculating. I do it automatically but it's dumb."

"I worked it out beforehand in the hole. I know you can do much tougher but my mental apparatus isn't what it used to be. I wanted to throw in some logarithms and cube roots but couldn't remember how they work. Settled for a lot of odd numbers. Thought that might throw you."

"It makes no difference odd or even."

"Your wits have to be sharp for what's ahead so I thought I'd give you a flash quiz just to help you hone up. It won't be long, lad. Seventeen times forty-one."

"Six ninety-seven."

"I know you can do tougher."

"Do you know a person or persons named Harry Braniff?" Billy said.

"Person or persons?"

"This Braniff person delivered an object to my room through the exit grating and I'm wondering if you know him or know who the person is who told him to do it."

"I have no standing around here."

"I listened to the object and it sounded like it might be important but I don't know in what way important."

"I have no standing, lad. I have no resources to call on. I live alone in a hole. I claw through dirt with a wire hanger and my bare nails, uttering nonverbal sounds as I dig deeper. There's nothing important I'm capable of doing except tell you what little I know and offer you the psychological security of my padlocked room if you can figure out how to negate the padlock. I have no current status."

"Person or persons unknown, I guess."

"I lit out for the hole because I couldn't break the code. What's doing on the code, Big Bill? The code about finished me. I grew to hate the thing and the people who devised it. Lost faith in myself. Cursed science and the natural limits of man. Finger counting is one of the few pleasures left to me now. Number systems are beautiful structures and none is more beautiful than the set of natural numbers and there's no better way to appreciate this beauty than to count your way upward, starting with the number one. You can count and count and count and count. No matter how long you count, how many unnamable numbers you utter beyond googolplex and glossolalia for how many years and decades, there's still one more number, it's still an open-ended sequence, it still outflies the imagination. I tried to break the code but the code broke me."

"I have a feeling the answer's very simple."

"The universe is so big, lad. What are we going to do about it?"

"I don't know."

"Neither do I," Endor said.

"A lot of it is missing, so it's not nearly as big as it could be. The value-dark dimension. A lot of the universe is trapped in there. We can't find it. That's why the galaxies aren't flying apart the way they should be."

"I thought they were flying apart in orderly fashion," Endor said. "Things flee. Everything hurtles to the edge and over the edge."

"Moholean relativity."

"This is new to me. Word of this hasn't reached me. They keep changing things on me. If it's not an addition it's a subtraction and if not a subtraction then a correction. Extremely depressing at times."

"Mohole told me all about it," Billy said. "He has a whole room just for vomiting."

"The history of science is crosshatched with lines of additive and corrective thought. This is how we try to arrive at truth. Truth accumulates. It can be borrowed and paid back. We correct our predecessors, an effete form of assassination, and then we wait either in this life or the next for the corrective dagger to be slipped twixt our own meatless ribs. Here it comes, *zip*, the end of an entire cosmology."

"A lot of people are worried."

"It's the size of things that worries people. No reason for the universe to be so large. It contains more space than I deem absolutely necessary. More time as well. Know who I envy?"

"No."

"Take a guess."

"Don't know."

"Low-gravity creatures," Endor said. "On a low-gravity planet the inhabitants are long, slender and delicate. This is how I think of the Ratnerians. I see them drifting across the terrain, almost ectoplasmically, a race of emanations merely flecked with solid matter. Yes. Beings nearly free of their planet's gravity."

"There is no planet. There's nothing up there but a couple of dwarf stars. The message came from somewhere else. This is what they're trying to find out more than what it says."

"This is new to me."

"Me too."

"What happens next?"

"Practically nothing," the boy said. "I keep my distance. I play around with the message but nothing more. That's what happens next."

"You go along with this?"

"I never asked to come here. I didn't care about the star code or even know if it was real. So now I'm just starting to get somewhere and they tell me to hold off. If that's what they want, maybe that's what I'll do. Out of spite. I believe in spite. Spite makes me feel good."

"Never misuse the freedom to invent," Endor said.

"What's that mean?"

The elderly former scientist cleared his throat for a full ten seconds, obviously building up to some kind of oration.

"Work till it hurts, lad. This is demanded of you. We all demand it. It's what you owe your chosen field. We insist on the highest striving of your intellect. There's only one way to create, as if your life depended on it, which it does. The message will tell us our place in this largest of all possible universes. No less than a total effort of your imagination must be brought to bear on this task. Every part is interconnected and all the numbers flow in proper sequence. If you don't give us every scrap of what you are, we die in strongly scented heaps. Whatever order can be conceived by the left-handed mind is yours to impose elsewhere. Whatever sense of form can be induced to rise out of the horizontal mist is yours to reapportion. Where perfect measurement beckons, no one but you is fit to sand the final beam. Mathematics is an expression of the will to live. Merely to play with it is to see your own basic nature crushed. Only the fiercest risks make existence possible. Throw yourself forward, lad. Devise forms that will explain the things around you. Wriggle out of your mortal silk. Avoid the body's wane in events of spectral perfection. Know the names of things and write them like a child in elemental lists. Who was it said names and numbers give us power over the world? Spengler no less. Never dismiss the intuition of the ancients, who believed that number is the essence of all things. The mathematical vision is not manifest in what is written and taught alone. Number is a metaphysic, the secret source of entire cultures, and men have been killed for their heresies and seductive credos. The whole history of mathematics is subterranean, taking place beneath history itself, misunderstood, ignored, ridiculed, unread, a shadow-world scarcely perceived even by the learned. Of adventure, greatness, insanity and suicide, it is nevertheless a history of nothing happening. *Of nothing happening.* Magnitudes correspond in terms of proportion. Variables in terms of function. But nothing ever happens. Statements are proved to be neither provable nor disprovable. Nothing has happened, yet everything is changed. Existence would be sheer dread without the verifiable fictions of mathematics. So sacrifice all, Big Bill. Fill every delicate invention with all your pain and every raging extract of your talent. Nothing less than sanity itself must be tipped into the scheme. Compulsions, tumults, fevers, epileptic storms. What is unlearned, along with your craftiest fabrications. Remember the savage and what he accomplished in his instinct for pure space and the mathematics of motion. Inventor of the boomerang. Yes, he pulled the string on space itself. The right side of his brain outprocessed the left. Intuition and motion and the conquest of time. It's the object of your labor, lad, to join the hemispheres. Bring logical sequence to delirium, reason to the forager squatting, language and meaning to the wild child's dream."

"All that?"

Endor began to cough and spit. The last of his strength had apparently been exhausted by the requirements of the formal speech he'd chosen to make and Billy imagined him on his back, arms and legs extended, chest pumping, warm spittle mingling in his beard with slime mold and the living mucus of his last meal. As time passed his cough assumed a tone of total desolation, the sound of a near bark, sufficient to define the residue of an existence.

"Three plus three times two."

"Twelve."

"See you at the hole," Endor said. "And, remember, there's a point after which it is possible to stop digging and take the free fall. Use your imagination. That'll tell you when to make the switch."

A long silence followed. He looked at the white tricycle on the screen. There was an electronic tremor and the picture went blank. He tried to get some work done. Endor's visitation left him feeling puzzled, maybe in part because it was nonvisual in nature. He decided to return to the meeting. Kyzyl escorted him to the door of the conference room. Puzzled, yes, but not unhappy. He liked being called lad, particularly by a bearded person. There was something pleasantly old-fashioned about it.

"But now a new theory has been put forth, one of vast implications."

He couldn't understand why anyone would wear a toupee that looked like a bowl haircut. As Bhang Pao spoke he made hand-washing gestures, each hand curling in and out of the other. Masha Simjian sucked on hard candy. The other two scientists listened in a bland daze. Billy took his seat in the corner and worked to perfect a look of peripheral interest. Bhang Pao, in a concisely passionate narration, discussed space-time sylphed and went on to summarize the rest of Orang Mohole's relativity theory.

"The laws are not equally valid there," he concluded. "Unpredictable events may flow from a given mohole or moholes. We don't know precisely what sort of events. Catastrophe, natural or unnatural, can't be ruled out. There is one hopeful note. The message of the star gods is still in effect. All we know is that the message-senders do not live on a planet in orbit around Ratner's star. Nevertheless they do live, they do exist, and this is cause for optimism if not unalleviated joy."

The door opened and Melcher-Speidell entered. In the midst of introductions Maidengut explained to Billy that the contributions of these two men in the field of alternate physics were so interdependent that the men themselves had come to be spoken of as a single individual, their names latched by an undying hyphen. Maidengut then carried two extra chairs to the table and everyone was seated. Billy was still in the corner. Lepro sat between Melcher-Speidell.

"There's nothing to get excited about," Melcher said. "When you talk and talk and talk about alternate modes of physical reality, as we've had to talk in our chosen endeavor, when you theorize and theorize, then it just seems to *happen*, whatever it is you're talking about, coming as no big shock, and this too shall pass is the way you tend to react is my reaction. We're just in the first stage. Nothing significant will happen until we're fully ready for it. This is the way it usually works. The idea begins to develop and spread. The thing or event becomes increasingly conceivable in hundreds of thousands of minds. The next stage is usually frightening imminence. The thing or event becomes frighteningly imminent. This is nothing special to get excited about and I want to say at this juncture how happy we are to have this opportunity of a faces-to-face encounter with the radical accelerate in our midst in order to reassure him that his work on the mathematical content of the transmission is no longer of vital priority status. The last stage is what really matters."

"Alternate physics, if it teaches us anything," Speidell said, "it teaches us that once you go across the line, once you're over the line and left without your classical sources, your rational explanations, the whole of your scientific ethos, once this happens you have to pause. You have to pause as we may have to pause someday in the future. You're over the line, sure, but that doesn't mean you have to keep going or hurl yourself into the uncharted void. This is nonsense. You pause. You reflect. You get your bearings. Alternate physics, if it's to move out of the theoretical realm, as it may have to one day, I guarantee you, with a vengeance, and into areas of direct application, must give us the bearings we need, or, lacking bearings to give, must soothe and support. We've come to an exciting time. Let's take the positive view and emphasize the challenge. I'm excited about this. I want to communicate my excitement but don't know how. I have my individual peculiarities. Things I cherish about myself. Private parts of me. I'm introspective. Fond of adults. Collect fruit and pennies. Like to take long walks on the beach. No better place to walk, incidentally. Sand toughens the calf muscles. You need this in the hypothetical sciences."

"Why or because is it," Lepro said, "that the number one speaker here to my right hand says in his own words nothing to get excited about and this is followed upon by my left hand here, who, why or because of the positive challenge, says excitement, excitement. Is this difference why or because of basic disagreement on essentials or why or because of semantics? Who accepts semantics, those of us at the table, omitting the corner person? I say no. You ask why or because not. I answer why or because it's too good to be true, that's why or because not. The beach is a diversion. On my left brings in his beach why or because he wants to keep us from thinking of the issue itself, which is that the sky above may be getting funny."

The one-way priority phone buzzed loudly. Simjian went to the panel, picked up the telephone, listened for a few seconds, sourly, and then turned toward Billy.

"It's for you again. A man who says he doesn't want to give his name but says you'll know who he is by the message. I'll try to repeat the message word for word as he relays it, although for the life of me I don't know why we should have to keep interrupting this conference in order to take messages for someone who's merely sitting in. 'Double companionship not feasible. But can be simulated repeat simulated. Finger-feelies, sensitizers, inflatable vulvettes. Workmanship tops, stop, atmosphere conducive to you-know-what, stop, soft lights and special scents, stop, promise memorable moments to all who dare yield to their burgeoning teenage sensuality, stop, all happening in my apartments atop the you-know-where. Discuss with no one repeat no one.' "

"I don't accept the call."

"That voice sounded familiar," Simjian said. "Was that who I think it was?"

"Yes."

"Because if it was, he's famous for his personal sleaziness."

"He's completely self-taught."

"Not to mention the tasteless events he likes to host," she said. "Degenerate ceremonies featuring objects and gadgets that mock our bodies."

"Speaking of ceremonies," Maidengut said, "I have some depressing news for almost everyone here. A torch-lighting ceremony is scheduled for the Great Hall. Tomorrow at dusk. All thirty-two of the resident Nobel laureates are supposed to be in attendance."

"What's depressing about that?" Simjian said.

"Nobel laureates only. Nobody else allowed. Pretty inconsiderate if you ask me. They might have included some of the rest of us."

"I've never seen a torch-lighting ceremony," Bhang Pao said. "I assume they light torches and hand them out. The torches are doubtless prelighted as a safety precaution and then everyone participating surely advances in a slow-moving line as the torches are handed out. After that I suspect everyone stands solemnly in place, holding his or her lighted torch as the ceremony unfolds."

"What's the ceremony all about?" Billy said. "I bet it has something to do with the aborigine."

"What aborigine?" Maidengut said.

"The white-haired aborigine. The nameless one. Somebody saw him this morning lurking around. I thought maybe they found him and wanted to do something nice, to show what they thought of him, the way he whirled."

"It's for Ratner," Maidengut said. "They're honoring Ratner."

"I didn't know there was a Ratner."

"He's being flown in from the States. His first visit here. Got the Nobel Prize for physics when he was a fairly young man and that was a long, long time ago. Wonderful occasion, really, even if they insist on restricting it. A great man. The Great Hall. Ratner himself."

Melcher-Speidell got up and left. The others soon followed—all but Maidengut and the boy. The former sat heavily entrenched, solidifying his relationship with the chair. He seemed to be waiting for a conclusive remark to be made or final question to be asked before he either left the room or fell through the chair and the floor beneath it. Billy paused at the door.

"The Ratner of Ratner's star?"

"The very same," Maidengut said.

This brief exchange completed, Kyzyl escorted the boy back to his canister.

10

OPPOSITES

He passed through twillig-shaped openings in the air, an infinite series of discrete convenient gateways.

Nobody seemed to know where the Great Hall was. He went to a nearby dining unit and checked the bulletin board ("advisory dispatch chart") for word of a torch-lighting ceremony. No word. No sign of Ratner's name. No directions to Great Hall. He read the lone note pinned there.

Vintage art films—8 millimeter
Sale or rent

1 – "Two in a Tub"
2 – "Aunt Polly's Banana Surprise"
3 – "What the Butler Did"
4 – "Volleyball Follies"
5 – "Frenchy and the House Dick"

Contact O. Mohole
Maternity Suite

By appointment only

He walked along a semicircular corridor, asking directions in vain, met in fact with squinted eyes and little sniffles, everyone reacting to this entity the Great Hall in similar fashion, civilized pygmies asked to climb sequoia trees, something ancestral in their replies, a captive skepticism shading every face. Eventually he came to a moving walkway ("linear glide") and stepped on. He'd never ridden on one of the linear glides, although he'd seen them once or twice in different parts of the building. It was a pleasant experience. You simply stood there, holding on to the moving strap above your head. The strap, similar to the kind found in subways, was suspended from a flexible-strength wire that enabled you to pull it down to suit your particular stature.

Only moments earlier he'd imagined he was moving through air-gaps cut to his shape, an infinite number of distinct apertures. Now, on the linear glide, he felt he was passing through one continuous hole. Precisely his height and width. A custom perforation. Even a special opening to accommodate his raised right arm. He moved in a straight line through a dim midevening monochrome, a kind of interior dusk, abstract murals on either side At one point a large figure, adumbral and shapeless, was superimposed on the geometry of walls and ceiling. Unerringly rendered shapes and amorphous overshadow. What was there about these surfaces that made the journey seem descendent and led him to believe he was breathing sheerest calculus? Strict precision strict. Down the line to dream the subliminal blend of number and function. Analysis rethought in arithmetical terms. Opposed positions.

Whole numbers providing the substance for the continuous torsional spring of analysis. Atomism and flow. Down the line past history's black on white. Ideal of proof ideal.

Every semirecluse has his amaranthine woman. Imaginary love-lies-bleeding. "But in this case," Softly had written, "the woman was not only real but a mathematician as well. This is Sonja Kowalewski and we can only guess at the levels of intensity during those afternoons when she arrives at his home for lessons. Twenty years old to his fifty-five. Aristocratic and social, while he is accustomed to life in remote villages. To someone fixed in solitude she must have seemed a brighter presence than he could bear. She is brilliant, attractive, Moscow-born, an Eastern jade (it is suspected) determined to have her pick of the schoolmaster's gifts. So we speculate on the density of their meetings. The quality of the sunlight in his parlor. The tone of their discussions on power series and irrational numbers. The very clothes she wears. His face, while she listens. Her eyes, adventuring. Is it within the student's vested right to consume the preceptor's soul? He is a bachelor, remember, while she is married (in name at least). Another level worth exploring. To empty each other of possessions. To negate each other's artificial names. In his regard for logic, proof, exactitude and caution, he tries not to dwell on his own belief that death is payment for risks not taken, and pours himself a beer. And for her part—what? Does she have fantasies about mathematics? Does she imagine that in his attacks of vertigo he spins from room to room, a scientist trying to cope with holiness, or perhaps himself immune, a germ-carrier of ecstasy? She titles a mathematical memoir: *On the Rotation of a Solid Body About a Fixed Point.* They pass their afternoons and when she dies (surprise) he burns her letters." Of, pertaining to, or resembling the amaranth. An imaginary flower that never fades.

In the wall ahead was an archlike opening through which the linear glide continued to move. The hole was about as tall and wide as he was. He stepped off the glide just as it whispered through the darkened arch. Adjacent to this opening was a door with a black arrow painted on it. The arrow pointed down. He opened the door and went down a flight of old stone steps, cracked in many places. The lighting consisted of a makeshift network of low-watt bulbs strung along the ceiling. He came to the bottom of the vertical shaft around which the staircase had been constructed. There was a large jagged hole in one wall and next to the hole stood a man with a plastic torch in his hand, flames two feet high.

"I'm Evinrude," he said. "You're very, very late."

"Is this the ceremony?"

"They're working out size places and they want the smallest last. That's the only thing that saved you."

"But this is the ceremony for Ratner, right?"

"Just to make it official, I have to ask if you're a laureate."

"Yes."

"In what field?"

"Mathematics."

"Because only laureates are allowed beyond this point," Evinrude said.

"Zorgs. I won for zorgs."

"What's that?"

"A class of numbers."

"Out of curiosity, would I know what you were talking about if you described them further?"

"No."

"Can people do things with these numbers of yours?"

"The average person, forget about, but in his book-to-be, right where I'm up to now, Softly says zorgs in their own way hark back to the nineteenth-century redefinition of the ancient and semimystical idea of whole numbers forming the basis of all mathematics. They hark back, he says. Softly can be funny that way."

"Who or what is Softly?"

"Head of the School of Mathematics at the Center for the Refinement of Ideational Structures."

"Correct," Evinrude said.

The torch he held was very large and Billy hoped they wouldn't give him one to carry, particularly if the ceremony was scheduled to be a long one.

"What happens next?" he said.

"I ask you why you're late."

"Nobody could tell me how to get here. I asked everybody I saw and none of them ever even heard of the Great Hall. It's not that I didn't ask. They just never heard."

"No wonder they never heard of it," Evinrude said. "You gave them the wrong name. It's not the Great Hall. It's the Great Hole. Whoever told you Great Hall was guilty of a misnomer. This is the old part of Field Experiment Number One. The building was partly built on an existing structure. Not many people know that. The old structure was buried, and so instead of destroying it or bypassing it they incorporated the old part into what they were putting up, a buttress for the foundation, because of the archaeology involved. This is where we're standing now. The old part. The temple cave. They still haven't figured out how to make it disasterproof. A sudden noise or loud report could bring it all down."

"What's this about size places?"

"It's to get a dramatic effect with the torches."

"We all hold torches?"

"The laureates," Evinrude said. "All the laureates get a torch and go to their size places and then light the torch and hold it."

"Why are they having the ceremony down here?"

"Ratner's people."

"What kind of people?"

"The doctor, the nurse, the organist, the fella from the bearded sect. They insisted on having the ceremony in the Great Hole because of first of all there's the old gentleman's health to be considered and the air down here is the right kind of air and because of second of all there's a sense of the past in the Great Hole because of its being part of a venerable structure and there's that to be considered, awareness of past, respect for heritage. The laureates agreed. Those that were consulted."

"I wasn't consulted."

"You were very, very late. Maybe that's why you weren't consulted. Ratner's people weren't late. They came thousands of miles but they got here on time."

"They weren't told Great Hall instead of Great Hole."

"Time to go in," Evinrude said. "Step lively, keep it moving, spread it out."

He dipped the torch and Billy stepped through the hole and walked down a flight of crooked stairs into a small dusty room with nothing in it but a bronze door and a stone bench. He sat on the bench and looked at the door. The particles in the air reminded him of chalk dust and he assumed all this powdery matter had simply floated off the walls and ceiling, further indications of the structure's fragility and age. The door opened, admitting a man wearing a mink fedora and a long black coat. His beard was white and untrimmed, reaching to his chest, and although its wispy attenuated ends made the boy think of surgical cotton sticking out of a box after a handful has been removed, he was sure on second glance that the beard was anything but soft, that its strands were coarse, firm and wiry, toughened by decades of misery and grit. The man's coat extended almost to his shoes. He approached the bench and Billy moved over to give him room to sit but the man stopped short of the bench, put his hands behind his back and leaned forward slightly, head inclined, lips beginning to move a few seconds before he actually said anything.

"The old gentleman wants you to present the roses."

"I thought you were the old gentleman."

"I'm Pitkin, who advises on the writings. I'm looking at the person he picked by hand to present him the roses face to face. He's one sweetheart of a human being. I advise him on the mystical writings. But if they forced it out of me with hot tongs, I'd tell them I learn more from Shazar Ratner than I could ever teach if I live to be—go ahead, name me a figure."

"A hundred."

"Name me higher."

"A hundred and fifty."

"Stop there," Pitkin said. "Many years ago he came back to his roots. Eastern Parkway. Strictness like you wouldn't believe. But the old gentleman he was tickled to get back."

"What kind of strictness?"

"The codes, the rules, the laws, the customs, the tablecloth, the silverware, the dishes."

"So then you're from Brooklyn, if your roots are Eastern Parkway.

205

I'm surprised I never heard of the old gentleman, being from the metropolitan area myself."

"He's a living doll," Pitkin said. "After you present the roses he has a word or two he wants to whisper up to you. You're the youngest. He figures you'll be worth telling. The others he wouldn't give you two cents for the whole bunch. Science? He turned his back on science. Science made him a household word, a name in the sky, but he grew world-weary of it. He returned to the wellspring to drink. They assigned me then and there. I know the writings. Many years ago, long before a kid like you was even formed out of smelly mush in his mother's tubes, I committed the writings to memory. They don't know this, the other elders, because we're not supposed to memorize. It's considered cheating when you memorize. When you memorize you lose the inner meaning. But how else could a dumbbell like me become an elder? Name me a way and I'll do it. Just between us chickens I did a little cheating. So what's the damage? Show me who I harmed. Once in a while I sneak another look or two to refresh myself. But only once in a while and just to refresh. This I vow and you're my sworn witness who I'm looking at. If I'm lying, may both your eyes drip vengeful pus."

"Why my eyes?"

"Because that's the oath," Pitkin said. "I didn't word the oath. Go ask who worded it why your eyes."

"It must go way back, an oath like that, to when they believed in exact cruelty to each other's parts of the body. Eye for eye. Tooth for tooth."

"You know the writings?"

"Just something I heard."

"To where did the old gentleman return to drink?"

"He returned to the wellspring to drink."

"We all memorize. The memory is there, so where's the harm in using it? Here I depart from the other elders. The elders say interpret the writings. Find the inner meanings. Seek the sacred rays from the world of emanations. The writings say the same thing. But not everybody can interpret. It's hard for some people to interpret. You should pardon me but it's true. Pitkin memorizes. If you can name me one thing wrong with this that I haven't already figured out for myself, I'll take off all my clothes and walk naked through Crown Heights."

"I've heard of it."

"So show a little mercy to someone whose whole life has been awe, fear and kilt."

"Kilt?"

"Innocence and kilt."

"You mean guilt. Awe, fear and guilt. There, that makes sense. You said 'kilt.' But it's definitely pronounced guilt."

"A corrector I got in front of me. I need this from a peewee quiz kid? This kind of talk I need from someone that I don't even know if his little shvontzie got trimmed by the knife?"

"One second please."

"Inches away from a filthy urinator and I have to listen to my spelling corrected by some smart aleck in arithmetic?"

"I was brought up to wash everywhere."

"Filthy-impure, not filthy-dirty. Ritual filth, the worst kind. One thing I want to tell you even if it breaks my heart giving advice to a speller. A little advice free of charge straight from the mystical writings. You ready for this? Quiz kid, corrector, you want to be instructed from the writings or you want to go through life waving your shvontzie like a monkey?"

"I'm listening."

"Learn some awe and fear."

"Is that it?"

"White monkey, speller, keep your business out of other people's noses."

Billy began to imagine that under the beard and heavy dark clothes was a young fellow arrayed in the latest resort finery, a slick casual warm-up act who would end his comic routine by dressing up in shabby clothes, sticking on a beard and stepping out in Pitkin's skin to do some involuted patter about ghetto life in stone-age Brooklyn.

"What did I say you should learn?"

"Some awe and fear."

The bronze door opened and a doctor and nurse entered. The doctor

207

held a huge syringe and the nurse was wheeling a device that consisted of a gallon bottle of colorless fluid and a thin black hose that extended from the bottle through a Pyrex vessel (filled with a semisolid material) and into a small clear cylindrical container. Paying no attention to the old man and boy, the doctor began to fill the syringe with fluid processed through the hose, vessel and tube. It was a complicated procedure and the doctor and nurse slapped at each other's hands, although with no animosity, whenever a faulty move was made.

"Some doctor," Pitkin whispered. "Only the worst cases he takes. If he sees you in the street having a heart attack, he walks right by. Tell him it's a tsetse fly in your lungs, if you're lucky he'll stop. He makes so much money you couldn't count that high. A house with grounds. Two big doors, front and back. A toaster that does four slices. His yacht he named it *Transurethral Prostatectomy*. Uses a colored nurse. See her? With the tube in her hand? Colored. Walk in any hospital right off the street and that's what you see. Uniforms, shoes, folded hats. Like anybody. Only colored. A total specialist, Dr. Bonwit. The old gentleman swears by him. Only because of Bonwit he came for the torches all this way. With Bonwit along he's willing to travel. Round trip we're paying. Ratner, Bonwit, Pitkin, the organ player, the colored nurse. We took up collections in the neighborhood. This is the respect people have for the name Ratner both before and after he turned his back."

"It's a back problem?"

"Turned his back on science."

"What's wrong with him then to make him have to travel with a doctor?"

"Not just a doctor please. A specialist. Never please say doctor to his face. You don't know this? What am I looking at here? How many kinds of genius did they tell me to watch out for? Pisher, where should you keep your business out of?"

"Other people's noses."

"A little awe and fear never hurt anybody."

"But what's the old gentleman suffering from?"

"Look it up," Pitkin said. "Turn to any page in the medical book and there he is. Swollen tooth sockets. Brown eye. Urinary leakage.

Hardening of the ducts. Hormone discolor. Blocked extremities. Seepage from the gums. The wind is bad. The lungs are on the verge. Bonwit gives the lungs two weeks. There's no breathing except shallow labored. The lungs, the lungs."

"What kind of wind?"

"Intestinal and digestive. Mixed wind. A little of each."

"What else?"

"The skin, the bones," Pitkin said.

"They must love him at Blue Cross."

"How are you behaving that I said you shouldn't behave like?"

"A white monkey."

"What am I looking at here?"

"A pisher."

"Moistness," Pitkin said. "His whole body is moist. The doctor, you should see him, night and day he works to keep it dry. Dedication at that price is worthless. You need heavy machines to keep a man alive. The face, the mouth."

Pitkin's lips continued to move and Billy wondered exactly how old this man Ratner must be if his advisor on the writings thought it suitable to refer to him as the old gentleman—an advisor with white hair growing out of his face at beard level and even above, crowding the eyes, and with lips that started moving before he spoke and did not stop until well after he was finished talking. Dr. Bonwit walked out now, syringe properly filled, and the nurse followed, wheeling the elaborate device.

"Is that for the old gentleman?"

"Nonclotting silicone," Pitkin said. "He doesn't like to see them fill up the needle, so they sneak around the nearest corner and do it there. Needles, who can look?"

"Didn't I hear something once about silicone that has to do with bigger breasts?"

"Watch with the language in front of an elder."

"Yes or no, are they injecting his breasts?"

"Get out from here."

"What for?"

"With language like that you address an elder?"

209

"I'm only asking."

"Get out from here."

"I do no wrong."

"They're injecting his face," Pitkin said. "His face collapsed coming over the ocean last night. A storm like nobody's business. Eagles on their hats they had to fly right into it. So now Bonwit builds up the face with a little shot. Poof, it fills right out. This is instant silicone, according to Bonwit, that fills you out, that coats the lining, that heats up the tissue and makes the moisture run off that's making trouble up and down the body. Good stuff. No clotting. He recommends."

"Not just for anybody."

"What can I say? He recommends. This is from his own words, Bonwit, that I memorized. With strictness like we got, who wouldn't memorize? This I ask. You're looking at an asker. If they put hot tongs on my body I might admit I could use another chance. Maybe with a second chance I could learn to interpret. Maybe it's less impossible than I think, dumbbell or not. But I'm asking who did I hurt but myself? An old man asks. True, I did a little cheating. I memorized here and there. I didn't look for the inner meanings. For years I'm sweating bullets over this thing. If they said I could have another chance I'd walk naked in the rush hour through a colored subway car. This I vow on a holy oath. If I'm lying, may you inherit a hotel with ten thousand rooms and be found dead in every room."

"These oaths are pretty dangerous to people just standing around listening."

"I didn't word them. They were worded five thousand years ago. You want to change the wording, go complain. Tell them Pitkin sent you. I'm in enough trouble with the cheating like a hot coal on my heart so I can't sleep at night, I might as well have that too, my name on a complaint by some pipsqueak speller from off the street. This is what happens with strictness. It has awe built in. The more you cheat, the greater the fear. Where's the impunity in this world?"

"Just don't start in with the vengeful pus."

"An oath is an oath."

"You don't have to use the worst ones."

"It's time to present the roses," Pitkin said.

They went through the bronze door, past the instant silicone apparatus and down several flights of stairs that seemed even older and more damaged than the stairs he'd descended earlier. He heard organ music below, a reverberating cavern-sized snore, and he followed Pitkin through a slit in the wall and out into the Great Hole, a vast underground chamber largely in a natural state (cool stone surfaces) but including remnants of ancient architecture (columns, half-walls, part of a platform) as well as elements of recent installation (fluorescent lighting and structural reinforcement). The lights were suspended from large portable appliances that resembled clothing racks. The organ, which was Endor's, the same neon pipe organ Billy had seen in the hobby room, was set on an outcropping of rock in a far corner. Aside from Pitkin, the only people he saw at the moment were the organist, now playing the kind of intermission music featured at hockey games, and the old gentleman's doctor, heading directly toward Pitkin. The two men exchanged a few words and then the bearded advisor disappeared into a dim hollow about thirty yards away. Listening to the organ, Billy recalled Evinrude's remark about a loud noise bringing down the entire Great Hole, if a hole could be thought of as something readily subject to being brought down.

"The old gent may or may not make it," Bonwit said. "One advantage is the air down here, crystal clear, a beautiful purifying agent for the biomembrane. Now here's how we'll work it. The laureates are in the antecave off the Great Hole and they're being instructed in torch manipulation. You don't join them until they file in and Sandow gives you a hand signal. Sandow's the man at the organ. After he gives the hand signal, the biomembrane is wheeled in by Pitkin and Georgette from that shadowy area with me leading the way. Then Sandow makes the opening remarks and the pigeons are released."

"When do I present the roses?"

"After the pigeons," Bonwit said.

"What's this biomembrane that's being wheeled in?"

"It's what keeps old Ratner alive. Ultrasterile biomedical membrane environment. This is the prototype model, fully operational but with still a few kinks. It's a total life-support system that grew out of the trace-element isolator used to keep lab animals germ-free. The old gentleman never leaves. This is the only nonhostile environment we could work out for him considering his state of deterioration. The bacterial count is zero. There are double airlocks for air current control. Pressure is regulated and there's automatic oxygen therapy when his system needs a jolt. It's even got a vapor duct to cut down the chance of self-infection. If he begins to fail, Georgette raises the shield and I crawl in and operate. The biomembrane is a self-sterilizing operating theater in miniature and it adapts to a postoperative therapy center, he should live so long, as the saying goes."

"Is Sandow a laureate?"

"Sandow is an organist," the doctor said.

"I was told laureates only. I can understand an MD and a nurse and even a person who reads from the writings. But if it's all laureates, why move that organ all the way down from where it was and include someone that didn't win? Except maybe he did win and only plays the organ on the side."

"Unless they give a Nobel Prize for pedaling, he didn't win. But it adds to the mood, an organ. I for one don't mind him around. It makes for more pomp, having an organ. 'LaMar T. Sandow at the keyboard.' Besides he's the old gent's lifelong friend. You want a friend to see you honored. I'm all for an organ at a function like this. It supplies a heady tone."

"What do you specialize in?"

"Everything," the doctor said.

Pitkin returned, bent and shuffling, a bouquet of white roses in his arms.

"The colored nurse told me to tell you the face filled out."

"Good," Bonwit said.

"I made believe I did a little reading. I gave a good show. It made him teary around the nose. Thick green nose-blow runs out of his eyes. From his nose you get nothing but water."

"What do *you* think of having an organ?" Bonwit said.

"We already got one. What, you want two?"

"Just want to know what you think. Fielding a few ideas."

"Why, somebody's against it?"

"That's right."

"Wait, let me guess."

"You want to give me the flowers?" Billy said.

"Against the organ, who could it be? Which person for his size makes the biggest corrections? Tell me if I'm warm if I move toward the speller."

"It belongs to Endor. They should have left it where it was."

Sandow broke off the intermission music and began playing a triumphal march. Pitkin handed Billy the flowers and went back to the dark corner, this time accompanied by Dr. Bonwit. The laureates started filing in, thirty-one of them, in size places. Multicolored neon, flashing intermittently, pulsed through the clear tubing that extended well above the organ. The torches carried by the laureates were as large as the one Evinrude had used to light the way into the original jagged hole. Although still unlit, the torches were being held as if each one were about to cough forth an assortment of fresh lava; that is, the laureates kept the plastic devices well away from their bodies, every head averted. They seemed to march accompanied by a terrible belief in their own potential for self-immolation. It passed methodically down the line, a bland handshake, freezing them to their processional drag-step.

The small parade came to a halt as Sandow lifted his hands from the keyboard and spun himself to the end of the bench, looking directly at Billy. Echoes of the organ music collided high above the floor of the Great Hole. Sandow tapped his right hand twice on the inside of his left thigh. This, it turned out, was only the first of two signals and he followed it with a little wiggle of the thumb. Billy, with the flowers, took his place at the front of the line. He realized now that the first hand signal had been meant for him (get in line) and the second for the doctor, the nurse and Pitkin (wheel in the biomembrane), for at this moment a massive transparent tank came into view. Its basic shape was simple: a cylinder on wheels, a blunt-nosed torpedo set lengthwise on a metal undercasing to which were fixed four scooter-sized tires. Dr. Bonwit walked ahead of the biomembrane, kicking small stones out of the way, and behind it were Pitkin and the nurse, pushing. Everywhere on the ten-foot-long tank were complex monitoring devices and all sorts of gauges, tubes and switches. It was by far the most elaborate health mechanism Billy had ever seen and he stood on his toes to get a look at Ratner himself but the angle wasn't favorable just then. What he could see, clearly, were a half-dozen large bright sponsor decals and stickers on both sides of the biomembrane and even on the blunt front end. Corporate names, brand names, slogans and symbols:

MAINLINE FILTRONIC
Tank & Filter Maintenance

STERILMASTER PEERLESS AIR CURTAINING
"The breath you take is the life we save"

BIZENE POLYTHENE COATING
UDGA inspected and approved

WALKER–ATKINSON METALIZED UNDERSURFACES
From the folks at Uniplex Syntel

EVALITE CHROME PANELING
The glamour name in surgical supplies

DREAMAWAY
Bed linen, mattress and frame
A division of OmCo Research
"Building a model world"

Sandow stood before the organ on the natural rock shelf and waited for the bearded man and the nurse to stop wheeling. When they did, all was quiet except for an underground stream nearby and the last sobbing echo of the triumphal march barely reaching them from a distant surface of the huge cavern. Sandow, a balding thickset man, wore a sort of Oriental smile, a pained look subtly altered by decades of erosion.

"I'd like to open my remarks by reaffirming my friendship with the old gentleman despite going our separate ways more than twenty-five years ago due to clashing ideologies, which explains my presence here, symbolic of a coming together, a let's-join-hands-type-thing, and what a setting it is, ladies and gentlemen, a basilica if I may use that word in a nonsectarian sense of earthen rock and the relics of an unknown civilization these many feet down to light our torches in tribute to this

214

gentle soul of science, who, when we were young men, he and I, espoused all there was to espouse in those benighted days of the principles of scientific humanism, including, as I recall, individual freedom, democracy for all peoples, a ban on nationalism and war, no waiting for a theistic deity to do what we ourselves could do as enlightened men and women joined in our humanistic convictions, the right to get divorced; but who, as I understand it, has now returned to the ideas and things from which so many of us were so eager to flee, proving, I suppose, that there's a certain longevity to benightedness, and I won't take up the time here providing you with a list of this great ex-scientist's current convictions beyond mentioning the secret power of the alphabet, the unnamable name, the literal contraction of the superdivinity, fear of sperm demons; so to enlarge on an earlier statement this is not only a coming together but a going away in a way, for having come to science and humanism, so has he gone, and in lieu of an eternal flame, which I had hoped to borrow for the occasion, we are here to light our torches to Shazar Lazarus Ratner, reasoning what better way to honor this man, this scientific giant, than to have the Nobelists light their torches from an eternal flame, which I'd wanted to get flown in from one of the nations in or near the cradle of civilization, simply borrowing the flame and returning it after the ceremony and they could bill us at their convenience but I was wary of pressure groups and I foresaw the remark from someone in such a group saying 'cradle of *whose* civilization,' for there is always this prejudice against Western civilization having its own cradle and calling it *the* cradle when other peoples have their own ideas of where the cradle is and even whether or not there is a cradle as we employ the term, being merely self-descriptive and not, I don't think, intending to pre-empt, none of which, as I thank you for your time and attention, has any bearing on the pigeons."

Apparently reacting to a prearranged word or phrase, one of the laureates stepped out of the line and approached a crate that was set beneath the natural stage where the organ was located.

"The pigeons," Sandow said. "Let us release the pigeons. The releasing of the pigeons, ladies and gentlemen."

The man raised the top of the box and about fifty pigeons came shaking out, like a series of knots unraveling on a single line, and flew toward the top of the cavern, veering just before they got there into an opening in the rock wall, merely a whisper now.

"The presenting of the roses," Sandow said. "The boy steps up to the great medico-engineering feat and symbolically presents the roses."

Billy strode to the tank and was lifted in the air by Dr. Bonwit and held standing on the curved surface of the transparent shield. Below, he saw the small figure of Ratner, pillowed in deep white. The doctor stood on one side of the tank, the nurse on the other, and together they supported Billy as he displayed the flowers for the benefit of the old gentleman.

"Ratner sees the roses," Sandow said. "The old gentleman acknowledges the floral bouquet."

The doctor and nurse lowered Billy to a straddling position on the tank. Bonwit turned a dial, activating a chambered device set into the clear shield directly over Ratner's face and about a foot from Billy's crotch. Immediately a bit of static was emitted from the interior of the biomembrane, apparently the sound of Ratner breathing through the bacteria-filtered talk chamber.

"The boy prepares to listen to the circulated words," Sandow said.

Bonwit took the flowers and inserted them in a sort of scabbard at the side of the biomembrane. Without the bouquet Billy was able to settle into a more comfortable straddling position. On his back Ratner looked directly into the boy's face. In a gesture of respect the latter leaned forward, trying to indicate his eagerness to hear the old gentleman's remarks. He was in fact neither eager nor respectful but the occasion seemed to demand gestures. Ratner wore a black beret and a long fringed prayer shawl that covered him from shoulders to feet.

"The old man speaks to the boy," Sandow said. "Sunk in misery and disease he speaks actual words to the little fellow on the tank."

The small ancient face was glazed like artificial fruit. The beret, however, gave the old man a semblance of heroic bearing. His arms were crossed on his chest, baby fists curled. What Pitkin had referred to as nose-blow was indeed being discharged from Ratner's eyes. Fortunately just a trickle. Far corner of each eye. Slowly the withered lips parted and the old man spoke.

216

"The universe, what is it?"

"I don't know."

"It began with a point. The point expanded so that darkness took up the left, light the right. This was the beginning of distinctions. But before expansion, there was contraction. There had to be room for the universe to fit. So the *en-sof* contracted. This made room. The creator, also known as G-dash-d, then made the point of pure energy that became the universe. In science this is what they call the big bang. Except for my money it's not a case of big bang versus steady state. It's a case of big bang versus little bang. I vote for little. Matter was so dense it could barely explode. The explosion barely got out. This was the beginning if you're speaking as a scientist. The fireball got bigger, the temperature fell, the galaxies began to form. But it almost never made it. There was such density. Matter was packed in like sardines. When it finally exploded, you almost couldn't hear it. This is science. As a scientist my preference is definitely little bang. As a whole man I believe in the contraction of the *en-sof* to make room for the point."

Billy raised his head and looked toward the laureates standing in line with their unlighted torches.

"He votes for little bang," he said. "The noise was muffled."

Then he crouched over the biomembrane as Ratner prepared to speak once again.

"The *en-sof* is the unknowable. The hidden. The that-which-is-not-there. The neither-cause-nor-effect. The G-dash-d beyond G-dash-d. The limitless. The not-only-unutterable-but-by-definition-inconceivable. Yet it emanates. It reveals itself through its attributes, the *sefiroth*. G-dash-d is the first of the ten sefirothic emanations of the *en-sof*. Without the *en-sof*'s withdrawl or contraction, there could be no point, no cosmic beginning, no universe, no G-dash-d. I learned this not long after I looked through my first telescope growing up as a boy in Brooklyn. But I failed to understand at that time."

Ratner paused here, apparently to regain his strength, and Billy glanced toward the others and made another capsule report, as he assumed they wished him to do, having traveled from every part of the world to be here for the ceremony.

217

"No universe without contraction. Grew up in Brooklyn, a boy, non-believing."

He turned his attention to Ratner once more. The lacquered face was unevenly puffy. Where teeth were missing, the inflamed sockets had bulged to the point of convexity, leaving a mouth divided between shaky teeth and burnt-out gummy nubs. Finally the old man's voice resembled a wind-up toy's, metallic and unreal, but Billy didn't know whether this was the result of his physical condition or the purifying action of the electronic talk chamber.

"We come from the stars," Ratner said. "Our chemicals, our atoms, these were first made in the centers of old stars that exploded and spread their remains across the sky eventually to come together as the sun we know and the planet we inhabit. I started out with binoculars, viewing the sky. It seemed remarkable to a boy like me, underfed and pale, with a small mental vista, that there was something bigger than Brooklyn. In those days of no television, the stars could be awesome to a boy, the way they swarmed, thin as I was, growing up, with binoculars. Later I got a telescope, my first, bought from a junk dealer, with a tripod, borrowed, and I stuck it out the window, top floor, and gazed for hours. Star fields, clusters, the moon. I read books, I learned, I gazed. Knowledge made me punch my fists against the walls in awe and shame. Our atoms were formed in the dense interiors of supergiant stars billions of years ago. Stars millions of times more luminous than our sun. They broke down and decayed and began to cool. Atoms from these stars are in our bones and nervous systems. We're stellar cinders, you and me. We come from the beginning or near the beginning. In our brain is the echo of the little bang. This is science, poeticized here and there, and this you can compare with the kabbalistic belief that every person has a sun inside him, a radiant burst of energy. Try to reach a mystical state without radiant energy and see what happens."

"Secondhand telescope," Billy said to the others. "Gazed at the stars and learned we're made of them. Pale and thin for his age."

"When I go into mystical states," Ratner said, "I pass beyond the opposites of the world and experience only the union of these opposites in a radiant burst of energy. I call it a burst. What else can I call it?

You shouldn't think it's really a burst. Everything in the universe works on the theory of opposites. To see what it looks like outside the universe, you have to go into a trance or two. According to Pitkin, G-dash-d could live anywhere. He doesn't need the universe. He could set up headquarters east or west of the universe and not miss a thing. But this is Pitkin. A rare attempt to interpret. The mystical writings. The mystical oral traditions. The mystical interpretations, oral and written. These exist beneath the main body of thought and thinking. You don't go into a trance reading the everyday writings. The hidden texts, try *them*. The untranslated manuscripts. The oral word."

Billy looked at the laureates, then shrugged from his position atop the shield.

"Written, oral," Ratner said. "Black, white. Male, female. Let's hear you name some more."

"Day, night."

"Very good."

"Plus, minus."

"Even better," Ratner said. "Remember, all things are present in all other things. Each in its opposite."

Billy turned and shrugged once more.

"I gazed constantly, learning, a young man, top floor still, gaining weight. Finally I realized a portable telescope no longer suited my needs and aspirations. I married a woman whose father had a house with a backyard. I thought here I could build what I truly needed, a ten-inch reflector with rotating dome. So with his permission and blessing we moved into his house."

"In the desert, I bet, for the clear air."

"In Pittsburgh," Ratner said. "There we lived and built. Halvah helped me, my wife, grinding the mirror, assembling the mount, measuring and cutting wood, sending away for instructions, pasting and hammering. I started to accumulate academic degrees, to go beyond amateur ranking. All that reading, it was paying off. I continued to gaze. It was awful, Pittsburgh, in those days. Smoke, soot, particles of every description. There was a steel mill two blocks away. I had to gaze between shifts. Many times Halvah's father tried to read to me from the writings. I paid no attention, acquiring my degrees, corresponding with leading minds in the sciences and technologies. He would hum as he read, a sound of piety, fear and shame. Smoke came pouring over the backyard. Thick black ash fell all over the dome. I had to stand on a chair and sweep off the top with a broom. I gazed whenever possible, I ate the cooking, I corresponded with the leading minds. Sometimes I punched the bedroom door, plentifully replete as I was with knowledge of the physical world. My father-in-law hummed, Fish, my father-in-law. I asked Halvah what kind of writings these were that her father never ceased to read from. I said Halvah what writings are these? I inquired of her what manner of writings her father so incessantly read. The mystical writings, she said. I resilvered the mirror, these being the days before widespread aluminum. He tried to give me instructions, Fish, in the secrecy of things, the hiddenness, the buried nature. Did I listen or did I sit in my dome, rotating, gazing, an occasional belch from the food?"

Billy reported to the others: "Telescope in a dome in the backyard. Marriage to the man's daughter owning the house. Science pays off. He gazes between shifts."

The metallic lilt of Ratner's voice, when again he spoke, seemed to possess an extra shading, a suggestion of querulous tremor.

"You know what you remind me of?"

"What?"

"Somebody who's giving only one side of the story," the old man said. "Don't think I can't hear that you're reporting only science, leaving out the mystical content, which they could use a little exposure to, those laureates with their half a million Swedish kronor. It was less in my day. And don't think I didn't notice all that shrugging when I was saying black-white, male-female, a little bit of everything present in its opposite. Because I noticed."

"Some things are hard to summarize."

"Give the whole picture," Ratner said.

"I'll do better."

"If you want to repeat, repeat both sides."

"From now on you'll see improvement."

220

"How many sefirothic emanations did the *en-sof* emanate?"

"Ten," Billy said.

"In words, what can we say about the *en-sof*?"

"I don't know."

"Something or nothing?"

"Nothing."

"There is always something secret to be discovered," Ratner said. "A hidden essence. A truth beneath the truth. What is the true name of G-dash-d? How many levels of unspeakability must we penetrate before we arrive at the true name, the name of names? Once we arrive at the true name, how many pronunciations must we utter before we come to the secret, the hidden, the true pronunciation? On what allotted day of the year, and by which of the holiest of scholars, will the secret pronunciation of the name of names be permitted to be passed on to the worthiest of the initiates? And how passed on? Over water, in darkness, naked, by whispers? I sat in my dome, rotating, knowing nothing of this. Nor of the need to exercise the greatest caution in all aspects of this matter. Substitution, abbreviation, blank spaces, utter silence. The alphabet, the integers. Triangles, circles, squares. Indirection, numerology, acronyms, sighs. Not according to Pitkin, however. If you listen to him, everything means exactly what it says. Not one ounce of deviation. Interpretation isn't one of his strong points, Pitkin. He's not so good, Pitkin, when it comes to interpreting."

Ratner's toy voice hissed and crackled through the chambered slot. The laureates were silent, standing in size places. Pitkin sat nearby on a large stone, silent, one hand covering most of his face, the mink fedora well back on his head, legs crossed and white flesh showing between the top of his black socks and his hitched-up trousers. The doctor and nurse were silent, respectfully set back about ten yards from the biomembrane, one on each side. Sandow was sitting on the edge of the organ bench, silent. Somewhere beneath them the hidden stream moved over smooth rock, making a faint smacking sound. From the boy's viewpoint the decals on either side of the tank appeared to be lettered in reverse. He looked closely at the old gentleman, tiny inside his prayer shawl, face gleaming with polymerized sweat.

221

"Go into your own bottom parts," Ratner said. "Here you find the contradictions joined and harmonized. This is a good place to look for the secrets you didn't even know existed. If you think I'm lying, knock once on top of the tank."

"I do not knock."

"The writings have a substructure, a secret element of the divine. Kabbalists delving into esoteric combinations of letters widened the meaning of particular texts. I allowed this much to flow from Fish's lips, progressing as a man, winning prizes in the sciences, sharing the marriage bed with my Halvah, stinky feet or not, ashes raining down. The way Fish hummed as he read. It began to get to me. What is there in these writings, I asked myself, that this man should hum? A noise of shame, fear and humiliation, my Halvah's father's humming. I refitted the tracks under the dome so it could rotate more smoothly. I learned physics to go with astrophysics. Radio astronomy to match my astronomy. I punched the walls with knowledge. Halvah gave birth, a baby, born screaming. The only nonmystical state where the opposites are joined is infancy. So perfect they often die, babies, without cause. What's your opinion?"

"I was an incubator baby."

"Then you know what it's like, living in a tank. Look who I am. Someone whose air is cleaned every four hours. A face that collapses at the slightest provocation. Climb in for a minute. Come, lift the shield. I want to whisper in your ear."

Pretending he hadn't heard these last few words, Billy looked away to make his report.

"The mystical humming of his father-in-law. A child is born. Punching the walls. The dome rotates with added smoothness."

Reluctantly he turned once again to the figure in the biomembrane.

"Don't look down your nose at esoterica," Ratner said. "If you know the right combination of letters, you can make anything. This is the secret power of the alphabet. Meaningless sounds, abstract symbols, they have the power of creation. This is why the various parts of the mystical writings are not in proper order. Knowing the order, you could make your own world from just reading the writings. Everything is built from the twenty-two letter elements. The alphabet itself is both male and female. Creation depends on an anagram."

"It's hard to picture."

"We have acrostics too."

"Do you have numbers?"

"Is Mickey a mouse?" Ratner said. "Of course we have numbers. The emanations of the *en-sof* are numbers. The ten *sefiroth* are numerical operations that determine the course of the universe. Constant and variable. The *sefiroth* are both. I could go into sefirothic geometry but you don't have the awe for that, being mathematical. *Sefiroth* comes from the infinitive 'to count.' The power of counting, of finger-numbers, of one-to-ten. We also have gematria, which you probably heard about, assigning numerical value to each letter of the alphabet. I won't even tell you about the hidden relationships between words that we discover in this way. It would be too much of a feast to set before someone who isn't ready for it, a lifelong eater of peanuts, by which I refer to myself as viewed in the face of Fish's revelations, gazing, a man, backyard, night upon night, galaxies and nebulas, my head filled with NGC numbers. The steel mill went on strike. I gazed like a madman. You couldn't get me out of the dome with threats to my child. I decided to study the sun. Adjustments, new equipment, unsilvered mirror, precautions. The sun is a frightening thing to view through a telescope, solar wedge or no solar wedge. I thought ahead to the helium flash. The final expansion. Having come from the stars, we are returned. The sun within us, the source of all mystical bursts, is perfectly counterbalanced by the physical sun that presses outward, swallowing up the orbits of the nearest planets."

Beneath the beret, Ratner's face sagged a bit. The lustrous muscles went slack and there was a suggestion of reinforced flesh about to melt.

"Picture this," he said. "From that great unstable period, the sun collapses drastically. It becomes the same size as the former earth. Now we're right inside it, mongrelized with three other planets, compacted down to a whiff of gas. The sun proceeds to cool, white dwarf, red dwarf, black dwarf, a dead star, dark black. No energy, no light, no heat, no twinkle. The end."

"Can I get off now?"

"We come from supergiant solar bodies, great hot ionized objects, and we end in the center of a dead black sphere. We're part star, you and me. Our beginning and end are made in the stars. Light, dark. High, low. Big, little. Go ahead, take it from there."

"East, west."

"Up," Ratner said.

"Down."

"In."

"Out."

"Give me a few, to test my fading powers."

"Love."

"Hate," Ratner said.

"Innocence."

"Kilt."

"Very good," Billy said after a thoughtful pause.

The old man lay back, panting gently. A few minutes passed. Finally he stirred himself.

"When the strike ended I went back to gazing by night. I studied eclipsing stars, flare stars, variables of every kind, reading star catalogues in my spare time, memorizing star tables, taking the cooking into the dome with me, a real fanatic. Also I feared the sight of Fish, always with the writings in his hand. He took books and folios into the toilet with him and stayed for hours. We could hear the humming from his bedroom half the night. He pushed his armchair into a corner and sat with his back to the room. This kind of transcendence I feared, a scientist, still young, pledged to the observable, welcomed into organizations, reaching a peak of knowledge, Pittsburgh, the backyard, my own dome, handmade, that rotated. The night sky was sensational. I made charts and calculations, identifying novalike variables, Cepheids, cool and hot stars, egg-shaped doubles. The child developed putative diarrhea, terrible, a living diaper. Did I realize I was being punished for knowledge without piety or did I sit in the observatory, scanning, light from the universe entering my eye?"

"Looks like trouble's coming," Billy said to those assembled in the

Great Hole. "He fears this person Fish who's always in the toilet reading. The kid is sick. A question is asked about piety and sitting."

"Come in and browse," Ratner said. "I know a few words I want to whisper in your ear. Come, pay a visit. Bonwit does it all the time, the doctor, holding his breath. A thing he denies doing to make me feel better. Come, let me whisper."

"I can hear you from right here."

"Pay a dying man a visit."

"I'll catch something. The shield might jam behind me and then where am I? I can hold my breath just so long."

"Browse a while."

"Put yourself in my place," the boy said. "What if the shield jams while I'm in there and then you die? What happens then? I'm probably taking a chance just sitting up here. All they told me was the flowers. Present the flowers."

"So this Fish," Ratner said. "This in-law Fish of mine. My Halvah's father. He begins to get to me with a remark passed at dinner about the hidden source of the mystical writings, doctrines and traditions. A secret beginning in the Orient. All this esoterica. Born in the East. Moving as if by stealth to other parts of the world. Always this obscurity. This secret element. I'll tell you an interesting piece of news. If you think I'm making it up, tap once on the shield. A dying man has no shadow. First heard from Fish. The person about to die lacks all shadow. Knock once if I'm lying."

"I don't understand the question."

"You know what you remind me of?"

"What?"

"A golem," Ratner said.

"What's that?"

"An artificial person."

"No such thing."

"According to instructions in the secret manuscripts, you get a little earth, run some water over it and then recite the letters of the alphabet in esoteric combinations with the four consonants of the t-dash-t-r-dash-g-r-dash-m-m-dash-t-dash-n. From this you get a golem."

"I'm almost ready to knock once."

"Light from the universe entered my eye," Ratner said. "I am in the dome, gazing, an ordinary night, through the eyepiece, open clusters, rich fields, my name being mentioned in the journals, this and that prize coming my way, a signer of petitions, the arts, the sciences, the humanisms, our child still in diapers, a tragedy, making watery excess thirty times a day, my Halvah up to her wrists in baby-do. Suddenly what do I see? A thing beyond naming. Not a thing at all. A state. I am falling into a state. Radiance everywhere. An experience. I am having an experience."

Breaking the long silence that followed, Billy spoke to the others.

"An ordinary night in the dome, getting famous, he starts to see something. The in-law Fish is winning."

Ratner's left thumb quivered slightly.

"There's nothing more I can say. I lived my life. Good, evil. Aphelion, perihelion. Hungry, full. Since then I have often fallen into states, passing beyond the opposites of the world. What use was a telescope after this? I had the states. Every experience was a new experience. It's something you don't get used to. Fish instructed me. In time I went back to my original roots, Eastern Parkway, the dispersed of Judah. We prospered as a family, learning fear, shame, piety and awe, my mind no longer filled to satiation with knowledge of the physical universe. Being pious I felt no need to punch the walls. They kept in touch with me, the leading minds, still an award or two, invitations every week. Only one I accepted, to visit Palomar, the two-hundred-inch reflector. I sat in the observer's cage right inside the telescope. Just the cage was bigger than my whole dome. I looked at some galaxies in detail. Nice, I liked it. When I climbed out they told me they had a special honor. A star. They gave a star my name."

"Falling into states," Billy said to the others. "Back to Brooklyn, the walls no longer punched. He visits Palomar. A star is named."

"Lift the shield and climb in," Ratner said. "I know some words to whisper. Come, take time. Make the sacrifice. A dying man needs visits. Be a sport for once in your life."

"Infectious danger."

ADVENTURES

"Hold your breath and lift out the shield. Take time. It's a worthwhile whisper or I wouldn't ask."

"I'm scared in plain English."

"We're all scared," Ratner said. "Who isn't scared? You, me, the laureates. Terror is everywhere. This I learned from the writings. Fish, humming, gave me his folios to take back to Brooklyn. Pitkin advises every day on the terror around us. Take demons, for example. You wouldn't think there's a connection between demons and the sperm in your testicles. The terror of onanism is that bodiless demons are able to make bodies for themselves from the spilled seed. Look at a drop of semen under a microscope and see how amazed you become at the concentration of life in that small area, the darting swarm, a phenomenon irresistible to demons. To be onanistic is to make children for the demonic element. You become the father of evil spirits. How can the pious and the G-dash-d-fearing campaign against such things? It's not easy, believe me. Nothing in the writings is easy. If I give the impression I abandoned science for the easy life, knock once. In returning to my roots I entered a world of strict mystery. A lot of loose ends, true. But great strictness in the numerology, the permutations, the legends, the symbolism, the esoteric combinations of letters, the compiling of substitutes for the ineffable name, the secrets of golem-making. In words, what can be said about the mystical state I entered while looking through the telescope in the dome in Pittsburgh, the yard covered with soot, double shifts at the mill?"

"Nothing."

"The first man was a golem before he gave names to things," Ratner said. "He was unformed matter waiting for a soul. Golem-making is laden with danger. What else can I say to a person who reminds me of one?"

The old gentleman's face appeared to be collapsing. Clear matter was being discharged from his pores as the face itself began to settle. This degenerative action was such that even the beret was affected. It slid forward a bit and to one side, coming to rest at a sharp angle over Ratner's left eye, much more rakish than the occasion seemed to warrant. His voice, running down, was a mechanized caw, barely a trace remaining of the desperate melodies of Brooklyn. He raised his right hand slightly.

"What is this but a place?" he said. "Nothing more than a place. We're both here in this place, occupying space. Everywhere is a place. All places share this quality. Is there any real difference between going to a gorgeous mountain resort with beautiful high thin waterfalls so delicate and ribbonlike they don't even splash when they hit bottom— waterfalls that *plash*; is this so different from sitting in a kitchen with bumpy linoleum and grease on the wall behind the stove across the street from a gravel pit? What are we talking about? Two places, that's all. There's nowhere you can go that isn't a place. So what's such a difference? If you can understand this idea, you'll never be unhappy. Think of the word 'place.' A sun deck with views of gorgeous mountains. A tiny dark kitchen. These share the most important of all things anything can share. They are places. The word 'place' applies in both cases. In this sense, how do we distinguish between them? How do we say one is better or worse than the other? They are equal in the most absolute of ways. Grasp this truth, sonny, and you'll never be sad."

Billy felt himself being lifted in the air. It was Dr. Bonwit, removing him from the biomembrane and setting him on the floor. Although he wasn't sure he liked all this lifting, he was glad to be off the tank. Observing size places he returned to the front of the line. Pitkin approached the tank, put his ear to the chambered slot and then departed. As Bonwit and the nurse busied themselves at the cart that held the silicone preparation, Sandow rose from the organ bench.

"Let us light the torches," he said. "The lighting of the ceremonial torches. The torch-lighting commences, ladies and gentlemen."

Holding a lighted candle, Pitkin stood now at the base of the natural stage. As Sandow called their names, the laureates proceeded in alphabetical order to touch the wicks of their torches to Pitkin's candle-flame. Then each returned to the line. As he waited for his name to be called Billy began to get nervous. He didn't know why; lighting a torch would be easy compared to straddling a biomembrane and being invited inside. Yet his nervousness grew. He actually feared the sound of his name being called. Person after person was summoned and the tension accumulated. He'd never experienced anything like this. He began to doubt that he'd be able to respond when his name was finally called. It made no sense. There was nothing to fear. It was just his name being spoken aloud as part of a series of names. His distress increased as Sandow reached the M's. What did it mean? His name had been called hundreds of times in a dozen places. Routinely he'd acknowledged it. It was his name, wasn't it, and he was the person who answered, right? He felt pressure building, a tightness in his chest and throat. Sandow got closer to T. There was no clearly defined threat and yet the pressure built. He'd faced worse threats with relative poise. From LoQuadro and the void core to Endor's hole's hole to Grbk and his nipples to Mohole's big greenie. Through all these nonspecific threats he had endured if not prevailed. The current threat, if it even qualified as such, was in a different category, he felt. The others, vague as they were, definitely qualified as threats. This one went too deep to be defined. (Existenz.) Maybe there was no word or phrase that quite described the tenuous nature of being. (Oblivio obliviorum.) To exist was to have being or actuality. To have life; live. To continue to live. To be present under certain circumstances or in a specified place. (Nihil ex nihilo.) Maybe he would not occur when his name was called. It wasn't merely a question of not being there to answer or of not being able to respond because of the pressure in his chest. Maybe he would not *occur*. (Nada de nadiensis.) The calling of his name might pre-empt him. The name itself might assimilate his specific presence.

"Twillig."

He realized he had no torch. No one had given him a torch. Nevertheless he walked over to Pitkin, not knowing what else to do and finding it a reasonably easy procedure. To counteract an intangible threat to one's sense of existence it may be necessary only to take a step from here to there. He looked up into the long coarse beard, feeling the sense of constriction begin to leave his body. Pitkin remained motionless, the candle burning at eye level.

"I have no torch."

"Well put," the advisor said. "You could make a career uttering truths."

"What happens next?"

"The old gentleman told me to tell you something even though you were in such a hurry you couldn't take time to pay a visit before the face collapsed and they had to inject. It was so serious they filled the needle right in front of him. That serious I never saw it. But he took time to give me a message, face or no face, even though a certain person I'm looking at was too much of a smarty pants to climb inside. He told me whisper to the golem in his ear."

After a pause, Pitkin's lips began to move. However, no sound emerged.

"What did he tell you to whisper?"

The lips paused a second time. When they moved now, however, words were soon to follow.

"The universe is the name of G-dash-d. All of us. Everything. Here, there, everywhere. Time and space. The whole universe. It all adds up to the true name of G-dash-d."

Another laureate's name was called and the man advanced to light his torch. Pitkin's lips were still moving. Billy moved out of the way as the remaining two or three people responded to Sandow's roll call. Finally all the laureates were back in line, this time with lighted torches. Sandow took his place at the keyboard and began playing a profound lament, the neon pulsing through the clear pipes in slow motion. Pitkin, still holding the candle, moved toward Billy in an earnestly furtive manner, sideways, inch by inch, eyes straight ahead, feet not lifted from the ground.

"For once in my life I talk without looking," he said. "You who I looked at before, hair-splitter, I'm only talking this time, making sure you're reminded not to fidget. Arithmetic monkey, keep your knuckles off the ground. One squirm and out you go goodbye. Even watch with the way you breathe. Never through the nose. You who I'm talking to."

"I understand you're growing a beard," Billy said.

Swiftly, with no excess motion, Dr. Bonwit had put on a surgical mask, raised the shield, climbed into the tank and administered the

230

facial injection, hunched over Ratner's shrunken form. Now he and the nurse wheeled the biomembrane toward a man-made opening beyond which, Billy assumed, an elevator waited. Pitkin followed them, his feet alternately gliding and bumping over the ground. Finally the biomembrane, its sponsor decals gleaming, disappeared into the opening, followed first by Pitkin and then, as the music reached a despondent coda, by the laureates in single file, their lighted torches casting shadow-tremors on the walls. This left Sandow, who climbed down from the stage and hurried out of the Great Hole.

This in turn left Billy, still shaken by the awareness that his own specific presence could seem so insubstantial, so nearly imaginary, a condition easily threatened by a one-word utterance. Pessimistic echoes were still diminishing as he headed through the opening. He came to a tall gate fastened across a shaft that was broad enough to hold a freight elevator. The elevator had already departed, however, leaving only the nurse behind, Georgette Bottomley, a slender figure dressed in white.

"They could fit all those people in one elevator?" Billy said. "Plus the tank too?"

"Plus the tank too but not plus Georgette."

"No room for one more?"

"I don't mind telling you I'm peeved off about that. Whenever doctor wants to get in his clientele's good graces, it means nurse have to wait. All my professional life I've been standing aside for the parade to go by. There's a chain of priority, you got to understand. This time it was doctor first, patient second, Nobel Prize winners third, rhythm section fourth, old man with beard fifth, Georgette in her accustomized place bringing up the rear. I'm good and peeved. I'll say it again."

"Where are you from?"

"United States."

"Whereabouts?"

"Hundred Thirty-eighth Street."

"I've heard of it."

"Ever been there?"

"Never been there. Just heard of it."

"Good and peeved," she said. "All my life I did without. I launched

231

my professional career so I could stop doing without. Doctor has a house with grounds. I always know when he's trying to impress somebody, because that's when he tells me to step off an elevator or get out of a moving vehicle. Business, industry and the corporation. Nothing under an executive vice-president gets into that office. We run checks so nobody can falsify their title. Doctor looks up their fannies and tells them they're doing just fine. When we get their waste specimen reports back from the lab, he calls them up and says fine, doing fine, keep it up. If they're out of town on business, he wires them about their specimens. Nice, fine, beautiful. He gives them encouragement. He praises their specimens. Oldest trick in the world but it always works."

"I guess that's how you get a house with grounds."

"Always I'm the one's got to make room, understand. But no point you and me swinging the heavy gloves. We got a long flight ahead. It's doctor and the beard I'm peeved off at."

"I'm not going back."

"Mean to tell me you're staying here?"

"I guess so."

"You standing there and telling me plane or no plane you are not hot-trotting your body away from this locale?"

"I stay until somebody says leave, I guess. Nobody's said anything as far as I know. I guess I stay."

"That fazes me. It really does. That fazes my whole composure."

"You think it's that bad here?"

"It's not a question of bad," Georgette said. "An accident is bad, which I've been at a hundred before I went into private practice. This place is no accident, no. But it's got such separate parts, seems like to me. Maybe it's just too new. All I know is one thing doesn't lead to another the way it should. I'm glad I'm going. I just wish this elevator had a button I could push so a light come on and we get out of here fast. See, that's what I mean about one thing not leading to another. Whenever you have an elevator with no button to call it with, that's when you wake up in the middle of the night with the menses cramps."

The freight elevator descended and kept right on going. Through the gate they watched it pass their level. A few minutes later they heard it coming up. When it stopped finally, Evinrude was aboard. He still carried the torch he'd been holding when Billy had encountered him in the vicinity of the jagged hole. This time the torch was unlighted. Georgette unlatched the gate and they stepped into the elevator. Evinrude lifted a projecting handle, starting them upward. He gave the two passengers no more than a grudging nod before directing his attention to the floor between his feet. After a long climb he depressed the lever and the elevator came to a stop.

"You, the nurse, you step off. The boy stays until we reach his stop. Stand back for the moving gate, watch your step stepping off, walk don't run."

They ascended again, two of them, moving in remarkably smooth fashion considering the fact that this was a freight elevator and not the smaller vibrationless kind. "And so irrational numbers were defined as convergent sequences of rationals," the manuscript had said. "The deft manipulation of such polar extremes, with resulting approximate values, may drive the purely logical observer to seal himself in a brickwork privy as a means of perverse defense against the cries of 'poetic truth' that so often accompany sequential definitions and (to cross the mathematical brink this once, and briefly) approximations of any kind." Evinrude stopped the elevator, opened the gate and led Billy into a gigantic storeroom full of equipment.

"This is where we expect them to surface," he said.

"Who?"

"The pigeons."

"The ones released in the ceremony?"

"They flew through a hole in solid rock and from there either back out again or into a ventilation duct that leads up eventually into this storeroom. If they flew back out into the Great Hole, that's not so bad. If they're in here or en route to in here, that means trouble."

"Didn't anyone know this would happen?"

"They weren't supposed to release pigeons," Evinrude said. "The subject was raised at a briefing. It was determined no pigeons. We drew up guidelines. We went to great lengths. But they released anyway, so now we have to retrieve. I happen to hate pigeons. I can't stand being anywhere near them. But it's my job to retrieve so I'll just have to submerse my feelings and go do it. All this because somebody ignored the guidelines."

"Pitkin, I bet."

"The duct's over that way."

"Why do I have to be here?"

"I need someone to help me deal with the pigeons. I didn't have the wherewithal emotionally to ask someone my own age. Besides, children know how to deal with animals. Adults have grown too far from their origins to be able to confront animals on a nonpet basis. The duct comes out of the wall behind that long row of tables."

They pushed through a dozen stacks of shipping containers. Deal with the pigeons, the man had just said. To Billy this sounded as though either a massacre or a bargaining session was in store. Evinrude still carried the unlighted torch, a circumstance suggesting massacre.

"So you do mathematics."

"I'm the one."

"The very word strikes fear into my heart," Evinrude said.

"Mathematics?"

"It goes back to early schooling. The muffled terror of those gray mornings getting out of bed and going to school and opening up a mathematics textbook with its strange language and letters for numbers and theorems to memorize. I didn't mind any other subject. But math struck terror. Everything about it. The sound of the words. The diagrams and formulas. The look of the book. Sometimes I find it hard to believe that humans actually do mathematics, considering what's involved. It's like a branch of learning in outer space."

As they got closer to the ventilation duct, Evinrude carefully inspected the floor as well as every item of equipment within reach.

"I don't think they're here," he said. "Because I'll tell you why. Wherever pigeons are, pretty soon the shithing starts."

"The what?"

"Pigeons are known for their shith."

"You mean 'shit,' don't you?"

"Did I say it wrong?"

"Definitely."

"There's not something called bullshith?"

"There's no *h* at the end. There's just one *h* and it's near the beginning."

"I should be standing here frankly amazed. I should but I'm not. Because I'll tell you why. All my life I've been making little mistakes like that. 'Shith' is just one example. I guess I learned it wrong."

"Where did you grow up?"

"In the outskirts," Evinrude said. "With a volunteer family. I had no parentage of my own. I think this led to oversights in my upbringing. Little gaps here and there. I'm weak in some areas. No doubt about it."

"Shit is universal no matter which language. Use my spelling and I guarantee you're safe."

They reached the duct. Evinrude flicked a switch, reversing the air current.

"If they were on their way this way they can forget it because once the air is flowing the other way the only thing they can do is relax and be carried back to the Great Hole. They're on their way down. We got here in time. They haven't surfaced. I definitely think that entitles us to something."

A single pigeon stood about sixty feet to Evinrude's right. Billy pointed it out to him. The pigeon began to approach, taking little pink-footed grip-steps. Evinrude held his torch out away from his body, then placed it gently on the ground, as though signifying his peaceful intentions.

"Why isn't it flying?" he said. "I can accept their presence in the air. When they walk I hate them. I just want to crumple."

"Then let's leave."

"Why isn't it afraid? It's walking right at us. I hate the way the head goes back and forth. They're full of disease in case you didn't know. Look at the funny steps it takes. They're very famous for disease. Watch out for your nervous system in particular."

"I'm going," Billy said. "Goodbye."

"I consider myself terrified. I'm consciously trying to inundate my feelings but so far no luck at all. I am really scared. I can hardly bear

235

to look at its little head gliding forward and back, forward and back. I hate the way it walks, don't you? Those scabby little feet. It's definitely headed this way in case you had hopes."

"I'm running," Billy said. "If I were you, I'd do the same. Come on. Let's go. Goodbye."

"I don't know how to run."

"Come on, hurry."

"I never learned," Evinrude said.

"Everybody knows how to run. It's easy. You just move your legs and then you're running. The brain sends a message to your legs and all of a sudden you're running. If you don't hurry up about it, I'm leaving. Just move your legs fast. Get your brain to send the message. Everybody can run. It's not hard. Try it and see what happens."

The pigeon took several more pink steps.

"It's not hard if you know how," Evinrude said. "I don't happen to know how. The subject of running is foreign to me. As a child I wasn't taught how to run and I've never been able to pick it up on my own. It's something I've always envied in other people, this marvelous ability to run."

11

SEQUENCE

There were times when he felt the lure of a submoronic mode of being. During such periods his mind turned opaque, making it hard for him to perceive the simplest incentive. It would be easy, he believed, to spend a lifetime in this stateless zone. Content to be organic. Content to perform only monotonous tasks. Content to forsake coherent speech. The spirit that informed him would swiftly dwindle, replaced by the soul of a plant. In time he'd dispense with voluntary motion and the natural management of his body. Content to smell himself and dream of downy molds.

This feeling always occurred when he was on the verge of solving a drawn-out mathematical problem. It seemed to mean, nearing the end, that he preferred to abandon all the structural forms, the intersecting perspectives, the entire weightless system of exact relationships; discard it all in exchange for the scantest condition of existence.

The intuition of mathematical order occupied the deeper reaches of cognitive possibility, too old and indistinct for tracing, predating even the analytical scrapings of logic and language. Because his work's natural tendency was to provide a model of his own mind, of himself as a distinct individual, he was puzzled by the lack of an adequate vocabulary for mathematical invention, by his inability to understand what made his mathematics happen. In retaliation, as it were, against the secrecy of his own constructions, he engineered a desire to subsist on minims of specific being. It was to this, the unknown self, that the basest nature was clearly preferable.

At the module he scribbled nonsense on a pad. This surprised him, this familiar indication that he verged on an answer, because it accompanied the solution of a problem that was anything but familiar, having (he was coming to see) none of the usual shadings and gradations. Sequence, form, unsuspected relationships were not really the issue here. But the process seemed the same as always. He could feel it happening, an emptying of both modes of consciousness, the asymmetric transmapping of fact and unorganized reality.

Beings that need no intervening substance to transmit their art, able to write with their fingers, laser-paint with eyes alone, creatures such would surely know this feeling, as of nature taking part in thought, the living brain that codes its own development.

He scribbled calmly, oblivious to everything but one emerging thought, feeling the idea *unerase* itself, most evident of notions, an idea with a history, scribbling, rule of ancient numeration. What breathless ease, to fall through oneself. Rudimentary being. Leaflikeness. A condition scaled down to noncomplex sensation. No, there was no way to name the process. Mathematical ideas exist between adjacent points on a line segment. He got up and walked around the room, unaware of sound and color and yet knowing, touching, seeing, hearing, breathing, sheer certainty, feeling it inside him, watching his own feet (what a funny word, hearing it, "feet," for the first time) move him ever more surely around the room. Thus the simple answer surfaced, deprived at first of linguistic silvering. In the seconds that followed he knew it in words.

Notation by sixty.

That had to be it, a positional notation system based on the number sixty. He knew that thousands of years ago two systems of numeration were used in Mesopotamia. Decimal and sexagesimal. The latter used a base of sixty instead of ten. Because the Sumerians had divided the year into three hundred and sixty days, they found the number sixty to be a more workable base in their astronomy. Notation by sixty also had the advantage over the decimal system in all work involving fractions because sixty has more divisors than ten. The vertical wedge used in Mesopotamia to denote the number one was also used for sixty. In the decimal system a given three-digit number is a way of expressing a quantity in terms of multiples of ten. Schoolchildren know that the number three hundred and twenty-four means three times one hundred (or 10^2), plus two times ten (10^1), plus four times one (10^0). In sexagesimal notation, the tens become sixties.

The message had been received in the form of fourteen pulses, a gap; twenty-eight pulses, a gap; fifty-seven pulses. He realized now that the total of one hundred and one units was not important. This total viewed differently, as one zero one, or binary number five, was equally unimportant. The fact that one, four, two, eight, five and seven are the digits of a recurring decimal had no significance whatever. The pulse total alone (ninety-nine) and the number of blank intervals (two) were also meaningless.

All that mattered was the original series of pulses: fourteen, twenty-eight, fifty-seven. In notation by sixty these are not three numbers but a way of expressing a single large number. To discover this number it is necessary only to multiply fourteen by thirty-six hundred (60^2), twenty-eight by sixty (60^1), fifty-seven by one (60^0). What was being transmitted then was the number fifty-two thousand one hundred and thirty-seven.

A man stood in the open doorway.

This, in our terms, was what the extraterrestrials were communicating. Their natural way of expressing this quantity, since they used powers of sixty, was in the form of the number 14,28,57. There was no reason why an advanced civilization should use a place-value system based on ten. Maybe they'd overcome all the problems inherent in a sixty-system and used it to much greater advantage than we use the decimal method. Of course, it remained for Billy to discover the importance of fifty-two thousand one hundred and thirty-seven. Now that he knew how to interpret the transmission, he could begin the task of decoding it. What did the new value mean? Obviously this constituted the second half of the problem.

For an unreal moment he imagined that the man in the doorway was an extraterrestrial, here to confirm his arithmetic. But there was nothing very exotic about the man and when he introduced himself as Dr. Skip Wismer, a NASA consultant on loan to Field Experiment Number One, Billy thought it a mere coincidence (of the nonexotic type) that he was associated with astronauts. Wismer went on to explain that since he had to pass this way to get to the demonstration, he thought he'd stop by and pick up Billy.

"I'm halfway done with the reason they got me here for. I guess it's okay to take a break."

"How do you know it's halfway?" Wismer said. "You won't know where the halfway point is until you're able to look back on the entire solution. Since you can't know what's ahead, you don't know how much you've done. This is plain common sense."

"It's a feeling. Very definitely says half. When I get it this strong I know it's true."

"You're claiming in effect to be digging half a hole. Can't be done, can it? Besides you're not even supposed to be working on the code. The source of the transmission is what we're primarily concerned with for the time being. In addition to which is the fact that the message was never repeated. Repetition in a case like this is essential. Without it, there's no reason to believe the pulse array is correct. Not to mention the computer retrovert we've just run that indicates error in the receiving equipment. Probably the switch-frequency generator."

"What's this demonstration you mentioned?"

"The Leduc electrode," Wismer said.

This didn't sound very promising. But since there was nothing else to do right now, he thought he might as well attend. First there was something he was determined to get rid of, namely the large green pill that Orang Mohole had forced him to accept in his apartments on top of the armillary sphere. He knew if he carried it around long enough, it would get him into some kind of tricky situation. He excused himself, went into the bathroom, closed the door, lifted the top of the toilet tank, dropped Mohole's greenie inside and was about to replace the porcelain lid when he realized something was floating in the water. It was a tiny cardboard matchbox. He took it out of the tank and slid it open. Inside was a tightly folded piece of paper, wet at the edges. He removed it from the box and unfolded it.

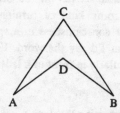

A	big (or little) bang	AC	matter expanding
B	*n*-bottomed hole	AD	gravity emergent
C	present time	CB	matter contracting
D	exo-ionic sylphing compounds	DB	gravity dominant
	∠ ADB	space-time sylphed	

Dr. Skip Wismer led him over a footbridge high above a miniature recycled waterfall and then into a sector called Med Comp.

"Large questions come to mind," Wismer said, "whenever I'm in the presence of someone with your kind of vast mental capacities. For instance, do you believe in someone or something larger than yourself?"

"That takes in a lot of territory."

"Scientist or not, I sometimes feel overwhelmed by it all. I mean the sheer allness, the sheerness of it all. To cite an example, what do you suppose happens to a person after death?"

"He remains in that state."

"My wife is dead, you know."

"Nobody warned me."

"What kind of system permits this sort of finality?"

"Death?"

"It's so definitive."

"Buried or cremated?"

"She's in an icebox in Houston," Wismer said. "Left her body to science."

"What will they do with it?"

"I hate to tell you."

"Stick needles?"

"At the very least," Wismer said. "The whole thing depresses and worries me, not least of all the question of what happens in the first few seconds after electrical activity in the brain ceases forever. Personally I think there's some kind of turning inside out. That's my theory. An unknotting of consciousness in a space of *n* dimensions. A turning outward. Not that I'd say the word. I'd rather commit the act than say the word. Particularly in front of a lady."

"What word?"

"Evaginate."

They entered a huge operating theater.

"So what's this electrode we're seeing demonstrated?"

"It's a device that would greatly simplify manned space missions. Probably increase an astronaut's capabilities a thousandfold. Which means I'll be a very interested observer today. Of course I don't know what *they* want to use it for."

Two men entered the theater. They were dressed in surgical gear—masks, caps, gowns, gloves. Dr. Wismer greeted them and then took a seat high above the floor of the operating theater. The room was full of wires, cables and monitoring devices. There was so much wiring in fact that nine or ten different colors had been used to enable technicians and others to distinguish between the strands. Wires were bundled, twisted and interlaced. They connected various machines, ran along the walls and floor, hung in clumps from a section of ceiling where panels had been removed.

"Ignore this mess," one of the men said. "It's the equivalent of making prophecies by studying an animal's entrails. Now that we've got the Leduc electrode, all this paraphernalia gets junked. My name is Cheops Feeley."

"I've heard of your medal."

"That's not the only thing named after me. There's a science fair, two research centers and a gypsy health clinic."

"You're a gypsy?"

"Lapsed."

"I heard your medal's given for work that's crazy in places."

"Madness content," Feeley said. "Nobody mentions it aloud but we all know that strict scientific merit is only one of the elements considered. The dark side of the award is what appeals to most people."

There was a large shipping container in a corner of the room. Billy noticed a scrawny old cat looking out over the top of the box. Cheops Feeley took a long step forward, putting both his hands on the boy's head, probing with his fingertips.

"You've got it, all right. Just as I suspected. I was sure it would be there."

"What would be there?"

"The mathematics bump."

"If there's a bump, it never hurt."

"It's a life passion of mine, skull conformation. Yours is very distinct. Definitely a bump for mathematics. That settles it."

"Settles what?"

"Everything," Feeley said. "You're definitely the person we want. The Leduc electrode is only part electrode. It's a bundle of extremely tiny wires able to stimulate and record brain activity. But here's the stroke of genius. These wires are attached to a microminiaturized disk that functions almost exactly as a computer does. But not just any computer. The Leduc electrode has Space Brain capability. And it's small enough to be implanted under someone's scalp. Through a tiny incision that leaves no scars. Once it heals. And the hair grows back."

All he could see of the men were their eyes, two sets, very steady, green here, hazel there, pinched in by mask and cap. Slowly the cat worked its way over the top of the box, followed by two others just as mangy. Billy looked up at Skip Wismer, who seemed to have dozed off.

"The Leduc electrodes are in that container to your right."

"Who's that on my left?"

"That's Leduc."

The other man nodded. At least, Billy thought, everybody's identified. One of the cats lazily climbed back into the box as three others emerged. Cheops Feeley went over there and lifted out a pink disk with wires attached. Terrific hygiene procedures. Watch him clean it off with some spit.

"We ordered blue and pink. But they only sent pink."

"Are they different besides color?"

Feeley shook his head.

"Here's our thinking on the matter. You with your enormous powers of abstraction. Space Brain with its unsurpassed superfine computations. A single dynamic entity. With no scars. And hair that's guaranteed to grow back."

"Sounds familiar, talk of this combination."

"We have massive backing. The resources of a very powerful cartel. Once the electrode is buried in your head, assuming you agree to such a procedure, all I have to do is notify them and you get paid a generous retainer for a period of time not to exceed the life of the appliance."

"They want to regulate the money curve, right? That's their only interest in life. The two strange talkers. Tell them my head stays shut."

"You don't have to decide now. This is just a trial run. I want to point out that subcutaneous implantation is no great problem in and of itself. Although there's a slight inconvenience in this particular case."

"Cat hairs."

"Listen closely," Feeley said. "The problem with the device as now constituted is that it tends to overstimulate the left side of the brain. This will result in an overpowering sense of sequence. You'll be acutely aware of the arrangement of things. The order of succession of events. The way one thing leads to another. This is a side effect of carrying the appliance under your scalp but it's not too great a price to pay for the kind of madness ratio we're getting, not to mention scientific value.

244

True, you'll find yourself analyzing a continuous series of acts in terms of their discrete components. Eating a sandwich will no longer be the smooth operation you've always known it to be. You'll experience, should you agree to host the electrode, a strong awareness of your hands, your mouth, your throat, your stomach, whatever's between the slices of bread, the bread itself. You might even find yourself in retrograde orbit, so to speak. Bread, bakery truck, bakery, flour, wheat and so on. There is so much involved. Our lives are so dense. The baker's hands, the farmer, his barn, the paint job, the latex, the trees. There is so much and all of it will be apprehended, as you eat the sandwich, should you agree to the implantation, in related sequence. In consecutive order. In proper succession. You'll be involved in a very detailed treatment of reality. A parody of the left brain. But is this reality of yours less valid than ordinary reality? Not at all. You'll be establishing fresh paths of awareness. Taking nothing for granted. Dealing with unlimited data. Every breath you take will be subjected to a thorough sequential analysis. Heart, lungs, nostrils, oxygen, carbon dioxide and so forth. There is so much involved and it's all right there for the asking."

The scabby cats seeped in and out of the box where the electrodes were stored. Cheops Feeley explained once more that Billy would be given ample time to decide whether he wanted to take part. This was just a test exercise, a dress rehearsal for the actual implantation. The procedure, should he agree to it, would be carried out in a chair-shaped operating table to save time between barbering and incision. He asked Leduc to get the table in question, as a practice maneuver, and then, handing the pink disk or "appliance" to the boy, went to look for a comb, pair of scissors and hair clipper. Finding himself alone with the dozing Dr. Skip Wismer, Billy moved in deliberate stages to the nearest exit. He eased his head out past the door frame and into the corridor, ready to follow it with left foot and leg. Someone was drinking from an ornamental fountain in a circular area about fifty feet beyond the end of the corridor. It was a man, dark-skinned and absolutely naked. Billy was motionless now, watching. As the man raised himself, his hands uncupping from his face, the boy could see that he was white-haired, although of indeterminate age, and that his chest was painted with geometric figures.

He stepped back into the operating theater. Leduc entered through another door, wheeling the chairlike device, which included among other things a battery of pen recorders poised to scribble brain rhythms on a continuous sheet of graph paper. Cheops Feeley arrived a moment later, carrying a barber's kit.

"Hercule, you do the hair," he said. "Just pretend, of course. Move the clippers over his head."

"I do not give permission," Billy said.

"Why so formal?"

"I'm just saying there's no point doing any more of this, because I'm not agreeing to do it. I don't know how I let it get this far."

"Nobody's going to force you. I thought I made that clear. Take part in the trial run, that's all we ask. Help us get our timing down pat. Then, later, should you change your mind, we'll be able to function smoothly, as befits an undertaking of this magnitude."

"How can a gypsy be lapsed?"

"A simple announcement usually suffices," Feeley said. "Now, please, take a seat in our device. Leduc will make clipping motions over your head."

"I get these foot cramps. I have one now. If I sit down, I'm finished. The only way to get rid of it is to give the blood a chance to circulate. That means to stay in a standing position."

Feeley looked at Hercule Leduc, who spoke for the first time, his voice blunted somewhat by the surgical mask he was wearing.

"It is convenient for you to believe you have a cramp," he said. "All of physical reality is a matter of convenience. Does A lead to B? Or is it simply convenient to believe that A leads to B? Both and neither. When we have succeeded in wedging an exception between the external world and our awareness of it, then we will discover that the divinity of the spirit of consciousness is based on the risks we are willing to take in order to fabricate pure terror and Olympian love. It was convenient for you to see an aborigine a few moments ago. This is poetic espionage undertaken by the senses to counteract the suspicions of void we harbor

246

regarding existence itself. We are most a victim of the principle of intelligence when we try to conceal our lonely terror and pursue a style of incessant self-deception."

Dozens of cats climbed in and out of the shipping container. The two gowned men conferred for a moment. Billy still had the electrode he'd been given earlier. He sidled over to the box and dropped it in among the cats and the other pink disks. Then he stood there shaking his foot as if to stimulate increased blood circulation in that area.

"Do I believe you?" Feeley said.

"About what?"

"The cramp," he said. "Hercule, do we believe him?"

"It's numb at the same time as it buzzes, if you want to compare it with your own both experiences."

"We agree to believe you on one condition," Feeley said.

"Let's hear."

"That, whether or not you agree to the implantation, you seriously consider being put in a package. Lecture tours, talk shows, a quickie biography, T-shirts, funny buttons. The ancillary rights alone could set us up for years. Endorsements, puzzles, games, mathematics LPs. The talent is obvious, it's there, you've got the bump. I see you taking on the world's greatest adult mathematicians in a series of international matches. Problems devised by a distinguished panel. Broad media coverage. Or maybe a package with an older person for contrast. You go on joint tours with deluxe accommodations. Discussion groups, lectures, wrist watches, funny buttons, debates. Can it possibly miss? I envision you dressed in a silver lamé kimono or a vinyl poncho. Once the incision heals. And the hair grows back. Leaving you without a scar. We'll package you with somebody you really admire. There must be one special figure in the world community of scientists. Who's your hero? Tell us and we'll get him."

"People from the Bronx don't have heroes."

It was Rosicrucia Sandoval who told Billy that the scream lady was dead. Rosicrucia was a short broad woman with breasts so bunched up and shapeless under her housedress that they appeared to be still in the process of formation. Her estranged common-law husband had been following her for months, his right hand inside his jacket, a theatrical mannerism meant to signify the presence of a weapon. Wherever she went she saw him, Sixto Ortiz by name, until finally she asked Faye for permission to use the Terwilligers' fire escape to get in and out of the building. Since the fire escape was at the back and led down to an alley, which in turn led to the basement doors of five different buildings, Rosicrucia felt she'd be able to move freely without being seen. Babe okayed the arrangement on the condition that she take the garbage with her on her way out the window. The setup lasted only one day because of the attack dog's reaction to someone coming in from the fire escape. Babe told Faye to inform the beleaguered woman that she had less to fear than she thought.

"Hispanics only shoot from cars," he said. "Tell her not to worry until he starts following her in a car. Hispanics shoot into crowds from speeding cars. Of course, there's always the chance he plans to knife her. A car is no good to him then."

About a month before the scream lady died, Rosicrucia sat on a folding chair in front of the building and, while keeping an eye out for Sixto, told Billy about the scream lady's recent operation.

"They gave her an ectomy. Three hours on the table. Complications, I heard. But now she's quiet since they did it. Only screams once, twice a day. It's how they quiet certain people."

"Ectomy," he said.

"That's right, ectomy, they did an ectomy. It's what they do to quiet a woman when they get to a bad age. Take out the hysterical organs. Three hours on the table plus. When she screams it's different now. Not so much an animal, you know?"

"Maybe they took out the wrong organ," he said. "They should have took the throat."

"The throat is not hysterical," Rosicrucia said. "Only hysterical organs come out in an ectomy."

That same day he entered the building behind his own and climbed four flights of stairs to the scream lady's door. He had dared himself to do it and so here he was. It was a period of his childhood in which he constantly dared himself to do disagreeable things. The strange piece of paper he had once snatched from her hand (cryptic numeroglyphics) was still hidden in one of his textbooks. But why, all daring aside, was he here? Maybe to ask her what the occult writing had meant. Or to hear her speak a single intelligible word. Or simply to look at her again. Nevertheless he was too scared to knock on the door. He dared himself again and again. (Knock or I'll kill you.) But he just stood there looking at the door. He looked at it until it opened. There she was once more, dressed in two or three bathrobes, exceedingly real, her presence fully developed in the dimness, a reminder of some cavernous fear. A sense of decomposition seemed paradoxically to replenish her body. Her power derived from this physical dwindling; she gathered strength from it, prospering on the horror in other people's eyes. Again she was barefoot and from an invisible hole in her throat came the same muted static. He backed off instinctively, edging toward the stairs. She hummed her static at him. Not once did she move, content to stand in the doorway in her furrowed robes.

"Put it in words," he said.

After a while she screamed. He didn't move. Motion at this point would have been disrespectful. He had never been this close to the scream lady when she was in the act of screaming and it was an occasion not without a certain commercial solemnity, resembling some authentic and quite powerful native rite at which attendance by tourists is permitted during specified hours. So he stood where he was, afraid to violate a tender balance between the woman and her act. For that second or two he lived within the scream. It vibrated inside him and overwhelmed the air around him—horrible, of course—much more than meaningless noise, her madness in its waveforms and repetitions occupying his body, madness measured in cycles per second, her willful disintegration taking over his mind. He watched her go back into the apartment. She didn't close the door behind her. He stood in the hall (daring himself) for several moments, or until the scream completely left his body. Then he followed her into the apartment, expecting to see stacks of old newspapers and filthy drifts of clothing that she'd gathered from the street and left everywhere to rot. But once out of the long entranceway he could see it was different, that she lived in stark circumstances, junkless, very little furniture, a cot to sleep on, both rooms nearly empty and yet far from bare. The walls. Because of the walls. Everywhere he looked there was black crayon script, her secret writing flung across the walls from floor to ceiling, uninterrupted by windows, doors, corners of the room. She sat by the open window, looking out on alleys lined with dented garbage cans. The small boy walked along a wall, trying to read the black wax, inhaling what she'd written, fumes from a hundred coloring books, that oily condiment he'd so often savored on his own two hands.

Secret weapons held sub ground NY under neath sub way & electric line voltage tunnels/Secret TV in walls & inter/de/ception of mail by name less agent person nil of danger/US net work/Goatspill to cat licks juice protest ants according St. Marx (13:13) hated for my names sake/Magna Carta 1215 + Napoleons waterloo 1815 = 3030 years war/CHECK ME ON THIS/ Addition my mission to US of ABC/Hellelujah days coming America Britain Canada/Dis (out of) ease agents functioning in lavatories/stairwells/basements to un (off of) seat the visible regime/Plague bearers/ Paid to un (take off) leash germ war fare on private taxpay level/Toilet seat pisces crab cause Cancer/ Poison insect bites give you/me Scorpio/Dread emitters of bull & ram para/lye/seize/Quote the zodiac at own risk & stay out of kid nap (SLEEPING CHILD STOLEN FROM HIS DREAM) & read Marx (13:17) woe to them that give suck in those days/None can eat/sit/sleep with out fear of contam or infestate by the name less provokers/ Banks watched All beds micro phoned Dark nes(t) spied on for signs of re VOLT ing/For many shall come in my name (13:6)/Sub neath be under ware: China = 3 + 8 + 9 + 14 + 1 = 35 centuries B.C. (SHOPPING DAYS BEFORE CHRIST)/ Coming up to sur face with secret dis (out of) guise of name & place/Meow Tse-tung/Confucius = Confuse/U.S. 551–479 B.C. = 72 = St. Marx 13/17/6/36: Lest coming of a sudden he find you asleep

All through summer the ripe nights were full of stroboscopic motion. Open hydrants lowered the water pressure and women screamed out of top-story windows at the boys and girls standing in the wide cockscomb spray they'd created by putting a bottomless keg over the mouth of the hydrant. Billy and his father stood on the stoop with a man named Consagra, a recent occupant, heavy and squat, said to be an illegal alien. Kids scaled the playground fence, ran and stopped short, jostled each other in elaborately designed war rhythms whose immediate purpose was the baring of homemade weapons, no more (in these early stages of the evening) than simple disclosure, a promise (as glancing as oblique light) of later improvisations. Whenever Consagra's attention was diverted, Babe would turn toward his son and make a crazy face—crossed eyes, buck teeth, bunched-up lips. People ate fudgesicles with the wrapper twined around the stick.

"There's a thin line between exterminator and roach," Babe said.

A squad car cruised past a man in the playground systematically breaking bottles. Figures came up from the basement rooms where carriages were stored. There were card games and radios. Naked children on fire escapes. Warm-weather flesh and the dismal ash of burning garbage. Inside, small bugs were sucked out of the dark to carom off the TV screen. Faye and Billy sat there watching a senile teenage epic ("Hey, kids, we're gonna be late for the luau") while Babe scoured ashtrays for a smokable butt.

"So what kind of movie?"

"Sit-throughable," she said.

"I'll need the set in ten minutes."

"Nertz to you, bozo."

"Ten minutes and counting."

"You only wish."

"What kind of junk is that to be showing the kid with skeighty-eight colleges showing interest? You should keep him away from awful stuff like that."

"It's a special kind of awful," she said. "You're not a movie person, so don't even ask me to explain. It's the kind of awful you have to have a feel for. Why don't you call Izzy with some batting stances?"

Much of local violence had garbage at its heart. People's leavings

251

were too significant to be consigned to grunting trucks, omnivorous burrowing machines that deprived the streets of their distinctions. In street fights, garbage was a weapon to be tossed. In arguments between neighbors it was garbage that was trailed across a doorway. Communal protests featured garbage mounds in flames. Garbage was a source of insult, a proud burden, a fester never ending, a mode and code of conduct (often air-mailed from windows to ease a burdened mind). The dead were sometimes found in garbage cans. Consagra looked across the street to the bottle-breaker speaking to the broken glass around him. Babe made crazy faces.

"Crabman versus the guinea wop," Ralphie Buber said.

The Bronx Zoo was several blocks east of Crotona Avenue. In a fairly remote part of the zoo was a series of ornate metal cages where the big birds lived. On rotted logs and long branches in the last of these cages the hooded vultures squatted. Impossibly large and indolent, bleak velvet-brown feather massed and hooked beaks stark as nickel silver, the five vultures dwelt in desultory camouflage, more majestic than the other birds (eagles, condors, hawks) because they did not beat their wings in grand futility, hating even freedom. Signs, omens, portents, auguries and foretokens. Even an auspex of old, gazing upon these adepts of dead flesh, might muse that bird divination had seen its better days now that squatting was the vogue.

"I wish there was a hooded vulture rental agency," Natasha said. "It would be perfect for people our size who want to kill themselves. You go to the agency and rent a vulture and it would pick you up with its powerful talon claws and fly to a great height and then drop you. They would be trained to drop you anywhere you wanted to be dropped. You could be dropped right in front of your own house if you wanted to get even with your mother and father for being your parents. Or you could be dropped over a big green valley or into a lake. Hooded vultures would be the best way for people our size. Imagine how everyone would feel, reading about the body being found."

Ralphie Buber spent his nights and days on the verge of a lunatic drool. Although he performed acts and committed social misdemeanors that far exceeded drooling, his basic nature seemed best defined by drivel and slime. He was oversized and extremely flabby and for these reasons smaller children liked to knead and beat him. Ralphie, seen purely in physical configuration, was designed to be punched by little fists. It was a daily occurrence, this informal mauling, as was his reaction to such assaults, an attitude of corpulence offended. Billy, for one, aimed many an unprovoked blow at Ralphie's haunches. It was never any problem avoiding a counterattack. Often the boy forgot to make one, staring at his assailant with the knowledge that something had been done at his expense but hardly an inkling what; and when he did respond it was with loose flesh bouncing and both hands tearing at his own hair, more dangerous to himself than others, a living marvel easy to evade. It was odd then that Ralphie of all the local oafs should choose to mock the bulky Consagra. Fusion and swirl everywhere. Multiple-flash effect. The street heavily textured with desperate energies. From the stoop of their building Babe and Billy watched Ralphie Buber approach holding a live crab stolen from the fish market. Consagra, who resembled poured cement, was wearing a sleeveless T-shirt, rolled-up chinos and work boots. He looked down at Ralphie with barely evident contempt, a slight narrowing of the eyes, a tension about the jaw, the hooded scorn a laborer has for discrepancies in the landscape.

"I'll bite off your ass," Ralphie said. "I'll stick my both pincers all the way in to your kidney liver. Then I'll eat your eyes, dumb nuts."

"Who you talk?"

"This is Crabman speaking. Attention all cars. I got a man on the stoop with his armpits showing. Sound the alarm, all units of the crab patrol. There's a man here that's acting like he's white, male, human. Free food on the stoop. Hurry all cars."

"Shut up you face," Consagra said.

"Crabs at sea, we have an imported human in the area. All units at top speed. This is Crabman signing off for now."

"I kill."

"This is Crabman back on the shortwave in his pale-green panel truck. Emergency call, sound the crab alarm. Free meal, free meal."

"Go the other street or I break you hole," Consagra said. "Keep talk, nice-nice, I come there kill."

"These here are called pincers, mister egg-fart face. They reach all the way in to your lung muscles. Crabman saying man on the stoop that tastes of steak meat. Last chance to get your free bites in."

Ralphie was talking into the crab's abdomen, using the creature as a microphone as well as alternate persona. When Consagra started down the steps, however, the boy thrust the crab toward him, employing it now as talisman or actual weapon. As he held the crab extended he made throttled aquatic sounds. Consagra responded by making a fist and biting it. It remained for Rosicrucia Sandoval to come outside and step between them, her disorganized upper torso making Billy think that two or three abandoned infants might be clinging to her breasts.

LET HIM WITH UNDERSTANDING RECKON THE NUMBER OF THE BEAST FOR IT IS A HUMAN NUMBER 666

A week's pay in his pocket, Babe came bouncing down the steps of a Third Avenue bus late one night and headed east alongside the high curving stone wall of a hospital for the incurably ill. When he first saw the other man the distance between them was about one hundred yards. He slowed his pace. The other man was just emerging from the unviewable part of the bending wall, figure more than man, something of a puzzle, coming as he did not just out of the darkness of Quarry Road but from a second surface really, a concealed extension of the curved line occupied by Terwilliger. There was no one else in sight and the only streetlamp was back near the bus stop. The other man wore a long coat and walked in a strange many-legged way, taking several short steps for every long slow stride Babe took. As the gap between the men diminished, Babe worried about that long coat. It was a dark coat, extremely long, much longer than his own coat, and this worried him. He couldn't imagine why anyone would wear a coat that long except as a weapons carrier or mobile receptacle for stolen goods. The other man, drawing closer, naturally began to grow to his true size (perceived from Terwilliger's viewpoint—as if he were the ultimate source of the other man's size) and at the same time he seemed to be getting smaller and smaller. But this was only because Babe had feared and expected someone very large and kept waiting for the other man's mammoth dimensions to be made known. Babe himself was six feet four. But his coat, in a relative sense, could not begin to compare with the other man's coat in terms of size and threatening color. The other man wore a hat and Babe did not. He kept his hands in the pockets of his long coat while Babe's hands were clenched at his sides. The high stone wall was to Babe's right, the other man's left. He was ready for anything the other man might attempt, too ready perhaps, over-prepared, displaying not grace but hysterical petty belligerence under pressure, for when they drew to within a yard of each other the quick-stepping man skidded on a bit of squashed fruit and Babe reacted massively, overreacted perhaps, jumping no more than an inch in the air but in that brief time and space twisting his body toward the other man (who was trying to keep his balance by running in place on the slippery fruit) and landing with feet strategically set apart, body firm and ready, well established in a lower and more advantageous center of gravity, hands now unclenched and knife-swiping at the air in short clean lethal strokes. "*Kill-kill-kill!*" he shouted. Again and again. "*Kill-kill-kill!*" The sound surprised even Terwilliger and in its pump-action ferocity literally knocked the other man off his feet. Babe could not stop shouting. The other man, now seen to be not only extremely small but also very, very old and almost surely Chinese, was on his back on the sidewalk, near the base of the wall. Babe was not able to come out of his frozen gladiator pose. The other man remained on his back, expressionless, his legs bent in and up with knees locked in at chest level, his small old hands crumpled near his face, the hat still on his head, the folds of his long coat parted by the upthrust legs. In time Babe stopped shouting. Slowly he began to circle the other man, careful not to relax his defenses too much, the right hand still slashing per-functorily at the air. The other man was pivoting on the small of his back in order to keep Babe's movements in his line of vision. It was a pretty funny sight, this old man turning while on his back like an armored beetle, limbs bent inward to protect his body, felt hat still on his head. As Babe, circling, reflected on the comic aspects of the situa-tion, his right shoulder brushed against the stone wall. "*Ya!*" he shouted. "*Wha-ya!*" He shouted just twice this time, only moderately startled by the contact, but the noise was sufficient to force the old Chinese into a supreme display of body fortification. Still spinning on his back, elbows providing most of the impetus, he slowly raised his head toward his knees, giving Babe a better look at his face, and then bared his lower set of teeth, digging them into his upper lip. Even with teeth bared the other man couldn't be said to have undergone much of a change in expression. His face was undisturbed, even serene, and it was possible to interpret the teeth-baring not as a gesture of self-defense but rather as a philosophical maneuver designed to show Babe that nothing less that a living skull occupied that old felt hat, an Oriental brain-case, a nearly timeless object indifferent to decay, erosion and the violent chemistries of men. In this manner, the one man supine and flashing his lower teeth, the other ripping at the air with his large right hand, they made one more full revolution on the dark and lonely sidewalk.

A path led him through a grove of ginkgo trees, their fanlike leaves dipping in the breeze from sea-light to dense shade. It was a narrow path, not often trod it seemed, rough-edging into grass and shrubs, leading nowhere special, the kind of country lane that peters out in carpetweed. Coming toward him was a woman wheeling a small carriage. She wore a long crystal-pleated sepia dress and was almost unendurably lovely, her face uncovered from some lost medallion, an ancient oval coin dug up and rubbed alive. Rose-white woman. She had eyes saturated in light, a fresh wet smile. Tall, a drifting walk, her body all radiant flux. Outside the strict limits of balance, evenness and line, all body-timed to lure the casual student into erroneous raptures about purely chance perfection, was a creature's awesome grubby joy in sensing the very air, detecting automatically those things beyond analysis. Brownish hair blown forward over her shoulders. Long hands, slender, cool and white. There was the baby carriage to be considered as well. Draped in semitransparent white fabric it was the single most surprising thing Billy had yet come upon at Field Experiment Number One. But he couldn't bring himself to think of anything but the woman, who had already paused, as he had, to pass a word or two. How did he react to her beauty? As a substance capable of being magnetized. She bounced the carriage softly, the merest creak issuing from its under-structure.

"I'm Myriad."

"Then I know your husband."

"Dear sheer Cyril."

"How's his arm?"

"Fine, thank you."

"When I saw him, he was just taking it off."

"Were you startled? He gets testy if people aren't startled."

"I tried not to show it."

"That was a mistake."

"I think he knew, because nothing testy happened. I'd like to see it take place again sometime, knowing the situation. I hardly got to see the stump. I'd be readier the second time. How's the stump?"

"Very well, I gather."

"Did he define the word 'science' yet?"

"He never tells me about his work," she said. "What about you and your work?"

"What do you want to know, outside zorgs?"

"I've been wondering if anyone could tell me whether mathematics has a muse. A spirit or bountiful power. A sort of would-be minor goddess to look after people like you."

"I never heard of one."

"Young people need looking after," she said. "Think of that beautiful boy Galois. People felt there was something secret in his character. They were right. The secret was mathematics. His father a suicide. His own death a horrible farce. Dawn in the fields. Caped and whiskered seconds. Sinister marksman poised to fire."

I need all my courage to die at twenty.

"Then there was Abel, not much older, desperately poor, Abel in delirium, hemorrhaging. So often mathematical experience consists of time segments too massive to be contained in the usual frame. Lives overstated. Themes pursued to extreme points. Adventure, romance and tragedy."

I will fight for my life.

"Look at Pascal, who rid himself of physical pain by dwelling on mathematics. He was just a bit older than you when he constructed his mystic hexagram. The loveliest aspect of the mystic hexagram is that it *is* mystic. That's what's so lovely about it. It's able to become its own shadow."

Keep believing it.

"The tricky thing about mathematical genius," she said, "is that its sources are so often buried. Galois for one. Ramanujan for another. No indication anywhere in their backgrounds that these boys would one day display such natural powers. Figures jumping out of sequence. Or completely misplaced."

He tried to smell her, wondering what she smelled like, a woman this sensational, but the fruit on the trees in the area supplied a strong odor of their own, unpleasant, overpowering whatever shy variation of jasmine or sweet cicely might have flowed from Myriad's pores.

"Numbers have supernatural harmonies, according to Hermite. They exist beyond human thought. Divine order through number. Number as absolute reality. Someone said of Hermite: 'The most abstract entities are for him like living creatures.' That's what someone said."

"People invented numbers," he said. "You don't have numbers without people."

"Good, let's argue."

"I don't want to argue."

"Secret lives," she said. "Dedekind listed as dead twelve years before the fact. Poncelet scratching calculations on the walls of his cell. Lobachevski mopping the floors of an old museum. Sophie Germain using a man's name. Do I have the order right? Sometimes I get it mixed up or completely backwards."

"You went too fast for me to tell."

"The spirit of obsession. Isn't that the crux of it? An entire life dedicated to a number, a figure, the properties of a geometric point."

"Too much obsession's no good."

"I know you don't believe that," Myriad said. "You say it only to preserve the secret."

"What secret?"

"The secret of your fierce existence."

"A geometric point has no properties, by the way. It just has location."

If, earlier in the day, he'd allowed himself to be barbered, slit open and computerized (as the lapsed gypsy had suggested), he would probably be standing here right now, left-brain-crazy, wondering about Myriad's birth, infancy, childhood, adolescence, young womanhood, marriage to Cyril, the lost arm, the honeymoon, the eventual conception, pregnancy and so on. He eased his way to the side of the baby carriage, in better position to look through the netting, if possible, in order to feed speculations, brain-crazy or not, on what kind of radical malformation of their baby's body would force parents to acquire a carriage so unusually small, so obviously custom-made, so shielded by overhanging fabric.

"Tell me about your mathematical dreams."

"Never had one."

"Cardano did, born half dead, his inner life a neon web of treachery and magic. Gambler, astrologer, heretic, court physician. Schemed his way through the algebra wars."

"Can I see the baby?"

"Ramanujan had algebraic dreams. Wrote down the results after getting out of bed. Vast intuitive powers but poor education. Taken to Cambridge like a jungle boy."

Though never less than stunned by her presence, all sepia and hoarfrost blush, he thought this woman slightly strange to be delivering such a grand harangue in the middle of a wood. Her remarks were somewhat formal and even vehement, as if she were trying to convert him, but as much as he liked the clear morning chime in her voice he knew he'd have no trouble resisting the force of her propositions on the extra-mathematical content of mathematics. A shadow-tailed arboreal rodent sat on a limb. The breeze freshened, creasing the gauzy fabric that covered the baby carriage. A sudden impulse made Billy want to run in circles around the woman and her perambulator. Run and whoop for the sheer stupidity of it, the utter dumbness, making a fool of himself for the sake of foolishness alone. A lancer's battle cry. A coon hunter's halloo. Run and shout and fall. But Myriad's beauty precluded this kind of nihilistic spree. He would have to stand and listen. Disagree if need be. Pout with ankles crossed like a mud-smudged little kid. The only thing that seemed inevitable was his presence at the lesson.

"Sonja Kowalewski wasn't allowed to attend university lectures. We both know why. When her husband died she spent days and days without food, coming out of her room only after she'd restored herself by working on her mathematics. Tell me, was it Kronecker who thought mathematics similar to poetry? I know Hamilton and many others tried their hands at verse. Our superduper Sonja preferred the novel. Did I get it right this time or backwards? I think I got it backwards."

"What's my chances at seeing the baby?"

"It has all its parts," she said, "and they're all in the right places. Still, it won't do to show it. 'Nothing,' said Napier, 'is perfect at birth.'"

"He was talking about logarithms."

She smiled and touched him briefly, the back of her hand, his brow, the trees and fruit, *yin hsing*, silver apricots, his life and hers, sequence of mephitic decay, the leaves, the bark, the tissue, the humus, the manure, tall, a drifting walk, hair blown back now, wind shift, as she glided behind the tiny carriage, their lives and hers, eldest sons and storied daughters, sand-reckoners, pursuing mathematics to its evanescent cave.

Rose-white woman, I want to die among your petals.

He went back to his room and waited. Then he practiced his signature for a while. He kept expecting someone to turn up. Or a note to come under the door. Or a drawing or poem. Or a message scrawled on the teleboard screen. Or a videotape delivered in some extraordinary way. But things stayed quiet except for a remote monotonous sound, as of people engaged in minor construction, coming from somewhere beyond the exit grating in a corner of the wall.

12

PAIRS

Robert Hopper Softly was a child-sized man with glaringly fair skin and a gift for leading people into situations they would never have entered on their own. There was a distinct sense of authority about him. His body, pathologically stunted as it was, possessed to full extent misfortune's power to reproach not only nature but symmetry itself. Softly in fact assigned supreme meaning to arrangement, proportion and equivalence but only insofar as these terms applied to abstract constructions. For himself, he did not wish to correspond. He was not part of a collection. With no adult in plain view could he be called reciprocally unique.

Head was disproportionately large, heavy brows shading his gray eyes. Hair was white-blond with pink tinges nestled at the roots. He had a shallow jaw and exceedingly wide mouth, a thumb-sucking machine, aggressively sensual, too much palpitating lip. It was clear he experienced pain with every step he took.

Being an important force at the Center for the Refinement of Ideational Structures he was hardly the sort to be attracted to fashionable schools of supersticism, to mysticism as science's natural laxative, to gymnastic meditation or standard mantric humming, and yet that residual smile on his face, that bare trace of masterful nasty charm, derived from a memory of his own early identification with (the magical aspects of) numbers. He recollected his naïve delight on establishing a relationship between his name—the letters of first, middle and last able to be correlated one-to-one-to-one—and the cardinal number six. This same number, viewed a bit differently, was a special element in the set of positive integers, being a mathematically perfect number, equal to the sum of its divisors. Here was the kind of coincidence a child of subnormal growth might be disposed to treasure like a flawless stone. Odd that he'd recall it now and even stranger the vestigial thrill he felt.

He was wearing two thirds of his three-piece suit. His shirt sleeves were rolled up and he carried his suit jacket over his shoulder, index finger through loop, as he walked along the corridor. In his other hand was a belted leather briefcase, scraped raw in places, old enough to have been his schoolbag in third or fourth grade, an object of sufficient romance, distinction and authenticity to be described as possessing moral and ethical substance. Inside were his hand-washables.

Billy at this point was sitting in pajamas on the edge of his twofold, pinky finger at belly level, idly mining some navel sludge. He blinked a few times, his body trying to respond to the fact that it was technically awake. A moment later a voice filled the room. It seemed to have no definite source. It simply filled the room (or *was* the room), an immense buzzing voice accompanied by a tiny echo.

"This is Knobloch reporting that a terrible mistake has been made. You were accidentally assigned to an experimental canister. The canister you've been occupying is actually a giant sensor. It records your heartbeat, your electrical brain activity, your oxygen intake, your eye movements, your cerebral blood flow and countless other functions that can be studied on EEG and similar tracings. Say 'I read' if you read what I'm saying."

"I read."

"Nobody's supposed to occupy that canister except on an experimental basis. You were put in there accidentally. The room is extensively shielded from outside interference. The walls, the floors and all the furniture are equipped with extremely superfine sensing devices. The only way you could avoid being traced would be to suspend yourself in midair. Literally everything you've done has been recorded, measured and studied. Except we didn't know until now that the tracings we've been getting belong to you."

"I read but do not understand."

"There's a signal output terminal that processes all the EEG record runs from various clinical sites. We were interested in the tracings of a particular EEG subject located in a high scrutiny habitat. We were very interested in this subject. We monitored around the clock. But evidently the output terminal sent us your functions by mistake. We weren't interested in your functions. You're not even supposed to be in that canister. That's an experimental canister."

"Who is this other EEG subject?"

"Tree Man II."

"I do not read."

"The ape. The chimp. That's what they call him over in Zoolog. The chimp whose phonetic structure they've rebuilt. We thought we were reading Tree Man's tracings. But apparently we were reading yours."

"What do they say, my tracings?"

"That kind of information is confidential," Knobloch said. "But now that we know you're in the experimental canister, we might as well take advantage."

"Take advantage how?"

"This is Knobloch preparing to de-transmit. Please remain in your present position for further voice contact. Do not move except as necessitated. Excess movement causes static."

263

There was a pause.

"Good morning," a second voice said. "This is D'Arco speaking. I am tall and rather fit, with finely chiseled features and eyes that bespeak a certain amount of worldly fatigue. Knobloch is stocky with pustules. While we've got you there, we may as well try a little something scientific. What I'm interested in is a person who hasn't strayed too far from his archaic collective memories. A child, in other words. It would be perfect if you were half your age. But I'm willing to grab what I can."

"I would rather I went back to work on the code, deciphering the code."

"No need to raise your voice," D'Arco said.

"I just want to be sure I am heard."

"By common consent the star code is no longer an ongoing project. I'm amazed anyone took it seriously in the first place. Radio signals that weren't even repeated. A jumble of pulses. How can you do serious work with that kind of unreliable data? What I'm interested in is a particular segment of your stage-four sleep."

"I have just now woken up."

"Sleep is a very active state, part of your waking life really. At times your heart rate and blood pressure soar. Your neural activity increases. There are rises in spinal fluid pressure and stomach muscle activity. Your little pee-pee-maker gets hard and fluttery. Under closed lids the most important thing of all is happening; your eyes are getting periodic exercise. Their rapid movements are coordinated in terms of conjugate function—a paired mechanism supplying a single vision. Without this exercise you might wake up to a double world. Which is the object, which the image? They are paired one-to-one."

"Sleep is part of waking?"

"When you dream in stage-four sleep, you connect with your own racial history. You glimpse a portion of your earliest being. Perhaps this is why there is no stage four after a person reaches seventy years. This stage just drops off, like a rocket booster. The segment I'm particularly interested in is called stage-four primal, which is characterized by a total lack of dream recall on the part of EEG subjects. Brain-wave tracings indicate that dreams do occur in stage-four primal. But no one has been able to remember one. With pregnant EEG subjects, we find bursts of fetal activity in this substage. Is there a connection between the subject's primal dream and the fetus' emergence from the uterus? The structure of the atom was conceived in a dream. But it wasn't a stage-four primal. Pure fable, myth, archetype, model, mold. This is how I characterize a primal. Dreams so shatteringly primitive the memory withdraws from them to relieve itself of responsibility."

Midway through D'Arco's recitation, Billy got up and jogged around the room, testing Knobloch's statement that excess movement causes static. It was true. The sound of D'Arco's smooth deep enveloping voice was interrupted by random bursts of noise. He tried standing still and quickly raising his hand. A small crackling warp in D'Arco's voice. He tried kicking his foot backward. A little hiss.

"Being a nonadult EEG subject," D'Arco said, "you haven't had time to drift away from your psychic origins, whatever these may have been, however replete with terror, darkness and fetal shrieks. Routine horripilation. We'd like you to sleep. Nothing more than that. You simply get into the twofold and sleep. Nothing will be attached to your body. The canister itself is sensor enough. All we want to do is record your stage-four primal. We want to learn what kind of dreams you have in that stage."

"But you said they're never recalled in that stage, being the shattering kind of dream."

"Very good," D'Arco said. "You've been listening."

"Also I have slept here ever since arriving. This means you already have plenty of tracings of mine."

"We thought your functions were Tree Man's, which means we didn't activate the current that could electrically stimulate the flash points in your temporal lobes, thereby enabling you, on awakening, to experience flashbacks of scenes from your primal dream."

"Is that the same as remembering?"

"It's better," D'Arco said. "The details are much sharper."

"So what happens now?"

"You go to sleep."

265

"I'm not sleepy."

"Knobloch will read to you," D'Arco said.

There was a brief silence.

"The history of zero is both interesting and informative," Knobloch read. "It is thought that zero was discovered in India by a Hindu many, many years ago. It is the shadow of pure quantity. On one side of it are the positive integers; semicolon; on the other side the negative integers. Plus and minus, minus and plus. You are getting sleepy. Your eyelids are getting heavy. You are falling into stage-four sleep preparatory to entering an undiscovered primeval dreamscape. Zero is an element of a set that when added to any other element in the set produces a sum identical with the element to which it is added."

He dressed quickly and walked out, hearing, before he closed the door, the static caused by his movements across the room. He gave his body a moment to replenish its supply of oxygen, energy and whatever else had been disrupted by the prospect of simple sleep—a prospect that caused decided terror, delayed or not. Then he went to the nearest elevator, waited for the door to open, stepped inside and pressed a random button. When he stepped off he saw two workmen hurriedly installing an office door and another man disappearing around a corner with a paint can in his hand. Billy went the other way. Something about the area seemed familiar but it wasn't until he walked past a barbershop that he realized he was in the vicinity of the hobby room. Pure luck, he concluded. Since this was a time of threat and since Endor's room was padlocked, the hobby room represented a welcome refuge, even if second best. Stage-four sleep recorded and traced. His brain waves on paper. Bursts, flat lines, spindles, jagged flashes. Dropping off. Falling to an alternate surface. The hobby room looked the same as it had when he'd encountered Siba Isten-Esru, the name shaman, Seven Eleven. Even the neon organ used in Ratner's torch-lighting ceremony had been returned from the Great Hole. He sat on Endor's tricycle and looked around. There was an eerie restfulness attached to being alone in a room of solid objects, this shadowy attic haunt so thick with reveries and dust. Weapons of holy wars. Pieces spilled from jigsaw puzzles. Trick decks of cards. Catgut, bamboo and iroko wood. He got off the vehicle and wandered into the depths of the room, passing among Victrolas, soda fountains and mummy cases. These last were very small, stamped OMCO RESEARCH, apparently designed for children, each case decorated with a chipped and faded likeness of the individual it once contained. In a steamer trunk he found a makeup kit. Among various pastes, wigs and cosmetics was a small black mustache, very somber, an emblem of anonymity more than a decoration, fit for a man who gravitates toward the darkest corners of rooms. He placed it over his lips and used his index fingers to press down. It seemed to stick fairly well. He pressed again several times as he strolled past the organ and tricycle back toward the door. Standing there were D'Arco and Tree Man II, the latter flat-footed, long-limbed, head thrust forward, jug-eared, a quizzical look on its face, profoundly self-mocking, the very expression Billy had come to associate with scholarship, distinctive mastery in learning. Not that the ape was so nakedly akin to some master of the classics. Just ambiguous was all, or appearing to be, teasing the known world, reluctant to share its puzzlement. One paw was held by D'Arco, who was well past middle age, his neck veins extending like bridge cables from his throat to the point of his chin. Wispy hair grew on his autocratic knuckles.

"Assuming you're asleep," D'Arco said, "your task at the moment is to wake yourself up. Just assuming, of course. Assuming you're asleep. The idea is to wake yourself up, assuming you're asleep, and identify the sound that corresponds to my voice. There's a specific matching operation that goes on."

"I admit I don't like this kind of talk."

"Of course, there's always the chance you'll wake up with diplopic vision. This will happen if your sleep, assuming you're asleep, is lacking in rapid eye-movements. You'll open your eyes to a world in which everything is paired. No unpaired things in the whole world. Countable objects. A set of sets associated with the number we call two. Assuming you're awake, which is no less likely, I should mention that this is the ape whose EEG tracings we thought were yours."

"The arms on him."

"His habitat is rigged exactly like your canister."

"Fingers, the toes."

"I think it's time both of you were returned to your respective EEG stations. Assuming one of you isn't already asleep and being recorded."

"If I had a scissor, I'd like to cut his toenails. Something about toenails that long makes me want to start cutting. What about you?"

"I'm a busy man," D'Arco said.

Tree Man looked at Billy and spoke, with grim effort, biting off the syllables as they emerged, slowly, units of digestive turbulence.

"All in fi nite sets are in fi nite but some are more in fi nite than oth ers."

From D'Arco came an avuncular chuckle, little spit-divots sailing through the air.

"The whole is e qual to one of its parts."

D'Arco wheezed at that, nearly doubling up.

"Pretty droll bunch, those folks over in Zoolog," he said. "I guess the brain adjustments and other work they did on the chimp could use some refining. But in the meantime I'd like you to take my other hand. Want to be sure you get to your canister and into the twofold."

As D'Arco moved toward him, hand extended, Billy felt ready to cower and spring simultaneously. There was a noise in the corridor, someone running, the sound of a voice delivering essential news, and they moved into the doorway to see Knobloch coming toward them at top speed, his mouth forming words as he ran.

"They're sending," he cried. "They're sending again. They're sending."

Fifty feet from the door he lost his balance and fell but rolled over smartly on his shoulder and was up and running again in the same motion, minus one shoe. He hobbled panting to a stop in front of them.

"They're sending, they're sending."

"Who is sending and what is being sent?" D'Arco said.

Knobloch looked at Billy.

"I hate you," he said.

"Why?"

"You saw me fall."

D'Arco clapped his hands a single time.

"Who and what?"

"Radio signals. Extraterrestrials. They're sending again."

"What's the nature of these signals?"

"Fourteen pulses, a gap. Twenty-eight pulses, a gap. Fifty-seven pulses."

D'Arco sagged visibly. Slightly lopsided, Knobloch merely sweated and tried to catch his breath. Billy stepped back into the hobby room, certain this was the end of all menace run amuck.

"I think we learned something here today," he said.

In the doorway the two men conferred. Billy wandered over to a small window in a far corner of the room. He looked down to one of the lawns and saw what appeared to be an impromptu parade. Two ragged lines of people. Some of them apparently carrying instruments. He was too far away, however, to hear any music. What he did hear, behind him, was Tree Man II padding down the corridor. When he turned he saw that D'Arco had also gone. This left Knobloch, stocky with pustules, to lead him to his canister, not before retrieving the lost shoe and putting it back on. In the canister he tucked Billy into the twofold and departed. In a matter of minutes his voice filled the room.

"Say 'I read' if you read what I'm saying."

"I read."

"Who discovered zero and where was it discovered?"

"Hindu, India."

"That concludes our voice check," Knobloch said. "Preparing to record stage-four functions. Preparing to record, preparing to record. Is subject ready?"

"No reply."

"Preparing to count down. Subject is counting down. Subject is closing his eyes and counting down from zero. Subject's eyelids are terribly heavy. Subject is drowsy as he begins to enter stage one. We have low voltage activity at this time. Decreased amplitude, increased frequency. We are recording at a paper speed of fifteen millimeters per second. Preparing to receive stage-one tracings. Preparing to receive, preparing to receive."

It was at this point that Softly entered the room. There was a second

269

of brilliant stillness. Sensational, Billy thought. Colossal, tremendous, stupendous. The special presence of the man, his ascendancy, the seeming contradiction of painful quaintness, were never more evident. He put down his jacket and briefcase. Then, as Knobloch's voice continued to deliver technical data, he approached the limited input module, stepped on a chair, reached into a small compartment high above the videophone and turned a silver dial. Knobloch's voice went dead and the room was totally silent. He stepped down from the chair, picked a loose thread off his shirt cuff and then put on his jacket. Billy climbed out of the twofold, moving at once to his side. It was over, over, over.

They walked together on the grounds. Billy carried Softly's briefcase, as he'd often done at the Center. It was a mild and windless day, sky high and bright, a day modeled on the rhythmic symmetry of a period of light before nightfall. When they entered the topiary garden they heard the ample blare of the parade as it steadily developed, then saw the marchers, dozens of men and women strutting in and out of the monkey hedges, most of them in costumes of various sorts, all wearing masks, men in one rank, women in the other, moving in twos, their masks improvised from newspapers, napkins, towels and sacks. One of the marchers shouldered a tuba, his paper mask fitted with a mouthhole, and other people played banjos, trombones, drums, clarinets and flutes. The noise produced was sufficiently dissonant to confirm the spontaneous nature of the event. In opera hats, bedgowns, bonnets, yellow slickers, periwigs, knickers and snoods they paraded under the sun, some of the "women," seen now at closer range, appearing to be men in women's clothing, as though to correct a deficiency and even up the pairings. A ten-foot muffler connected several necks.

"I'm willing to believe this is International Children's Day," Softly said. "There really is such a thing, you know."

"I didn't."

"They've kept it from the children."

"I didn't know you were expected, Rob. You never told me a thing. What do you think of this place?"

"Needs a fluted column or two. But don't get depressed, we won't be here much longer."

"Where are we going?"

"I'm working out the details."

"Somewhere together?"

"Sure, together, absolutely. This whole operation needs to be drastically altered. When I agreed with U.F.O. Schwarz that you were uniquely suited to unravel the transmission, I didn't know things would be handled so casually. There hasn't been enough systematic thought put in on this."

"But I'm a lot closer than anyone else got to a solution. The number they're transmitting is what we would call fifty-two thousand one hundred and thirty-seven. I'm sure of that and all I have to do is go on from there."

"From there to where?" Softly said.

They walked slowly across a level expanse of grass. Softly, forced to move in mechanical tick-tock fashion because of permanently dislocated hips, lifted a tin of small cigars out of his side pocket and lit one up. He seemed to haul himself over the ground, hitching with every step, his stomach working as hard as his legs to produce some locomotion. Fields. Number fields. Algebraic number fields. Star fields. Electrical fields. Metrical fields. Field equations. Unified field theory. The grass had recently been cut and possessed that nearly toxic freshness of nature in recuperation, a savor of arrow poison more seductive than the wildest lime. The two moving figures were about a hundred yards from the building, which was hard to look at in this midpoint hour, having been designed to play with light, to magnify and angle it in veering octaves so that the whole structure resembled a burst of solar art.

"They mixed up my tracings with an ape's."

"What kind of ape?"

"Chimpanzee."

"They're the most intelligent," Softly said.

They sat on the grass to rest. Billy stretched back, face lifted to the sun. After a moment he became aware that Softly had taken off his jacket and placed it over his head so that his face was in shadow beneath the upturned collar. Always doing things like that, the boy recalled. Usually these things were funny, dumb and strange and it was only after some time had passed that he would realize there was an element of intelligence at work. In this case, he decided, it was Softly's pale coloring that provided the motivation, his susceptibility to sunburn.

"I think we have to attack the code in a radically different way. However we look at it, this is one of the most important events in the history of mankind. It has to be dealt with in the purest way possible. Do you see what I'm getting at? We have to be absolutely lucid. We have to be exact to a degree never before attained. The slightest intuitive content has to be eliminated from our finished work. See what I'm leading up to?"

"Let's have the gory details."

"One way of viewing mathematics is in terms of number. I guess you know what the other way is. I'll say the word in a more expressive language just so there'll be no doubt exactly what it is we're talking about."

"I wish you wouldn't."

"*Logik,*" Softly said.

That distinctive quality of parade music, a summons to come running, to gather together in public and allow whatever loyalty imbues marchers and band members to quicken likewise the communal spirit and reduce all colors to one; that special emotion, as the music drops into time and distance, is swept pathetically away, to be replaced by a faint wonder at the depths of regret that often follow such fleeting revelry.

"I think I feel sick."

"Logic is the scrub brush the mathematician uses to keep his work free of impurity. Logic says yes or no to the forms constructed through intuition. So-called intuitive truths have to be subjected to the rigors of logic before we can take them seriously, much less use them in our work. Remember, we're dealing with beings of extraordinary capacity. How can we expect to communicate without a ruthlessly precise system of symbolic notation? Now I know your accomplishments. I understand your feelings—don't think I don't. But you have to admit that much of what you've done as a mathematician has been devoid of true depth. Brilliant instinctive skimming, to be sure. Unprecedented, in fact. But skimming nonetheless. We have to eliminate contradiction and go beyond all those lax attitudes that make true scientists want to crumple up whimpering."

"I don't like the sound of it."

"Neo-logistic, it's called, technically."

"I definitely feel sick."

"Don't get your balls in an uproar," Softly said.

Cigar smoke drifted out of the gabardine tent, not quite concealing Softly's faint smile. In slow motion his left arm emerged from the jacket to give the boy a chummy cuff on the shoulder.

"I find it interesting that Gottlob Frege produced his first landmark work on the logical foundations of mathematics exactly one hundred years ago. Almost as interesting is the fact that Einstein was born that same year. And that Dodgson published a book on non-Euclidean geometry—organized in dream form. Of further interest is the coincidence that a critical split in mathematics resulted from work being done on infinite sets about that time."

"Why is this interesting?"

"Because I find it so."

He dug a little hole for the cigar and gently buried it. Funny, dumb and strange.

"As we redefine and strengthen, I think we'll get closer and closer to the prospect of a genuine exchange with the extraterrestrials. We have to seek a level deeper than pure number. That much I'm absolutely convinced of. So let's not drag it out."

"I got halfway there, Rob. I found out they use a system based on sixty. I know it didn't take any complicated work to figure this out but that's exactly the reason we don't need this big change in our thinking."

"Even if you sit down and solve the code later this afternoon and solve it in a manner convincing to one and all, this still wouldn't mean we've found an effective way of exchanging information with the extraterrestrials. What we need and what I'm trying to get the groundwork started on is a logistic cosmic language based on mathematical principles."

"It'll take years and years until long after we're kaput to even reach them out there with an answer. So what's the difference?"

"That's not the point, mister. Field Experiment Number One may smell like a brand-new shower curtain but its aims are important ones. If we're going to behave as a single people, as rational human beings who inhabit the same planet, we desperately need goals and pursuits that can unite us. Finding a way to speak to intelligent beings on another planet is one such pursuit. This place wasn't called Number One accidentally. Others are being planned. Beacons in the shit-filled night. If we succeed here, we'll be providing impetus for similar projects throughout the world. One, two, three, four, five."

"I need this speech?"

"You can make it work," Softly said. "You with your one-of-a-kind touch, your fantastic grasp of connective patterns, of relationships and form, of hypothetical states, of the ways in which an isolated concept ties into the whole body of mathematics. Think of it. A transgalactic language. Pure and perfect mathematical logic. A means of speaking to the universe. Whatever small forays have been made in this direction in the past are about to be completely overshadowed by our efforts at Number One."

"I thought we weren't staying."

"It depends on events," Softly said. "We'll be here in general but elsewhere in particular, I suspect."

They began to walk again. It was still possible to hear an occasional parade sound, very faint at this distance, tiny rips in the air, the brief repeated *pop* of tearing seams. Softly kept the jacket over his head.

"I think we're free to break off, split away, to follow a new course. In line with the rigorous approach I'd like everyone to stop using expressions like 'Ratnerians,' 'superbeings,' 'extraterrestrials' and so forth. It's a radio source we're in touch with. If Moholean relativity is the real thing, the source isn't even where it seems to be. So why assume it's a planet orbiting a star? Remember the homely old adage: 'Belief in the causal nexus is superstition.' So let's from now on be sure to use the term 'artificial radio source.' And let's find a more precise name for the so-called beings who are presumed to have initiated the transmission. How about 'artificial radio source extants'? ARS extants. Just so we know what's what."

"Getting tired?"

"From talking more than walking. Hard to adjust to the fact I'm walking with someone who doesn't tower over me. The size we share makes it easier for me to imagine you in the palsied grip of middle age, hee hee, which in turn makes my own years fall away like dry leaves. The fate of man, recto verso, is to go to his grave in a rented hearse-o."

In time they returned to the vicinity of the cycloid structure. A woman opened the gate that led from a small enclosure known as the abstract garden. She walked toward them, carrying a small piece of luggage and some books.

"Look at the ass on that."

"What ass?" Billy said. "She's coming toward us."

"I like to anticipate."

Softly put his jacket back on and they settled into adjacent chairs in the abstract garden. The paraders had evidently passed this way, leaving tokens of their frolic. A man with a pointed stick jabbed daintily at pieces of paper and stray fragments of costume.

"So in conclusion," Softly said, "what we've got to do is restate and strengthen our method of reasoning. Make it exact and supremely taut. Introduce distinctions and fresh relationships. Argue our propositions in terms of precise ideographic symbols. Submit our mathematics, in short, to a searching self-examination. In the process we'll discover what's true and what's false not only in the work before us but in the very structure of our reasoning. There's been no concerted attempt to eliminate slackness and ambiguity from the work you've done up to now. I've got news for you, mister. The goddamn fun is over."

They were alone in the small garden. The afternoon had lost some of its rabid glare. A smell of mown clover rose from the earth. It summoned a special presentness, that particular time-sense in which animal faculties conspire to rouse the spirit, the ordering force of memory, and Billy was stirred to relive some elemental moments separately blessed within the flow of past events. They could be counted, the times in which he'd guided a length of string through the hole he'd nail-scraped in a chestnut, the lumps of clay he'd thumbed and gouged into some amorphous model, the cherry pits he'd buried and people he'd learned to believe. They could be counted, the times in which he'd flexed his toes in dense wet sand, the bites of ice cream he'd chunked out of dixie cups with a flat wooden spoon, the caves he'd made in his mashed potatoes, the pages he'd detached from his composition notebook, tearing down along the row of wire rings, and the white flakes that bounced down out of the air as a result, also distinct and countable. They could be named and listed, the places he'd hidden from danger, the nights he thought would never end.

Softly got up, stretched and headed abruptly toward a remote rear entrance of the building. The boy followed, carrying the briefcase. It wasn't until he walked toward the reflecting surface of an electronic door, now sliding open, that he realized he was still wearing the false mustache.

276

REFLECTIONS

Logicon Project Minus-One

Everywhere dense the space between them seemed a series of incremental frames that defined their passion's dark encompassment, man ostensibly engrossed in dressing, woman nude and on her side (a horizontal dune anagrammatized), neither failing to be aware of the sediment of recent links and distances, that variable material suspended in the air, living instants of their time within each other, sweat and re-echoing flesh serving to confirm the urgent nature of their act, the industry involved, the reconnoitering for fit and placement, the fundamental motion, the pursuit of equable rhythm, the readjustment of original position, the effort of returning to oneself, of departing the aggregate, and in the slightly pasty daze in which they now remembered their fatigue, their sense of well-merited weariness, it was possible for each to examine even further the substance of that space between them, so reflective of their labor, the odors transposed, the strand of hair in the mouth, the experience of whole body breathing, the failure (or instinctive disinclination) to produce coherent speech, the bright cries, the settling, the eventual descent to slackness, the momentary near sleep in milkiness and cling, the recapturing of normal breathing tempo, the monosyllables and blocks of words, the raw awareness of the dangers of exchange, the oddly apologetic uncoupling, mutual recognition of the human demonology of love. She rose from the bed, not without a glib tickle of the springs, this done with a bounce of her amazing buttock, the left, notable for its star-shaped birthmark. He sat atop a footstool, engaged in double-lacing his shoes, taking time between knots to watch her dress, an operation that seemed to portray the correspondence between position and time, one action generating the next, step-in, shake-into, hoist-on, her limbs and torso covered now, fluidly moving woman, her eyes appearing to follow the delicate pebbling sound of Softly's voice. She sat back on the bed as he spoke, the bottoms of her feet identically smudged with dust, arms enfolding her raised knees to form a body-hut that wobbled. Softly rubbing his pale stubble took time to glance inside the folder she'd left propped against the footstool. He spoke a moment longer (about terms, formulas, sentences and proofs), then got up and hurried out of the room, moving with his customary lurch. Had he happened to turn, a step beyond the doorway, for a final word or sweet and simple farewell nod he might have found himself a trifle mystified by the wry smile on his lover's face.

I TAKE A SCARY RIDE

The boy was packed and waiting when Softly arrived in his canister. His pants were pressed and he wore his good sport coat and tie. His fingernails were clean. The part in his hair was nearly straight.

His shoes were shined. The mustache was gone. While Softly nosed his way around the room as though they were about to move in rather than vacate, Billy picked up his suitcase and headed toward the door.

"Not that way."

"What other way is there?"

"Straight down."

"Explain please."

He watched Softly approach the metal grating located near the base of the wall. This, of course, was the emergency exit point for the whole sector. Softly unclasped the grating and set it on the floor.

"We can't go in there except for man-made or natural disaster," Billy said. "They told me that. I nodded my head to show them I understood their statement. Floods, fires, wars, earthquakes."

"Do I get to pick one?"

"I don't like going down there for no reason."

"There's an emergency all right. I thought all along this would happen and it has. Cable traffic is heavy beyond belief."

"So what is it, some kind of alternate physics situation or the bottom is falling out of space or water doesn't boil at the boiling point anymore? Because around here that's the kind of emergency you get."

"Tensions," Softly said.

"What kind?"

"The worst kind. International tensions. Mounting international tensions. First there were states of precautionary alert. Then there were enhanced readiness contours. This was followed by maximum arc situation preparedness. We can measure the gravity of events by tracing the increasingly abstract nature of the terminology. One more level of vagueness and that could be it. It's not just a localized thing either. We're dealing with global euphemisms now. Exactly how soon it'll break out depends on when x, representing the hostile will of one set of nations, and y, the opposing block, slip out of equilibrium in terms of capability and restraint coefficients. We could frame any number of cutie-pie equations but we've got more important work to do."

"So how far down do we go? Is there a basement with a shelter right under here?"

"We go deeper."

"Where they keep the proton accelerators? I think that's about as far down as the building goes."

"Deeper."

"I know where. Where the balloon is that they keep in that big room, the balloon for astronomy. That's about thirteen levels down. Or the Great Hole. We go to the Great Hole, right?"

"Deeper," Softly whispered.

"Deeper than the Great Hole?"

"What I find most satisfying about this structure is the fact that it comes in more than one part. The first, naturally, is the cycloid. The second is the first in reverse, completely below ground level. Same shape upside down. Same distance down as up. Nothing goes on down there in the sense of official goings-on. It's nothing more than an excavation. But it fulfills the concept."

"I think I'll stay here."

"I call it the antrum. Just a fancy way of saying hole in the ground. I've had the floor of the excavation fixed up a bit. Just the bare essentials. And I've selected the very best people to help us in our work. Every one a supersavant. It took all the persuasiveness I could muster. I think the world tensions helped. In this kind of chancy muddle everybody agreed the only way to stay intellectually fresh was to put ourselves in a state of total isolation. Consider yourself lucky to be working with these people."

"I'll take my chances with the global phrase-calling."

"Follow me down," Softly said.

On his hands and knees he backed into the exit hatch. Billy handed down his suitcase and followed. After descending a long metal ladder they had to step over a series of sewer pipes to the edge of a catwalk. It was hard to see, the only light being provided by a dusty bulb. To one side was a stack of beams and thick boards set on sawhorses, all apparently left by workmen. They crossed the catwalk and headed toward another light, avoiding puddles as they went. This time the bulb was inside an open shaft. Softly cranked a lever and eventually a small elevator ascended and stopped, roughly at their level. It was really the frame of an elevator, much of its wiring exposed, no paneling at all, a few yards of hexagonal mesh closing in all but one side. In this lame cage they were lowered into the excavation, a journey that took them through storage and maintenance areas, restricted sectors, down along porous shale and rock, past timber underpinnings and assemblies of masonry and steel that formed support for subtunnels and emergency access routes, the elevator suddenly dropping into open air, free of its shaft, cabling into the darkness of the inverted cycloid, air currents, oscillation, a bucketing descent through drainage showers and rubble-fall, the cage shaking so badly that Billy sought to convince himself there was a pattern to the vibrations and changes of speed, a hidden consistency, all gaps fillable, the organized drift of serial things passing to continuum. Gradually the elevator slowed down, steadying its descent. Then it fitted into its housing, a sort of armored toy-box located on a platform about a dozen feet off the ground. The riders stepped out and walked down makeshift wooden stairs to the very bottom of the vast excavation. An awful lot of trouble, the boy thought, just to fulfill a concept.

A short distance away was a series of cubicles for working and sleeping. Larger units included a first-aid room, a kitchen, a primitive toilet, some field telephones. Everything was set on a slightly curved surface of clay and rock and there was nothing above but darkness. Oil drums, wooden crates and natural debris were set around the cubicles to keep dislodged rocks from bouncing in. A generator droned nearby. Water dripped, splashed and occasionally cascaded in the distance. It was cool down here but not uncomfortably so. The smell of earth was firm and gripping, mineral-rich, and humid air could be felt on the tongue like the taste of a lead penny.

"Frightening ride, I freely concede, but better this than a block and tackle descent," Softly said. "If we ever short-out down here due to flooding, that'll be next. Up and down we go, sitting in a loop of high-grade rope."

In Billy's cubicle were a cot, a footlocker, a large shiny blocklike chair and a TV table on casters, this last item meant to serve as a desk. The partitions were about twice his height. There was no door, just an

entranceway; no ceiling; a clay floor. Softly left him alone to do his unpacking and Edna Lown lowered herself toward a kitchen stool, moving
slowly as befitted her bulk, a cigarette aslant at the corner of her mouth.
He opened the lone piece of luggage but found that only half his things
could be pressed and kneaded into the locker. The rest he left in the
suitcase, which remained unclosed at the foot of the bed. Then he sat
in the chair, not accustomed to free time, Lown's blouse littered with
pale ash from her cigarette. Softly took his ease across the table, watching her thumb through a sheaf of papers, hair fairly gray and worn in
an uneven page-boy cut, clear eyes set in a broad strong face, sedately
aging woman, tank-driver of the neo-logistic school, her thumb ac-
celerating the page count now.

"Where is he?"

"Cube one."

"Will he fold under pressure?"

"He's my protégé, Edna."

"What took you so long?"

"Had to talk to someone about some questions bearing on incidental
matters related to the project."

"We work in absolute privacy, Rob. I won't give an inch on that.
Neither will Lester. This seclusion business was your idea. Now don't
start bending."

"Edna-doll."

"You've got tendencies."

"We work without outside interruptions. That was and is my formal
promise."

"When do we see him?"

"Anytime you're ready," Softly said. "Is that the latest notation
work?"

"I'm not happy with it."

"Of course you're not happy. This is a revolution in the making. All
science, all language wait to be transformed by what we're doing here.
I am the leader. Nobody's happy until I'm happy and I won't be happy
until we've finished what we've come to do."

The boy did not move when they entered his cubicle. Softly sat on the bed. The woman remained in the entranceway, examining the apathetic figure in the chair. She wore glasses with dark frames and round lenses.

"We expect this will be a long and intensely productive period for all of us," she said.

"I haven't even shut my suitcase. That's how long I'm staying."

"Events aren't influenced by one's wishful application of significance to commonplace objects. Whether your suitcase is opened or closed, we'll be here quite a while."

"This is a lady dentist talking."

"Behave yourself, Willy. I told you the fun's over. Edna Lown is here at my request, my entreaty, my urgent supplication. Learn from this woman."

"Naturally I'm familiar with your work," she said. "I detect a strong computational strain running through it. Not much sense of discrimination. Not much use for logic. Paradoxically yours is the kind of intellect we need. The basis of mathematical thinking is arithmetic. The whole numbers and how we use them. On the other hand the basis of arithmetical thinking is pure logic. We can trace the foundations of arithmetic to a handful of logical propositions. It seems to be the rule for top people to come to mathematical logic only after considerable work in other areas. That's nice. I like rules, regulations, formats."

"It seems to me if I remember correctly they got me here to explain a message from outer space. Do I keep on doing that too or do I just work on this other stuff?"

"You can play with the code in your spare time," Softly said. "If you sincerely feel the ARS extants are using a nondecimal system, attack it from that angle. I think what they're using is what we're looking for. A universal logical language. Help us develop that and the code will take care of itself."

The woman spat a grain of tobacco from the tip of her tongue.

"Mathematics is a model of precise reasoning, subject only to the requirements of an inner discipline," she said. "It's an annex of logic. Nothing more. All the rules of what we call 'number' derive from logical propositions. Logic precedes mathematics. And since the fundamental elements of logic have no content, mathematics has no content. Form, it's nothing but form. It stands on thin air. The symbols we use are everything. What they represent we discard without the slightest misgiving. The focus of our thought, the object of our examination, our analysis, our passion if you will, is the notation itself. And this is what our work will involve to a large extent. It's nothing you haven't done before really. The emphasis is on classes rather than numbers. That's all."

"Is that all?"

"I enjoy listening to my logic-mongers talk," Softly said. "They make the creation of an artificial language seem anything but difficult. Remember, Willy, the greatest work is both simple and inevitable. That's my final word for the moment. I'll leave you with Edna now. See you in a few pangs."

"What's that?"

"There's no day or night down here. The body makes its own time, usually very different from what we're accustomed to. Waking time we measure in pangs. Hunger pangs. Sleep time we measure in lobsecs. This refers to a Lester Bolin snore cycle. Lester's Edna's associate. The average full-length sleep is about half a dozen lobsecs."

"Don't you think that kind of talk offends adolescents?"

"Willy, if you think Edna is sensible, there's always Lester to contend with. I remember telling him once how interesting I thought it was that the first use of zero as a number probably took place a great deal earlier than the usual estimates would have it and in Indochina no less, where we can imagine a sort of common abstract boundary between the Taoist concept of emptiness and the Hindu notion of void. He flailed, literally flailed at the air."

"Of course, there was Cantor," the woman said.

"I'm late for an appointment."

"After all the breakdowns, depressions and seizures, after he died, finally, didn't they find in his papers a statement to the effect that mathematics can't be explained without a touch of metaphysics?"

"Juju mama mumblety-peg."

"Obviously I agree," she said. "I just mean it's curious enough to be interesting, not unlike your emptiness and void. What does our young man think?"

"If it's in his papers, I guess that makes it history."

"History is full of interesting things," Softly said. "It has no worthwhile statement to make to us, however, in our current preoccupation. We're permitted to deduce, at least at the outset, that everything is either *a* or non-*a*. What we're not permitted to do is say that everything is either the Great Wall of China or something else. In our present circumstance we don't even know the Great Wall exists. We've never heard of it. So let's forget about history."

I GET A LITTLE BACKGROUND

Edna Lown spoke for a time on the possible form an interstellar vocabulary might take. She pointed out that a "grammar" would have to be communicated gradually through the medium of radio signals of different wavelength and duration. It would be a step-by-step operation, the elements of our synthetic language defining themselves as they were transmitted and, we trust, deciphered. There would be no inconsistencies or exceptions to rules. As we formulated our cosmic discourse, basing it on principles of neo-logistic thought, we could make our transmissions increasingly abstract and difficult, assuming, we hope safely, that those on the other end had correctly interpreted previous transmissions. In this way we could progress from "*a* plus *b* equals *c*" all the way to a definition of "truth," if indeed this word is subject to definition. The radio signals in combination would be the equivalent of a set of ideographic units written in Logicon. Connectives, binding variables, arrays of signs gradually emerge from the radio noise. The concepts of "plus," "minus," "equal to," "is implicit in," "can be interpreted as" soon accumulate in a solid body of planet Earth knowledge. He sat in the chair listening to her as Softly emerged from the shaft, hurried across the catwalk and headed toward the metal ladder. In her room the young woman sat on her bed trying to make sense of the notes she'd written earlier in the day. She seemed to have trouble expressing anything resembling annoyance or frustration; all such displays were inevitably absorbed by her utter presentableness. Well-tailored pants and shirt. Trim figure. Roundish, soft and overpretty face. Whenever she gestured in the direction of vexation, the act automatically endowed itself with a glow of tomboyish pathos, much too adorable to be taken seriously. Hair coasting over the juncture of jawbone and ear, slightly upcurled, the palest of browns. Eyes overripe with sensibility. Softly was halfway out of his pants before he'd taken a couple of steps into the room.

"Let's go," he said.

"What is this, a nuclear holocaust copulation drill?"

"I'm in a hurry."

Softly seminude resembled a Roman sculptor's serious jest. He appeared ludicrous only to the extent that parts of his body were still bound in cloth. Elsewhere nothing was in miniature and it could be maintained, as now he removed the final stretchable sock, that naked he was even more imposing than when fully dressed, his chest fairly broad, his head more closely related in size to the rest of his appendages, an illusion fostered by the balancing factor of his sex organ, a piece of equipment that seemed to hold him together, structural bond and esthetic connective.

"Rob, I'm kind of busy."

"So am I, so am I, but I took time to come up here. You don't have to undress completely. Just give me something to aim at. A suitable accommodation."

"Unfunny," she said.

"Come on, let's get moving."

"These notes are all messed up. I can't read my own notes. How will I ever get a book out of this?"

SEE LESTER EXIST

Lester Bolin glanced at the envelope and strolled over to cube one, where his associate was saying that any civilization advanced enough to have constructed an apparatus for receiving radio transmissions from other parts of the universe would most likely be able to interpret any series of messages based on strict logic. In fact the artificial radio source extants would probably have less trouble understanding a message from Earth than we ourselves experience every time we try to decipher fragments of an ancient language found buried somewhere on our own planet. This seeming irony, she said, merely emphasizes the absence of logic in our spoken languages.

"In any case Logicon is not designed to be spoken. As we go along we'll doubtless see it reveal an innate resistance to being articulated."

"By humans," Bolin said, standing in the entrance.

"Lester's been working on an experimental *thing*. He believes he can get it to speak Logicon."

"Sorry I'm late, all. Cut myself and couldn't stop the bleeding for the longest time. Isn't there supposed to be a limit for that sort of thing? Coagulation? Doesn't blood clot on schedule or something?"

"How'd you do it?" Billy said.

"I was opening my mail with a long thin instrument consisting of a flat-edged cutting surface terminating in a handle."

"A knife?"

"If you want to put it that way."

"Lester's notion of a joke," Edna said. "Lester's a joker. Except jokes don't work very well down here. This is dead time. You can't cut it."

Bolin was a large man who gave the impression of being unmade. It wasn't simply that his clothing fit badly; certain items either missed connections with other items or were connected in the wrong way. The back of one trouser cuff was stuck in his sock. The reckless knot in his tie failed to conceal the fact that his shirt was fastened, starting from the top, with button *a* in hole *b* and so on down to his belt buckle. Part of his shirt was tucked into his shorts, the elastic band folded over his belt for an interval of several inches. His hair was thinning up front and he seemed to want to pat it often. Softly took a cigar from the little metal box. Minor rockfall on the north slope. Mushrooms, mosses, algae, phosphorescent fungus. The trancelike sleep of sated bats digesting upside down. Bolin stepped outside a moment, returning with a chair. Edna Lown stood a few feet to one side of the entranceway. The simple act of sitting was for Lester something nearly ceremonial, his rump and thighs settling ever deeper, investigating the chairness beneath them, and Billy felt this was a man intent on compressing every second in order to discover the world-point within, a *serious* man, look how he *enjoys* his sitting, watch his scraping feet, see him *exist*, a man (Softly mused, of sitting men in general) concluding an infinite sequence of states of rest to begin this period of self-limiting motion. Constant temperature, humidity, darkness.

"My husband, when we were married," the young woman said, "didn't recognize my handwriting. We never left notes for each other. We never wrote letters, even when separated for months. It was always *dring-dring* the telephone. Isn't that remarkable? What we've come to? His own wife's handwriting. My own husband's. Both ways it worked."

"Is that why your marriage broke up?" Softly said.

"We forgot to have fun. That's what happened. No kidding, we just forgot. There he goes. A fleeting figure in the dawn."

"And now you can't even recognize your own handwriting."

"I can recognize it all right. I know it's mine. I just can't read it. So don't draw full circles."

"Remember, you don't talk to anybody unless I give the word. Edna will not like this. It will take every last ounce of my massive powers of persuasion."

"Is smoking allowed in this crate?"

"I want you to straighten out those notes so I can have a look. That's the first order of business. Then you see my friend Terwilliger. Then we go back up. I don't want to push things. I need Edna's good will. This is a smuggling operation. You are being smuggled in. When you're finished interviewing the boy, you will be smuggled out."

"I'd rather stay in the antrum."

"You will be smuggled out," he said.

Serious people. No way no how, Billy thought, to avoid them in this setup. That one sitting inside his chair. The other one standing there in a blouse, a skirt and desert boots, her age and size wearing those tall shoes, not that you can blame her, this setup down here, not even any planks over the ditches. Envelope resting on Lester B.'s knees. Serious very serious. As Lester and Edna spoke of the discipline they would all have to exercise in order to succeed in this venture, Billy put his right index finger in his mouth and bit away part of the fingernail without detaching it completely. He then used this jagged fragment to scrape dirt from under the fingernails of the other hand. Eventually he reversed the process (left index finger, right hand), feeling good about the whole thing, partly because it seemed so ecologically sound. After a while he thought of his own funeral, another favored pastime, resorted to whenever his mood needed a boost, his self-esteem a measure of support. There he is in a heartrendingly cute casket lined with napped fabric, white and velvetlike. Everyone he's ever known shows up for the wake. They stand about solemnly, shopkeepers and doctors of philosophy, dozens of boys and girls, colleagues by the score. Their sorrow at his passing mingles with his own self-pity (as he watches). It's fairly obvious. There's not much doubt about it. Guilt. They feel guilty. What they feel is guilt. They bear this terrible guilt for not having treated him better, loved him more, valued his life above their own.

Jerks.

Inside the drained body little eruptions of rot are already taking place. What once was composed of water, fat, protein, minerals, skeletal ash and assorted fluids is at this moment undergoing structural alteration of the most extreme sort. Mulch, glunk, wort and urg. Nameless wastes. He felt a slight weakness in his upper arms, which probably explained why this part of the death reverie failed to entertain to its usual degree.

"So what's it like," Lester Bolin said, "being a radical accelerate?"

"If that's what I am, it's the only thing I've ever been, at least as far back as the time I first knew what numbers were, so I can't compare it with anything else, which is probably in general the thing you're looking for, I mean more than, less than or equal to what it's like not being a radical accelerate, if I heard the question right."

"In its own way, a remarkably exact answer," Lown said. "Note the use of 'if,' 'only,' 'at least,' 'as far back as,' 'anything else,' 'probably,' 'in general,' 'more than,' 'less than,' 'equal to,' 'like,' and finally 'if' again. Good to excellent answer."

LESTER TELLS US ABOUT ROB

"I'm lowering my voice, so watch my lips. Softly. What Softly's got is a nonhereditary child-size condition. Rare sort of thing. Diagnosed right from the beginning. He was an abnormally small baby, I mean really small, lopsided as well, badly proportioned. He said considering what he looked like in infancy and early childhood he's lucky to have emerged as a 'viewable' adult. Apparently the thing was caused by a chemical imbalance in the mother's womb. As I understand it, he's not a dwarf per se. He told me this himself. I never expected to hear this kind of intimate revelation from someone like Rob. The problem with his hips was there from the start. Part and parcel. One night he just sat himself down and told me the whole thing. I admire the man more than I can say. To have accomplished what he has under such negative conditions. Here, this was delivered to me by mistake."

He tossed the envelope on the bed and followed Edna Lown out of the cubicle. They stopped off in the kitchen, where Softly was pouring tea.

"So?"

"He has to get used to us," Edna said.

"He will in time. Any trouble develops, let me know and I'll work on it."

"How long have you known him?" Lester said.

"He's been at the Center for a couple of years. I first met him several years before that."

"What about your other friend?" Edna said.

"Who's that?"

"How long have you known her?"

"What other friend?"

"There's a young woman in your cubicle."

292

"She's sitting on your bed," Lester said. "Surrounded by sheets of paper. Sorting them."

"No problem."

"Who is she, Rob?"

"Journalist, she's a journalist. Extremely adept and very cooperative. Doesn't do anything without checking with me first. Comes to me for verification of every note, quote and so on. Will not interfere with the work. Will not make a nuisance of herself. She is no problem, believe me. I'm orchestrating the whole thing. Nobody gets anything out of this project that we don't want to give."

"She's writing an article, is she?" Edna said. "A sort of general background article on Logicon. Is that the idea?"

"Book, she's writing a book."

"Rob, I don't like this."

"It's a little book, Edna."

"What else has she written?"

"Little books," Softly said. "All her books have been little."

I READ MY MAIL

Billy decided to take a walk around the area. He got up slowly, envelope in hand, and went along the crude lane that separated the rows of cubicles. There wasn't much here that he hadn't already seen when Softly led him in from the elevator. He didn't go more than a few yards beyond the protective barrier of crates and oil drums. From this short distance the units for living and maintenance resembled a secure campsite, the only source of light in the giant earthen bowl. He was aware of the presence of water. Somewhere up on the slopes water was running along bedding planes and joints. Maybe it was right under him too, dripping into hollows, seeping, cracking rock apart, collecting and finding outlets, only yards below, wells and falls, deep pools, wide living rivers. He sat on a rock and looked for the first time at the front of the envelope Lester Bolin had given him.

Consortium Hondurium
c/o Liberian Ship Registry Inc.
The Guano Exchange
Tax Shelter Liechtenstein

> Mr. William D. Terwilliger Jr.
> School of Mathematics
> Center for the Refinement of Ideational Structures
> Pennyfellow, Connecticut
> USA

Please forward

The thought of mail depressed him. He would have to open the envelope and read what was written inside. It seemed so burdensome. Worse, it was bound to remind him of the task ahead. Linguistic fission. Less than the measured heft of ordinary language. Less than sentences and phrases. Less than words. Less than word fragments. Less than number words. Less than the customary signs and symbols. Less than the usual graphics.

Space Brain Computer Quiz
WIN! WIN! WIN! WIN!
Magnetized plastic symbols

May we congratulate you on the fact that we have selected your name from a carefully guarded mailing list of some of the world's most distinguished intellects and professional people, culled from hundreds of other lists. This makes you eligible to win an unlimited number of brightly colored redeemable plates embossed with precoded symbols. All you have to do is correctly answer the enclosed bi-level quiz questions designed and formulated by the world's most famous computer—the fantastic Space Brain!

Eerie and Uncanny

This phenomenal control-process system—more adaptable than anything in the eerie world of science fiction—has not only designed and pre-printed the deducto-magic quiz on the enclosed quiz card but is pro-grammed to scan and grade your personalized entry. If you are a selected winner, your redeemable wallet-sized laminated plates will be enclosed

294

in next month's quiz. A dozen consecutive winning entries—one for each month of the calendar year—will entitle you to redeem your plates at one of our centrally located redemption centers in your color-coded area of the world. See map attached.

Pay—then play

Every statement on the enclosed quiz card has a pair of answers. SIMPLY CHECK THE BOX NEXT TO THE WORD THAT IS MOST LOGICAL. In order to play, you must first pay the preselected entry fee for your particular mailing list. This figure is computer-stamped on the back of your quiz card. All arrangements subject to the provisions of Space Brain leasing agreement. Void where voided.

ENCLOSED QUIZ CARD

Do not use numbers to indicate logical words. Simply check (√) the correct box. Only perfect solutions win. In the event of a tie, all entries subject to disqualification.

In a tricky situation it is your best friend, above all others, who would find it easiest to _____ you.
- ☐ deceive
- ☐ believe

The faster you run from nameless danger, the _____ you get.
- ☐ queasier
- ☐ wheezier

For one of tender years, it is best to approach life and its logical opposite, adult constructions both, with whatever degree of _____ you can hurriedly muster.
- ☐ fatalism
- ☐ natalism

People who live in caves eventually go _____ .
- ☐ wan
- ☐ yon

The practice of _____ would be difficult to introduce into alien cultures.
- ☐ embalming
- ☐ salaaming

The radio doesn't normally give listeners a chance to hear a _____ .
- ☐ chap snap
- ☐ lune rune

Active people are _____ than people who just mope around feeling sorry for themselves.
- ☐ healthier
- ☐ svelthier

Faced with temptingly equivocal data, the annotator immediately begins to _____.

☐ validate   ☐ salivate

Being concealed, the woman's starring _____ was difficult to interpret.

☐ role   ☐ mole

Some children have to be _____ into playing certain games.

☐ coaxed   ☐ hoaxed

Logical thought is indispensable to _____ in the midst of this, the most ambiguous of all possible worlds.

☐ surviving   ☐ conniving

Amusing, isn't it, how it's always the most rational of individuals, positioned securely in the dark, beyond reach of even the faintest trace of sunlight, who refuses to entertain the notion that under these or similar circumstances he'll ever be _____ by his own shadow.

☐ heightened   ☐ frightened

After observing that the introductory bulletin accompanying the quiz card was stamped with the attesting emblem of a notary public, he made his way back to the cubicle, where a young woman was waiting.

"Hi."

"H'o."

Her visit was brief and the interview she conducted, although it had its opaque moments, was pretty easy to take. She rolled the TV table over to the chair and took notes as they talked. Billy sat on the bed, his back against the partition.

"I'm Jean Sweet Venable. I'm sure Rob's told you about me."

"Terwilliger, William."

"I'm sure you were warned about a writer on the prowl."

"Never heard of it."

"Rob gave me permission to research this whole project and eventually do a book. Sounds fairly intriguing, this Logicon business. The fact that someone like you is involved makes it all the more so."

"What's your question?"

"Do you calculate in longhand or on the typewriter?"

"I use a pencil."

"What are some of your other work habits?"

"I write in the dark."

"That's exactly the kind of thing I want."

"I write in the dark."

"Give me more like that," she said. "I pounce on stuff like that. I eat it up."

"Are you something Rob keeps on the side? Because it's fine with me but you have to understand he probably doesn't take this book you're doing too seriously. Wherever he goes there's something on the side."

"I'm fairly well known in my own right."

"For what?"

"My books."

"Have I heard of them?"

"So I don't think this is a case of somebody keeping somebody else on the side. *Eminent Stammerers*. That was my first. Got a fair share of attention considering the limited scope of the subject matter. I've done scores of magazine pieces."

"Anything else I might have read or know of someone who did?"

"*The Gobbledygook Cook Book*."

"Sounds familiar."

"Fourteen weeks on the list."

"Not bad."

"So I don't think, despite appearances, that this is a case of somebody not taking something too seriously."

"Keep believing it. I do."

"What's the essence of your work?" she said. "I want to know what happens inside your mind. What *is* mathematics? Poincaré talked about getting flashes. Do you get flashes? He also said, I think he was the one, that mathematics is the art of giving the same name to different things."

There was a trace of hoarseness in her voice, of lightly sanded cunning, somehow at odds with her appearance. Certain words she spoke seemed almost to vibrate with the kind of ironic connotation difficult to isolate from its sexual core. There was in addition an offhand and even cavalier element to her note-taking. She scribbled what he said. Line after line of catchpenny scrawl. Not even remotely legible. Maybe, he thought, she was just thinking ahead to the next question.

"What else should I ask?"

"I write using big letters."

"I like it," she said. "Now this business of deciphering what the ARS extants are saying. Is this being abandoned in favor of the Logicon project?"

"I am keeping going on it."

"You're a good subject," she said. "Give me some more like writing in the dark with big letters. Most subjects insist on telling me about every so-called fascinating job they've had since the age of puberty, or what good athletes they used to be, or the year they spent in a beach house in shorts. I much prefer the offbeat item. Give me more, give me more."

She liked to stand clutching herself as she talked. Hands under opposite elbows. Only one hand to elbow if she had a phone or drink in the other. Leaning back against the nearest large object as she talked. Sometimes her right foot scraping the floor. Her head sometimes tilted left. Jean believed in very little. All around her all her life people went around believing. They believed in horticulture, pets, theosophy and yogurt, often in that order, flickeringly, going on to periodic meditation, to silence and daunted withdrawals. Despite their belief in staying single they all believed in marriage. This was the collectivization of all other beliefs. All other beliefs were located in the pulpy suburbs of marriage. To entertain other beliefs without being married was to put oneself in some slight danger of being forced to be serious about the respective merits of these beliefs. Dishevelment would result. True belief. The end of one's utter presentableness. Recently ex-married, Jean had not yet detected flaws in her presentableness. But this was because she had not yet experienced the onset of the danger of belief. The links were thrilling if indeed true links, if more than mere envisioned instants.

"I think we should wear uniforms," Bolin said.

So, if she had been standing and talking, which she wasn't, being en-

298

camped by now in Softly's cubicle, "sorting impressions," trying to read "notes," there would have been on display some related version of that casual posture, that sleeveless V-neck sweater, that knit shirt, the acute crease in those flannel pants. Her husband had left without warning one morning. No hint since of whereabouts. All around her people accused him of cowardice. If willing to grant this, she realized she would have had to concede the corollary, that to live with her in wedlock required courage. (Is that really logical?) A certain marital valor. An intrepidity and grit. She didn't hate him, miss him or wonder where he was. Never a thought of some swell revenge. Among the things she didn't believe was that we learn from experience. Nothing of value accrued to her from the fact of his disappearance except for one insight, that there seems to be in men a universal mechanism, a preconscious warning hum that is activated upon mention of certain details of a woman's prior life. And so each man she met, on being told of her husband's sudden departure, would himself suddenly depart. It began to take on the rhythm of a biological cycle. All of them assumed she had made life unbearable. No doubt an expert in chaos administration. A magic-wielding bitch despite her utter presentableness. Discovery of the chromosomal hum did not interest her much, being useful only when she was in bed with someone she wanted to wake up in bed without, in which case she had only to remember not to go to sleep without first mentioning that one morning without warning her husband had left. All around her all her life all the others believed, forever attending classes to solidify old beliefs and obtain knowledge that would lead to new beliefs, grown people going to school for instruction in coloring with goo, in lifting the dress to sit on the pot, in spitting out buttons to prevent strangulation, believers, flickering.

"How are the notes coming along?" Softly said.

"Accumulating nicely."

"They should be ready by now. I want to see them when they're ready."

"I'm changing systems," she said. "It's just a question of switching over to this new system. Everything's in order. It just has to be systemized anew."

"Do it up top."

"I want to stay."

"Edna and Lester won't like it. They want absolute assurance nobody's hovering, nobody's listening, nobody's otherwise disturbing their concentration."

BILATERAL SYMMETRY

It had been Bolin nonstop for a solid hour. Maybe more, maybe less, hard to tell. Billy thought he saw a light high on the southwest gradient, there and gone, a pale beam shifting. He was in his chair. Lester Bolin was sitting on the ground at the juncture of two partitions. Bolin on bilateral symmetry. Bolin on symbolic notation. Bolin on the subject of uniforms. Team jerseys with LOGICON sewed across the front. His left leg was bent at the knee, the other leg stretched out flat, and he ceased gesturing in accompaniment to his remarks only to raise his left hand from time to time in order to simulate a grooming motion over the scrubby tract above his forehead.

Exact correspondence of form and constituent arrangement on opposite sides of a dividing line or plane, Softly thought. He rejected the idea, never proposed, that there might be someone or something on the other side of an imaginary median line to match his parts and their relationships and into which he might theoretically flow. He was bundled into his bed, thumb-sucking, trying to stifle the chill that had penetrated his body on the most recent descent. Several blankets and a thick quilt. His thermal jammies. In the kitchen Lester was boiling water for tea. Edna was out near the barrier trying to get the shower to work properly. In cube one, the boy was unwavering in his marsupial sulk. Fill fill fill. Softly thumb-sucking made a series of tiny plectral sounds, as though pinching an inflated balloon. He felt a period of depression coming on. Arrival as scheduled. Activity and high excitement. Then this immense gloom. He consoled himself with the thought that it wouldn't last long and more pointedly with the clinical knowledge that a person afflicted with cyclothymia, the technical name for this condition, was known, of all things, as a cycloid. How utterly lovely. What depths of stability and equivalence. What splendid *Einheit* or unity. Day and night of manic-depressive psychosis. Sun, heat, maleness. Moon, shade, femininity. Bless all Celestials and may they dualize forever. Pangs and lobsecs. He took his thumb out of his mouth, stepped from bed, opened the briefcase that held his hand-washables, felt around among the underwear and socks and came up with a small cylindrical inhalator. It was trademarked NorOmCol and had a screw cap, which he removed in some haste. He fitted the device high into his left nostril and squeezed once, *I went to a Chinese restaurant to get my laundry back*, releasing a colorless vapor. *Whoosh.* Wonder what a microscopic view would resemble. Noradrenalin transmission appearing on the slide like a neon sea. Cells unable to reabsorb. Active brain, racing pulse. Is this stuff psychoto-mimetic is the question. Or is it "madness"-inhibiting? He put on an old robe and slippers, pondering which came first, state of mind or effect produced by chemical agent, his nostril pleasurably scorched.

> I went to a Chinese restaurant
> To get my laundry back
> They served it up on the half-shell
> Without the usual crack:
> *Yan tan hoakery poke*
> *Bloody hum de dum*
> *Divy tivy artichoke*
> You are *it*

He went into the kitchen, where Bolin was pouring tea for Edna Lown, who sat before an ultraviolet lamp. Waving off a cup of tea he circled the table a few times before climbing a stool near the entranceway. Edna wore sun goggles.

"Laughter," Bolin said.

"What do you mean by that?"

"Ha ha. Just another way of saying ha ha."

"Why don't you simply laugh?"

"I am laughing. Ha ha. A sound indicating amusement or glee. Middle English *ha ha*. Old English *ha ha*."

Heterology refers to lack of correspondence between bodily parts, as in structure, arrangement or growth. An adjective is heterological if it denotes something that doesn't apply to the adjective itself. What about the adjective "heterological"? Is it heterological (this is Softly thinking) or not heterological? Let's work our way through the successive reflections of this logical dilemma. The mind that makes it to the other side needn't concern itself with bodily parts and whether they match or not. For isn't it true, historically (I permit myself to slip, this once, through my own blockade), that people have maintained a fascination for the subplot of erotic potential in small bumpy misproportioned men (not that I wish to exaggerate my own unevenness), perhaps suspecting us of possessing cyclic drives and impulses traceable to our more "natural" state of being; that is, our obvious lack of grace (which means, here, both effortless movement and divine favor, stressing the latter); or believing us capable of providing something deeply feared and longed for, nightmarish fulfillment, incubus asquat on the belly of a sleeping woman.

"Sign over Spanish barber shops," Lown said. "*Algebrista y sangrador.* Bonesetter and bloodletter. Trying to solve the flow."

The slope was dark. There were matches and candles in the pack, however. A crack of flame by the light of which a man might refuel a carbide lamp. At her desk Edna removed the heavy glasses she wore and then reached down and unlaced her desert boots. An unspoken sigh rose through her frame. The easeful stress of mellow bodies settling. Eyes closed now. Lips moving: broad-stroked Mayan lips moving slightly. What we conclude must be true in all possible worlds. True false. Tautological contradictory. Easier to reason without a sense of passing time. No systematically recurring event such as sunrise to provide a means of measuring an interval. Rest now rest. Continuous variable. Limit of an infinite sequence. Cut ever nearer the true value. Close in. Klōz in/n/n/n/n. Edna had grown children; that is, sons and daughters now adult, living with husbands, wives and real children in suburban Bellevue or some slight variation thereof. (Where's gramma, dad? She's living in a cave, shut up.) This piece of furniture was all that could be scavenged in the way of a desk, being a former chair taken apart and put back together by Lester Bolin inventively rearranging.

Despite the constant need for enterprise, the lack of material comfort, she liked it here. This was true work, what her life was all about, a summation, the terminating act of a long career that had often verged on greatness. The careers of each of them—Lester, Rob, herself—had proceeded along fairly similar routes, touching here and there, pausing to curl one inside the other, ever so lightly, never before this close to braiding together in a significant way. The atmosphere of crisis would prompt them to work harder and better. The lack of comfort. The imposed proximity. Rest now rest. It was all so enfolding. Across the fiction of pure space they studied each other intently, parents of their own bodies, listening to the listener, all gravid with formal deduction. She opened her eyes. Maurice Wu. And put her glasses back on. Yes rested well rested. Time to shake off the dross of ordinary language. Maurice Wu squatting in the guano fields. She heard Bolin begin to snore. What she found truly remarkable was the fact that it had taken her so very little time to adapt to these ridiculous living conditions. On a typewriter stand in Bolin's cubicle was an old Royal portable with a sheet of paper sticking up out of the roller. Set on the ground between the legs of the typewriter stand was a shortwave radio. Next to the stand and the radio was a small plastic desk. On the desk was a framed photograph of Lown and Bolin formally posed on a small lawn on some campus somewhere, each of them half turned toward the camera and half facing the other person, hands behind their backs, Edna's left leg extended a bit, Lester's right leg likewise set forward, the photographer's insistence on balanced composition (whatever the level of humor intended) evident most of all in the centering element of the entire picture, this being a waist-high twin-handled jug of indeterminate markings, each handle pointing (as it were) toward one of the standing figures. Above the radio, the stand, the antique machine, the desk, the photograph, draped across the full length of one partition, was a banner inscribed as follows:

BREATHE! GLEAM! VERBALIZE! DIE!

He completed the mixture, relighted the lamp, fitted it once again to the miner's hat. He put his work gloves back on. He snuffed the candle.

He put the candle back in the pack. Getting to his feet he shouldered into the pack and put the hard hat back on his head. Besides the gloves, helmet and pack, he wore coveralls, kneepads, high socks and climbing boots. He carried a canteen and sleeping bag separately from the pack. After several heavy shrugs to redistribute the weight on his back, he began the long passage down the southwest slope to the tired lights at the floor of the antrum.

ROB DOES A TRICK

Softly fully dressed went to cube one. He was thinking of Jean Sweet Venable aswarm in bedsheets hundreds of feet straight up. Of her works he had read only *The Gobbledygook Cook Book*, deeming it serviceably useless; a good example, in other words, of what he expected (and would demand if need be) of her current assignment. He found his protégé in the stiff gleaming chair, sitting with legs crossed, a novel posture for the boy.

"Is there anything I can do to cheer you up?"

"Stand on your head."

Softly did this, fairly easily, not without first putting a folded towel on the spot where his head would settle. Showing little strain he righted himself. Then he sat on the towel, an act evidently requiring more effort than the headstand did.

"What else?"

"That's enough for now."

"I want you to be happy, Willy."

"I'm trying."

"We need you. You wouldn't be here otherwise. This is the most important thing any of us has ever attempted. Otherwise you wouldn't be here. Let's trust each other, you and I. A secret pact. Mutual love, trust and brotherhood."

"I trust you."

"Then why aren't you cooperating with Edna and Les?"

"I'm here when they want me."

"You have to show a willingness, an enthusiasm. This isn't some boring homework assignment in junior high. Show something. Make me proud of you."

"I'm here for the asking."

"You're a mathematician," Softly said. "You work till you drop."

"That's pretty much what Endor told me."

"Sure, sacrifice."

"The hole he's living in is equipped with a hole of its own."

"You have to put yourself on the line, everything forever, and you haven't been doing that, Willy. Let me tell you why we're lucky, you and I. Something you've never thought of. Size, our size, because of our size we don't have to pump blood nearly as far as most people. Most people have to pump to much greater heights. We save squillions of miles of blood-pumping effort. Don't have to worry about high blood pressure or arteries popping open. Cheery news, don't you think?"

"Does the outside world know about any of this?"

"The outside world? What do you mean by the outside world?"

"The people anywhere but here who might be interested in this project. Do they know what we're supposed to be doing here?"

"I don't know what you mean when you say what we're supposed to be doing here."

"I'll start with the way it's been happening up to now."

"Sure," Softly said.

"The signal from Ratner's star. The people who tried to figure it out before I got here. Endor leaving for the hole. My getting here. The events. My working on the code. My being told the signals are not coming from Ratner's star and that it's all because of a mohole. More events. The second signal the same as the first. Your getting here. The Logicon project."

"So what's the question?"

"Do they know about this out there? Other people in science? Does anybody know what's going on here?"

"Absolutely no one."

"How come?"

"Pressures, because of external pressures," Softly said. "The last thing we need is a whole bunch of people commenting, jumping up and down, making judgments. The last thing we need is coverage."

"Stand on your head," Billy said.

When he was seated again Softly took a newspaper clipping out of his wallet. He unfolded it and waited for the boy to reach over and take it.

"Meant to show you this earlier. Nothing very important. Just thought you'd like to see the kind of company you've been keeping."

Make Formal Prize Announcements

STOCKHOLM This year's Nobel Prizes were made official today after delays owing first to the local outbreak of hostilities and subsequently to internal disputes surrounding the awards for peace, economics and physics. The appropriate Swedish and Norwegian committees jointly released the official list without comment.

CHEMISTRY—Walter Mainwaring, Canadian; Cosmic Techniques Redevelopment Corp.; for research in exo-ionic sylphing compounds.

PHYSIOLOGY/MEDICINE—Cheops Feeley, Kurd; the Cheops Feeley Foundation; Field Experiment Number One; for developmental work in the scar-free implantation of microcomputerized electrodes.

ECONOMICS—No award.

PHYSICS—Orang Mohole, Austro-Mongol; Relativity Rethink Priorities Council; Sexscope Gadgeteer Inc. (consultant); Field Experiment Number One (visiting member); for theoretical work in the Moholean structure of the value-dark dimension.

MATHEMATICS—William Terwilliger Jr., American; Center for the Refinement of Ideational Structures; Logicon Project; for studies in zorgal theory.

PEACE—No award.

LITERATURE—Chester Greylag Dent, unaffiliated and stateless; for what the Swedish Academy described in its original announcement of the award as "recognition of a near century of epic, piquant disquisitions on the philosophy of logic, the logic of games, the gamesmanship of fiction and prehistory, these early efforts preparing the way for speculative meditations on 'the unsolvable knot' of science and mysticism, which in turn led to his famous 'afterthoughts' on the ethereally select realms of abstract mathematics and the more palpable subheights of history and biography, every published work of this humanist and polymath reflective of an incessant concern for man's standing in the biosphere and hand-blocked in a style best characterized as undiscourageably diffuse."

"How come they have me down for Logicon? I haven't been here long enough for any Swedes to know where I am."

"They made a routine request for information," Softly said. "As usual in matters pertaining to you, this material passed across my desk at the Center. All anybody knows about Logicon is the name. I had to account for Lester and Edna being here. Also for our absence from the Center. But nobody knows the actual nature of the project."

"But what if I said no I'm not going."

"I felt you'd trust me enough to come with me. Trust. Let's trust each other, Willy. Let's help each other be."

"I'll try."

"Incidentally I'm negotiating with Mainwaring. I want to get him here if at all possible."

"Who's that?"

"First name on the list," Softly said.

"Chemistry. Walter Mainwaring. Canadian. Cosmic Techniques Re-development Corp."

"He may be the only person in the world who understands the full implications of sylphing."

"How does that help us?"

"You never know, he might come in handy, somebody like that. We're negotiating now. I want him here badly. He's the last one I need. The final one-of-a-kind mind."

"Edna, Lester, me and him."

"Lown, Bolin, Terwilliger, Mainwaring and Wu."

"Who's Wu?"

"Oriental gent," Softly said.

Sooner or later he had to get up and go to the toilet. On his way back he heard his name called. It was Lester Bolin speaking from bed. Billy approached the entranceway of Lester's cubicle. He saw the banner, the photograph, the typewriter, the radio, the man himself, the narrow bed consisting of canvas stretched on a collapsible frame, the sheets and blankets at one end of the bed, bunched up, supporting Bolin's head. Lester wore a sport shirt and pajama bottoms.

"How do you like it down here?" he said. "Like it?"

"Hate it."

"Intensity," Lester said. "Everything's so concentrated down here. I'm having a great time. Want to go up with me later? I have some work to do on the model. Sources of power are handier up there. It'll be computer-driven. Parts will operate electromechanically on instruction from Space Brain. This is preceded and followed by an operation called logic rendering. The result, with luck, will be a control system that speaks Logicon. Of course we have to perfect the language first. That's our primary job. Take that paper out of the typewriter and look at it."

$$) -: o/o :k.: k' ""(-($$

"What does it say?"

"If the word 'proof' in this context applies only to arrays of sentences that make an assertion about an object language L, then in fact the proof itself, as opposed to the word 'proof,' shall be evident only in terms of the language M, or metalanguage, in which we draw necessary conclusions about the object language L, this method M also being subject to formal study through investigations carried out in M prime, or meta-metalanguage, the purpose being to preserve selectness by using only those statements that consistently refer to themselves," Bolin said.

The boy went back to cube one and got into bed. Isochronal rockfalls. Cave openings all along this route. More guano for my artifacting. The caves set into the slopes of the excavation contained a number of *megaderma*, or "false vampires." These were cannibal bats that rampaged among the roosting species, all of which were covered with tiny bloodsucking insects which themselves provided asylum for even smaller parasitic blood-fleas. Whole lot of sucking going on. Which could be the reason, thought Wu, why medieval gnome-worshippers in the mountains of central Europe believed that the crystal mixture of hydro-magnesite and water possessed distinct medicinal properties and may have been right, they might, for wasn't it used centuries later to stop the flow of blood? Moon milk. Dehydrating agent and coagulant.

EDNA GETS ANNOYED

"I don't know what to call you," he said. "What do you want to be known as?"

"Mrs. Lown."

"Maybe I'll get out of bed later and come talk to you. Right now I'm in bed."

"We have work to do."

"Being in bed is the work I'm doing right now."

"Don't be smart."

"I think I have a fever."

"I'll leave this material on your desk," she said. "Then I'll come back for it."

"What's the point of that?"

"I expect you to read it in the meantime."

"How will you know if I do or not?"

"Really this is childish."

"I could fake it," he said.

"You've no reason to behave this way."

"Okay, I'll read it."

"We're professionals, after all."

"I'll read it right away."

"Please read it," she said.

"I will."

"Do you really have a temperature?"

"They're common for my age," he said. "Growing takes place with a fever."

"That's quite a stack of reading you've got before you. I'm afraid you have to put up with my handwriting. If your eyes get tired, close them.

As long as your eyes are closed, you might as well sit in front of the radiation lamp Lester Bolin brought on down. It compensates for lack of sunlight. You can borrow my goggles if you promise to return them."

"What does Lester Bolin want to be known as?"

"Mr. Bolin," she said.

Once she'd been a character in a novel. How distressingly strange it was. The woman in the book wasn't like her at all, at all. Yet she'd recognized herself immediately. Such essential differences. The name he'd given her. Impossible to think of herself with a name like that. The one word of dialogue he'd written. Nothing at all like something she might say. But she'd seen herself at once. Jean Sweet Venable. The mind of the character was completely unlike her own. The clothing. The body. The mannerisms. A carefully wrought set of individual mannerisms. Carefully. Wrought. But they weren't hers, you know? No resemblance whatever. Still, she'd seen herself at once despite the differing circumstances, setting, dialogue, mind, body, clothing and mannerisms. What was it he'd done to bring her face to face with this representation she tried so forcefully to deny? How did he manage it? Son of a bitch. What did he know? Nothing more than anyone could learn by sleeping with someone. My star-shaped mole. That was the only thing she'd recognized as being literally hers. The character sat in cafeterias. The character was disheveled. She sat at tables still wet, bearing the elliptical traces of a washcloth. People talked to themselves. They pushed food into their mouths with their hands, pecking at their own fingers, never less than watchful of the possibilities of theft and death, poised cunningly over free glasses of water. They all carried shopping bags. The character was surrounded in her cafeterias by men and women with shopping bags and none of them shoppers, none at all, not one. It said so in the book. Collectors. Epicures of refuse. People tired and hungry after days of poking through trash cans. Collectors (talking to themselves, force-feeding) of bottles, cartons, bags, paper cups and other terminal necessities. Those without empty dented milk cartons will learn how foolish they've been when the time comes. Emblematic birthmark on the buttock. This was the only thing, superficial or otherwise, he'd used as perceived. This and her inclination to predict. Jean loved to make predictions. On marriages, divorces, breakdowns, booms and crashes. It was not these similarities, however, but other things, merely superficial in the book and resembling nothing she'd ever said, done, thought about or looked like, these other things, it was these that impressed on Jean a sense of resemblance between her and the character based on her. How painfully strange it was, searching the pages for signs of her own persona. Surfaces, guise and conscious intentions. The kingship of printed fiction. Its arbitrary power. Its capacity to gain possession of a person or thing by ineradicable prior right. The character had fainting spells. The character sometimes sat all night in doorways. The character's underwear stank. The character was never far from the presence of ugliness, the physically ugly, from the plane of misshapenness. She, Jean, carried air-mail stamps in her handbag. She had a shoetree for every shoe. What did he know? How much and how? Son of a bitch bastard.

Softly pushing in and out.

Defenseless love is suicide. Under that open sky nothing falling survives the rigors of identification. Where once men and women sought communion in sexual love, innocent of the need for programmatic valuation, they now deploy themselves across a level of existence composed of silences and daunted withdrawals. The theme of modern love is isolation. No longer is the lover prepared to experience sentimental pain, that traditional embellishment that gives desire a degree of symmetry. We did not fall into the trap of matter in order to be redeemed by love and thrust upward into the world of pure form. Clearly we did not, she thought. No longer can lovers regard sex as the mysterious chrism of their life together, as nature partaken, the rayed balsamic flowers worn by a woodland god. Sex is painted on the very walls, spread on white bread. Lovers, then, once their secret language has been despoiled by synthetic exchange, are forced to disengage their love from biology and keep it in seclusion. What replaces erotic language? Oral sex, she answered brightly. Tongues wagging in appointed crannies. Lap, pal, left to right. Unsuspecting mouth devoured by the genitals to which it presumes to communicate its moist favors. Defenses must be built to save the lovers from what unfolds around them and then again within their love itself to shelter each from the other's patent treachery. What is defenseless love but an invitation to nipple-pricking pain? Knowing the rules, we all shout at the jumper to jump. On the other hand, she thought, love does not speak to theorists.

"Evil pelvis," Softly said. "Unscrupulously seductive mouth. Belly a bowl of fruit. Labyrinthine navel. Resilient milky thighs. Cute pudendum, hee hee. Lickable armpits. Predatory eyes. Surging breasts. Hair rare. Smile terribly foudroyant. Backside a-twinkle."

Maurice Wu unencumbered by equipment and heavy clothing crossed the path to cube one. He was still a fairly young man, slender, appearing cheerfully relentless atop a long informal stride.

"Unfunny, ass, and totally inaccurate needless to say."

"Call me names and see how far you get."

"I want to see Edna next."

"Next we do this."

"We just did that."

"We do it again."

"I'll settle for Lester."

"How lucky for me to be so crudely unattractive. What tinctures of wetness it loosens from your innermost loam."

"God how horrible."

"Admit it, bitch; my titmanesque frame, my gross and pettish mouth, collapsing jaw, unnatural skin pigment, my eye color; admit the jingle you feel. I kiss my own thumb every day on waking. Think what little chance I'd have as an idealized Hollywood dwarf. Get used to my lewds and moods, sweet Jean, foul runt and lecher that I am, because I control the flow of material and nothing of note gets said to the likes of a keen journalist like yourself without my considered okay."

"You don't have baggy flesh," she said. "It's baggy flesh I count on for my cheapest thrills."

"You think this is a lark, don't you?"

"You're firm, Rob. I give you credit, your age."

"You think you walk in here and just talk to some people and organize some notes and there it is, the whole story, all ready for the bookbinder's tools."

312

Bolin and Lown left their cubicles.

"This area of the world is rich in caves," Wu said. "Up on the slopes there are openings, if you look closely enough. Some of the caves they lead to are first-rate. Tons of guano. Just a question of burrowing under."

"You go in it and look?"

"Countless decades of accumulated bat shit."

"What do you find underneath?"

"In this particular excavation, nothing that goes back very far. Pottery and bones mostly. I've found stuff in other places that goes back so far your flesh would crawl."

"Fifteen centuries."

"Don't make me laugh," Wu said.

Bolin put the pot on, nodding to Softly as he passed. In the boy's cubicle Maurice Wu stood leaning with his elbow up high against the partition, hand on head.

"Understand you're running a fever, Willy."

"Hello, Rob," Wu said.

"Hello, Maury. Hi, Willy. Understand you're running a fever."

"It's not much."

"Starve it," Softly said.

"Okay."

"What do you think of Maurice?"

"I barely met him just now."

"What I value most about Maurice is this flair of his for syncretistic thinking. Sweet and sour pork. Diametrically opposed entities partaking of each other's flesh. It permeates all his thinking. The reconciliation of opposites. Childish and dumb but I love it. Did you read the notes Edna gave you?"

"It's like Weierstrass wanting to take things like continuity and limit and base them on the integers."

"I told you never mind that stuff, mister. Forget about historical figures. Pretend you never heard of those people, places and things. Besides it's not 'wire-strass.' Did you read the notes Edna gave you? Edna gave you notes to read."

313

I GET INTERVIEWED AGAIN

Bolin was intent on composing the whole of Logicon on his old portable typewriter. Why not? If he and Edna and the youngster were sufficiently stringent in their methods, a handful of symbols would suffice. That plus the alphabet. More than enough to work with, ideographically. This sort of notation would appear at times to resemble cartoon obscenities. Nevertheless the meanings and relationships concealed by ordinary language would stand out sharply. In normal times Lester lived with his wife in a converted barn. The horse stalls they'd turned into dinettes. The haymows were now sleeping lofts. They'd found a hand-cranked washing machine and made an end table out of it. Elevator descending. A plant stand was formerly a butter churn. They bought Tiffany glass for their spirit lamps. A Civil War whiskey barrel became a pre-Revolutionary soup tureen. Conclusions must follow necessarily. We must compel acceptance of conclusions.

"Did you know you'd get the prize?" Jean said.

"I had a hunch."

"Where were you when you heard the news?"

"At Rob's house."

"Give me more."

"I was sitting in a chair. He came in and told me. Then we shook hands."

"That's not too terribly interesting," Jean said. "Give me something better."

"That's what happened."

"I want better than that. You have to give me better."

"How come you keep riding back and forth? Why don't you just stay down here?"

"I'm not allowed," she said. "The logic-mongers might object. Come on, slyboots, give me some more."

"Rob said I wouldn't have to make a speech. Then he did this trick he does with turning his jacket inside out without taking it off. That's all that happened."

314

"I understand whenever Rob lectures at the Center, the place swarms with mathematics groupies."

"Who do you want to know about, me or him?"

"You're not giving me anything to pounce on. You were a better subject last time."

"Talk about pouncing, better not bring your husband around if you have one. Rob doesn't care what he says in front of husbands."

"Our marriage failed for lack of fun," she said. "Fun is the only way to survive. A marriage is doomed without it. Think of all the time you have to spend alone, the pair of you. You have to renew, renew, renew. It's time that wrecks marriages, obviously. For a long while we managed well. This is because we made sure we had fun. We played tricks on each other. We stuck out our tongues. We called each other on the phone and used funny voices. These weren't necessarily impulsive acts. Often there was a great deal of premeditation involved. We thought it was essential to do these things and so we worked at it, we worked at it very hard, so very hard. And it was successful for the longest time."

"But then you ran into trouble."

"We used to scare each other a lot," Jean said. "Of all the kinds of fun, this was probably the one that worked best. Jumping out of doorways at each other. Pretending to be dead. Screaming into the telephone. I loved pretending to be dead. I was terrifically good at it. He was never completely sure it was just fun. There was always an element of doubt in his mind. When he'd lean over me for a really close look, I'd jump up screaming. That would keep our marriage going for another week."

"I'm surprised it wasn't longer."

"I know it sounds foolish. Between us, we totaled I don't know how many years of very expensive higher education. Still, we felt we had to do these things to keep from going stale, you know? One morning he got up and left as usual. He always left before I did. I can barely remember his face but I know he left early, he liked to leave early, he liked to be the first one in the building to hit the streets. That was the day I realized we'd had no fun in a long time and I knew at once this was the reason we hadn't been getting along. I made it a point to get home first that

315

evening. Emptied a large bottle of aspirin. Hid the tablets. Put the bottle next to the bed. Got into the bed—torso nudo for documentary shock effect. I sprawled and waited, trying to look puffy. But he never came home. That was the day he'd decided to leave for good."

"Sure it wasn't sex that caused the trouble? Maybe you just never brought it out in the open."

"Sex was fine," she said. "It wasn't sex at all. Sex was the least and best of our worries."

"How many times a night?"

In the kitchen unit they worked and talked. Cigarette ash was scattered over Lown's blouse. She slipped her feet out of the desert boots and discussed Lester Bolin's latest work on notation, which she considered far too cumbersome, overburdened with content. It was pleasant to sit with Rob and Lester, exchanging ideas and objections, seeking to extend the technical possibilities of their method by making it ever more reductive.

"It's like doubling to get half," she said. "A negative number doubled yields half the original value. A series of doubled reflections gets continually smaller by half. I don't think we'll be rewarded with a sense of genuine precision until we get as close as possible to a kind of beneficially corrective infinite regress. Lester, I think you'd profit immensely by clearing your work through our young man."

"I showed him some stuff very recently. He just walked out. It seemed to depress him. I'm anxious to work with him but he just isn't interested. I wonder if we really need him. Do we really need him?"

"I'm reminded of a family that lives across the road from me in Pennyfellow," Softly said. "Years ago they adopted a very small child, an Asian girl, orphaned by the bombing. In a matter of days she became the focus of that home as none of the natural children in the family ever did. This is because she possessed something unique. Moral authority. Time and again I heard one member of the family chide another for piggishness, insolence, bad grammar, always saying in effect: 'What will Phan think of us when she's old enough to understand?' Remarkable, the sheer authority of that small round object. Because she was tiny, virtually mute, because she was Asian, an orphan, a victim of war,

316

Phan was the ultimate moral force in that household, a living contradiction of nearly everything the family had once held to be eternal; that is, justice, truth, honor, so forth. Now I don't say my pal Willy is a moral force exactly. But I do believe his presence here has extramathematical significance. True, as Edna says, mathematical thinking is based on the whole numbers, Willy's specialty, and it's also true that his powers extend to related areas and that once he gets deeply involved in what we're doing here he'll probably put us all to shame, his mind working like a beam of light searching out a target. But Lester, when Lester asks whether we really need the boy, that's a valid point. After all, we're dealing with a form of mathematics that substitutes classes for numbers. This is what makes him reluctant to enter. He knows he may have trouble finding his way around. Nevertheless I maintain we absolutely need him. He's our living contradiction. His intransigence speaks against us. We need him to balance things. He's the listener, the person we need to judge what we do. This is the power of the young. They know what's right, if not what's left."

"It's unlike you to put things on a human level," Edna said.

"Does it erode my formal authority?"

"It's a pleasant change, truth be known."

"Jean Venable would like to spend some time with you and Lester. Journalist I told you about. Briefest of interviews. In and out. Give her a feel for the subject."

"Sorry," Edna said.

"Everything she writes crosses my desk."

"That's not the point."

"Lester-pet, what about you?"

"I don't think so, Rob, no. The last thing we need is that kind of distraction."

"I'm going back to work," Edna said.

"How's it coming?"

"Fair to good."

"The boy will respond," Softly said. "He's very young. These are strange circumstances. He'll come around. Wait and see."

Lacing her boots she thought how close they'd be coming in the final stages to the rudiments of primitive number systems. Repetition, order, interval. Lester's shoes were scuffed and battered and she could see them pressing into the earth, which was his way of thinking and working, a concentration downward. Softly's shoes were quite immaculate, set neatly parallel, almost touching, his feet swinging in little arcs several inches off the ground. She began to rise, cigarette in mouth, as Billy went through the handwritten notes she'd left him. The first phases of communication would center on the integers. The symbols that compose Logicon will eventually have to be recoded in the form of suitable radio signals. What we have then, he read, is English to Logicon to radio-pulse idiom or systematic frequency fluctuations. The statement "every number has a successor" becomes asterisk-N (or some such) in Logicon; this in turn, pending advice from the technical end, becomes something like pulse-pulse-gap, the point being that with a few key modifications, a juxtaposition here, a repetition there, we can establish a scheme of affirmation and negation, assent and denial, giving simple "lessons" in number and following up with some kind of basic information as to where we are in time and space. The most likely thing we'd have in common with the ARS extants is interest in numbers and in celestial events. Earth people, who differ widely (spoken and written languages, etc.), share use of the Hindu-Arabic number system. Also it's instructive to note that calendar-making is one of our earliest cognitive labors and evidence of interest in lunar cycles, eclipses, so on. Strange, she thought, how the integers, which are discrete, and our attempts to chart time, which is continuous, may well combine to give us a common area of reference with extraterrestrials. However, if she correctly interpreted the remarks on Moholean relativity made by Softly some time earlier, it was plain that we here on Earth do not know the location of the artificial radio source. So either we must figure it out or wait for them to tell us. In fact she didn't really care whether we ever replied to the original signal. She viewed the Logicon project as an intellectual challenge and nothing more. An advance in the art of mathematical logic. A breakthrough in economy and rigor. The transformation, in Softly's phrase, of all science, all language. She had no strong conviction that Logicon was essential to celestial communication. It would be, in her view, a breathtaking addition to the body of human knowledge, period. As far as she was concerned it might be easier to step directly from English to radio-pulse idiom without an intervening form of discourse, no matter how strictly logical. Her handwriting began to collapse and he read only one more section, this being Lown's estimate of how the expression "*a* plus *b* equals *c*" might actually be transmitted. There would be a pulse followed by a double time interval to indicate an operation pending, in this case addition, the plus sign itself signified by a particular kind of beep or dash. Repetition, order, interval, she thought, continuing to rise from the kitchen chair.

FEMALE HAIR DOWN THERE

He heard Lester Bolin begin the first snore cycle of this particular sleep period. His things, Billy's, were still divided between the footlocker and the suitcase and he didn't know and had no intention of finding out in which of these containers his pajamas were located. There was a single light in the antrum right now and it originated in the cubicle farthest from his, a periodic surge of candleflame, Softly's quarters, diagonally across the path. He heard a sound above the snoring, very faint at first, a gentle impact somewhere on the slopes, repeated more than once. He stepped out onto the path and immediately saw something come over the barrier and bounce several times, barely visible, its forward motion ending in the gravel and soft clay, the object spinning in place, a rubber ball, eating out a slot for itself, unmistakably a Spalding Hi Bouncer, still rotating as he walked toward it past Maurice Wu lodged in a sleeping bag in a corner of his cubicle, past Edna Lown motionless in her bed, past Lester Bolin asleep on his cot; a spaldeen, as it was commonly known, just an ordinary faded-pink rubber ball that had bounced down from the top of the excavation. He picked it up and turned toward the opening of Softly's cubicle, detecting motion in the shallow glow and knowing what it was before he actually sorted out the allusive shapes. Jean Sweet Venable was in bed with Rob, moving over and around him, uncomplexioned in the dimness, a fine-

319

grained and purposeful figure. Billy was stilled by the sight of her. The very notion of "female hair down there" had long been a source of contemplative ache and wonder; to see it, actually set eyes upon a woman's pubic hair, filled him with a stunned hush, a reverence for the folklore of the body. But what they were doing now, man and woman, had no connection to beliefs, legends or culture. It seemed to him that the sex act was something no one could make up in a story. He watched reluctantly, afraid they would perform some variation of the act, assume a position of such deft fury that he might once again grow feverish, his mind and body unequal to the burden of sexual possibility. That people might do nameless things to each other caused him some concern; he did not care to witness the unimaginable, particularly as it applied to crypts and fissures of the body. For the moment, at least, the lovers remained within the limits of his own borrowed knowledge. It was hard work, sex. Jean was breathing through her mouth, Rob through his nose. They seemed to be striving toward something that existed beyond a definitive edge. Her legs were ill-adapted to this event, too long, the sole flaw in the composite. Odd how the force of Softly's physical innocence produced abnormality from model proportion. Jean's breathing became more rapid and she began to speak as though in tongues. It was here that the lovemaking abandoned its industrious manner, its claim to uniformity and craft, and started to resemble an act of appalling power, an incoherent labor meant to be performed in the dark or near-dark. He was in awe of what they were doing because they themselves seemed driven to it and lost in it. Her head at a slant, her body moving loosely beneath the impetus of Softly's more systematic cadence, Jean continued to utter fabricated babble, terrible for Billy to hear because he did not associate it with intensely compiled delight but rather with an obliteration of self-control and the onset of an emotional state that bordered on prophetic frenzy. There was no sequential meaning to this, no real process of thought and repetition. The sex act did not have organized content. It was unrelated to past and future time. It was essentially unteachable. It did not represent anything or lead necessarily to a conclusion, a sum, a recognition that someone or something has been part of a structured event.

No one could have made this up if it hadn't actually been known to occur, whatever it was, whatever the body's need for this brief laboring void. He began to back away now, Jean's voice winding down, Softly thinking:

> Olleke bolleke
> Rubisolleke
> Olleke bolleke
> Knull

Back in cube one he tossed the ball into the open suitcase and sat in the chair. Bolin had stopped snoring and stared into the darkness directly above. He and his wife were the kind of people other people liked to describe as being devoted to each other. But he rarely thought of her now. She was in the converted barn and he was in the antrum.

"Say something."

"I thought you wanted me to shut up," Jean said.

"Then shut up."

Maurice Wu slowly dressed, thinking of the slopes, the bat caves set within the slopes, the guano fields spread across the bat caves. He hummed a smudge of breath on each lens of his spectacles, then wiped the glasses on his shirttail before slipping them on. Man more advanced the deeper we dig. This revolutionary thesis was beginning to develop urgency. He'd seen evidence of it in the field over the past several months —elaborately notated bone objects, increased cranial capacity. But the notion itself—that at a certain layer of soil the signs of man's increasing primitivism cease abruptly, to be replaced by a totally converse series of findings—this idea had been too radical to take firm hold in his mind until recently, when, in Softly's presence, he'd felt the first trifling stir of implication. Wu had assumed the entire series of layers had been disarranged by haphazard burial practices or some kind of earth spasm in the area of the dig. He realized, however, that the findings showed far too much consistency and sense of progression (however negative) to be explained away in this fashion. The indications were in the field. Man's mental development shows signs of surging upward as we dig past a certain point and continue down. Layer by layer there is evidence of greater complexity. Working in the area of the Sangkan Ho strata, he and his colleagues had traveled farther back in "primatal time" than anyone before them, a fact confirmed by potassium-argon dating. Eventually they'd come upon the partial skull of an adult hominid of small brain capacity and only the most elemental toolmaking skills. Considering what they'd previously found, the appearance of these remains was not surprising. But several feet deeper, and about half a million years earlier, were decorative tusk fragments. Below these were signs of fire maintenance, signs of complex tool types and weapons, signs of pottery making, signs of elaborate costumes. Below these was clear evidence of a culture versed in seasonal processes and number thinking. There were tools that bore lunar notations—systematic chartings of the phases of the moon. There were bone objects engraved with planetary observations. There were limestone slates that carried records of pregnancy and birth. All these patterns had been verified in the laboratory through microscopic analysis, the markings clearly indicative of a culture that perceived the notion of time itself as a nonrandom process that enabled humans to reckon their acts and conduct their lives against a fairly predictable setting of climate, geography and celestial event. Deeper, there were clay huts and drainage systems and below this was a flat stone that could not be clearly analyzed as decorative or notational; it was marked with a quartz engraving tip as follows:

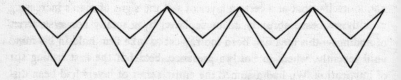

Bats in flight, Wu concluded, pleased that the engraving suggested his avocation. Then it occurred to him that he might be holding the stone upside down. It was at this point that he was lured from the site by Softly's abrupt summons, later to be informed by colleagues that below the stone they'd found skull fragments, vertebral and pelvic components, hand and foot bones, teeth and an upper jaw—all of which pointed to a male "hominid" who not only had a brain capacity equivalent to modern man's but also (judging by his noncranial parts) resembled us in body size, manual dexterity, posture, locomotion and even the way he chewed his food. So it was that Wu speculated as he crossed the path to Billy's cubicle: what would the remaining levels reveal: bronze, iron, plastic, neoplastic? He entered striding.

"Tell me about mathematics."

"What's to tell?"

"I understand it's a crazy way to live."

"What are you doing here anyway?"

"Visiting," Wu said. "Saying hello."

"I mean here in the antrum. Rob has us here for different reasons for each person. What's your reason?"

"He hasn't told me."

"Why not?"

"I don't know."

"How will you find out?"

"He told me to ask Mainwaring when Mainwaring gets here. But he hinted Mainwaring wouldn't tell me either. Wouldn't or couldn't. I don't mind waiting. I like it here. I go artifacting and study the bats. Hobby of mine for years."

"What do you learn from bats?"

"Bat lore."

"Give an example."

"Depending on the hemisphere, bats fly out of caves in leftward-tending spirals or rightward-tending spirals. Taking the globe as a whole, we see that bilateral symmetry is preserved."

"Where did you meet Rob?"

"The Chinese-American Science Sodality. A few years ago."

"What was he doing there?"

"Rob has a deep interest in things Chinese. He was born in China. Did you know that?"

"He never told me about an event like that."

323

"In fact his physical condition is a result of something called Chinese gnome disease. This is a crippling illness that was prevalent in a particular area of China for an entire millennium. It attacks the bones and muscles, preventing normal growth in children and reducing adults to a gnomelike state. It wasn't until recently that the cause was found. A lack of certain minerals in the water."

"He never told me that."

"Maybe because you're not Chinese," Wu said. "I'm Chinese."

"What's your field?"

"Prehistory."

"How far back?"

"Practically out the other end."

"Are bats known to be dangerous?"

"Just the opposite," Wu said. "We should do everything we can to see they survive and prosper. This is because their waste material is useful as fertilizer. Maybe you don't know it but the economies of entire countries are based on the export and domestic use of bird droppings. Skirmishes have already taken place between neighboring countries disputing the ownership of coastal islands where millions of sea birds do their shitting. Bats are next. The commercial market for bat guano is already growing. It won't be long, people being what they are, before some individual or group tries to get a monopoly. Of course, going back to your question, you don't want to get bitten by a bat with rabies. If you don't have the antibodies you'll get infected, which means you acquire the consciousness of the animal in question and become antagonistic to water. Crazed bat consciousness. I think about it from time to time when I'm crawling through a bat cave."

Before leaving, Wu reached in his pocket and took out a crumpled letter, saying someone had evidently left it in his cubicle by mistake.

Man, woman or child:

You have been nominated to be part of our chain. The document you are reading, rest assured, is not an ordinary chain letter. It is unconditionally guaranteed to be effective, having been devised and mailed with the help of computer time-sharing techniques of unprecedented scope and accuracy.

324

Our mailing list is brutally selective. Only the world's leading intellectuals are part of our chain. These are men and women whose work has been accepted for publication in those leading journals of opinion whose lists of subscribers and contributors are readily available in return for cash considerations.

We have been commissioned by a vast research organization to undertake this project. In the past we did purely abstract work in the area of the world-market money curve. Since moving our operation beyond the legal maritime limit, we have broadened our scope to include actual cash transactions. It is our current conviction that the idea of money must yield eventually to money itself. Money facilitates the exchange of goods and services and is of vital importance to central planners who wish to gain control of specific world-market commodities most in demand at present and likely to continue as such.

Now that you know us better, our immediate concern is that you maintain the chain. This letter has traveled around the world sixteen times. No one has broken the chain. Most chain letters continue to circulate due to the age-old force of superstition. We expect more of the members of our chain. To break the chain is to disrupt nothing less than a mass speculation on the will to exist. We count on your cooperation in this matter.

By now a question has probably occurred to you: "What do I get for maintaining the chain?" There is no simple answer to this question. It would be easy for us to say: "In a matter of days you will receive something wonderful in the mail." We make no such claim, however. The chain is its own justification and reward. The terms of our contract clearly specify that we say no more on the matter.

To maintain the chain, you must draw a straight line through your name where it appears below. Then you must mail this letter to the person whose name has been placed directly below your own:

Chester Greylag Dent

This letter has been in circulation for years and years. Don't be the one who breaks the chain!

Billy noticed the raised seal of a notary public in a lower corner of the page. Below the seal, in diminutive italic type, were the words: *Central American Intercorporate Control Combine (formerly Consortium Hondurium), Elux Troxl, prop.*

325

INTERVIEW

"Who are some of the influences on your work?"

"Softly."

"In what way?" Jean said.

"He shows me how to use what I have. He was a pretty good mathematician himself. He knows how to bring me out."

"Rob's a living influence. What about people long ago? Old masters. The titans."

"Rob explains their work to me. He takes me through it step by step."

"What about Sylvester and Cayley?" she said. "Strong influences? Mild influences? In betweens?"

"Not too many people know about most mathematicians, no matter which century they belong to. How do you know about them?"

"Research."

"I don't see what they have to do with a book on the Logicon project."

"The more I research mathematicians, the more I know about you," Jean said. "I want to know all I can about all the people here. I can't achieve any depth unless I do that. That's why I ask about influences. Was it Sylvester or Cayley who said the best inventions of analysis result from our probings of the continuous as it exists in our own perception of space? Direction. In mathematics, don't you try to build a sense of direction into ideas like space, time and motion? Make it a game, isn't that it, with specific rules that govern every operation."

"We're not allowed to talk about this," he said.

"What do you mean?"

"Rob doesn't allow it. He said to skip people in history. He wants me to concentrate on Logicon."

"Is this a formal ban?"

"I'm only telling you what he said."

"We can say what we want, pigsney. Don't let Rob talk you out of anything."

"Would you be interested in some special material for your notes?" he said.

"Absolutely."

"I have a hunch I'm going to die soon."

"More," she said. "More like that. Give me everything you've got."

Not what something really is, Softly thought, but how we think of it. Our struggle to apprehend it. Our need to unify and explain it. Our attempt to peel back experience and reveal the meaning beneath. The task is to attempt a logical design that may or may not duplicate the structure of the thing itself. His desk, unlike the others in the antrum, thrown together and wobbly, was an elaborate sectional apparatus with automatic drawers, a pop-up typewriter, modular shelving and a built-in pencil sharpener that operated on batteries. The desk ran parallel to all but one side of the cubicle, where the entrance was located. The cubicle itself was considerably larger than the other living units, hardly suited to the word "cubicle" in fact. The bed, adorned with huge silk pillows, had little in common with the cots elsewhere in the area. Sweating excessively Softly undid the belts on his leather briefcase, lifted the worn flap and began sifting among bottles, tubes and packets of stimulants, relaxants, euphoriants, deliriants, sedative-hypnotics, local anesthetics and animal tranquilizers. Among the collection a sample-sized bottle made him smile, containing as it did the high-grade synthetic intensifier he'd given Maurice Wu to chew soon after the latter had first arrived in the antrum. The label included a warning: *Insightful experiences may intensify existing psychosis.* Far from showing panic reaction, however, Wu had emerged from a period of chills, irregular breathing and slurred speech with a tentative and rather engaging idea about counter-evolution. Softly found what he wanted now. He lifted out a vial, twisted off the cap, removed the cotton packing and shook a capsule into his hand. He swallowed it without water and then got into bed, wearing socks, slippers and his robe. He became drowsy almost at once. His perspiration smelled less tense and septic. Another ephemeral chemical event, he thought. Opiate receptors functioning nicely. Sense data less demanding. He stuck his thumb in his mouth, thinking suddenly of the peculiar demonic genius of street games, the secret vernacular

327

passed down for centuries, the sense in so many games of something fearful transmitted through certain words or the wile of simple touch. He began to vomit calmly. Tag—you're *it*. What was *it* but something or someone too evil to be named? Hoodman blind. Hango seek. Skin the cuddy. He raised his head from vomiting position, eyes closed (to avoid seeing the ejected matter), and then leaned back on one of the pillows and thought of the game he and the boy had more or less jointly invented, halfball, a "meaningless formal game" designed to be played almost anywhere—street, pasture, alleyway, an empty green in summer's murmuring dusk. Elements of rounders, baseball, tag, cricket, one o' cat, stickball and children's verse. The task is to work out an abstract scheme which may or may not reflect the composition of the thing itself. Convenient fictions, he thought. Děń sə-tē, he thought. Water flowing along a gutter on a city street. A figure trying to hail a cab. Umbrella and suitcase. This was Mainwaring, a well-barbered man of middle age—tall, ruddy, fit and trim, emitting an executive scent. He knew the large puddle beyond the curb was an invitation to cab drivers to veer this way and splatter his clothes but he wasn't worried, being certain he could step aside in time and seeing the entire process (from the driver's viewpoint) as an exercise in perceiving functional relations between entities (puddle, figure, vehicle). It was his conviction that taxi drivers are no more than theoreticians of massive insult, delighted by the *prospect* of splattering or maiming, having no inherent need to think beyond relationships to the literal disfigurement of objects or people. The truly brutal ones were bus drivers. Give a bus driver a nearly empty bus during an off-hour with no one waiting at the designated stops and he'll go smashing down the avenue, pupils dilated, a convulsive hum bubbling up from his throat, Softly opening his eyes, the great painted van careening down on stray dogs, derelicts, children, an interior point system in effect. He dipped the umbrella and a cab stopped just short of the puddle.

"The international airport," Mainwaring said.

"Right or left side of the street."

"Either, I suppose."

"Near corner or far?"

Edna Lown's spectacularly archaic undies were hanging up to dry. Nearby, working, was the woman herself. This happiness puzzled her. Every symbol she wrote in her notebook seemed to possess the resolve of a finished work, an isolated operation neatly free of assumption and shaved of the danger of intuitive reckoning. This work was all there was. Her life had been reduced to a process of selection and refinement. This was merciful, she believed, considering the atmosphere of horror that so often prevailed in the world outside. Nothing in her work was accidental. This is the single theme variously affirmed, tested and modified. She realized she hadn't seen her own face since taking the ramshackle elevator down. The past, the whole chromium world, none of it was more than meek recollection, the negative image of colleagues, family and friends; of university towns, fellowships and travels; of visits to suburban Bellevue. It was puzzling, this happiness she felt, an extended measurement of the textures we're able to achieve beyond the sum total of events that compose our lives. In this hole in the ground Edna knew she lacked nothing, wanted nothing, could easily dismiss all past associations and all prior honors. She lived in the grip of scientific rapture. The complicated longings of the woman who had made her way in the world (through the force of intellect alone) were so subordinate now as to be nearly nonexistent. Ambition, love, friendship, the pleasures of giving and of winning away, the comfort of professional acceptance, the soul's snug glow at the failure of others—all those fitful inclinations, those urgencies and yearnings were so much dead air compared with this simple and total absorption, *holism*, a state of unqualified being. Edna Lown was entering herself just as surely as if she'd been able to bend her arms into her mouth and swallow them to the shoulders; arms, legs, torso; a bewitchingly comic meditation technique; leaving the head balanced on a cushion, head and skull, abode of the layered brain, everything we are and feel and know; the universe we've made.

The small craft began its vertical descent. Despite the many hours of travel, the plane-changing, the time zones, Mainwaring remained fresh, his hair brushed straight back, faintly gray in places, his jaw seemingly locked into position with cotter pins. Across the aircraft's fuselage was the inscription: OmCopter SkyHop. The entire journey had been made at night. Different parts of different hemispheric nights. One long night.

Edna's wet underwear dripped onto a stack of papers she had set on the ground. She read the previous session's notes. These were notes essentially for her own nonspecific use, not the kind of background material she'd given the boy to read and not more immediate work directly applicable to the Logicon project. She'd been jotting down these particular notes and others like them for a number of years, simply to order her thinking, to clarify certain general areas she believed worthy of investigation. It is both silly and useful, she thought, feeling completely relaxed now, very ready, working well ahead of the pencil.

    f. It is both silly and useful to conclude that human speech derived from the cries of animals.

    g. As conjectured, it was specifically the mating calls of animals that directed early men and women toward their own variety of speech. Language thus became a communication associated with sexual activity. This connection imparted to language an erotically powerful duplicating property.

    h. I'm tempted to say: it also made talking fun. Words became a playful analog of sexual activity.

    i. All language is innuendo.

    j. We imagine the (primitive) child learning to speak in the arms of its mother. Here we have the essence of play. Mother and child. Language and sexuality.

    k. Thus language, classed by gender, is undoubtedly female.

Jean Venable sat in her room high above the antrum. Her notes were all over the floor, unreadable, and there were packets of research material stacked under the bed, unread. She was beginning to think Softly had been right when he'd accused her of viewing the whole thing as a lark. If she were to make a prediction she would predict that she was on the verge of something strange. A decision about her book. What it should and shouldn't be. "Strange" in the sense of previously unknown; in the sense of unfamiliar; in the archaic sense of alien or foreign. What kind of rotgut prose would she write about a project she hadn't really been interested in since the very beginning? What was she here for if not to test herself against the dangers of true belief? What good was solitude to a writer if it didn't lead her into something deeper in the way of living and thinking? The fact that she was having nearly continuous sex with a child-sized man seemed to confirm (in an inexplicit way) that she was ready to take a nervous little step into the coiled room she'd seen from time to time mingled with the reflections in a train's dusty windows or in the glass halves of a tenement's outer doors. Sex with Rob was very much a part of the isolation she'd been submerged in since coming here. Not that she didn't enjoy it on "a purely physical level." Softly was an antidote to fantasy. His very dimensions mocked those drowsy episodes she used to devise apart from reality. What were these mental images but fairytales for adults, whimsical tintypes that did little more than confirm the childish appeal of illogical relations (maidens, amphibians etc.)? From her reaction to the bluntness of Rob's marred body, his special unalterability, the abrupt initiatives of his sexual nature, she readily inferred that fantasy, her own, had reached its vanishing point, an event that returned sex to those locations she felt it had long abandoned, between the actual legs, in and around the actual mouth, on the breasts and under the testicles and in the hands, on the tongue, in the actual hole. Together they filled a natural space. There was a real feeling of bodies giving out, signs of rashes, skin burns, bruises and teeth marks, her mind distantly aware of chancing the wastes of nonentity, a prospect that forced her to speak her physical involvement, to pant out sounds against this break in the continuity. Funny how she and Rob avoided every preliminary gesture, even a hint of a kiss or nonfunctional caress. Kissing him would have disgusted her. It was his organ of copulation her body craved, the Latinate folds between her legs that stirred him to ithyphallic meter. Funny all right. It made her laugh at past loves, at the banality of the past itself.

1. In no time at all we enter the cloud of modern thought. Here the limits of childhood involve the shattering of perspective. This could just as easily be called the formation of perspective.

m. Growing, the child perceives a difference between itself and its class. The child's mother is no longer the sole teacher of "words." The erotic content of language begins to dissolve.

n. The "truth" about language is not available to us. Only play-talk, the lost form of knowledge, can express what is otherwise unspeakable. Is there a connection between these sentences?

o. Play-talk is the natural mode of brute locution. It alone is free of disguise and ambiguity.

p. What do we mean when we say that the function of a logically perfect language is to set severe limits? It's possible we have things backwards. We should ask ourselves whether we are correct in establishing more boundaries or in completely destroying what now stands.

q. Great scientists never fear being slightly wrong; their errors, if such, are total.

r. I'm tempted to say: to pass beyond words as we know them is "to mate."

s. The secret task of logic may be the rediscovery of play.

Charming, Edna thought, perhaps a bit wearily, hearing Softly's peculiar footfalls as he went past her cubicle, picturing him in a suit, vest and dark tie, those resplendent little shoes, all of which he was in fact wearing as he made his way to cube one, where Billy was found to be in bed, hands clasped on his head, knees upraised, a general sense of adolescent languor in the air.

ROB TALKS IN QUOTES

"Where's the ball?" Softly said. "I'm in the mood for some exercise. Some distraction. We all need a little distraction."

"What ball?"

"Didn't I see you pick up a rubber ball recently?"

"A rubber ball," the boy said. "I brought it in here, I think."

"Get it out and cut it in half."

"What for in half?"

"You really are socked in, aren't you?"

"Halfball, is that it? You want to have a game of halfball."

"About time," Softly said.

"I don't want to play."

"You love halfball."

"Not in the mood, that's all."

"It's your game," Softly said. "Yours and mine. Get the ball, cut it in half and let's go play. Maurice cleared away an area just beyond the crates. He's cutting down a mop handle now. Jean's going to play too. You like Jean. You and Jean get along. I've taught them the rules. Edna and Les will watch. It's more fun with spectators."

"I thought the fun was over."

"You need a fresh dose."

"Maybe I'll feel like playing later on."

"Wee Willy, hit 'em where they ain't."

"I want to either stay right here in this dirt room or get completely out of the whole place."

"Look, we'll go out on the 'field,' loosen up a bit, play one game of halfball and then you can come back here and 'rest.' Halfball is a beautiful game. You love halfball. It's exactly what you 'need,' some 'exercise,' a period of 'distraction.' So what do you say, hey?"

"I want to stay here."

"Why the sudden obsession with immobility?" Softly said. "What kind of dopey routine is this? Some kind of mystic trance you're falling into?"

"No."

"Because if it is, you know what I have to say to you."

"I know."

"Musjid pepsi kakapo."

"What else?"

"Huwawa djinn."

Billy had always enjoyed the unfamiliar word clusters that Softly used to counteract serious remarks about religion, the supernatural or the fuzzier edges of quantum physics. What he didn't like was his mentor's very occasional tactic of pronouncing certain words as though they warranted quotation marks. The practice seemed to have a source deeper than mere sarcasm. Softly sometimes employed this vocal rebuke, if that's what it was, in circumstances that appeared to be completely unsuitable. He would refer to a table, for instance, as a "table." What sort of inner significance was intended in such a case? It was one thing for Softly to use a sprinkle of emphasis when speaking of someone's "need" for "rest." But when he put quotes around words for commonplace objects, the effect was unsettling. He wasn't simply isolating an object from its name; he seemed to be trying to empty an entire system of meaning.

"If you're not ready to play, are you ready to work?"

"Definitely."

"You'll do whatever Edna and Lester ask?"

"Yes."

"See, I told them you'd come around. And I haven't even had to get mean. My displays of adultism are minor legends wherever children congregate."

"Do I have to play halfball?"

"No," Softly said. "Just give me the rubber ball and I'll have Maury cut it in half."

The game was played on the negative curvature of the small clearing. Softly removed his jacket and tossed it to Lester Bolin, who sat with Edna on a crate. The fey spectacle about to unfold brought to Edna's face a look of delighted expectation laboring to hide the strain that went into its manufacture, as though she were attending a garden party for the criminally insane. Wu cut along the seam of the rubber ball with his penknife, then pocketed one half of the ball and gave the other half to Softly, who began to warm up, being the bunger, or thrower. Jean had a lot of trouble holding on to his deliveries. The ball behaved erratically once or twice (when Softly tossed it end over end) but very smoothly at other times (when he gripped it along the edge and hurled it in a sidearm motion straight in or went three quarters to fashion gracefully breaking slow curves). Wu stood off to the side taking lazy stylized practice cuts with the sawed-off mop handle. The field was marked with rocks and cans set apart from each other in complex patterns. When everyone was finished warming up, Softly addressed the spectators.

"Strict rules add dignity to a game. At specified points in the contest, certain verses have to be recited, certain moves and countermoves have to be made. There are no bases, as in baseball. There is no wicket, as in cricket. However, there are runs, hits, errors and breaks for tea. In halfball, errors count in the errormaker's favor. Imagine a scoreboard if you will. Runs, hits, errors. The final result depends on all of these, not just runs. It is the total array of digits that determines the winner. If a player keeps making errors, he adds to his sum. Once his errors get into double figures, the total spills over to the run column. Therefore, you say, it is necessary only to make error after error in order to win. Not so, I reply. For while one player is making errors, his adversary is scoring runs. The errormaker must balance the gains he is making in his error column against the gains he is allowing the other player to make in the run column. I am the bunger. Jeanie is the munch. Maury is the doggero. Normally we'd have a lippit as well but I think we can do without. As the game progresses, we switch positions. The objects scattered on the ground are either skullies or wacks, depending on the situation. The purpose of each will become clear as we go along. Please don't leave until we're ready for tea break. It annoys me no end when people leave before tea break."

Softly, a lefthander, threw some billowing curves to Wu, keeping the ball down and in, mixing in an occasional flutter pitch that he kept hauntingly outside, presumably away from the doggero's power. Finally Wu managed to hit the ball—a weak grounder that spun and wobbled in circles of ever decreasing limits. At this stage the munch and doggero addressed each other.

"What's your trade?"

"Lemonade."

"Where do you ply it?"

"Where we dry it."

"Dry what?"

"Apricot."

I MEET MAINWARING

From his bed, hearing the voices, Billy tried to remember how old he was when they'd invented the game, realizing for the first time that he'd actually had little to do with any of it, that it was almost all Softly's—the rules, the verse, the reliance on connective patterns. His hands were still clasped on his head. He moved them forward and back, the top of his head shifting with the movement. He liked that feeling. After a while he thought of a scantily clad woman with enormous breasts bazooms boobs titties. She was "scantily clad" only in the sense that he told himself such a condition prevailed; the fact was he couldn't quite picture the flimsy items she was supposed to be wearing. He tried to include himself—that is, an image of himself—in the painted haze. For some reason it was extremely difficult. He didn't really care that much. As long as they let him stay where he was. As long as they didn't force him to be logical. He heard someone moving in the cubicle next to his and went to see who it was. The man unpacking introduced himself as Walter Mainwaring, Cosmic Techniques Redevelopment Corporation.

"We both have something in common."

"The Nobel Prize," Mainwaring said.

"Right."

"My father was a mathematician. Didn't give me a middle name. Just an initial. X. Idea of a joke, I suppose."

"What are you here for?"

"Rob is eager to know more about sylphing compounds. I'm not sure how he plans to apply this knowledge but I'll be happy to tell him what I can. My latest work involves aspects of mohole identification. Know what that is?"

"No but it sounds funny."

"Things are funny up to a point," Mainwaring said. "Then they aren't funny anymore. Alternate question. Do you know anything about Moholean relativity?"

"I know Mohole the person."

"Mohole's work happens to tie in with sylphing. What this all leads to remains to be seen."

"He wears padded shoulders and swallows greenies."

"I gather Rob's assembling a team. Good. I like teamwork. I believe in teams."

DOGGERO and MUNCH: "Bunger, bunger, let us go forth; the sun, the sun is shining."

BUNGER: "Fall down a well and never tell and I'll let you be born in the morning."

The boy returned to his cubicle and got into bed. Eventually he heard Softly announce the tea break. There was a minor landslide on the north slope. Jean Venable and Maurice Wu remained in the playing area while the others went to the kitchen unit for tea.

"Full name please."

"Maurice Xavier Wu."

"Where did you get the Xavier?"

"My father was a missionary," he said.

"Where?"

"U.S. of A."

"Did you grow up there?"

"Off and on."

"Did you date American girls?"

"Did I date American girls?" he said. "What kind of book are you writing?"

"I try to ask whatever comes into my head," Jean said. "It's a new technique I've been developing. But I think I may abandon it. Nothing but junky things have been coming into my head. Everything's up in the air right now. Don't tell Rob I said that. I'm sort of going through the motions, frankly. But keep it to yourself."

"Maybe we should do this another time," Wu said. "I'm preparing a journey up the slopes. Some caves here and there I'd like to look into. I have to get some supplies together. Then I have to polish my *wu-fu*."

"Let me ask this one thing," Jean said. "What's your role in the Logicon project?"

"You're not taking notes, I see."

"I'm not taking notes. You're right, aren't you?"

"Maybe by the time I'm back down here, Rob will have some firm plans for me. Don't know yet exactly what's on his mind. In the meantime I'm having a good time seeing the caves."

"What's a *wu-fu*?"

"It's a medallion I wear around my neck whenever I go into the field. It's a circular thing that has a cluster of bats set into it. Bats with their wings extended. The bats themselves form a sort of circle around a symbol of the tree of life. The Chinese are probably the only people who think of bats in connection with good luck and a long life. Anyway, before I go into the field I like to sit on a mat and polish my *wu-fu* for exactly seventeen minutes."

"What does that do?"

"Nothing," he said.

"I think I understand."

Jean feared dishevelment. The silken puckers above her shirt cuff. The winning fit of her handsomely tailored pants. It was no joke to imagine what her life would be like without a firm commitment to utter presentableness. She'd been thinking a great deal about dishevelment lately. Increasingly she wondered, thinking of images in the glass halves of tenement doors, in the jigsaw spill of silver that had always seemed to crunch beneath her shoes in the worst parts of town. With each new cycle of wondering came the fear experience, a sensation she tended to characterize not just as fear but as "fear itself." This was the comic element at work. An attempt to overdramatize for comic effect. Jean had always thought of herself as too modern and complex to experience the kind of primal fear that would qualify as "fear itself." She found it difficult to appear pestered much less frightened. The soundly proportioned near neutrality of her figure, her looks, her manner; the supremely intact rightness of it all—these were meant to accompany brilliantly modern inner rifts, spaces and vague negations. But she was beginning to see that somewhere on the edge of these ponderings on the subject of dishevelment was the essence of fear itself. What depths of immense bedraggled dishevelment she feared, and why, it was hard at the moment to say. She had never heard anyone speak of this kind of fear. All around her all her life people recounted episodes that involved fear of heights, fear of depths, fear of slipping away, falling off, dropping into; fear of earth, air, fire, water. Where was fear itself, the backward glance of a woman in unspeakably soiled rags, collector of shopping bags, victim of spells, mumbling to herself in the stale corner of some cafeteria? Fiction, Jean thought, sitting surrounded by her notes, dozens of stunningly disordered pages spread across her bed; fiction, she thought, idly biting the skin on her index finger.

In the kitchen they listened to the water boiling. Bolin still held Softly's jacket, keeping it neatly folded on his lap.

338

"Dent is terribly, terribly old," Edna Lown said.

"Old Dent," Softly said.

"Too, too old to be of any conceivable help to us."

"Lester-pet, how can he help?"

"I can't perfect the control system without a metalanguage. Logic rendering just won't work. The machine won't be able to render Logicon or speak Logicon until I figure out how to separate the language as a system of meaningless signs from the language about the language."

"The old problem," Edna said.

"Old Dent," Softly said.

The water boiled furiously.

"Does anybody know how to get in touch with him?" Lester said.

"He has an appointments secretary," Softly said. "The only way to get in touch with old Dent is to try to reach this man known as the appointments secretary."

Bolin poured the water.

"How's our young man doing?" Edna said.

"He promises to work. He'll do whatever you and Lester want. I suggest you begin with the latest notation."

"What about the game?" Lester said.

"What game?"

"Expression of surprise."

"Game, game, what game?"

"The game I'm holding your jacket for. The halfball game. When do we go back and finish?"

"There's no time," Edna said. "Rob's got a lot to do if he really plans to get together with Chester Greylag Dent. Appointments secretary or not, the man's nearly impossible to contact."

"Unlisted number?" Lester said.

I DON'T FEEL SO GOOD

Temperate by nature, ever serene in fact, Lester Bolin was not upset by the panting laughter with which Softly responded to his question about an unlisted phone number. He simply dug his shoes into the dirt, glancing toward Edna for some sign of an explanation. His work on the computer-driven control system (known, like the language itself, as Logicon) had been going very slowly. He had constructed a frame to house the wiring and inner mechanisms. As a sort of joke, he had given the frame a box-shaped "head" and cylindrical "torso." The next step was to build a formal language, void of content, into the circuitry. Concurrent with that he had to design an inbred body of statements about this symbolic language; this would be a second form of discourse, less stark, less empty than Logicon itself and therefore able to provide a basis for analysis and description. It would have to be a system that enabled the creators of Logicon to discuss their language in a context other than the language itself and that furthermore allowed the control system's mechanism to make meaningful statements both *in* Logicon and *about* Logicon.

Gamete sac gonad scrotum, Billy thought, recalling the sense of confusion he'd felt upon learning that the urethra functioned as the male genital duct, having always believed that organs, ducts, valves and canals ending in the letter *a* were exclusively female. He felt weak, sweaty and depressed. Once again he clasped his hands on top of his head, moving them forward and back, enjoying the tectonic sensation. After a while he slipped completely under the covers, alone with his own smell.

For this higher kind of calculation, Lester Bolin was using sheet metal, sponge rubber, various plastics; tubes, relays, a tape playback system; timing sources, transistors, a monitor system; any number of electronic components; box-shaped head and cylindrical torso. As a further joke of sorts, he was designing the model in such a way that it would operate only upon insertion of a coin.

Chester Greylag Dent lived quietly in his custom-made nuclear-powered submarine, endlessly circling the globe. Of late, however, he'd chosen to hover, first at one thousand feet, the normal test depth for conventional nuclear submarines; then at ten thousand feet, far below the zone of light, just idling there in the dark and cold among deep-lying viperfish and giant eels; then at twenty thousand feet, below all plantlife, below the nodding work of winds and currents; and finally at an incredible thirty-five thousand feet, dead sea creatures drifting down, sponges, gouged-out shells, segmented worms feeding on detritus, fossil imprints in the sediment, the silt itself hundreds of millions of years old, never unsubmerged, the quietest place on earth.

The helicopter in which Robert Hopper Softly dozed was heading oceanward over a cluster of volcanic islands. The craft was equipped with four different submarine-detection systems but because the submarine in question was lying dead at such tremendous depth, the more powerful sonar equipment of a tracking ship had been called into play. After the helicopter set down on a pad at the bow of the tracking vessel, Softly went immediately to a restricted area of the ship for a look at the active acoustic detection monitor. Signals from a huge mass of submerged metal were being received and separated from the background of oceanic noise. Softly proceeded to the afterdeck and stepped into a reinforced deep-diving cylinder that was then lowered into the sea on cables. The cylinder's base was designed to match the shape and size of a submarine's escape hatch. Its descent, which took several hours, was electronically guided by the surface vessel, as were the final maneuvering and coupling. To Softly all motion appeared to be taking place in an aneroid medium, some kind of thick gel. Affixed at last he knocked on the submarine's hatch. It was opened by Jumulu Nobo, an abnormally large Negrito who served as Chester Greylag Dent's appointments secretary. Softly was led through the pantry and wardroom, not without noticing that the hatch was equipped with a long metal police lock and that the bulkheads were wallpapered in cheerful colors and patterns.

"Trouble finding us?"

"Minimal," Softly said.

"Chet's asleep now but I'll be glad to answer any preliminary questions you may have."

They eased into facing chairs in a small compartment outfitted in wicker and equipped with French doors. Nobo wore a maroon jogging suit with matching sneakers. He explained that several of his Malayan forebears, all of exceedingly short stature, had migrated to Louisiana, settling in a town called Oslo, Norway, where, eventually, young Jumulu grew to adolescence and early manhood, the first of his people to exceed four feet in height.

"I wanted to study marine biology," he said. "It sounded so clean, so virtuous. Who could ever claim that a marine biologist was wasting his life? At my disposal would be a mass of remarkably interesting facts about the matchless organisms that populate the oceans of the world. But then I heard a voice. It told me to keep searching. In places like Oslo, Norway, Louisiana, people tend to hear voices. Anyway I kept searching and in time I wandered into the multifaceted presence of the great man himself."

"And here you are."

"I manage with a crew of eleven, a housekeeper and a eunuch. We don't have an easy time of it. But the rewards far outweigh the sacrifices."

"Gratitude for your hospitality obliges me at this point to express amazement at the very existence of a submarine able to reach such depths without breaking apart."

"Chet outlined the basic design himself. I can tell you this much. One, this is not a spindle-hull design. The entire craft is delta-shaped— a pair of sweptback wings or fins without a body proper. Two, we have what we call a flooded outer hull. Sea water enters through small openings. This makes us more pressure-resistant than ordinary underwater craft. Three, the special metals we used for the inner hull make a thoroughly reliable weld."

"I'm impressed."

"We're all very happy with it. Of course, the hull groans from time to time."

"So I notice," Softly said.

"Perfectly normal. No cause for concern. Anticipated in the specifications."

Despite his assurances Nobo himself seemed ill at ease. He kept brushing imaginary dandruff out of his hair and occasionally stuck a finger in his ear and shook it vigorously. He appeared in addition to be a master of the darting glance. Sounds in the hull; the crossing of Softly's legs; static on an intercom nearby—all evoked the swiftest of flinching looks from the appointments secretary. Whether this was his natural manner or a result of being submerged for extended periods was a question that didn't interest Softly, who found himself distracted by the delay in seeing old Dent and therefore failed to take any more than the most casual notice of the details and intimations that weaved through the ensuing chat.

"Did you happen to see a freighter nearby when you were aboard the tracking ship?"

"Don't think so."

"They've contacted us a number of times," Nobo said. "We prefer to ignore them."

"Who are they?"

"The freighter is Liberian. The people aboard apparently represent a Honduran cartel."

"Consortium Hondurium," Softly said. "They came to feel a consortium is more stylish than a cartel, at least in name. So they changed over. In fact they're still changing. Been through several corporate names, I believe. Elux Troxl. I know his work. Interested in abstract economic power."

"Not any more."

"How do you know?"

Nobo got up and began jogging in place, his glance darting to different areas of the compartment.

"According to their messages, they're interested in cornering the guano market. Bat guano as fertilizer. They've apparently located a rich source nearby and they want to lease this vessel and any other vessel in the area in order to help transport whatever they can haul out of the bat caves. They've not only moved their corporate headquarters to a freighter; they've changed their name again."

"What is it?"

"ACRONYM."

"What's it stand for?"

"We were wondering about that," Nobo said.

"Knowing a little about Troxl, I would guess it's probably a combination of letters formed to represent the idea of a combination of letters. Nobody knows Troxl's real name so maybe there's a grubby logic to the whole thing. He excels at time-sharing. He also deals in mailing lists, chain letters, coupon analysis, subscription research, that sort of thing. Really huge companies sometimes hire people like that to undertake tedious but necessary projects. He's a notary public as well, which gives him a sheen of respectability in a fly-by-night sort of way. To my knowledge the only nonabstract professional activity he's ever been associated with involved the fire-bombing of zoos and animal hospitals. This was done to get people to contribute funds. Troxl's fund-raising organization handled the whole thing, of course. The vast outpouring of money went to rebuild the zoos and hospitals in question. The donors' names remained with Troxl. In this way he compiled enormous mailing lists, which he sold to other fund-raisers, to direct mail houses, to test-market organizations, to the subscription departments of various print media and to government agencies. With the money thus amassed he leased time on computers all over the world in order to control the fluctuations of the money curve."

"On the surface," Nobo said, "just another semi-treacherous entrepreneur."

"With a rather unsavory associate."

"Grbk."

"You know about him?"

"He was mentioned in the latest communication from the freighter. I think they want to impress us with their pureness of heart."

"Mentioned in what connection?"

"He's under house arrest aboard the ship."

"On what charge?"

"Heinousness," Nobo said.

A slight bland lad entered the compartment. This was Bö (boo). As the Negrito continued to run in place, the young man, head bobbing, whispered something in his ear.

"Chet will see you now," Nobo said.

"Good."

"He's in the west wing."

"Very good."

Bö took Softly toward the bow, where they went past the sonar sphere and then made a sharp turn into the other sweptback portion of the submarine. They walked through a series of compartments, all numbered in bright red paint, some resembling rooms in a country cottage.

"Don't you get depressed?" Softly said. "I mean being under so long."

"I'd rather be down here than on the surface. Last time we were on the surface I fell overboard. I was surprised when nobody seemed to notice. First I yelled. Then I began to count. I screamed numbers at them. I got all the way to forty-three before Jumulu noticed. It was my instinct to die with a number on my lips rather than a boring plea for help. So tacky and dull. With my degree of heightened self-awareness, it was just about impossible to thrash around out there shouting help, help."

"Did your life flash before your eyes?"

"My life constantly flashes before my eyes," Bö said in a voice tenderly bereft of resonance. "I try to pick out interesting moments as they go by. But I can never find any."

At ninety-two, Chester Greylag Dent was a dusty figure wrapped in an elegant shawl. Once tall and broad, he'd seemed to wear away, his physical presence now limited to a rather fragile central reality. He was nearly transparent, his upper and lower regions beginning to curl toward each other as though to assemble themselves about his navel, that passionate stamp of gestation. He sat in a sprawling deck chair, occupying only one fourth of it, his knees drawn up under the shawl. As Bö left, Softly sat in the other deck chair, this one not equipped with a leg rest. The compartment was otherwise unfurnished but there were books, manuscripts and correspondence scattered everywhere. Dent's hair was reddish brown with a blond streak through it.

"I think of myself as the Supreme Abstract Commander."

"Nice to see you again," Softly said. "It's been many years."

"Bit of a lickspittle, that Bö. Still, there's no better way to fashion an element of depraved antiquity than to have a eunuch aboard."

345

"When we first made radio contact with your appointments secretary, using, with special permission, the U.S. Defense Department's submarine communications system—an interesting setup, by the bye, that utilizes the earth itself as a reflector to bounce radio waves up to the ionosphere—he said you no longer received visitors. So I'm particularly gratified that we were able to arrange a get-together."

"Besieged for decades," Dent said. "We rarely surface now. Rarely even move. Jumulu screens all communications."

"Then you personally have no contact with the outside world," Softly said.

"I keep a post office box in Newfoundland. But we haven't surfaced there in a very great while. All these bits and pieces of mail lying about are from five to ten years old. If I haven't answered them by now, I don't expect I ever will. Will I?"

"What do you do to pass the time?"

"I think of myself as the Supreme Abstract Commander. That's what I do."

"Very good."

"I also formulate ideas on this and that topic."

"I thought as much."

"As you know, I've been referred to more than a few times as the greatest man in the world. Why do you suppose that is? Is it because of my books, my speeches, my innovations in so many diverse fields? Is it because I renounced my dual citizenship in order to become stateless? Is it because I returned my academic degrees, my honorary degrees, my medals, my plaques? Is it because I chose to disown my children, my grandchildren, my regius professorships? Is it, do you suppose, because I have always insisted on viewing us not as a collection of races and nationalities but as a group that shares the same taxonomic classification, that of Earth-planet extant? Surely the proclamations of greatness that collect about my name go beyond these factors to include the life choice I've made. To suspend myself in the ocean zone of perpetual darkness. To inhabit an environment composed almost solely of tiny sightless feeble-minded creatures palpitating in the ooze. What do you think, Softly?"

"Something to that, I suppose."

"True greatness always involves a period of complete withdrawal. To withdraw completely is to appeal to the romantic instincts of people. Blind little sluglike organisms. That's about all you can expect to find down here. Too cold and dark for anything else. I believe this accounts in large measure for the proclamations of my greatness and I would remind you that they come from every quarter of the civilized world."

Dent's voice had a whistling sort of tone, very reedy, and it seemed to quicken as he approached the end of a statement, as though the voice were issuing from a tubular conveyance which he feared was about to implode.

"Why have you come, Softly? Make your point. There must be a point you came to make."

"I'm involved in a project called Logicon. We're trying to devise a totally logical system of discourse with the idea of using it eventually as an aid in celestial communication."

"Have you drained the system of meaning?"

"We're doing that now."

"Have you established a strict set of rules?"

"We're working on it."

"Have you taken measures to safeguard your system of notation from vagueness and self-contradiction?"

"I'm confident we can do that."

"Have you devised an alternate system to test the original system's consistency?"

"That's the problem," Softly said. "That's why I'm here. We need a metalogical language to build into our computer-driven machine. We'll save a tremendous amount of time and labor if we can refer to a source of artificial intelligence that functions on both levels—Logicon and meta-Logicon. Throughout your career you've had great success in model-building, in the development of new materials, in advanced design and so forth. This submarine is an obvious example."

"I'm far too old to help in this matter," Dent said. "True, I spend some time every day dictating ideas which are then typed, privately printed in our offset room and bound in leather. But my ideas are no longer mathematical in nature and haven't been for a great many decades. I've written extensively on the subject but haven't actually *done* mathematics since my twenties. Your problem is essentially mathematical. You need someone able to draw on vast powers of creativity."

"I've got Lown and Bolin."

Dent yawned and shivered simultaneously.

"Who else?" he said.

"Your fellow laureate Terwilliger."

"Billy Twillig sat on a pin. How many inches did it go in? *Four*. One two three *four*."

"Nice," Softly said.

"He can solve your problem, can't he?"

"He hasn't been cooperating. He won't even sit in front of the sun lamp. The others take turns. All but him. Maybe that's what's got him down. Lack of sunlight, real or synthetic. There's a form of depression people suffer in northern regions during the sunless months. It's called polar hysteria. Maybe that's what he's got."

"Probably he doesn't like sharing the limelight, that one. I know that one's work. Original but full of quirks. That kind of mind never succeeds at collaboration. Pride, arrogance, vanity, insecurity. They go together. Ego, instability, fear itself."

"You have no advice to give me then after all the preparations I made, not to mention the traveling, the search, the descent, all of which, excluding the preparations, have to be repeated in the opposite direction."

"Arithmetize," Dent said.

"Arithmetize?"

"The system must reflect the metasystem. Or vice versa. Provide each sign with an integer."

"An integer?"

"If your electromechanical relay system is a continuous one, you must match it with a discrete-state mechanism. After all, Cauchy played with discrete and continuous groups. He was also a royalist who gave money to the poor."

"Why bring that up?"

"Balance," Dent said. "That's the best I can do. Every invention has an element of balance. Beyond that I have nothing to say except that problems are inevitable. As you well know, the more consistent the system, the less provable its consistency."

"Who does your shawls?"

"I use this man in Sausalito."

"You must give me his name," Softly said.

Dent asked him to ring for the eunuch. There was a buzzer on a panel nearby and Softly pressed it once, wishing he'd never thought of making this trip. Bö soon arrived with a chamber pot. He sat it on the floor next to the old man's deck chair and then left the compartment.

"This is in the nature of a drill."

"Of course," Softly said.

"I have a calculus."

"A calculus?"

"A stone. A urinary calculus. An abnormal mass in my bladder. Have you ever passed a stone?"

"No."

"We drill every day. Getting ready for the event itself. The passing of the stone."

"I hope you're not in pain."

Dent seemed to be thinking of something.

"Logic merely fills the gaps," he said finally. "The main technique is the mathematical technique. Granted, much of mathematics is exceedingly comic. But this only makes us believe in it all the more."

"My immediate concern is metamathematics."

"Hilarious," Dent said.

"A universal logical structure able to speak about itself in metalogical terms."

"Extremely mirth-provoking."

The hull groaned loudly. Jumulu Nobo stepped into the compartment and explained that it was time to play rock-paper-scissors. Old Dent liked to play in Japanese. When Nobo, hands behind his back, reached the count of three, Dent thrust a clenched fist out of his shawl. Nobo at the same time flung out his right hand with index and middle fingers extended.

"Ishi!"

"Hasami!"

There was a brief pause.

"Rock breaks scissors," Dent said.

"I hate to lose."

"A fact that makes my pleasure even keener."

Again Nobo counted to three.

"Hasami!"

"Kami!"

The hull groaned. Softly thought of the immense pressure being brought to bear, the shatter-capacity of the sea at this depth.

"Scissors cuts paper," Dent said.

Softly watched them play for an hour. Finally Dent made a gesture and got to his feet. Nobo picked up the chamber pot and held it just below the old man's crotch, undoing the single metal clip in Dent's pajama bottoms with his free hand. A long time passed.

"Stay to dinner, Softly?"

"Must get going, I'm afraid."

"We're having hamstring," Nobo said. "A big favorite back in Oslo, Norway."

"Really must run," Softly said.

"Hamstring, maw and rootage."

Bö led him back around to the escape hatch and unsecured the police lock. Eventually, in the helicopter, Softly noticed a freighter almost directly ahead. He asked the pilot to go down for a closer look. Deck hands were visible here and there but no one of obvious consequence. However, the ship's name was easy to read, having been lettered on the hull in Day-Glo paint.

Goo Fou Maru
Seagoing Headquarters for
ACRONYM
Operating beyond the 3-, 12- and 48-mile limits
Not subject to international search procedures
Trespassers will be prosecuted

Softly had his briefcase aboard the helicopter and he found an anti-depressant inside and swallowed it quickly. A fairly mild rise it gave him, just enough to keep him intact until he reached the ordered dense environment at the bottom of the great excavation.

Maurice Wu in long johns and sweater scrubbed the chrome reflector of his carbide lamp with foaming soap. Then he checked his first-aid kit for bandage roll, tourniquet, sterile gauze compress, one-shot antirabies serum, boric acid solution. He poured some carbide from a gallon can into a small plastic container. He put spare parts for the lamp into an even smaller watertight pouch. Having already polished his *wu-fu*, he slipped it around his neck. Then he put on kneepads, coveralls, high socks, climbing boots and cotton gloves.

Billy left his cubicle.

In the next unit Mainwaring and Bolin studied a number of documents that the former pulled out of his attaché case, where these papers and others were filed, tabbed and partitioned. Regarding organization in general, Bolin thought of his own tendency to make lists. The best part of list-making was the satisfaction he derived from crossing out each item as it was attended to. In any graded series of human gratifications, he was sure this pleasurable sense, that of business-neatly-completed, would occupy one of the lower orders. Still, it was a constant source of irreducible delight, the crossing-out of things.

Jean Venable stepped over a generator cable and headed onto the path between the rows of cubicles. She saw Billy coming out of the first-aid unit and walked with him back to his quarters.

"Not ill, I hope."

"Just checking out what they have in there. Not much. I thought I'd walk around a little. See what's doing."

"Do you employ certain time-wasting devices to put off the start of another day's work?"

"No," he said.

"Do you experience an emotional letdown when you complete a theorem or whatever?"

"Cut it out."

"Just wondered," she said.

He realized he was causing a one-man clutter and so he got into bed, dressed in the same pants, shirt, underwear and socks he'd been wearing when he first entered the antrum. Jean arranged herself sidesaddle on the TV table that was supposed to be his desk.

"Come on, slugabed, cheer up."

"Sure."

"It finally came to me," she said. "A beautifully lucid moment."

"What?"

"Sooner or later I always know when something's wrong. I knew it was something really basic this time. Then it came to me."

"What?" he said.

"Lucid but frightening," she said. "My book."

"What about it?"

"I'm making it fiction." she said. "The thing that was wrong was that I didn't really have a book as things stood. It wasn't willing itself into me, excuse the metaphysics. It was all very forced. But then I realized what I wanted to do and it was frightening. Fiction. I'm going to write fiction."

"Why is this frightening?"

"Because I don't know how to write fiction. I'll have to make everything up. I'll have to change everything. About the project. About the people involved. Everything. The sounds, the smells, the touch. The appearance of things and the essence of things."

"Why the smells?"

"I plan to make strict rules that I plan to follow. Reading my book will be a game with specific rules that have to be learned. I'm free to make whatever rules I want as long as there's an inner firmness and cohesion, right? Just like mathematics, excuse the comparison. Let's see, what else? Don't tell anyone we've had this talk. That's what I wanted to be sure to remember to tell you."

"I won't."

"Don't say anything."

"I won't say anything."

"If Rob finds out, I go flying out of here headfirst. And I want to stay a while longer. I need technical stuff from Edna and Lester. I need to find out if they can actually do what they've set out to do. I need to learn what this new man is like, this man Mainwaring. And meanwhile I'll be secretly writing and planning and scheming."

"When Rob sees he's not getting the book he thinks he's getting, I don't want to be around."

"It's not really his fault, I suppose. Those occasional rages and flurries of insult and all the rest of it. I suppose if I'd been raised under the same circumstances, I'd not only be temperamental and even hostile at times but most likely I'd be the same size he is. His size, after all, is everything, isn't it?"

"Raised under what circumstances?"

"Total emotional neglect," she said. "Rob was abandoned by his parents and raised in a foundling home. According to records he later dug up and examined, he had no organic abnormalities at the time. But see they kept him in a small dark room unattended for hours on end. I'm talking about extended lengths of time. He spat up food and swallowed it again. He suffered from insomnia. Then he lapsed into periods of prolonged sleep. This inhibited his growth hormones with results that are all too obvious."

"That doesn't explain why it hurts him to walk."

"On that subject I have a couple of things to say. His emotional deprivation resulted in all sorts of otherwise unexplained respiratory infections as well as a marked decrease in muscle tone. This could account for his hip trouble."

"What else?"

"It could be an act," she said.

He picked some lint from the bedsheet and blew it off his fingertip to another part of the same sheet.

"Why would he want to put on an act?"

"Maybe he wants pity. Maybe he thinks it helps him maintain command. People sometimes embellish their afflictions in order to create a specific effect. Maybe he thought child size alone would make him a comic figure. He felt compelled to seek a tragic tone, to gain a more complex kind of attention."

"Anyway this isn't the only story I've heard about Rob's disease. Lester Bolin said it had something to do with his mother's womb being unbalanced, the chemicals not mixing right."

"I don't know anything about his wombhood," Jean said.

"And then Maurice Wu told me that Rob was born in China where he got this so-called gnome disease because of the water having no minerals. So I've been through this before."

"All I've told you I heard from Rob himself. Except for the dislocated hips being an act, of course."

"Which is just a guess."

"They don't seem dislocated when we're in bed," she said.

MORE ON BATS

Everyone was impressed by the confident gleam on Mainwaring's face. Everywhere he went in the antrum he carried an attaché case full of documents that tended to support what he consistently referred to as "the latest findings."

"It was Gauss who worked out a proof of the binomial theorem in which n is a negative integer," he said. "I don't mean to impinge on the other fellow's area of competence but it seems to me that n may be a vital element in the present scheme of things."

"How so?" Bolin said.

"As you well know, the physical universe tends to provide an arena for the utilization of totally abstract mathematical ideas long after these ideas are developed. Happens time and again. What first appears to be worth preserving solely for its beauty is often found to have direct application to the world of matter, energy and the life processes. So: if Moholean relativity is valid, we may find that the concept of an indefinite number of dimensions is more than a purely abstract piece of Gauss-inspired mathematics. As of this moment, the value-dark dimension continues to be pure theory. What we're doing at Cosmic Techniques, my home base, involves trying to identify an actual mohole. According to Mohole himself, there are moholes numbering n."

"I'd like to hear more about it."

"If you're sure I'm not impinging," Mainwaring said.

"Please keep going."

"My father was a mathematician, you see, so there's a distant affinity."

"My father designed war toys," Bolin said.

"We are presently engaged in sylphing. According to Mohole's theory, wherever there are exo-ionic sylphing compounds, there are moholes. This is why we say a mohole is space-time sylphed. And what we're trying to do is identify areas in space where mohole-trapped particles, X-ray emissions and so on are absorbed by sylphing compounds. On a contour map such an area would take the form of an absorption hole."

Wu checked his backpack for trowel, pocket magnifier, dental pick, brush with soft fine bristles, nylon cord, cable ladder, whistle, dehydrated food, lengths of manila rope, candles, compass, the first-aid kit, the container that held the extra carbide, the pouch that held spare parts for the carbide lamp. He left the pack sitting on his sleeping bag and went across the path to visit Billy.

"See you in a while."

"Don't tell me you're not scared going up there."

"Maybe a little."

"Wading through that stuff."

"The guano."

"You're scared, I think."

"The right kind of scared."

"Bat-cave-osis."

"Want to come with me?" Wu said.

"I'm not budging."

"See you in a while."

"Ever see a bat get born?"

"No," Wu said, "but they do it pretty much the way we do. And I guess if you attach nonbat emotions to the event, it's just as happy as human birth and just as sad," thinking that darkness possesses a measure of vestigial light, the yin-influenced veiling of the sun, a unity

355

in this occultation. He'd scrutinized astronomical inscriptions on ancient Chinese oracle bones. He'd written a brief study of the relationship between mathematics and fortune-telling ("techniques of destiny") in early China. He'd toured the temple caves of the Northern Wei dynasty. He'd investigated China's history and tried to analyze the intrinsic rhythms of its language and character. He'd learned the language itself. He'd spent long periods of time in the land itself. From all of this he hoped to gain nothing more than a feudal sense of security. He did not pursue self-identification, a centralized response to one's own distinctness, as much as community, and there it is again, common possession, *this* including a measure of *that*, the number one (even if negative and printed in black, as was done by the Sung algebraists) seeking a perfect balance, a positive complementary sun-cut force with which to interlock. What he wanted from that microscopic China in his mind was some affirmation of the fact that he was not alone.

"Why sad?" Billy said.

"The birth of a baby equals the death of a fetus. This experience re-creates itself throughout our lives. Wish me luck."

Arithmetize, Softly thought, semihysterically.

Lown and Bolin had a whispered conversation in the former's cubicle. Her desert boots were unlaced and the cigarette she was trying to smoke kept going out. Lester was dressed in a combination of pajamas and golf togs.

"Could it be the other way around?"

"Everything could be the other way around."

"And probably is," she said.

"That's the trouble."

"So go ahead."

"At any rate," Bolin said, "he explained that Mohole's model of the universe is a stellated twilligon with an *n*-bottomed hole."

"I see."

"This is also called a terminal mohole."

"Sounds ridiculous to me."

"I didn't want to say anything to him."

"Childlike."

"That's what I thought," he said. "That precise idea occurred to me."

"Which isn't to say it's not valid."

"Right-o."

"I suppose metamathematics would sound just as childlike to Mainwaring," she said. "And we both know nothing is more valid."

"Better keep your voice down, Edna."

"So go on."

"At any rate," Bolin said, "the whole thing apparently springs from forces that were created in the first split second after the big bang."

"The big bang," she said.

"Because Ratner's star lies within a suspected mohole, which is a fractional part, as I understand it, of the value-dark dimension, meaning no spatial area and no time, it was thought the signal picked up by the synthesis telescope was originating from Ratner's star. But it wasn't."

"This part I already know."

"It was just that the mohole had trapped the signal and sent it our way. Ratner's star is a binary dwarf. Couldn't possibly sustain a planet of any size."

"A binary dwarf," she said.

"Mainwaring and his people are trying to identify an actual mohole at the same time that they attempt to trace the signal to its real source."

"Yes."

"Unpredictable cosmic events are implicit in Moholean relativity."

"Yes," she said.

"If there are moholes, the physical laws in a mohole probably change, depending on the observer, where he is, whether he is moving or at rest, his rate of speed if he is moving."

"I see."

"A mohole has little or nothing in common with a black hole. A mohole is part of the innate texture of space. It is not a singularity, a collapsed object, a gravity pit. It is simply what is out there, numbering n."

"A black hole," she said.

"In the last analysis, moholes are impossible to talk about. What we're really doing is imposing our own conceptual limitations on a sub-

357

ject that defies inclusion within the borders of our present knowledge. We're talking *around* it. We're making *sounds* to comfort ourselves. We're trying to peel skin off a *rock*. But this, according to Mainwaring, quoting Mohole, is simply what we do to keep from going mad."

LESTER TRIES AGAIN

Softly at his desk was in a state of intense excitement. Funny things happening to the tissue at the back of his brain. He kept inserting pencils in the battery-operated sharpener, thinking that the interval aboard the submarine had at least renewed his appreciation of the dedicated tone that obtained in the antrum. It was all beginning to fit together. Wu would have time while artifacting in the dark to develop further his "contralogical" theory of human evolution. Mainwaring appeared to be efficiency, calm and self-assurance incorporated; was clearly making correct probes; might even be inclined to try a bit of synthetic intensifier in the spirit of hale fellows well met. Lown and Bolin were proceeding apace, more or less, lacking only the raw gut power of Terwilliger's methodology, a circumstance which might by this time be completely rectified, hope I hope I hope. What the boy had to overcome was the pain, the dread, the risk involved in being logical. Historical development of the word "boy" might be instructive fun to trace with him some time. Make him aware of the soft treatment he gets around here. Ox, oxhide, he thought. Neck collar, knave, servant. There was Jean. Jean's book fit in. Jean's book would detail the ingredients of their triumph while making no reference to what was really going on. So Jean's book definitely fit in, not to mention Jean herself, chilled silver in the candlelight, pleasant to smell, slow to anger, an easeful creature experience, sidereal distinction of her left buttock, make of that what I will, snug in the gunnels of her wraparound legs. Women are at their best when ☐ oppressed ☐ undressed. Of course this kind of elegant ideational structure depends in the end on technically precise mathematical language.

We used to crush pieces of chalk with the butt end of wooden guns that had a nail and a rubber band and you could shoot off small pieces of linoleum at each other. We used to fill up socks with the powdered chalk and smash each other on the back. We used to say: *"Halloween! Halloween!"*

This is where zorgs fit in, the technicality, the precision, the mathematics, the language. Strict rules, Billy thought, feeling tired and limp, watching Lester Bolin come into the cubicle and pull the chair over to the cot and extend a sheet of paper in the general direction of his mouth. He took it and looked at it as Lester waited for him to react. He did not react, however, and after a while Lester got up and went away. What was strange was that Billy, looking at the page, fully realized the beauty of Logicon or at least its potential beauty as seen in the nearly surreal cleanness of its ideography: nothing unnecessary, nothing concealed, a sense of what he instinctively regarded as "extreme Chinese formalism," the mechanical drawing that *is* the machine.

```
(e) ...X'  ...x'  ...  )((x): y-y'
(d) n(x')  "O"... II (n)x'        wf
(c) Fx * dG(y, ) * S.b(u, numX * )
```

He got out of bed, took the blanket off the cot and spread it over the TV table. Then he crawled under the table, wedging himself between its plastic legs before proceeding to even out the edges of the blanket so that it completely shrouded the table and the person under the table. He felt foolish but determined. The foolishness of the gesture only strengthened his resolve. He thought of a characteristic of his. Whenever people expected him to like something, he either didn't like it or concealed his liking of it. He supposed he didn't want his feelings to be anticipated by others. But in this case it wasn't his feelings that were the issue, or liking something or disliking it. He didn't really know what the issue was and he was sure no one could tell him. All he knew was that in a very short while he no longer felt foolish.

BREATHE! GLEAM! VERBALIZE! DIE!

Wu's backpack was stenciled with the letters MXW. He filled a canteen with water from a larger canteen. He reknotted his boots. He was just starting to roll up his sleeping bag when Softly entered his quarters, followed by Mainwaring, Bolin and Lown, Lester's eyes shifting (Mainwaring noticed) as he appraised Wu's cubicle. For one thing there were no chairs. For another there was no cot. There was no desk either and no sign of luggage. Wu dragged the backpack into a corner and sat down on top of it.

"Before you get going," Softly said, "I'd like you to fill these people in."

"Sure," Wu said. "On what?"

"Events."

"You mean events in the field?"

"The field and after the field," Softly said. "These people know nothing about it. They need to be filled in."

"It's like this," Wu said. "We were in Sangkan Ho under the auspices of the Chinese-American Science Sodality. We seemed to be witnessing an unusual thing taking place. After a certain point, the deeper we went the greater the complexity of the tool types, of the culture in general. This is after a certain point. Up to that point, everything was normal. After that point, we found a progressive increase in complexity."

"Interesting," Mainwaring said.

"Everything we found was carefully analyzed. The methods of optical confirmation are very advanced. And we don't anticipate the slightest controversy as to our dating techniques and so on. The controversy we may get will be the culturally based sort of thing that doesn't question the findings but only the implications of the findings. This is simply a case of people not being able to accept revolutionary truths."

"To be expected," Lown said.

"We're in no hurry to publish," Wu said. "There is plenty of work to be done. When Rob no longer needs my services, I'm heading back to the field. It wasn't until I left the field and came here that I first realized the extent of what I'd seen in the field."

"Man more advanced the deeper we dig," Softly said.

"Charming," Bolin said.

Someone using a crayon had written out the number eighteen on the undersurface of the TV table. To read the word he'd had to roll his eyeballs way up. The blanket smelled of stale traffic, the corroborating truth a laboratory of research onanists might produce in their methodical throbbing and desperation for pictures. His body filled the space between the blanket walls. He had never before been so aware of himself as a biological individual. He smelled, he sweated, he ached. Between himself and his idea of himself there was an area of total silence. What would happen if this space could be filled with some aspect of that collective set of traits that enabled him to qualify as a persisting entity? He put his hands under his shirt and rubbed his chest and stomach. He was growing, he was aging. The greater sag of his left testicle, natural as it was, seemed an intimation of some massive dysfunction soon to manifest itself. Death he felt to be anything but senseless. In ways he could not put into words, it appeared to be a perfectly reasonable occurrence. A logical conclusion, in short. But in thinking about it, in preparing (as it were) to evade it, he seemed to lead himself into a series of inexpressible mental states. These were states that weren't so much bleak as negative, lacking some fundamental element. He felt there was something between or beyond, something he couldn't account for, between himself and the idea of himself, beyond the negative mental invention; and what he knew about this thing was that it had the effect of imposing a silence. That was as far as his thinking went on the subject. There was nowhere else for it to go, he believed. In a while he began to feel better about the site he'd chosen for his life and thought.

Googolplex and glossolalia.

Jean was alone in her room on her bed working a needle and thread. Earlier she had written a number of pages and now she was trying to busy herself into a different line of thinking. She mended this and that. She bit apart thread. She mumbled instructions to herself, not very successfully. The results, that is, were not successful, dangling buttons, loosely stitched seams; the mumbling itself was quite flawless. Oh, well, worship of the body always ends in fascism. Of the body and the body's armor. What had surprised her in the relatively brief time she'd spent at the typewriter was the very direct correlation between writing and memory. Writing, in this case, being of the nonjournalistic type. Memory being not just the faculty of recollection but the power to summon the density of past experience. The author of *The Gobbledygook Cook Book* (as she sometimes thought of herself) had never before realized the degree of concentration she might succeed in reaching simply by staring into the keys of a typewriter and now and then tapping on one or more. Writing is memory, she thought, and memory is the fictional self, the powdery calcium ash waiting to be stirred by a pointed stick. She didn't believe the book she was determined to write would include a great many of her own past experiences, at least not as they occurred in the special trembling weather in which she'd stood. Still, memory might yield the nuance and bone earth necessary to make fictional people. Having herself been a character in someone else's novel, she tried to anticipate the nature of the successive reflections she might eventually have to confront. She sat on the bed, playfully mingling the words "fear itself fear itself fear itself" into the instructions she mumbled concerning needles and threads and a different line of thinking.

He heard someone step into his cubicle, Billy did. Pretty heavy meant probably Bolin. Wu took long sort of bounces. Rob hobbled. Edna Lown with desert boots dragged her feet. Mainwaring, he didn't know how Mainwaring walked but he bet on Lester, judging not only by the weight expressed in those footsteps but the accompanying sound, paper rattling in someone's hand and almost definitely paper being sailed onto his cot, a single sheet, Softly thought, beatific Chinese, lovely how my Lester-pet does his stuff on an old Royal portable, quaint as a puking babe on some far-off plain, if only now the object of our concerted love will blink to indicate his willingness to play.

I LOSE MY BREATH

When everything was quiet the boy slipped out from under the TV table and without even looking at the bed or the piece of paper on the bed went down the narrow trail of clay and gravel to the barrier nearest his own quarters, where he found among the boulders, crates and oil drums a very large section of heavy canvas which he struggled to dislodge from a numb mound of rubble, finally taking it in tow and heading back to cube one, time to rest, to catch his breath before proceeding to stand on the chair and place the edges of the tarpaulin if that's what it was over the edges of the partitions of his cubicle, getting off the chair to move it several times to new locations until the placement was complete, time to rest and resettle, so that what he had now was a canvas roof with enough material left over to block all but a few inches at the bottom of the entranceway, his immobile home, not that he was foregoing the blanket-shrouded table, oh no, here we go, down and in, the enclosed area's concealed zone's secluded figure.

We used to ring people's bells and run, crossing the street in zigzags, building to building, wedging broken toothpicks into the cracks around the doorbells of people we didn't like or who we thought would probably want to kill us if they could. In the Chinese laundry the old man kept an ax under the counter and what we used to do was pick one person to go stand in the doorway and make meat-cleaving motions with his or her hand until the old man reached under the counter and then you could run but not before you screamed into the store: "*Halloween! Halloween!*"

He took excessive pleasure in the progress of his fever, luxuriating in the unprecedented smell of his sweat, a chemical stench that led him to credit his body with greater toxic power than he'd believed it to possess. His clothing was drenched, emitting a stink of its own, as did the blanket that hemmed him in and the canvas beyond that. He alternated between chills and periods of dawning warmth, his body at the mercy of these fluctuations, his mind "asleep" in elements of form, in angularity and curvature. Salutary hallucinations. Miner's hat with headlamp. Phlegm deposits in his lungs or someplace. Perseverations. Spitting in the dust. Thinking of bats. Repeating a phrase. There were few things more pleasantly disgusting, he believed, than watching his own spit hit the dust, half quivering with fragments of earth, a tiny spoonful of drool. He curled up tighter, head between his knees, hands in the dirt, happy in his sub-reckonings, his dumbbody whiff, his spittle glisten, the persistent images of pure form, the sense that he was accompanying himself out of some systematic pattern.

Wu put on his miner's hat with headlamp. Across the path Mainwaring sat back in a swivel chair, his legs crossed on top of a small filing cabinet. His umbrella and suitcase were in a corner. His attaché case was on its side in the middle of his cot. This will not take long, he thought. This will be handled with dispatch. As such projects go, this one gives promise of being very elegant. It would also seem to lend itself to expeditious performance on all fronts. Promptness, efficient speed, general dispatch. It must be the antrum that gives me this feeling. Compulsion to perform according to standards. Convergence of a number of ideas at a single point. That is undoubtedly what Rob is aiming at. To approach the same point from different directions. To tend toward a definitive conclusion, result or balance. This woman standing here telling me she has been granted permission by "our friend Rob" if it is all right with me, this standing woman, to conduct an interview concerning my particular area of competence. There goes Mr. Wu.

"Sit," he said.

"You were probably warned about a writer on the prowl."

"I don't imagine I have to apologize for the accommodations."

"What is your role in the Logicon project?"

"I'm associated with a firm called Cosmic Techniques. We're in the process of developing an echolocation quantifier, patent pending, and we believe and hope and trust that this device will help us locate that part of the universe where the artificial signals originated. Concurrent with this, we are trying to identify a mohole, something that's never been attempted before."

"Speaking more slowly, would you describe this quantifier in detail?" Jean said.

"Restricted information."

"How do you plan to identify this mohole?"

"Without getting too technical, I would say that the latest findings tend to support the theory that wherever there are moholes, we can expect to turn up a trace of exo-ionic sylphing compounds, or vice versa. With a very stylized computer-generated map of the galaxy and using observations made by the synthesis telescope here and fed to our facilities in Canada—that is, to Cosmic Techniques—we are ready and willing and able to sylph; that is, to locate absorption holes, or places in space where dust, gases, cosmic debris and electromagnetic information are being absorbed by sylphing compounds, as I explained to Mr. Bolin, pleasant man and very capable, I'm sure."

"If I had to put what a mohole is into words, what would I say?"

"You'd have a problem," Mainwaring said.

This sitting woman intent on duplicating what I say, always a partial shock to find someone who thinks enough of fact to get it absolutely right, this woman sitting here at half my age. I have been photographed for the newspapers half a dozen times. I have been interviewed for this and that publication on more than a score of occasions. I have, let's see now, been called on the telephone and asked for my opinion on the latest findings perhaps a dozen times. I belong to this this this this this organization. I have won that that that and that award. I own nineteen dress shirts.

t. The codes to language contained in play-talk are the final secrets of childhood.

u. Is it silly to say that there is only one limit to language and that it is crossed, in the wrong direction, when the child is taught how to use words?

v. Does this mean that to break down language into its basic elements is to invent babbling rather than elementary propositions?

w. Is play-talk a form of discourse *about* language? That the answer is in the affirmative seems undeniable.

x. I'm tempted to say: babbling is metalanguage.

Edna Lown was beginning to think of this set of notes as a subprofession, her cryptic existence in an alternate system of relationships. Puzzling, isn't it, how I'm beginning to look forward to this scribbling, making time for it, setting aside more immediate things, sneaking it into what's supposed to be an inflexibly tight schedule. It was quiet in the antrum. Lester Bolin was between snore cycles and there was no sound at all except the clear faint measures of water flowing in the distance. There was no reason for Edna to regard her note-taking as a secret occupation and yet she did, thinking of it often while engaged in other tasks or in conversations with Lester and Rob. It's like something I keep behind a closed door, she thought. A bed, she thought. To meet with someone behind a closed door, a man or woman (or woman?) who is not known to any of those who know me. To engage in these meetings between scheduled events. To never change the sheets on the bed behind the door. To barely know the person not known to those who know me. To be in this sense a witness to my own adventure. Wandering, she thought. I am wandering badly. A thing she rarely did in the extreme setting of the excavation. Some fairly large rocks came bouncing down the slope and crashed (judging by the sound) into a sturdy cluster of oil drums. Yes I love it here.

y. To maintain that things belong backwards is a facile argument intended to emphasize the difficulties involved in making observations and conducting experiments.

z. Is this always true?

a. We think we know that a child's intuition of geometry neatly reverses the series of historical developments in this field. Beginning with invariant spatial relationships, the child proceeds to closed and open structures; to the properties of figures extended through space; to the elements of point, line and plane.

b. To a geometer this is regressive development, or history inside out.

c. The child knows these things before it knows words.

d. It may be important to seek connections.

e. It may be important to ask whether the child's day-to-day geometry, this grasp of certain principles of space and sequence, automatically confers on childlike babbling an element of mystical sophistication.

f. On the other hand we may be back to facile argument.

g. What is unexamined and superficial is often "cured" by obsession. This too, of course, suggests the inside-outness of things.

h. Fragmentation.

i. Forced dispersion of a fixed idea.

j. Does the scattering of the fragments of a scientific obsession reflect the physical and mental state of the person seeking to be cured of facile argument?

k. Mathematics.

l. Half-blind Euler pacing at his slate. Lagrange in his despondency pondering the blank spaces in his art.

Softly had never set eyes on his own semen. He regarded this fluid not primarily as a transporting medium but as some defensive secretion of the body, a reaction (perhaps) to danger or excessive stress. Danger from what source? The excessive stress of intercourse? He didn't ask these questions in so many words or examine the reasons why this secretion might be defensive. He hated the feel of semen on his thighs or on the sheet beneath him, bleak lick of damp, that adhesive resistance to the possibilities of flow, the chill synthetic stickiness of it. Thinning there in cubic centimeters. Approaching the "appearance" of transparency. Sugar fuel in that plasma to rouse my sperm from its quiescent state. To maintain its fertility. To boost its movement into the female apparatus. But do I know for certain there is sperm in my ejaculate? Noughts and crosses. Shepherd's score. Hopscotch. Cybernetics. Precisely why he avoided the sight of his own semen was another question he didn't ask in so many words. It was a sight to be avoided, that was all. What could you say about your own semen and why you hated the feel of it and avoided the sight of it? It was not a subject to be nudged toward some finished insight. So Softly thought, the same Softly (all too aware of the irony of it all) who believed in the wholesomely promotional idea that sex is not what you do but what you are. This made the fluid in question an ambiguous topic at best.

He left Jean (muttering) on her stomach and took the elevator down to the bottom of the antrum, Jean (on her stomach) not unloved, not unmarked by the incidental menace of this loving, by Softly's roistering maul, good luck to her arms and legs, physically a shade slack, he thought, lacking all in all her customary purpose and zeal, that expressive force through which her body explored some silent ideal of spacelessness, moving now against the sheets to rewarm herself and wearily to clean his nervous semen from that itching patch of lower belly. He went straight from the elevator to the crude shower stall near the barrier. Here he undressed, eyes averted from the center of his body, and stepped with terrible suddenness into what proved to be no more than a trickle of freezing water, enough at any rate to freshen his armpits, crotch and feet. He hurried into his clothes, body taut against the cold, and walked on down to cube one.

There was a dusty tarpaulin draped over the entire cubicle. It covered most of the entranceway as well. Softly leaned way over, lifted the canvas and stepped inside. Moldy gloom. There was a blanket over the plastic table that was supposed to serve as a desk. He assumed the boy was under there. It didn't seem absurd that the boy would be under there. It was sort of Willy's way these days. On the bed was a piece of mail. There was also the chair to be noted. The footlocker. Finally the suitcase. The suitcase was opened, its contents giving every indication of having gone untouched since the time they were first carried down here.

Softly sat in the chair and took one of the small cigars out of the tin he carried in his jacket pocket. He lit it up, squirming further back into the seat. He recalled that Lester Bolin had once told him how boring it was to teach game theory to sophomores. That was a long time ago. That was Lester on the brink. Now he was inescapably within the confines. Prenex normal forms. Recursive undecidability. The pure monadic predicate calculus. A firm foundation for analysis is all that got it going. EXERCISE: Prove that every consistent decidable first-order theory has a consistent decidable complete extension.

Uga boo
Uga boo boo uga

"That's my cigar smoke you smell. I don't want you to think the place is on fire."

"I'm very calm."

"Calm," Softly said. "Wonder what our young man means by that."

"It's easy to concentrate in here."

"He must be trying to lift the general morale in the place, declaring his readiness to concentrate. On what, of course, remains to be seen. This must be a phase of the polar hysteria syndrome that the experts are not ready to confirm just yet. Utter calmness. Readiness to concentrate."

"What's polar hysteria?"

"He's able to squeak out occasional questions, it would appear. Very encouraging indeed. Sunlessness. That's your problem. Aggravated sunlessness."

368

"Keep believing it."

"Any plans for making an appearance sometime in the near or distant future?"

"I'll play it by ear."

"He gives every sign of being alive, at any rate, and in tentative control of his faculties."

"That brings up an interesting point."

"We're all anxious to hear what sort of points are deemed interesting by people who spend their time crouching in shrouded environments."

"You got this whole thing started down here by talking about the tensions going on in the outside world."

"True enough."

"Maybe I'd like to know what's happening lately."

"Things, if anything, are worse," Softly said. "We're getting reports about aggression and counteraggression. The meaning of the term 'counteraggression' defeats me for the moment but I suppose in this kind of situation there's bound to be a certain amount of muddled thinking."

"I'd like the talking to end now."

"Wants to be alone, does he, with his newly discovered sense of calmness? Desires the kind of quiet even blankets and waterproof coverings can't guarantee? Plans to concentrate, does he? Chooses to listen to his circulating blood as it bears tender nutrients through his body? Decides he needs an interval of quiet breathing, right? Intends to invent the nonce word that renders death irrelevant."

"Somebody's getting carried away."

"It's very uncomfortable in here," Softly said. "Do you know that or not? If not, why not? This canvas I find depressing. You've never behaved this way before. I think I'll keep talking just to annoy you."

Immense bedraggled dishevelment.

Because it was possible to get infected without even being bitten. It had been known to happen. There were cases on record. Because of the saliva in the air. Or because of the parasitic insects floating around. Or because of the guano. Or because of the urinous mist surrounding the colony itself. So this possibility alone was reason to think of a bat cave not as a place inhabited by bats, inviting to bats or even swarming with bats but rather as a place that was *bat-infested*.

Jean Venable wearing a raincoat walked into Softly's cubicle and finding it unoccupied sat down and waited for Rob to return, which eventually he did, Billy's head coming out from under the blanket, Softly moving right past Jean and seating himself formally at the elaborate desk, where he pretended to engage in a series of engrossing tasks, the boy's head withdrawing again, damp wool, the humidity of stilled midnights.

I AM NOT JUST THIS

There is a life inside this life. A filling of gaps. There is something between the spaces. I am different from this. I am not just this but more. There is something else to me that I don't know how to reach. Just outside my reach there is something else that belongs to the rest of me. I don't know what to call it or how to reach it. But it's there. I am more than you know. But the space is too strange to cross. I can't get there but I know it is there to get to. On the other side is where it's free. If only I could remember what the light was like in that space before I had eyes to see it with. When I had mush for eyes. When I was dripping tissue. There is something in the space between what I know and what I am and what fills this space is what I know there are no words for.

I TAKE A DRINK

"If you're busy, Rob, I'll go, although it's silly, isn't it, this artifice."

"You have something for me to read, do you?"

"I want to interview Edna," Jean said.

"I thought you might have some notes for me to go over, or even some prose, actual prose, a first draft, you know, not so finely styled but full of raw technical data or something on that order. Didn't you tell me you were devising a new system of note-taking or note-arranging or whatever? Aren't you that person? I want to read, Jean. I want something to look at. I want to be of service to you. Don't talk to me about artifice please. We're supposed to be doing a book. You write it, I read it and make helpful suggestions. This is the arrangement. This is what you're here to do."

"Fine, fine."

"Edna doesn't want to talk to you," he said. "But I'll talk to you. I'll tell you anything Edna can tell you."

"Let me go over my questions here."

"Whenever you're ready."

"What about Lester?" she said. "Will Lester want to talk to me?"

"Seriously doubt it."

"Am I allowed to enter his presence and request a few moments of his time? I've talked to everyone else at least once and after all these are the key people, more or less, aren't they? I mean this is the Logicon project and they're the mathematical logicians. I want to hear their unfiltered ideas, opinions and convictions. What kind of journalist would I be if I settled for less than a face-to-face encounter?"

"Let's have sex," he said. "Take off your clothes and never mind the people here. The people here are working, sleeping, climbing the slopes, camped under tables. To even things up, I will take off my clothes at the same time you are removing yours. This equalizes things."

Coiled room, she thought. A nervous little step into the coiled room I've seen from time to time to time. Oh, well, how could you have nearly continuous sex with a child-sized man and expect things to progress in a routine manner, as in the non-half-crazy world of people the same size. Look at him in this weak light, how eager to mock my past, how aware of my cooperation in this undertaking, the return of my body, the canceling of subscriptions to reverie, fancy and illusion. Touching me just his touch I think insane. From time to time mingled with the reflections in the broken glass I pass in the street or in the windows of trains crossing dead sections of town, bodies nodding under the glass halves of a tenement's outer doors, I see this room occupied by a female figure inside concentric rings. Oh, well, how could you be a man the size of a child and possess a touch that could be anything but insane, if only halfway so. I laugh at past loves, at the dreary predictability of the past itself, which may or may not make sense. Darker the better with him. Hate to see all that face-making and bizarre dimpling. Here we are now, set inside ourselves, let him have his say or nay, ruttish tyrant, cycloid, stunted pasha whirling in his silk pillows.

Once more the boy's head protruded from the blanket. He heard water running somewhere and after a while he crawled out from under the blanket and sat on the floor of the cubicle, listening intently. Sitting in the dirt was pleasant, although he was sure there was no calm that compared with the calm prevailing under the table. In time he crawled over to the segment of canvas that covered most of the entrance and he peered beneath this overhang into the dimness at the bottom of the antrum. He heard the running water. Not on the slopes this time. Closer to this level, swelling, looking for an outlet. Chill water moving through joints and break lines and over flowstone formations. Cavern water rich in nitric acid that dissolves limestone to widen existing holes. Cave-maker, Wu thought, hearing the same sound, thinking the stream might be traveling upward, carving out an embryonic cave, a living structure with a cycle that ends in death, wondering how much trouble it would be to order a rubber dinghy, neoprene wet suit, aqualung and water-proof spotlight, dismissing the idea on the grounds he would not be here long enough to see it through. The higher he climbed the darker it got. Along the rippling beam of the lamp, his eyes sought an opening.

Billy left his cubicle and walked quietly toward the barrier and out over it. There was water nearby. He could feel as well as hear it. Where the floor of the antrum curved severely upward he put the heel of his shoe to a large flat stone and kicked it right through the natural hatch in the earth where it had been wedged. Water roaring engaged his senses. He lowered himself into the nearly vertical crawlway, knowing from the roar that it was only several yards long, and then braced his shoulders against one surface and his feet against the other and de-scended with some difficulty to solid ground. He could see almost noth-ing but knew he was on the edge of the underground river. It was fully a river in power and sound. It came flowing past him, carrying clay, silt and organic debris, carrying limestone to redeposit, straight on past, leaving him only a hint of its animal presence, that complex and adaptive motivation that directs living things toward the strangeness, beauty and freedom of repeated sequences. Naturally he put his hands in the water. It was cold enough to make him tremble and when he cupped his hands and brought some water to his lips to drink he felt some seconds later a brief assertion of pain behind his right eye. Mildly frightening. When it subsided he simply listened to the river, feeling no special need to see it, photograph it or take samples home to study. He had *tasted* it, after all. Some element of river-taste would subtract itself from the recollection of that unit of pain and he would learn again that hidden inside everything he knew was half of what he was. The river carried with it a near-sweet breeze, although not really that, nor a mineral redolence, nor whatever quality of freshness might result from its continuous onward movement, but something more complex, traveling with it from its source, that clarified whatever distance intervened between the river and the mind through which it flowed.

Speaking outside herself, Softly thought. Sex inevitably enriches itself during those transmanic times in which to speak sensible phrases is to contravene the meaning of the act. Assuming there is sperm in my ejaculate, have my sperm cells successfully collected in my epididymis, storing themselves in that convoluted parlor while they approach the basking trance of their maturity? Important to contemplate the mechanics of one's spermatic duct system. In this way we distinguish ourselves from lower forms of copulating life.

The darkness he found had grades or stages. Where the water flowed it wove the dark into something whole. Beyond the river, or where he thought the other side must be, the darkness was not as absolute, stretching into distances that could be recognized as filling specific limits. He sat and listened, trying to detect some modulation in the roar.

SELF-BETTERMENT

Lester Bolin barely awake summoned the young woman by gesture into his quarters. He sat at the edge of the bed twirling an index finger through the thinning area of his hair as though trying to produce an ultimate flourish with dessert topping, Jean thought, noting to herself that particular men seem to have been born in pajamas, friendly tentative suicidal men, their bodies no more than stuffing for those loose-fitting playclothes. She sat in a chair with a note pad in her lap and watched Lester settle into a thoughtful yawn.

"Rob said it was all right to ask you if it's all right, you know, to talk to me."

"Why are you wearing a raincoat?"

"Clothes are a mess."

"I accept that," he said.

"Need to be cleaned and things."

"I'm Mr. Bolin."

"What can you tell me about the Logicon project that might be in my technical grasp?"

"I'm working on this thing, this sort of machine, and what I hope to do is I hope to get it to speak actual Logicon. It'll save us huge amounts of time and trouble if all the most time-consuming and trouble-making aspects of Logicon can be handled by this control system. I'm using the most advanced materials and a lot of old-fashioned ingenuity. Mrs. Lown doesn't think Logicon can be spoken. She says it's inherently unspeakable. But I think I can provide meaningful sounds for our notation, which means all we have to do is come up with a metalogical language."

"So far I'm with you all the way," she said. "Please keep on going."

"Would you like to see my male member?"

Drowsily he plucked something from the midmost hollows of his pajamas. It was vividly sleek, a Pop Art penis, not at all like Bolin himself, all rumple and shrug. After a while he put it back in, more or less as an afterthought, it seemed to Jean, and not until he'd resumed his comments on Logicon.

"It hasn't been easy. You'll never get me to say it's been easy. And the toughest aspects are still to come. This is important so watch my lips. Metalanguage. We spend nearly every waking moment, Mrs. Lown

374

and I, trying to perfect an alternate system that we can use to analyze the consistency of the original system."

"That's it in theory," she said. "Now how will the control system actually function in the sense of electronically or whatever?"

"I don't think that's in your technical grasp."

"I was afraid not."

"I don't think that's in anyone's technical grasp who hasn't studied the matter from every angle over an extended period of time. I'm only being candid when I report that I myself have run into a great many problems in this area and expect to continue to run into a great many more problems. Now, I've spoken to you candidly and at length despite a certain amount of inconvenience, despite time lost that I could have used to better effect, i.e. the project itself, and despite repeated statements by Mrs. Lown and by me that contact with people outside the project would serve absolutely no purpose as far as our work is concerned. Despite all this I've granted you an interview. There's something you can do in return."

"What's that?"

"Show me your fuzzy-wuzzy," Lester said.

"Is it important to you, seeing it?"

"It's not important, no. When you say important, I'd definitely answer no. Not a matter of life and death by any means. If you don't want to show it, just ask whatever questions remain on your list and we'll go our separate ways."

"I'd rather not show it around too much."

"Fair enough," he said.

"Questions on my list," she said. "Rather than questions on my list, I'd like to ask you, if you don't object and even if you object strenuously, why you exposed what you call your male member and why you asked me to show you what you call by an even sillier name."

"Who could answer a question like that?"

"Do you do it often?"

"Of course not."

"Is there something about me that sort of drove you to do it?"

"There's something about me, I guess."

"What?"

"Who could answer?" he said.

It was at the precise second Billy lifted the canvas and stepped into his cubicle that Softly entered his own quarters, having just left the kitchen, where he'd had some timeless tea with Edna Lown, feeling suddenly glum gloomy morose dejected depressed, these states of mind unfolding in the irreversible succession of a thing singly perceived. From his briefcase he seized a packet of TriOmCon, tore it open and placed a pale tab under his tongue. He sat amid the pillows on his bed, *ratchety ratchety come and catchety*, eventually leaning over to untie his shoes and then removing the rest of the clothing and stretching for his robe, wondering in this interval of reaching out to finger the patterned fabric why it was that with the coupled obstacles of child size and cyclothymia he had to endure as well the thought-provoking if minor abnormality of a right testicle that hung noticeably lower than the left. What revenge was this on the left-flawed proportion that customarily prevailed? Balance of sag and nonsag in egg-shaped structures. Bilateral symmetry. He invented a zero-sum bi-level game with table of matching strategies. T's testicles, S's testicles. Left, right. Plus, minus. Never commented on (that I can recall) by a woman in a position to know, whether supine, astraddle, lotus-blossomed or otherwise, probably because they are so intent on the dynamics inevitably brought into play by the size of my body itself, a fact perhaps more important to their pleasure than my gracelessness, the violating aspects of my sexual presence. Child size. The innocent candor of their desire for something cherishable. In bed in his robe he tried to sustain a brief interval of unsullied stillness. Traveling upstream in microns per second, he thought. Rounded head, long tail. Traveling into warm weather and the medium of half masticated life. I am still "depressed." This should not be the case. I will stay in "bed" until it passes.

Billy noticed for the first time that the piece of paper left on his cot was not another display of Bolin's notation but another piece of junk mail, evidently delivered to Lester by mistake and then deposited here. It was a promotional item that included a small plastic key in an acetate seal. He sat on the cot and began reading.

Addressee:

Lacking in poise, self-confidence, the ability to gesture convincingly? Millions everywhere are discovering the dynamics of elocution. Our simple techniques will enable you to speak and gesture in public as never before. These self-training methods are revealed in our—

SELF-BETTERMENT CRASH PROGRAM

—by which you spend only minutes a day learning how to promote yourself with poise and lasting assurance, whether in business dealings, at social functions or in casual everyday conversation. Discover for yourself how our easy-to-follow rules will give you the skills you need to make a good impression every time you talk or gesture. Our booklet—

YOUR KEY TO ADVENTURES IN ELOCUTION
(the plastic key appeared here)

—can be yours free of charge when you agree to enroll in our Self-Betterment Crash Program. To receive this free booklet (and to be automatically enrolled at money-back rates if not pleased), do absolutely nothing. Those wishing neither booklet nor enrollment should write at once to: ACRONYM; c/o AAAA&A Guano Mines Ltd.; Dept. Aleph-Null; Aboard the Goo Fou Maru; c/o the Large Black Mooring; Kwangchow Bay. Postcards cannot be accepted.

All three items he'd received belonged in the category of junk mail but it was clear that this particular piece differed from the computer quiz and the chain letter in a major respect. It included a key. A tiny plastic key, to be sure, but still a key. A notched and grooved implement designed to open a lock. With his thumbnails he attacked the acetate seal and finally succeeded in freeing the little key. It had the cheap weightless feel of something you'd find at the bottom of a cereal box. Designed to open a lock. But what lock? He heard someone coming along the path and immediately lifted the blanket and got under the TV table. Heavy-footed Bolin again. Logician on the hoof. Again the sound of a single sheet of paper wafted toward his cot. When Lester was gone the boy crawled out from under the table and approached the lone page that rested in the middle of his bed.

```
(b) Num bow   (w) HA (m) ...   )
(a) (u,v) : ** : Xc tr Y    (()
(z) ! ... .  Irr Y: TTTTTT      $
(y) (X w(h)ee(( * )(      ,: /
(x) F* #i **-&lem........i'i'i'
(w) n(dG):        'O' @###'        d
(v) "                         "
(u) n(x)'' Ymaj.O: !. f()mii.
```

He crawled back under the table. He spent a long time thinking. Nameless danger. Time of inevitable terror. "Visit my room." A place in and of time. A place to sit and think. Who'd said that? "Visit my room." Endor. Endor's room. It was Endor who'd told him that. When you are faced with nameless danger, so on and so on, "visit my room." A place to sit and think. A room to comfort you. But Endor's room was padlocked. Endor's room had been padlocked since Endor left for the hole. He didn't have to think much longer. The key. The plastic key sealed into the junk mail. The tiny plastic implement designed to open locks.

A LOT HAPPENS

Billy changed his clothes and headed for the elevator. He turned a handle and the skeletal lift began to ascend. Eventually he crossed the catwalk, climbed the metal ladder, unlatched the exit grating and stood, slightly out of breath, in the canister he'd once occupied. Nothing seemed very different. He went out into the corridor, expecting to see some evidence of the kind of global tensions Softly had talked about both before and since their descent. He didn't know precisely what sort of evidence he'd expected. Sandbags maybe. Fire marshals. Boldly printed instructions for finding shelter. Blastproof cabinets full of canned goods and water. Large arrows painted on the walls. Morale-building slogans. First-aid hints. But nothing seemed very different. People came and went. The play maze was where it had always been. Linen carts were lined up along an extended section of the hallway. The voices of men and women he passed gave no indication that people here were under special stress. He found a "goal guidance phone" in an alcove and dialed INFO.

"This is tape sector B."

"I want to know Endor, where he's located, his room floor and number. Capital E-n-d-o-r. I want his room's location."

"Please state your medical history and then wait for a coded response detailing what medication, if any, is indicated as advisable in this instance. Remember, cold compress for swelling. Hot compress for tight muscles and that ache-all-over feeling. This message brought to you by the Wakefield Foundation, suppliers of medical products and chemical preparations to a generation of satisfied users."

"Being tape, you can't switch me to another line, right?"

"For simultaneous translations, dial SIMO. Your medication tape is pending. Dine internationally next time you're in Beirut. Abco-Panzer welcomes you to the newest showcase in its chain of fine eating establishments."

He hung up and stood there a while, looking around, a model of studied frustration. There was a phone directory in a horizontal slot precisely at eye level. Endor's name was listed and so was his room number. Billy took an elevator up there. The hallway lighting was harsh and it was obvious the walls and floor had not been cleaned for some time. There was no one around, a fact that intensified the tone of institutional dinginess. As he approached the door, it occurred to him that yes, of course, Endor's room would be set up to provide a perfect contrast to this sense of desolation. The padlock was still in place, an extremely large device attached to a metal fastener. He took the key out of his pocket, recalling his visits to the hobby room and the sort of emotional warmth generated by Endor's cluttered effects, imagining further what the room he was about to enter would look like, seeing it very clearly as he slipped the key into the cylinder. A drawing room with gothic hall chair and carved rosewood sofa. A fireplace with cast-iron grate and tasseled fabric overhanging the mantel. There would be a high-backed armchair with buttoned upholstery. There would be a hearth rug and a table with a chamber candlestick next to a chess set and a silver bottle stand. A drawing room with windows draped in layers of cloth, with a bookcase and bubble-back chairs and a mahogany tea caddy. On the walls would be large inspirational engravings and creamy portraits. Above would be a metal chandelier with frosted globes to spread the gaslight. A lacquered sewing table with mother-of-pearl inlay. A writing desk with a brass-stoppered inkpot and a curved tray for pens. On the mantel there'd be a clock as well as a vase with artificial flowers, both contained in bell jars. A drawing room with a large cabinet, shrouded in velvet, that held a tea service in bone china painted with assorted species of heather; that held biscuit barrels, toddy warmers, potpourri dishes with scroll feet, sporting ale jugs decorated with scenes of autumn; that held fruit dishes, gilded coffee cups and saucers, stoneware vases with waterweed motifs, ornamental plates that glowed in rose-splashed luster. A drawing room that provided to those who entered a sense of contentment, serenity, joy, well-being and comfort.

But it wasn't like that at all.

The room had hardwood floorboards that needed waxing. From the ceiling hung a single light bulb, unshaded. There was a rocking chair, plain in appearance, located in the far corner. A rectangular segment on one wall was cleaner than the rest of the wall. The imprint of whatever had been there indicated that the object extended from a line a few inches above the floor to a parallel line several feet below the ceiling and that it was about as wide as a pair of men standing abreast. The only other thing in the room was a Coca-Cola wall clock.

High on the northeast gradient Maurice Wu spotted a small opening in the hard earth and commenced inching his way in feetfirst. In minutes he was standing in a narrow passage full of dripstone formations whose intricacy made him think of the valves and piping of the body. He walked through a calcite basin into a small chamber. Here he decided to take off his pack and sit down a while, not really feeling the effects of the long climb until he was settled in a restful position, the labor of the ascent recalled in his breathing, a series of deep respirations easing off eventually into murmurs of de-accelerated fatigue. He looked around him now. The light from his headlamp caught a rimstone pool in the middle of the chamber. Not much else of immediate interest in sight.

The sound of rushing water he'd heard on his way up the slope was so faint now as to be part of the texture of the silence in the cave. As always in caves he felt he was here to remake himself. It was as though his senses had automatically emptied out just as he'd slipped into the opening. He was entering with a sense apparatus featureless and unformed. Caves were a test mechanism for the redevelopment of his animal faculties. Because the environmental demands were few, he was able to record the smallest irregularities in the silence and semidarkness with brilliant quickness and clarity. This enabled him to build within himself a separate presence, something unremembered, a receptive mentality that seemed to make him part of something more than the living cave around him at the same time as it set him adrift from what he could only regard as his distinctness, his Wu-experienced causal reality. At any rate he was less fearful here (although stimulated by such pure awareness that it amounted to something very much like fear, if fear could be called restlessness in expectation of danger) than nearly anywhere else. What we need, he believed, is a way to reinvent the human brain. As now constituted it can be viewed in cross-section as a model for examining the relative depths of protohistoric and modern terror. Cycles and swamp terrains of fear and periodically recurring depressions and earliest wetland secretions of dread (brain stem and midbrain), not to mention Mr. Mammal as paranoid grandee of the grassy plains, that (limbic) region of emotional disorganization, falling sickness, psychosomatic choking, another way of saying terror of the veldt, he thought, which is fear not really of lurkers in long grass but of the veldt itself, its terrifying endlessness, its obliteration of both singularity and pluralism, its lack of soul-cozying nooks, its tendency to disappear into itself, leaving us, he thought, with the geometry, music and poetry of our evolved, cross-referencing and highly specialized outer layer of gray tissue (cerebral cortex), not to mention celestial mechanics, medicine, the research and development of wars, not to mention voiceless cries in the night, utterly neomammalian this last activity, a cortical subclass of fear itself itself itself, thought Jean at her typewriter, staring at page twenty, numbered but otherwise blank, and wondering what it would take to "remember through" one's individual being on out into phylogenic space, that part of us not subject to conscious observation, out through breast-seeking mother-clinging babyhood into that segment of our ancestral mentality possessed in abundance by nonprimate forms of animal life, not to mention the *age* of the human brain, Wu thought, its unique status a matter of millions of years of neural variation from the brains of our taxonomic relatives. Oldness was becoming an obsession of his. Everything and everybody were turning out to be a lot older than anyone suspected. It began for Wu when he first learned about the charcoal-burning hearths and human skulls found half a century earlier in the caves at Chou-Kou-Tien. Everybody everywhere was being re-evaluated. In the Transvaal, Mexico, Europe, Indochina, the East African rift valley. Flint tools, jawbones, bark paper, shell necklaces, ivory weapons. One way or another the findings were pushing everything back, with ramifications broad enough to include the possibility that truly upright "men" coexisted with relatively erect "hominids."

"Hee hee," Softly remarked to Lester Bolin.

A nullifying plunge through history's other end to all those ancient and naïve astronomies of bone and stone.

He smelled it then. Having crossed the rimstone pool to wander at the other end of the chamber, he stood absolutely still, noting the acidic moldy odor of bat shit. He saw a crawlway leading to another chamber. As he emerged from the crawlway the carbide flame opened up into an immense petalous moon-vase of light, revealing the chamber to be much larger than the one he'd just vacated. He stood at the edge of the guano deposit. They were everywhere, roosting, probably by the hundreds of thousands, bats upside down, apparently blinking in response to the intruding light, their eyes becoming constituent glint-points of a vast flash effect that surged across the broad ceiling. Packed together as tightly as the colony was, it resembled some slowly gathering cave disease, a tissue anomaly that carried its own alien pale pigmentation. He stepped into the guano, careful of his footing, relieved to see it was only knee-deep. He checked the heights of the cave for cannibal bats, *megaderma*, never failing to find it incongruous that someone of his sensitivity would look forward (however buried the urge) to seeing these spike-nosed marauders attacking, killing and eating smaller bats. He didn't think they even belonged this far north but here they were, one gliding past him right now, impressive wingspread, nose-leaf, outsized ears, long pointed teeth, a bat fond of dismemberment, quick enough to kill in flight, capable of plucking the odd gecko from a temple wall. Of course, it was those aspects of the event considered apart from the actual killing and eating that appealed to him, considered apart from the seizure behind the smaller bat's ear, considered apart from the fact that *megaderma* eats everything but wings and head, considered apart from the blood and body fragments. It was the abstract phase of things for which he reserved his virtuous appreciation. The bat's flight path. The bat's sound-beaming apparatus. The mathematics of a moving target. The evolutionary logic that provides cannibalistic bats with fangs that enable them to grasp and slash.

    m. Speech therapists regard certain words as "cues to anxiety."
    n. Since words are attempts to relay impressions about the world, we must ask what shattered aspect of the world causes people to experience a conflict between the need to speak and the anxiety that weaves through a particular word.
    o. Are there as many shattered aspects as there are people who experience conflict?
    p. I'm tempted to say: together we blurt out the components of world consciousness.
    q. This leaves unexamined what has remained unsaid.

In Endor's room the boy rocked in the wooden chair. It was strange how a nearly bare room could seem so dense with exhausted thought. The bulb hung at the other side of the room. The clock was on the wall to his right. On the wall facing the clock was the imprint that extended from a line a few inches above the floor to a parallel line several feet below the ceiling. It was not unpleasant to sit here rocking. The fact that the chair was a rocking chair made a difference, he felt. In a conventional chair he would have been more bored than he was. The rocker definitely belonged. It was just right for this kind of room. When Endor had mentioned the "psychological security" of his padlocked room, he must have had the rocker at least partly in mind.

There were no windows. Across the clock's face was the word "Coca-

Cola" in upper and lower case letters. The clock was not the digital type, which definitely would have been out of place here. It was an old clock with pointed hands. Digital clocks, he felt, told time too bluntly. He had to concentrate for a second or so before he was able to place the digits in a meaningful context related to morning, afternoon, evening, an appointment here, a train to catch there. It may have been that most arrays of numbers had deep associations for him—mental connections that tended to develop freely when he looked at a clock that had no dial, no moving hands, no slashes to mark the minutes. But it was more than that. Digital clocks took the "space" out of time.

It didn't take him long to realize that the hands on the clock in the room hadn't moved since he'd entered. This was in no way surprising. In a room with scuffed floors and an old rocker and a single dim bulb hanging down, it appeared to him that a stopped clock was more or less appropriate. He took it to be an element of the restfulness that Endor had claimed for the room. Although disappointed at first, Billy was beginning to think that Endor knew what he was talking about. A place to think. A room to comfort one. A measure of security. There was something about the near bareness and the relative placement of the objects violating this bareness that made him feel the "inexpressiveness" of the room had been designed in highly precise terms. No lacquered sewing table or creamy portraits or mahogany tea caddy. Something else, however. Maybe just the rocking. The fluid viewpoint produced by this rhythmic motion. Maybe the light. The degree of grim scrutiny suggested by a naked bulb. Maybe the lines in the floor or the sound of the rocker or the tone of exhausted thought. The more bare an area, it would appear, the deeper we see. It was beginning to occur to him that something about the Coca-Cola wall clock was a lot more interesting than the fact that it was stopped.

What the clock said, the time it told, was twenty-eight minutes and fifty-seven seconds after two. It was there to see, clear as could be. The second hand had stopped precisely on the mark denoting fifty-seven. The minute hand was exactly two marks shy of half past the hour. The hour hand was between two and three, shading toward two.

Two (p.m.) was the fourteenth hour after midnight. Fourteen hours, twenty-eight minutes, fifty-seven seconds. This of course was the pulse array transmitted by the ARS extants. Fourteen, twenty-eight, fifty-seven.

At first something had been missing. The twenty-eight was there. The fifty-seven was there. It had taken him the length of several breaths to realize that two o'clock, if viewed as postmeridian time, corresponded to fourteen hours.

He had been right in believing the ARS extants used a positional notation system based on sixty. As he'd already determined, their number 14,28,57 corresponded to our number 52,137. It wasn't until now that he realized the significance of the latter number. Seconds after midnight. Time. They were giving us the time. It happened to be the case that the sixty-based system coincided with our current method of keeping time. What he envisioned briefly was a paired set of figures appearing in a drizzle not dissimilar to his own brand of handwriting:

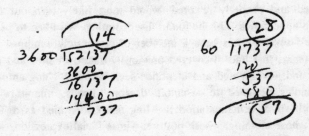

The code then was just barely mathematical. There had been little to solve really. The simplest arithmetic did the trick. What was required was merely to see that the numbers in question referred to a time of day. The ARS extants were intent on alerting us to a particular hour, minute and second. No more than that. Apparently they wanted us to know that something might happen at twenty-eight minutes and fifty-seven seconds after two p.m. on a day yet to be determined.

That was it then. He'd deciphered the message, found the answer, cracked the star code. Not through mathematics as much as through junk mail—a plastic key that fit a particular lock.

He thought of the people who'd preceded him and failed. Those before Endor. Then Endor himself. He wondered now about Endor's motive in mentioning this room in the first place. Was it just security and comfort he cared about? Or did he know the answer was written on the face of that clock?

It was possible that Endor was living in a hole and feeding on larvae not because he'd failed to figure out the message but because he'd succeeded. In other words he'd interpreted the answer in a negative sense. A very negative sense. A sense so negative he'd gone looking for a hole in which to live.

In the lunar urn of the bat cave Maurice Wu excavated an area littered with broken pottery. Together the shards began to suggest certain characteristics he'd spotted in other pieces and it wasn't too long before he was ready to guess that these were fragments of a lead-glazed pottery bowl (early Han), the thickness of the glaze at the rim indicating that the piece had been fired upside down. The bowl, if assembled and properly restored, would most likely turn out to be simple in appearance. This he found disappointing. Wu liked to be dazzled. He'd several times been a member of elaborately equipped prospecting teams that had discovered previously unknown sites and eventually found, investigated and identified such items as T'ang amphoras with handles designed to resemble dragons' heads; miniature jade vases with spiral ornamentation; a Ming figure identified as a Taoist divinity whose clothing, whose posture, whose facial expression, whose accompaniment of symbolic animals had associations that branched back hundreds and thousands of years, every such conjunction subscattering then into increasingly cryptic motifs involving taboos, legends, reincarnations, composite gods. How enriching he found this sort of thing, never one to overlook the fact that religion and art probably began in caves and having always viewed religion as nothing more or less than an integrated system of art in which a superhuman element is variously invoked, beseeched, prattled at and adored. A religion's success or failure, for him, was based solely on the conscious efforts of its practitioners to express their veneration in ways that reflected, expanded and altered the mind's conception and the senses' external arrest of what

386

is beautiful. In Wu's scheme of things, Hinduism, for example, was an overflowing success, a plague-chronicle of diversities, cycles, soul wanderings and richly depressing cultural practices; while, for instance, the eerie Protestant disciplines that stressed hymn-singing and Bible-reading struck him as being deficient in those contemplative delights that color the oriflamme of art. Guano dropped nearby. He troweled and sorted in the dimness, wondering why it was that systems of religion were so often used as frames of reference for the clarification of ideas that were in no way related to spiritual attitudes. Self-contradiction. The flailing brilliance of initiates in those unspecifiable realms deemed so central to being. Newton resorting to the idea of God as an absolute encompassing structure in his theory of mechanics. Leibnitz in the heyday of his mysticism using binary arithmetic to try to convert the Emperor of China to Christianity.

Wu mused on latent history. Not the negative chronology of years B.C. but a class of intelligible events too fine to be collected in the sifting mechanism that determines which sets of occurrences are to be recorded and analyzed as elements in a definite pattern and which examined merely for their visibility as the coarser of the particles in the mesh. Latent in any period's estimation of itself as an age of reason is the specific history of the insane. Diametrically opposed entities, Rob had said, partaking of each other's flesh. Does syncretism really permeate all my thinking? Lost historic categories. Appearing neither in patterns nor as radioactive flashes. One might extend this search for lost categories to a subject as choicely off-putting as guano. The history of guano mining. Worldwide guano markets. Effects of guano on agriculture, trade, society. Bird matter vs. bat matter. Soil renewal and patterns of economic decline. Techniques of vacuum-pumping bat guano by the ton into enormous cylinders which are hauled out of the caves by an aerial conveyor system, and the profits thereof.

Not far from the fragments of pottery he found a circular bronze mirror, its reflecting surface shattered, the rest of it in remarkably good condition. This was by far the most interesting thing he'd come upon since he'd started exploring these caves. He estimated its period as late Warring States, which coincided well enough with the lead-glazed bowl.

He used his pocket magnifier to examine the back of the mirror, its concave rim, the concave band encircling the small fluted knob at the very center. Between rim and band was the ornamental field. He was both surprised and undazzled by the mirror's design element. Abstract geometric patterns executed in thread relief. A ring of figures that made him think of the ambiguous markings on the stone at Sangkan Ho. What was surprising was the fact that the design was so purely non-representational, apparently empty of any attempt on the craftsman's part to stylize animal or other figures or in any way to sacrifice reality to principles of design; most likely there'd been no thought at all of an antecedent reality. What was undazzling about the mirror was the fact that it was so completely free of the swarming ornamentation, the animal motifs, the dragon scrolls, the cosmological diagrams, the visual puns, the syncretistic juxtapositions and the *b'ai kiu* or play-verse as well as other types of inscriptions that characterized centuries of Chinese mirrormaking. He spotted several corroded areas that would have to be swabbed with a chemical solution to remove the offending copper chloride, an agent of what is known as bronze disease. Of course, oldness was one thing. Europe, Mexico, the Transvaal, the East African rift valley. Oldness was one thing but reverse evolution was something else; probable mental progression in the wrong direction; advancement backward. It was one thing that the findings were pushing human origins back to a point in time much more remote than anyone had believed possible; it was quite another thing (as he was reminded in thinking of the Sangkan Ho stone) to find signs of advancing culture the deeper we probe. With his trowel he drew and marked a figure in the powdery dung.

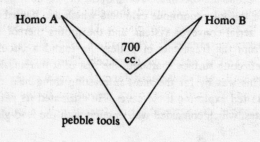

So we begin to see not only that we go back much farther than previously estimated but also that there is no aspect of the natural history of the brain or femur that makes it obligatory to deduce that evidence of our extended lineage must show ever increasing primitivism—smaller and smaller cranial volume, cruder tool types, nonhuman skeletal organization. Given the questions that still existed concerning the early atmosphere of the planet and the age and nature of the first living organisms, given the factors not yet taken into account (there are always factors not yet taken into account), given the relative speed with which complicated molecular systems developed and the nonrigorous estimates of the time involved for these designs to elaborate themselves, it seemed to Maurice Wu that an element of poetic truth might be contained in the speculation that humans and their precursors filled that huge primordial blank in the fossil record (a blank just beginning to be systematically roughed-in). Not being a specialist in biochemistry he had the advantage of nearly free-reined conjecture and used it to imagine a form of accelerated evolution (a process consisting, after all, of nothing more than life plus time) taking place in some lost fold of our genetic beginnings, long before the firemakers, the cave painters, the crafters of bone daggers, the brachiating primates, the bipeds who sucked nonopposable thumbs. This expeditious, this somewhat cursory emergence would be followed, in his scheme, by a gradual decline to the point where cranial capacity measured well under a thousand cubic centimeters, which is precisely where things at the Sangkan Ho strata began to get interesting. Poetic truth usually raises more questions than the fledgling poet is inclined to answer; nevertheless, he believed, we are on to something here.

Billy kept on rocking, enjoying the illusion that the room was gradually emptying itself of exhausted thought. Dense sensations reduced themselves to points, lines and planes. The unshaded bulb. The rectangular imprint on one wall. The pattern made by the grain in the hardwood floor. The hands on the clock. The angle at which light climbed one wall. The continuous functional shift in the room's configuration (noun to verb) due to his movement in the rocker. Something may happen at fourteen hours, twenty-eight minutes and fifty-seven seconds on a day yet to be determined. The correct number of objects. The objects spaced at fitting distances. The distances defined in varying degrees of light and shade. The light and shade informed by a converse moderation. Space and periodic solids. Continuously filled transitions. Acts of the time-factoring mind.

Several ravaging bats swept past an outcropping of rock and then flashed toward the ceiling. Wu was unable to observe the subsequent kills at the precise time they took place (due to *megaderma*'s quickness and his own delayed reaction) but did manage to "re-record" events (or fit them together) as the discarded parts of a number of roosting bats hit the floor of the cave. Deciding to inspect these particular inedibles, presumably wings and heads, he got up and walked toward the other end of the cave, filled with a childlike mingling of aversion and thrill, the severed and no doubt bloody extremities concentrated in an area dense with limestone formations. When he got there he realized he would either have to squeeze past some jagged rocks to reach the leavings or enter the area through a small crawlway. In a prone position he began to work his way through the opening, which was of no greater length than his own body but more cramped than he'd expected. He was nearly to the other end when the flame in his headlamp went out. The darkness was total and he was frozen to the stone. He tried to think beyond the level of unchecked hysteria. The core of his immobility was a whirl of (psychic) motion. He told himself to remain calm. He tried to fight the illusion of rush, of speed, of overwhelming events. He couldn't move his arms to reach the matches in his coveralls. With a lighted match he could easily find his way to the backpack on the other side of the cave. In the backpack were candles. In the light of one of these candles he could easily refill the carbide lamp. But he couldn't seem to move. He told himself to think into this problem calmly. After a while he was able to grasp the possibilities. Either he couldn't move because his fear had made him rigid. Or he was wedged. He realized he was not breathing properly and then felt chills in his upper body. He tried to gauge his panic, to talk to it, to determine its contents. Again he told himself to proceed with utter calm. He summarized the situation and calmly measured the depths of his terror. It was difficult to maintain a thought for more than several seconds. He attempted to concentrate on the problem of movement, on involuntary rigidity versus being wedged. This is unreal fear, he told himself. This is fear based on unreasonable foundation. This is unfounded fear. In a series of incomplete summaries he tried to tell himself what had happened, where he was, how he felt, when he would be able to move again. But being wedged. The possibility of being wedged kept occurring to him. Being wedged meant something he did not give a name to. There was still the feeling of speed to contend with, the rush of events (although obviously nothing was happening), this uncontrollable hurry in his mind, this nullifying plunge. He tried to recall precisely what had happened. Was darkness all that happened? Or did his shoulders become stuck in the crawlway as well? He wasn't sure. He couldn't remember. He was afraid to try to squirm backward. He thought this might confirm his being wedged. He thought his feet, his toes might be able to move slightly, his hands, his fingers, thus establishing that it was not fear that caused his immobility. His body itself would be stuck fast. Then he would know he was wedged. There was no dark adaptation, or adjustment of the eyes, in this total blackness. This was not just complete absence of light but a state of its own, the quality of authentic darkness, that aspect of nightlikeness which makes distinctions impossible. This dark had a special presence. It was far from empty. It was not just nonlight. It had a nature that dated back. It had intrinsic characteristics. It was animal. Be calm, he thought. Analyze the fear and you will control it. He began to wail then. It happened before he knew what was taking place and after a while it seemed that he had given himself over to this lamentation as one enters an irreversible state of being. What came out of him was a series of prolonged near-rhythmic sounds, intense and pitiful, marked by the fact that he was able to sustain each high-pitched cry far longer than might have been considered possible under the circumstances, any circumstances.

r. To avoid the associations commonly attached to certain words, we have renounced ordinary language in our theoretical study of patterns of reasoning.

s. In using symbols to denote logical operations, we have done much to eliminate imprecision, nuance, emotion, the variety of evocative "meanings" that cling to spoken and written words.

t. In advancing toward conclusions that are by nature unshakable, we have attempted to set aside intuition.

u. Mathematics is only as correct as logic allows it to be.

v. We have developed in fact such tightly precise levels of argument that they have led us into the midair anxiety of that engine-stalling aspect of metamathematics in which we see only too clearly the innate limitations of formal systems, the overthrow of proof, the essential incompleteness of the axiomatic method.

w. We are left trembling with success.

x. Can we theorize on the existence of a link between the rigor of this logical undecidability and the strict limits that language has set around itself?

y. Language is the mirror of the world.

z. What we have yet to learn how to say awaits our impossible attempt to free reality from the restrictions it must possess as long as there are humans to breed it.

Wu was engaged in a lifelong effort to become Chinese. His crossing between the spheres was becoming burdensome in many ways, with the result that what had been a tendency to examine and strengthen the Oriental aspects of his identity was now a demanding need and more. The cultural parts could not be equated; the languages were noninterlocking; the souls did not shine in each other's light. These, it seemed, were the obstacles he faced. His own life then was a bitter contradiction of that dyadic principle of thought in which an element complements its opposite. State of being one. Singleness of purpose. Constancy and accord. Ironic that these intuitive Chinese objectives were precisely what he saw no hope of attaining in the years that remained to him (relative youth notwithstanding). During his stays at one or another division of the Chinese Academy of Sciences he was never able to believe that his presence was any more than an *exchange* of some unspecifiable sort, a form of reciprocal scientific politeness in which a rather anonymous prehistorian from the West is allowed to stride casually in and out of the Institute of Vertebrate Paleontology and Paleoanthropology, occasionally speaking the language to colleagues, who (as per terms of contract) answer him in elaborately meaningless phrases—this entire affair, down to the length of his stride, subject to duplication in a Western university (or some such) with a slightly Westernized Chinese scientist doing the striding and with English the language in question.

Vocal sounds in meaningful patterns.

The language itself, Chinese, was a deeply woven structure through which he tried to guide his intercultural assumptions. To become Chinese was to rethink oneself, to yield to alien verities. Whatever was in him of that nation and race had to be allowed to find its way to definitive expression. The vagueness of such an undertaking was precisely what made it seem impossible; the generalities that had to be exposed in layers; the set of personal characteristics that had to be restaged somehow; the primary source that had to be found; the embedded part of him that had to be read and understood: 本

Wu, risking the well-ordered foolishness of the man who leads an overexamined life, was determined to resist the prospect of failure. At some accessible level of his being, the prevailing theme, he continued to believe, was simple unity. The single-cell mechanism of man in nature. The rote-prayer of centuries of science. To be only part Chinese was to be an archery target for the honed ironies his own predicament had given precise dimensions to. His thinking led in nearly every direction to some outsized metaphor, *this* the object of his ironic perception, *that* the impediment to his personal search.

The cave was silent. He resolved to investigate this silence, to examine it systematically, to measure it in detail. It was true; he was sure of it now. Silence prevailed in the bat cave. This meant his wailing had stopped. He still felt moist chills in his back and chest but his breathing was fairly regular now and he was no longer wailing, not wailing, released from the need to wail. Events did not appear to be overrunning him any more; there was no illusion of speed to contend with. Everything was clear and getting clearer. Why had he been so confused before and why was he so nearly lucid now? He was not wedged. He knew this as surely as it is possible to know a thing. It was necessary only to squeeze backward out of the crawlway. He was certain of this. It was obvious. All he had to do was squirm back out, get a match from his coveralls, light the match, find his way to the backpack, remove a candle from the pack, light the candle, get the extra carbide, refill the lamp. This he did, all of it in a matter of minutes, and it was simple and done and over, all fiction, Jean thought, wondering what it would take to "remember through" the ochre and soot of cave art to the very reason why these earliest of artists descended to the most remote parts of caves and applied their pigments to nearly inaccessible walls, the intricate journey and the isolated site being representative perhaps of the secret nature of the story told in the painting itself, all fiction, she thought, all fiction takes place at the end of this process of crawl, scratch and gasp, this secret memory of death. Breathing evenly now he reached under his coveralls and sweater to touch his *wu-fu*, a reassuring moment, the bat pendant cool against his fingertips, cool and faintly moist from the sweating he'd done. No longer, he thought, am I running for commissioner of shit. Time to report to Rob and get on back to the field and leave these nocturnal flying mammals to excrete in peace. After relighting the lamp he put the residue formed by the old carbide in an airtight container, where it could not harm anything living. He heard the roosting bats begin to squeak and whistle. There was motion here and there. Some were airborne now, a few, the great majority still chloroformed in roosting posture, suspended in their self-enfolding fur. As he gathered his things together, the whistling became gradually louder and more bats pelted down off the ceiling, small and barely definable presences, the dim light stung by their veering taps and caroms. Wu sat next to his pack, wondering where the opening was that would let them find their night. Crazed bat consciousness, he thought. I must have sounded part bat for a while back there or a wailing male banshee assigned the death of the fairy folk themselves. Wings everywhere. The cave appeared to be a crumbling substance transformed continually into something that grew more and more desperate to be relieved of this endemic unrest. No special pattern disclosed itself, the bats clustering in generally circular subdivisions of larger masses, the blast of beating wings increasing in volume, *megaderma* still in evidence here and there, cruising in their homicidal flight paths, their private little eddies of disruption and blood, all the bats guided by orientation pulses of ultrasonic frequencies, the animal charms of echolocation, he thought (children more sensitive than adults to high frequency bursts), these pulses beamed through the nostrils of bats in flight but how interpreted on their return, he wondered, deciding ears alone were not enough and that the brain must be involved, some clever acoustic center that enables each aeronautic creature to classify in transit the nature of the object that intercepted and returned the original beamed sound. The cave was like a living madness now. Bats perhaps in the millions. It was becoming easier to detect the spaces between bats than individual bats themselves. Then even these spaces began to vanish. Wing-thundering echoes on the level of some heart-stopping natural calamity bearing down on a town. Wu began to laugh. He didn't know what was going on. He'd been in dozens of bat caves but had never witnessed the mass exit and could not place it in some logical context. It was an incoherent event. The incredible storm roar of wings. The sense of insane life rising out of what had been only moments earlier a set of limestone surfaces. The sheer number of bats. The frenzy of their withdrawal. He watched small groups of bats separate themselves from larger clusters and fly on out past a limestone column toward what he assumed was the passage that led to open night and he imagined himself on the other side of this opening, able to watch the colony emerge, first in small sets and groups and clusters, then larger units, these advance swarms followed by the main body, all flying close to the mouth of the cave as the rest of the bats came pouring out, the withdrawal taking a very long time, circles stacking up, increasingly precise figures in a vast wavering column, the wind blast deepening, the column growing taller, the cave emptying finally, no longer the slightest wisp of individual motion, all one now, a great spiraling flight that whispered into its season beyond the trees. And because he liked to be dazzled, Wu in his corner of the cave, pondering the reflecting mechanism of this means of navigation, sat laughing into the night.

I SIT A WHILE LONGER

Billy rocked in Endor's chair as Edna slept as Softly left his bed, took the elevator, crossed the catwalk, climbed the metal ladder, emerged from the canister, walked through a series of corridors and stopped before a particular door. What was unusual about this door was the fact that it had a metal bolt on the outside. Softly slid this bolt into its socket, then headed back toward the elevator.

Jean Sweet Venable stayed awake to test her own steadfastness, the persistence of her bleak resolution to confront the pain of being self-aware. The onset of the danger of true belief. The end of one's utter presentableness. The imminence of fear itself. (She relied on the convenience of titles.) What a settlement of sheer plantation ease we might occupy if only we could choose to hide now and again from thought, perception, feeling, will, memory and morbid imagination. Sleep is no help. The period before sleep was her time of greatest mental helplessness, in fact. A sense of semiwaking awareness artificially induced. Anesthesia not quite complete. Involved mental processes of deadly repetition. Blank horror. Fear in spaceless combinations. A fixed design that included death and something else as well. Sleep itself is an improvement but not always. The period after sleep is usually not as bad as the period before sleep but there are times when it is worse, when the lack of control suggests once more a treacherous anesthetic. Why isn't it possible for us to rest from time to time in some tropical swoon of nonentity? Because no matter the drugs, the cures, the sleeps, the disciplines, the medications, there is no escaping (she was on the floor now, looking for a particular blank page) the unlikelihood of escape. Maybe she had concluded prematurely that the woman in the book wasn't like her at all, at all. The name he'd given her. Impossible to think of herself with a name like that and yet names are the animal badges we wear, given not only for practical necessity but to serve as a subscript to the inner person, a primitive index of the soul, and how could she be certain, sibylline instincts or not, that the name the novelist had given her would not in the end find its rightful soul to wear. The dialogue he'd written. Nothing at all like something she would say and yet how could she know what word or words were still to be spoken. The character had fainting spells. The character sometimes sat all night in doorways. The character's underwear stank. Successive reflections. Halfway through *Eminent Stammerers*, Jean had imagined herself as a Modern Library Giant. Sticking with her title even after she discovered that it was not quite as technically precise as *Eminent Stutterers* would have been, she filled a limited number of pages with a relaxed commentary (it wasn't the deepest of texts) on the neurosis of the speech tract; on the possibility that stuttering (interruption of word-flow) is, like glossolalia (extended word-flow), an example of learned behavior that calls for negative practice or unlearning; on the phenomenon of being alienated by one's own voice; on word-fear as a threat to sanity. She wondered, now, crawling for her blank sheet, how she'd ever expected to complete the multitude of pages necessary to qualify one's book for candidacy as a Modern Library Giant. Surely to those who suffered from it (Aristotle, Aesop, Darwin, Dodgson, Moses, Virgil, among those eminent enough to be mentioned in the text), stammering to some extent represented the "curse" of verbal communication, the anfractuous blacktop route from the pure noise of infancy. It was also a "recording" of one's mental processes, a spontaneous tape of that secret pandemonium to which childhood is often prone. Imagine, nonstammerer, the terror of this simplest question: "What is your name, little girl?"

What she'd completed thus far, since abandoning the idea of a non-fiction book on Logicon, amounted to no more than a thin scattering of pages. Some of these pages even had words on them. A few, yes, a very few had words scribbled and typed here and there, starting from the top. The others, which she considered no less a part of the thin scattering of first-draft material, were lacking in formal content, although clearly numbered and therefore distinguishable from each other. The very page she was on the floor searching for happened to be numbered but otherwise blank and yet distinguishable from the other pages not only by number but in the nature and quality of the words she had not yet set down on this page. To overcome one's tonic block; to master words; to live without the inner will to stammer. Her own speech had never been hesitant, spasmodic or in any way labored. What satisfaction was there (if any) in the foreknowledge (if any) that one was on the verge of a stammer? Is there a special kind of mind (scientist, fabulist, poet) that believes in the necessity of continual psychic testing, that needs to see confirmed its own logical picture of living hell? Her childhood had been relatively free of stress. She had walked, talked and played without serious complication. "Gigg" (it had been reported to her by those who called themselves her parents) was the first word she spoke. A giddy girl, a thing that whirls. The page she'd been looking for was under some clothes that were under the bed. She studied it, easily perceiving that the certain kind of writing that would eventually fill this page was different in look, in sound, in touch from the writing she would entrust to any of the other blank pages, as indeed these remaining blanks would differ from each other. Of course, from this clear and easy perception it was just a short step to the visionary insight that it was not necessary to fill in the blank pages, to entrust any kind of writing at all to these pages. These pages were already complete. *She knew* what they would look like with words on them. *It was not necessary* to think of these words and set them down on these pages. From her knees she studied the room itself. Everywhere she looked in the room were these pages, almost all of them numbered and blank, dispersed over the various surfaces of her strewn clothes. Immense bedraggled dishevelment. She stayed awake to prolong that state of near sleep that represented the most treacherous level of helplessness. It was like spending one's life stupefied in the worst of ways, permanent hesperian depression, the mind able to comprehend nothing but its own fear, the unlikelihood of its escape from self-awareness. So these pages then, these numbered pages would one day contain a fiction of her making. It would be complete when the pages were complete, hundreds of them, or thousands, blank nearly every one, easy to imagine with certain kinds of words on them. Jean decided she needed air, night air, she needed out of here, if only for the briefest time. She could not open the door, however. The door was apparently locked from the outside.

The first Latin word she'd ever spoken (according to those who claimed to be her teachers) was *pupilla*, which has the roundabout charm of meaning "little orphan girl" while it refers to the pupil of the eye, a connection based on the fact that when a child looks at her own miniature reflection in another person's eye, she sees a female figure locked inside concentric rings, a lone doll in a coiled room, a little orphan girl, herself, confined in the pupil of someone else's eye. Whose eye is this, Jean thought, that I am looking at so closely? What do I expect to find mingled with my own reflection in the center of that frigid iris? She took off her clothes, reclined on the bed and waited for her child-sized lover to open the door and, as he did, to enter the room and the woman in the room in nearly simultaneous strokes of motion.

Softly feeling better about things was in his quarters in his bed in his pajamas, a dynast in the lounging bliss of a culminating vision. What did it matter that divergence from type had long been identified as the inescapable trait of those maladapted to their surroundings? Size, what was size? Pigmentation, what was that in the light of the passionate science of the mind? The antrum was a cave, in effect. In caves, remember, there is no need for special size, for skin color, even for eyesight itself. The unpigmented thrive here. Microscopic mossy life. Degenerate optical apparatus. To be unfit elsewhere is to count oneself among the naturally select in this inverse austral curve. Eek what a break—is that a nose or a hose?

"Lester."

"I come in?"

"All means."

"Rob, I've been meaning to ask."

"Find yourself a chair."

"What did Dent say?"

"Dent, Dent?"

"You went to see old Dent."

"The submarine," Softly said.

"You never told me what he said."

"What did I ask?"

"You asked about the metalogical aspects of the problem."

"He said arithmetize. I remember now. He said replace every assertion with a number-theoretic statement. He was sitting in a deck chair."

"Sure, arithmetize," Bolin said. "Obvious enough. But how does that help me with the machine? In concrete terms, what do I do? How do I wire? What goes where?"

"He said something about the relay system. It sounded vague to me. I wouldn't worry about it, Les. The important thing is the language, not the machine. I don't even know why I made that trip. There was a eunuch aboard. Dent had a stone. What's that on my desk?"

"It's a bronze something. Mirror. Encased in plaster and burlap with just enough showing. Genuine artifact, my guess."

"Maurice Wu must have left it. A gift from Maury, I'll wager. He's just come down from the slopes. Cover it up, will you? Put that robe over it."

"The glass isn't much use anyway, Rob."

"Cover it up," Softly said.

Bolin thought it might be interesting to match the logical symbolism of the characters on his typewriter with a highly distinctive metalogical notation—a sort of Nazi typeface (super-Hollywood-gothic) with broad counters and thick slurping serifs. It would set off a strict contrast, command attention, forcefully highlight the existence of logical rigor. At this stage, however, he didn't know how serious he was about the idea.

For the machine itself he planned to use logically coded values rather than numbers except in the metamathematical sphere, where the need to arithmetize required numbering of the formal expressions (if he could figure out how to do it), the natural number series in this case beginning neither with zero (*Peano, Hilbert*) nor with one (*Dedekind*) but, for technical reasons involving logical constants and their negations, with minus-one (*Lown, Bolin*).

Logicon Project Minus-One.

The machine's metallic luster delighted Bolin. The coin slot was nearly completed. Lester loved the coin slot. He'd long considered the possibility of using lipstick or paint or crayon to make formal markings on the "head" and "torso." Abstract ritualistic figures. Protogeometry of some kind. Imagine Rob and Edna when they saw it. Imagine them putting coins in the slot and hearing the thing speak Logicon. Old-fashioned ingenuity, Bolin thought, recalling without apparent reason the faultless professionalism the young woman had shown, the reporter, when he'd made that indelicate request in the midst of their interview; the peerless near hesitation she'd utilized between his request and her reply-in-question-form. ("Is it important to you, seeing it?") He'd revealed his sex organ to her for the most innocent of reasons. Although he couldn't identify this reason specifically, he was convinced of its innocence. He'd shown his and asked to see hers. It was what people did. Usually people did this in more socially complex ways. In his momentary innocence he had done it directly. This by most standards made him either a menace or an object of pity. He knew he was neither. What he'd done was in its own way a case of enigmatic tenderness, performed and articulated in the sheen of recent waking, an act made defenseless by this very circumstance, the bewitchment of the intellect by sleep. Revealing his genitals was a form of dreamy speech. This was the thing he'd done, the exchange he'd attempted, but he didn't know why any of it had happened. Probably his motive could not be known. His motive most likely would have to be traced to one of those impulses so close to the electrochemical essence of things that microwires in bundles would have to be sunk into the skull and the basis for his action reduced to an investigation of neural events, or oscillating shapes on graph paper. But ritualistic markings, he thought. They were bound to be amused by that. This primitive android control system. This synthetic talking primate. His wife was in the converted barn and he was in the antrum, joined now in Softly's quarters by Walter Mainwaring with an armful of documents.

"News," he said.

Softly issued a general call and in moments Edna Lown and Maurice Wu entered the large cubicle. Everyone's attention was directed toward Mainwaring, who, as he sorted the documents on his lap, working with his customary brisk efficiency, manifesting his usual confidence, looking trim, fit, ready and fresh, was wondering exactly what the ingredients were in that synthetic intensifier Softly had convinced him to take a little while ago, claiming on its behalf (Rob's actual words) "a tendency to produce insights unattainable by other means" and there was no doubt he was feeling fine at the moment, possibly at a mental peak, although he didn't know whether this justified the anxiety of having to undergo an initial period of strangely spaced breathing and rambling speech. Softly's whitest smile. They were eager to hear him begin.

"We have not, repeat, have not yet detected evidence of an actual mohole anywhere in the galaxy or beyond. However, we feel we are making progress. At Cosmic Techniques, my home base in Toronto, we have sylphing teams working around the clock. It's important for us to find a mohole because analysis of the sylphing compounds may help us confirm the latest findings, which you'll agree, I think, are rather startling, however tentative. Using information gathered by satellites, balloon-borne instruments and, most of all, by a device of recent concoction called an echolocation quantifier, we believe we have traced the radio signals to their source."

"Tell us," Softly said.

"The source of the message is planet Earth."

"Fascinating," Lown said, drawing out the word in tentative awe.

"The signals originated from somewhere on this planet. Were absorbed in some component of the mohole totality. Were eventually reflected back this way, where they were picked up by the synthesis telescope at Field Experiment Number One."

"That is something," Bolin said.

"Our analysis indicates that the missing matter in the universe is probably contained in moholes, as was theorized by Mohole himself. That the radio signals were definitely artificial rather than some kind of natural emission. That these signals almost surely originated in a solar system x number of light-years from the center of the Milky Way and located in a spiral arm on the galactic plane and furthermore on a planet relatively close to the solar hub of this system, a planet having a sidereal period of revolution about its sun of x days at a mean distance of x point x million miles and an axial rotation period of x hours and x minutes, the precise figures in this bottom folder, and an average radius of x miles and a mass of x times x to the x number of pounds."

"Marvelous," Softly said. "That is absolutely marvelous."

"Sylphing is an entirely new process. Once we penetrate the secrets of moholes, the lawlessness, if you will, of the mohole phenomenon, we think we'll really make some wonderful progress in understanding the structure and constituent dynamics of the universe."

"Walter, you're a marvel. I knew you'd come through."

"We still have to confirm, Rob."

"Just as I said back then, Walter's the last one I need to fit all the elements together. The final one-of-a-kind mind. Maury, speak to us. Your turn. Tell us what you've come up with."

Maurice Wu sat slumped forward, nodding slowly, elbows resting just above his knees, palms joined and fingers pointing down. He took off his glasses, held them up, gazed into the lenses, slipped the glasses back on. Once more he leaned forward, nodding.

"Okay, cranial capacity as well as noncranial parts. This is way down past stunted pebble-tool hominids. We get modern posture, modern brain capacity, modern locomotion. Work at the strata is proceeding very slowly. Everyone is determined to be exceedingly cautious. Analysis of whatever is found has to be painstaking almost beyond belief. Removal of encrusted debris. Reconstruction of shattered bones. Microscopic examination. Okay, so what's the next level going to yield? How far back will the strata take us? To what sort of living thinking entity? Right now all I can report, aside from whatever I've already told you, is that part of a jawbone has been found. I've just been notified. It includes a fixed replacement for several teeth. Bridgework, in other words. As yet, nobody knows quite what the material is that was used to make the bridge."

"Lovely," Bolin said.

"In my own mind I've been convinced for quite some time that what the dig seemed to indicate was in fact the case. In the very distant past on this planet, there was a species of life that resembled modern man both outwardly and otherwise. Intellectually I've managed to accept this without reservation. Now, thanks to Walter, we know precisely what these people were capable of doing, technologically. They were capable of beaming radio signals into space. In time we may learn much more about them. You know, while Walter was talking, I was prompted to recall that some time back some experts in reactor engineering were having trouble explaining the details of what they believed to be a spontaneous nuclear reaction in a uranium deposit over a billion years ago. Not everything fit in. There was a chain reaction all right. The unique composition of the uranium told them that. But the conditions that would invite such an event to take place spontaneously were not likely to have been present under the circumstances that prevailed in that time and place. So."

"There we are," Softly said.

"I don't know what it means," Wu said. "But there we are. Possibly the reaction was intense enough to cause a series of rather sizeable explosions."

"Why speculate?" Softly said. "We have what we need."

"Exactly," Bolin said. "A lovely, lovely model."

"Good to excellent," Lown said.

"I mention the uranium business," Wu said, "only to suggest the possibility that our original evolutionary thrust was followed by a period of degeneration that might have been connected to radiation diseases and such. Then, at a crude toolmaking level, things swung upward once again, taking us to the point we now occupy. The answer we've arrived at here is probably the answer we've known, at some dim level of awareness, since the beginning. We've used a prescribed form, a rite of science it could almost be called, and it's included more thrills and chills than even the strata probably contains."

Mainwaring looked up from his notes.

"To summarize," he said.

They all looked at Mainwaring.

"In the untold past on this planet a group of humans transmitted a radio message into space. We don't know whether these people were directing their signals toward a particular solar system, toward a huge cluster of nearby stars, toward the center of our galaxy, toward another galaxy; or whether they knew of the existence and nature of the mohole totality and were perfectly aware that their message would return to planet Earth at a specific time in the future—a message, moreover, that was more likely to be preserved and detected, when we consider earthquakes, erosion and continental drift, in the form of a radio transmission than in a time capsule or other kind of sealed device."

"Applause," Bolin said.

"Now all we need to finish up the exercise," Softly said, "is Logicon on a platter, served up by Edna and Les. It's important we know how to reply to the message, regardless of content either way."

"We get back only what we ourselves give," Mainwaring said. "We've reconstructed the ARS extant and it turns out to be us."

Edna felt she could have done without that last wad of self-important discourse. She and Bolin went into the latter's cubicle and set immediately to work. On the typewriter stand was the old Royal portable. A sheet of paper stuck up out of the roller. Set on the ground between the legs of the typewriter stand was the short-wave radio. Next to the stand and the radio was the small plastic desk. On the desk was the framed photograph of Lown and Bolin formally posed on a small lawn on some campus somewhere, each half turned toward the camera and half facing the other, hands behind backs, Edna's left leg extended a bit, Lester's right leg likewise set forward, a large and not very interesting jug positioned evenly between the standing figures (solely for compositional effect, it was clear), the artificial dignity of the picture enhanced by the fading gray tones and the shopworn frame. Above the radio, the stand, the typewriter, the desk, the photograph, draped across the full length of one partition, was Lester's antic banner. The narrow bed consisted of canvas stretched on a collapsible frame. The chair lacked one arm. Bedclothes were scattered over most of the desk. Everything, she thought, looking into the dirt between her feet. Everything is here.

AN UNUSUAL SOUVENIR

Billy dialed INFO.
"Speaking," a male voice said.
"Is this tape I'm talking to?"

"Far from it."

"Good, I want this person's location. She's a visitor. Her name is Venable."

"Last name first."

"Venable."

"Male or female."

"She."

"Guest sector twenty-one."

"What direction is that?"

"Depends, doesn't it?"

"Depends on where I am, I guess."

"I would think so," the voice said.

"Faggot."

It took him a while to find the area. The doors were not only closed but unmarked. There was no one around, leading him to think it must be night or very early morning. One door, however, had a bolt lock on the outside. He knocked and heard Jean's voice, far away, a dim mutter of unrest. He unlocked the door and went inside. She was in bed under several layers of clothing, blankets and sheets. The room was littered with typing paper, all of it seemingly blank. Jean looked desperately weary, her face empty of all animating force. Nothing there but features, the shape, the extent, the proportions of distinct parts in a sand of white silence. He stood nearer the door than the bed.

"Am I awake?"

"Yes," he said.

"Good, because that's necessary."

"Good."

"Because without it I wouldn't be able to feel I was definitely myself really."

"Can I ask what time it is? I don't see a clock but maybe you have a watch in your clothes."

"I know the time in my head. I've been keeping time to help me stay awake. It's past dawn, I think it's well past dawn. That's generally where we are. I've been keeping mental track."

"Good."

406

"Why is this good?"

"Because this way we have hours before it happens because I think this is the day it might happen, whatever might happen, if anything, and I'd hate it to be only minutes. Otherwise, if not today, why wouldn't there be a calendar or something in Endor's room showing the date too? I wanted to tell you. Then I have to get back down and let the others know."

"Did you ever not feel your body was yours?"

The overprettiness was gone, the sense as well that she'd made a space between what she thought and what she sometimes said, the girlish lilt, the winsomeness that halfway guards fitful pain, questions of fearful intelligence. Lost too was a feeling of what poured forth from her, what lights, signs of sustained engagement, that earthly luck of youth unculled, the connections, net measures of being, and her willed incompleteness, the not quite committed nature of her self-acquaintance, a mind that partly clings (till now, the agon) to some ghost of other-ness. What remained could be called the experimental beginning of it all. She thought it might be what had always been there. She glimpsed it now and then, obscurely conscious of what there was in common be-tween this and that, struggling to remain awake, to think and be, to see the incurable self. Always the buried hope of an auroral moment. That magnetic dawn of first existence. What remained was not subject to analysis. It was simply what had been won, or yielded to, depending on your view.

"Did you ever not feel the presence of one particular part of you, like when you were little and you wondered under the covers if your foot was really there and being afraid to look or feel?"

"It's probably something I'll remember better when I'm older."

"Assuming you make it."

"Descartes was buried without his right hand."

"What happened to it?" she said.

"Someone took it."

"Souvenir?"

"Exactly."

"That's a wonderful story," she said. "It'll keep me awake for hours."

Edna Lown in the one-armed chair studied the old photo on the desk nearby, failing as always to see the humor Bolin saw in that stilted pairing of figures. They worked for a long time then. Lester told her about his idea for a Nazi typeface to provide a graphic stress of the contrast between Logicon and meta-Logicon. Ideal lead-in to a rest period, she announced. Again she studied the photograph, realizing finally what it was that had troubled her about the picture all these years, what (besides its failure to reward one's comic sense or to mellow the dead ends of reminiscence) had led her to feel something was faintly irregular about the whole thing. It had nothing to do with that dumb jug or the ceremonious adherence to strict relationships or her miserably ill-fitting clothes. It was a question of left and right. When the picture had been taken, her place was to the left of the container, her right leg extended. This long it had taken her to recall it clearly, the gothic arches in the distance, the elms, the armored Buicks full of existential freshmen, her own body in relation to all of these, the tennis courts, the dousing sprinklers on the lawn. In the picture she is being "pointed at" by the jug's rightside handle and it's her left leg that is extended. Of course, the reverse was true of Lester. Fact versus picture. The photo had always had this indistinct tone of wrongness about it. Now she knew what caused it all. The picture was flopped. Somehow the negative had been reversed and on the resulting print she and Lester had not only changed places in relation to the container but had undergone a corresponding adjustment in individual left-rightness. There and here. Then and now. It was almost as though they'd spent the intervening years contesting each other's placement on either side of a vertical axis of symmetry.

"I understand Mainwaring's got something already."

"What's he got?"

"I understand he's got a mohole," Bolin said.

In his swivel chair Mainwaring was readying himself to report the latest findings to Softly. He didn't at this stage know quite how to fit this information into the model they were on the verge of completing, lacking only the final touches on the transgalactic language itself, the means by which they'd be able to "reply" to the ARS extants. In a sense it was odd to be replying to people who (in a sense) no longer existed. But the important thing, according to Rob, is that Wu has postulated a novel evolutionary sequence and that I have traced the radio signals back to Earth. The very uselessness of Logicon, according to Rob, is what makes the project a pure act of the intellect and therefore supremely enriching. If it had been determined that the ARS extants were not Earth-dwellers but extraterrestrials (the message originating, say, in a solar system on the other side of the galaxy), the entire project, according to Rob, would have been endangered. To transmit an actual reply to the actual message-senders (or their succeeding generations) would be to miss the point of the whole thing. Besides, spoke Rob, *we* are the succeeding generations. Mainwaring sighed. He headed down the path toward Softly's cubicle. He was eager to leave, to get back to Cosmic Techniques and some semblance of normality, if you could call mohole identification a normal sort of pursuit. What he'd learned from his sylphing teams came as a shock and a half. They'd done it, all right. On their color-contour map (generated by telescopic data and computer analysis), they'd found themselves staring into the colorless puddle of an absorption hole, a spot on the map indicating an area in space where every kind of emission from every type of source is being absorbed by exo-ionic sylphing compounds.

"Lock it behind you," Jean said.

Softly in bed listened as Mainwaring with that uncharacteristic dampness on his brow explained that this was the first hard evidence ever gathered of the presence of moholes in the universe.

"And you've analyzed the compounds and therefore confirmed the path of the radio signals."

"True," Mainwaring said.

"Thank you, Walter. You're a winner in every way."

"There's more to it, Rob."

"Important?"

"I don't know. I'm honestly not sure at this point."

"Because we're about ready to call it a night."

"This is something hard to evaluate right on the spot."

"So if it's not tremendously urgent, let's let it go for some other time."

"What they've apparently discovered is that we are in the mohole, if that's the way to phrase it. This solar system appears to be what we call mohole-intense. We are part of the value-dark dimension. All along we've been anxious to identify a mohole somewhere out there. We felt it would help us confirm the path of the radio message. And it has, it has. In a wider application we were sure it would shed valuable light on the mohole phenomenon itself. But we never anticipated finding a mohole so close to right here, to us right here. Evidently it's just happened, it's extremely recent, we're right in it. Everything around us on out at least to the most distant planet and right in to the sun itself, our sun, we ourselves, all of us, people, matter, energy, we're part of a mohole, we're in it, we're mohole-intense."

"I don't feel any different," Softly said.

"Rob, we don't know. That's it. We don't know what it means. This is space-time sylphed. We're dealing with Moholean relativity here. Possibly dimensions more numerous than we've ever before imagined."

"All that's boring. What the senses can perceive. What the senses can't perceive. Nimbus fizgig remora."

"We used zorgs," Mainwaring said.

"I thought you used zorgs in tracing the signal."

"We didn't need them for that. We needed them for validating the existence of the mohole."

"That was the original plan. To use zorgs in tracing the signal. That's where zorgs were supposed to fit in."

"It didn't work out that way."

"Not important," Softly said. "Nothing to worry about."

Mainwaring watched him get out of bed and dress. Then both men left for the elevator. Softly looked into the darkness as Mainwaring explained that he wanted to check incoming cables for more news from his sylphing teams. Slowly the elevator climbed, making the usual noises.

It isn't necessary to write down the words. You know what it will look like page by page and that's enough to know. That's everything really. There's a whole class of writers who don't want their books to be read. This to some extent explains their crazed prose. To express what is expressible isn't why you write if you're in this class of writers. To be understood is faintly embarrassing. What you want to express is the violence of your desire not to be read. The friction of an audience is what drives writers crazy. These people are going to read what you write. The more they understand, the crazier you get. You can't let them know what you're writing about. Once they know, you're finished. If you're in this class, what you have to do is either not publish or make absolutely sure your work leaves readers strewn along the margins. This not only causes literature to happen but is indispensable to your mental health as well. But me, see, she thought, but me now, that's another side of it. Blank pages. The prose stays with me, the characters, the story, the setting. Only I know what's on those pages. Those pages are intelligible, nonviolent and sane. This is the sane way to write if you're insanity-prone and I've found it all by myself when Softly entered her from a kneeling position, her lower back and pelvis upcurved from the surface of the bed, his hands at her hips drawing her into him, body (hers) swollen and bruised, arms (hers) extended back toward the headboard, hands pushing out from that panel to drive her more fully onto his body or to make his body unconditionally part of hers. It was the briefest of sexual episodes. She was nearly herself, she felt, a body restored to its secret petitioner, her voice as she spoke into his furry ear (a routine oozing curse) reminding her of the street croak of diggers in vacant lots along the edges of that ultrasculptural city you might have scanned from the windows of your undependable train. He backed off the bed with spit on his lips and that streamlined marine glisten at the center of his body, aquatic flopping cold-blooded organ, neon gleam of it, wet with her vulval wash. His strength did not surprise her. It is something we all superstitiously assume. One's various afflictions provide the material for secret competence. Pulled from the bed she reached back instinctively to find a grip, a hold, a firm piece of something, coming away with a sheet in her hand, warm, she thought, dragged along the floor, not the least surprised by his strength, left then, the closet door coming open, waiting politely with her warm sheet, pushed and bounced inside, homunculus, madman, my child-sized lover, all buttoned in this little dark, this orphaning eye of the night, *a-choo*, coats and dresses in my hair, hate to wait the fate of the turning key.

But he didn't bother locking the door this time. He closed it, left it, dressed and returned to his quarters. Lester was boiling water for tea. Edna as well was in the kitchen area. Their voices dulled by fatigue. Excessive reflex action, Softly thought. Restlessness, excitation, over-alertness. Need to supply myself with some enforced relaxation. He undressed, put on his thermal pajamas, tossed his briefcase on the bed and then crawled in under it. He undid the straps and searched inside for something to sniff, swallow or lick, anything at all as long as it contained an appropriate moderating agent. Mainwaring stood in the entrance. He was dressed in jungle fatigues. Stenciled on the flap of his breast pocket were the initials WXM.

"Rob, it's me again."

"Sure, why not?"

"I was working on a letter of resignation. I'd planned to leave it on your desk. But since you're here I think it's only right we do it face to face."

"What brought this on?"

"Man to man," Mainwaring said. "What brought this on? What brought this on was the most recent communication. It's all in my letter. Do you want to see it?"

"You decide."

"It's in my pocket."

"Neatly folded, I presume. Either that or it's the tiniest resignation in corporate history."

"Do you want to see it now?"

"Read it to me."

"Maybe that's best."

"Whatever," Softly said.

Mainwaring remained in the entranceway.

"To Robert Hopper Softly," he read. "As you may or may not know, Rob, our parent organization, OmCo Research, has just been acquired in a complicated stock deal by ACRONYM, a long-term international speculative monopoly that operates beyond maritime limits. In cases such as this, reorganization is standard procedure. Therefore it is reasonable to assume that such wholly owned OmCo subsidiaries as Cosmic Techniques Redevelopment Corporation, the Center for the Refinement of Ideational Structures, the Relativity Rethink Priorities Council, Field Experiment Number One, the Affiliated Friends of the Logicon Project, the Chinese-American Science Sodality and other model-building organizations will either become defunct or will be restructured beyond present recognition. At the very least we can be certain that the services of all current personnel involved in policy-making will no longer be needed. It is therefore with sincere regret that I submit my resignation."

"Is that it?"

"End of statement."

"Acquired by ACRONYM."

"Elux Troxl."

"None other."

"Or whatever his name is."

"Guano holdings," Softly said.

"Right."

"A nonabstract proponent of actual living shit."

"Guano stockpiling, price-fixing and eventual distribution," Mainwaring said. "The whole operation computerized to an extent and level of complexity never before known."

"I like your outfit, Walt."

"Rob, since your identification with OmCo is greater than anyone's, I assume you'll also choose to resign. It's best all around. I personally urge it. This is what I honestly think and feel and believe."

I MAKE AN ENTRANCE

He knows enough to know he doesn't have to lock the closet door. It happens in stages like my pages. Coats, dresses, fabrics, materials, yard goods, cloth. Plenty to do here. Many ways to keep awake. No lack of activities. Touch the cloth, smell the fabric, cover my feet with the sheet. Sleep is no help. The period before sleep is my time of greatest mental helplessness, in fact. Sleep itself is an improvement but not always. The period after sleep is usually not as bad as the period before sleep but there are times when it is worse. Death is creeping logic. It is creepingly logical. Death and something else. SYNONYMS, she thought: *insanity, lunacy, madness, mania, dementia*. Those nouns denote conditions of mental disability. *Insanity* is a pronounced and usually prolonged condition of mental disorder that legally renders a person not responsible for hĭs or hûr actions. *Lunacy*, a romantic form of *insanity*, can denote derangement relieved intermittently by periods of *madness*. *Madness*, a more general term, often stresses the crazy side of mental illness. *Mania* refers principally to the excited phase of manic-depressive psychosis and we all know who suffers from that particular disorder, his hyperactive priapic clock ticking to its own internal time. *Dementia* implies irreversible mental deterioration brought on by obsessive thoughts of such organic disorders as death. I could easily easily easily open the door. Or:

They had tea in Softly's quarters for a change. After listening to Mainwaring read his letter of resignation, Softly had decided to switch from a relaxant to a stimulant. He sat among his pillows, cup in hand, and smelled the dark souchong.

"What happens now?"

"You keep working, Lester-pet. You finish the notation."

"What about Mainwaring and Wu?" Edna Lown said.

"I guess they'll be leaving soon."

"I have this urge," Bolin said.

"Tell us, Les."

"I want to call you Bobby."

Softly felt his brain racing toward some chemical event of a highly suspect nature. He sipped his tea. Pulse rate. Blink rate. Degree of nausea. Sweatiness of palms. Flushedness of face. He sipped his tea once more. Edna makes good tea if Edna made this tea. But I think it was Lester, who wants to call me Bobby.

"Forget it."

"Watch my lips," Bolin said.

"Really, Les, forget it."

"Watch my lips."

"All right, I'm watching."

"Bobby."

414

"An experience I wouldn't have missed," Softly said.

"Were you watching?"

"Very carefully," Softly said. "What about Edna? Was Edna watching?"

"Intently," she said.

"Bobby."

"Forget it," Softly said.

"I've always had the urge. I don't know why really. Odds are we won't be here much longer. Notation's coming along. So I thought I'd indulge myself once and for all. Indulge the urge. It's kind of fun to say."

"Bobby," Edna said.

"Exactly."

"Bobby, Bobby."

"I've really enjoyed it here," Lester said. "Never guessed I'd be able to produce steadily in this kind of isolation. I feel like Kepler in his little black tent. Kepler had this tent he used to carry around with him. Whenever he felt like making some observations, he set it up in a field or wherever. A one-man tent. Small, tight and dark. A tiny hole for his telescope to fit through. He'd sit in the dark and observe. The whole sky pouring through that little hole."

"Shut up," Softly said.

Billy nearly tripped on the generator cable. He heard the voices and headed directly for Softly's cubicle. He halted about a yard inside the entrance. The others reacted to his arrival with looks of flinching inquiry. Maybe he'd slipped their minds. (Oh, yeah, him, wonder where he's been.) He watched them, awry in this mild surprise, slowly recompose themselves, reaching back for faces and manifestations.

"I have deciphered the message," he said.

"What a charming announcement," Softly said. "I didn't know you could even get the elevator to move. You have, I assume, been doing some wandering."

"I went to a few places up there but got lost a lot too, especially coming back."

"We're glad to see you, really and truly, but no announcements please. I think we've had enough of those."

"Something may happen at a certain time."

"Not interested."

"The pulses are meant to be seen as time on a clock. When it gets that time, I don't know but something may be meant to take place."

"Look, mister, the message is indecipherable. The only value the signals have is that they got us going on the Logicon project. The message was sent from this part of the galaxy, this solar system, this planet, and it was sent 'millions' and 'millions' and 'millions' of years ago. That's all we have to know about the message. Our remaining task is to frame a reply in a universal cosmic language. It doesn't matter what the reply is. Content is not the issue. So don't go around telling people you broke the code. There is no code worth breaking. If, by some accident, you have happened upon an interpretation that appears to make a moderate amount of sense from a mathematical viewpoint, we don't want to hear it."

"So what am I here for?"

"You're here to help Edna and Lester on Logicon," Softly said. "And if there is a category of nonaccomplishment existing beyond total and contemptible failure, I believe this is where the results of your participation belong."

"What about before we came down here?"

"That part was a preparation for this part. You needed the background, the activity, the other side of the problem. It's not possible to fulfill a concept unless you set it up properly."

"Anyway, I broke the code whether you like it or not."

"You're beginning to sound like some kind of idiot savant."

"Make remarks."

"Maybe you'd rather do absurd calculations in your head than something worthwhile, something invaluable to science and the mind."

"Go ahead, say things, I don't care."

Edna Lown got up and left, returning a moment later with a fresh cup of tea.

"If this mohole business is true," she said, "maybe we ought to hear what our young man's got to say."

She left Softly's quarters again, returning this time with Mainwaring, who could barely contain his eagerness to accept the burden that specialized knowledge entails in times like these.

"Yes," he said. "It's possible that something extraordinary is going to happen. Where we have space-time sylphed, the level of unpredictability is extremely high, we feel. The laws simply aren't the same. In a sense we're wasting time even discussing it. There's nothing to discuss."

"Don't talk like that," Softly said.

Bolin made a proposal. The short-wave radio. If something funny's taking place, somebody somewhere's probably detected it, or the first signs of it, or a partial hint at least. The short-wave radio. An announcement. A bulletin. Something. Anything. It's the quickest way we have to get information.

He jogged down the path to his cubicle. They waited, saying nothing. Lester returned with the radio, set it on a chair and raised the antenna. Then he placed himself in a facing chair. The antenna was enormous, more than twice Bolin's height. He began to turn dials, picking up atmospheric static, moans and cries, ships, taxis, fire engines, beeps from research satellites. Mainwaring edged his way to Billy's side.

"We used zorgs," he whispered.

"For what?"

"Identifying the mohole."

"Zorgs are useless."

"We used them," Mainwaring said.

"Practically nobody knows what they even are."

"Softly knows, doesn't he?"

"He's one of the few."

"Softly explained how we might use zorgs. I briefed my sylphing teams. Without zorgs we would never have found the mohole."

"Amazement."

"Except Softly wanted us to use them in tracking back the signal. But we didn't need them for that. We needed them for the mohole."

417

"Very amazing."

Bolin had picked up a newscast that was interrupted seconds later by a bulletin concerning a suspicious person barricaded in a commercial building somewhere.

"A hole is an unoccupied negative energy state," Mainwaring whispered. "Hole theory involves 'pair creation,' which is the simultaneous creation of a particle-antiparticle pair. Holes move, just as moholes seem to move, just as a discrete particle can separate itself from a continuously dense array, leaving behind its antiparticle or hole. What Softly pointed out was that zorgs provide a perfect working mathematical model of hole theory."

"I never thought it."

"Zorgs allowed us to attack the sylphing problem in ways that were otherwise inconceivable. We had to learn to view zorgs as events rather than numbers, just as particles are events rather than things. The discrete-continuous quality of zorgs is what really helped us work out the necessary mathematics of Moholean relativity and made mohole identification practically inevitable."

"Pretty interesting."

"Things are interesting up to a point," Mainwaring whispered. "Then they aren't interesting anymore."

"The idea of zorgs applying."

"Experience and pure thought. The mind and the world. External reality and independent abstract deduction."

"How come you're in camouflage?"

"These are jungle fatigues. I've kept them pressed and handy for a good many years. Don't know why really. But this seemed a good time to slip them on."

Softly motioned for silence.

"Our mobile units are standing by," the announcer said.

There was a pause.

"This is mobile unit twenty-two," another voice said. "The barricaded suspect has been exchanging gunfire with the police for several minutes now, every abrupt report echoing clearly in this deserted commercial district, unprofitable relief from the silence that weighs so heavily at this early hour in the wilderness of cities. From the beginning a police official has been speaking through a bullhorn, his supercharged voice adding a faintly theatrical quality to the proceedings. Mist is settling on the area now, successive webs of condensation. In this grainy weave of near light, every lull between shots is filled with a sheltered sense of bedtime lazing, the feeling we all know of idle security, of high-and-dry privacy—a deception, of course, like any airy moment of disentanglement, but at the same time not a totally false picture of the somewhat muted urgency that prevails here this morning, events unfolding in the embodying harmony of a sonnet. From atop police vehicles the familiar swivel lights range through the haze as the suspect reloads and fires, perhaps aware of the classic nature of his predicament, the energy field he momentarily inhabits, the solitary trance of power, the levels of encounter and isolation he has caused to bring about. The act of sighting down the barrel of that weapon may be the release he has always sought. An ambulance, white with dark trim, purrs sullenly nearby. A marksman in a bulletproof vest raises his weapon and takes aim. This is what it's all about, isn't it, listening audience? A brief seizing brilliance in the immediate air. A death-rendered flash of perfect equilibrium. In the fog and mist of a remote warehouse district, this is mobile control returning you to our studio."

"Hi, back with traffic, weather, recipes and reviews. This note from the science desk. An unscheduled total eclipse of the sun will probably take place later today, more or less, it says here, on the other side of the world. Some minor delays on airport access roads. Details upcoming. Another water-main break during the night but first I'm being motioned at here, so let's go right now to mobile control."

"The suspicious person has been calling down a series of unintelligible remarks. He is standing in the window, shouting, now firing, now shouting, a figure somewhat melancholy to contemplate in the tempering medium of this thick rich mist. The official with the bullhorn is shouting back at the suspect. Electric hysteria begins to spread. The police are rapid-firing now, perhaps a dozen marksmen on the street, on rooftops, in doorways and windows. It is evident that the police and the suspicious person have agreed to abandon nominal reality as we pause here for a test of our clear-signal testing apparatus, a test, a test, this is only a test."

Softly moved his index finger across his throat, leading Bolin to turn off the radio. They all sat or stood in place.

"Eclipse," Lown said.

"Just a rumor," Softly said.

"Maybe it's not unscheduled," Bolin said. "Maybe it was due all along."

Mainwaring shook his head.

"Noncognate celestial anomaly."

"Don't talk like that," Softly said.

"Is science dead?" Bolin said.

"I would dearly love to know what's going on," Lown said.

Mainwaring shrugged.

"There's nothing to say. This may be just the beginning. There's nothing any of us can say to clear things up."

"Don't talk like that," Softly said.

"When does it happen?" Bolin said.

"He said later today," Lown said.

"Whose time?" Softly said.

"Later today must mean later today his time, the radio's, wherever that was," Lown said.

Mainwaring made a face.

"Obviously it won't be long. Whoever's time and wherever the broadcast originated, the eclipse will happen. That's all that matters, I would think and feel and suspect."

Softly turned his head into the fattest of the silk pillows. The others left his quarters, filing out slowly, Terwilliger, Lown, Mainwaring, Bolin. Although his face was pressed into the pillow, Softly's eyes were open. Words in isolation or combination are meaningful; connect; reflect. Think clearly, he urged himself, turning his head and looking up into the dark vast space that composed most of the antrum. Some small rocks tumbled into the barrier. He heard his colleagues in dialogue. We must re-term, confirm, he thought. It will help us think clearly, help us prepare for the conditions that may accompany this noncognate celestial anomaly. To know for certain when, what, where and how; this is necessary, looking straight up, hearing the generator shift to a more sonorous drone, reaching for his robe. Shit, piss and corruption. This was a phrase that went back several decades (in the special context of his own life) and when it entered his mind, Softly reacted as he did to every unbidden recollection of childhood and adolescence, with a sense of abomination so pronounced it caused clear physical discomfort, caused him to sweat, to tremble, this state of aversion intensified by the fact that in putting on his robe he had uncovered the bronze mirror Wu had left on his desk. Quickly he reached for a towel.

A DESPERATE MEASURE

Softly walked over to Wu's cubicle now, seeing Lester leave the kitchen and head down the path to his own living unit, where he sat at the plastic desk and immediately began making simple lists of things, using paper and pencil. Bolin's customary satisfaction in crossing out each item on a given list as that particular errand or mental task was attended to did not begin to match the pleasure he now derived from listing things and crossing them out with no attempt at an intervening activity, mental or otherwise. He concentrated on the simplest of lists, writing down the days of the week and then crossing them out, one by one; the names of the objects in his immediate field of vision; the names of the probable objects behind him; the articles of clothing he wore; the months of the year; brands of cigarettes; makes of cars; his favorite flavors; world religions; state capitals; countries and their chief exports. Finally he began to list the integers. He wrote down the integers not by name but symbol, listing roughly a dozen, sometimes more, before going back to do the crossing out. The integers were immensely pleasing to list, much more so than any of the other categories, the sequences arrayed like numerical paternosters. Why hadn't he realized earlier that to list something and cross it out is far more satisfying than to list something, act upon that listing and only *then* to cross it out?

a. I'm tempted to say: give me a cookie.

Maurice Wu was packed and ready to leave. It seemed Maurice was always coming in or going out, always rolling up sleeping bags or latching backpacks. This time he was going out, of course, and not just to do some miscellaneous caving on the slopes. There were no chairs and so he didn't invite Softly to have a seat.

"Hear what's happening?"

"Yes," Wu said.

"We have to confirm. I want to confirm. Frankly I can't stand not knowing for sure. Will there be an 'eclipse' or not? Do we just stand around 'talking' and wait for it to happen?"

"I was leaving."

"Stay," Softly said.

"There's my fieldwork. I want to get back to the field. I'm really eager to leave."

"A while longer."

"How do we confirm something like this? Something like this isn't subject to confirmation, is it?"

"Think."

"Anyway, they said it's going to happen, didn't they?"

"Just a rumor at this point."

"It was on the radio, wasn't it?"

"They said 'probably happen,' 'will probably take place.' "

"What we need is something completely out of the ordinary."

"Think, 'Maury.' "

"Didn't I hear something recently about some woman they brought in who's supposed to be able to perceive things beyond the range of the immediate present?"

"No good," Softly said.

"She's just some woman from the slums somewhere who's supposedly got this unexplained insight into the future. Didn't I hear she's in one of the complexes? Being pored over by experts in this and that discipline. Being wired, prodded and so forth. Something completely out of left field. That's what we need."

"Nammu zendo baba."

422

"Granted, it's a desperate measure."

"I want to keep it scientific. No seers, diviners, soothsayers or clairvoyants. This is a scientific project."

"I'm trying to think of her name. I've been hearing about this woman. An interesting case apparently. She has fits apparently or goes into trances or spells. Then she does her stuff. I remember thinking her name sounds like a Greek-American soccer team. Do the field telephones still work? I can call upstairs and find out what's what."

"It contradicts everything I've always believed."

"Bend a little," Wu said.

"I'm not enthused about this."

"Better than nothing."

"In fact I hate the idea."

"Skia Mantikos."

"What's that?"

"Her name," Wu said. "It means 'the shadow prophet.' "

Lester Bolin stood in a room without furniture and looked directly into the "head" of his metallic Logicon. Edna Lown in kimono and desert boots was slumped over her desk. In his hand, Lester's, was a device containing an automatic switch that operated on photoelectric command. Wu coming out of his own cubicle and heading toward the field telephones next to the first-aid unit saw Billy come out of the first-aid unit, his left thumb encircled by a fresh bandage. Softly back in bed, Mainwaring making sure his documents were packed, his file cabinet emptied out, his umbrella at the ready. The density of time enveloped everything.

"So what's with the finger?"

"Cut it when I opened my latest piece of junk mail."

"Called a paper cut," Wu said.

"Except I noticed at the last second the mail wasn't supposed to be for me. Addressed to R. H. Softly. So I dropped it in there before I fixed my cut."

"Did you see the gift I brought him from the bat cave?"

"No."

"An ancient Chinese mirror."

"What's it worth?"

"Priceless."

"That much?"

"At the very least."

"You made a big mistake," the boy said.

"Why?"

"Better not let him see it, that's all I'm saying."

"Why not?"

"He hates mirrors. He never goes anywhere near them. You better go get it before he gets back."

"He's back," Wu said.

"It's probably covered up. That's why I didn't see it. He covers them up. That's what he always does."

"Why?"

"You want to ask him?"

"I guess not."

"Where you going anyway?"

"Make a phone call."

"What, Chinese food?"

"Funny," Wu said.

"Ordering out?"

"It's this person I want to get in touch with. A desperate measure, I grant you. But she may be able to tell us what's going to happen."

Edna Lown in kimono and desert boots was slumped over her desk, thinking. Bolin stood in a nearly bare room in a storage and maintenance area next to the upper part of the elevator shaft, looking at the squat object that itself stood among scrap metal, sawdust, lengths of wire. Wu cranking a field telephone, Mainwaring testing the effectiveness of his black umbrella. In his hand, Lester's, was a device that emitted an immediate click whenever he pressed his thumb on a button. He took a coin out of his breast pocket. He didn't know what to expect. In the unlikely event that he had assembled the control system with absolute precision (unlikely because this was the first such venture he'd attempted and because it was all so homemade), the machine would be capable of producing combinations of sounds that coincided with the ideographic units he and Edna had devised as written language. Mainwaring changing clothes, Softly in his bed scanning the latest mail.

REFLECTIONS

This announcement is neither an offer to buy nor a solicitation
of an offer to sell the securities referred to below.
The offer is made only by the Prospectus, copies
of which may be obtained only from exchange
agents or designated notaries public.

AAAA&A GUANO MINES LTD.

Literally millions of shares.

Price contingent upon fluctuations of world-market money curve.

Softly stopped reading here, thinking I am old, I will die, no one
cares, her upper body slumped forward on the desk and what an implausible object it is, she thought, this material structure of mine, each
of its lower extremities encased in a sodden boot, the rest of it bleakly
scaled in this woebegone kimono, the photoelectric command at the
end of Bolin's hand, thinking I am old, a thick-lipped gray-haired
plodding woman, head resting on her arms, eyes closed, pack of cigarettes at one elbow, glasses with dark frames and round lenses at the
other, Wu's middle ear conveying vibrations inward, sounds, auditory
signals, the implausibility of my parts, she thought, never before so
wretchedly apparent, everything pointing in a different direction and
Softly thumb-sucking in bed, her momentary depression, if that's what
it was, based, she believed, on the fact that she had come to the end of
her "nonspecific notes," the jottings she'd been adding to for many
years, the closed door of her professional life, realizing (a) that the
notes indeed were finished (although she could not have said how she
knew this so conclusively) and (b) that these fairly random observations
were in fact the ever-circulating substance of her life's work. These investigations, these exercises in connective thought, these secret odds
and ends comprised the essence of her scientific intent more than
Logicon ever would. A witness to my own adventure. It was as though
she had mistaken another's life for her own. Why, suddenly, did the
major undertaking of her career, this neo-logistic song of the universe,
seem less important than her notes, which, she well knew, were never
meant to be more than probes, a series of little scribbles that might fill
the off-hours. It was crazy, wasn't it? In her depression and fatigue

425

(thinking I will die) she knew only that the notes explained her life, *were* that life, devices of the punchy brain inside her. It was a mistake really, what she'd always taken her life to be. That was someone else's life. *This* was her, Edna, belated rectifier of mistakes. To barely know the person not known to those who know me. To be in this sense a witness to my own adventure. Whose body have I been wearing all these years? Is it one body for many people or exactly the reverse? What gross colonic events, may I ask, are taking place in the area of my sigmoid flexure, Softly thought, stressing to himself the importance of such inquiries, Mainwaring pausing here to breathe the aged and tannic fragrance of his suitcase, Edna's eyes opening on pages of notation, thinking I am old, I will die, no one cares. Bolin inserted the coin in Logicon's "navel." In his pocket, Lester's, was a piece of paper that contained: arrays of symbols; the meaning (in English, more or less) of each array; the corresponding phonetic speech units (Logicon) that the squat object would emit—that is, if Lester had assembled the machine correctly. For example, the array "/:nK" corresponded to the statement "the function letter f contains n number of f-less transforms" and both of these corresponded to the sound "fu ling ho," as Lester had worded it on paper. He stood in a storage and maintenance area looking directly into the partially exposed upper portion of his primitive android control system, which itself stood among coiled wires, sawdust, fragments of scrap metal. Lester depressed a button on the device in his hand. There was an immediate click. This wasn't as interesting, he realized with surprise, as making lists of things and then crossing the things out, one by one. As he waited to learn whether or not Logicon had an innate resistance to being spoken, something else occurred to him. If we are mohole-intense, it doesn't really matter, does it?

THINGS GO THE OTHER WAY

"Are we all here?" Softly said from his bed. "Where's Walter that son of a bitch Mainwaring with his ever-popular sylphing compounds?"

In time they assembled along the walls of Softly's quarters. Edna with a cigarette drooping from the corner of her mouth. Billy trying not to look so eager to be entertained. Lester cradling his short-wave radio. Mainwaring clean-shaven and subdued. Softly himself.

In walked Maurice Wu, halting just a yard inside the cubicle and then stepping aside, with faintly absurd politeness, as the woman appeared in the entranceway. On Maury's face was a sense of that draining tension that ghosts over the eyes and stretches the bravest smile to idiotic limits. For a moment he seemed to pose formally, as though for picture-taking. Then nodded and began.

"She's been apprised of the situation. She knows what we want to know. They have her on what they call a maximum output cycle. She's been up and at it for exactly twenty-three hours. Productive stress, they call it. Okay. What happens next is anybody's guess. She's apparently got this routine she goes into. I saw some of the preparations myself. Let's hope that's the worst of it. I guess I stop talking now and join the rest of you."

The woman wore what appeared to be a simple sheet, its ends stitched together to provide her body with rudimentary protection. Her lips were likewise stitched, literally sewn together, one of the preparations Wu had referred to. White thread hung down below her chin. Blood-crusts covered her mouth and jaw. The act of sewing and the presence of the thread itself caused her lips to jut out from her face to a grotesque extent. Impossible to judge this woman's age or place of origin. Her face, aside from the mouth, showed signs of a life clearly lacking in material comfort. Pockets of discolor. Meager sunken flesh. Eyes destitute of lenient experience. With arms bent upward she stood in the filthy sheet and stared into her curled fingers. Then she began to turn, slowly, her bare feet pressing into the earth.

They watched in silence.

Her body, performing nothing more than this slow rotation, appeared to assert the prestige of emptiness; it might take the shape of whatever swerved in its direction. She stared into her curled fingers, eyes going blank, the scant identity within them receding in nearly measurable stages. She seemed to reach a special level here; paused; then whirled, a series of rapid turns. Her body shook briefly and she fell, remaining motionless, her face in the dirt, for an extended period of time.

Under the covers Softly's hand tried without success to promote an unequivocal erection.

She began to roll in the dirt. As she did the sheet gradually parted up her back, thread becoming undone. Her face was blotted with earth and accumulating pain. All along her unwindingly pallid body, this tidal index to a madness spaced with art, were further traces of this beaten life of hers, bruises here, broken skin, indentations. Whatever was meant to happen would not involve the others in some collective ecstasy. This woman's jurisdiction, the ascendancy of her vacant gaze, was turned completely inward. Her territorial range was nil. She unraveled before them an imbecile beauty, senseless and deserted, the negative telling element of her life. This was the power of her physical presence, of these nameless spins and tremors, that she was a mind and body able to empty out and in some decompressing play of painful craft eventually to refill herself, or so it seemed to those who watched as now the sheet completely parted, woman no longer rolling, face down on the twisted sheet, arms still bent up and tucked under her now. Birthmarked on her right buttock was a star-shaped geometric figure. All watching knew it was a pentagram, secret emblem of the ancients. The woman rose to her knees, keeping her back to the others. She raised both arms in the air, hands closed. One by one then, in synchronization, she pointed the fingers of each hand upward, thumb, index finger, middle finger, pinky finger, ring finger. She did this repeatedly, beginning to moan now, and like the other things she'd done these latest exercises drew their effectiveness (no eye strayed nor mind wandered) from the very obscurity that motivated their performance. Although she was not facing her audience it became clear once more that she was reaching a special level of enactment. She moaned steadily. The muscles in her back contracted. She continued "to count" into the air, as though fashioning a correspondence between whole numbers and the systematic maze of nature. Then she lowered her arms and, using hands to help her move, turned, still on her knees, toward those watching. She tried to open her mouth. No longer·content apparently to make a single unmodulated sound, she strained against the binding thread, using facial muscles alone, hands at her sides. Several stitches loosened, causing fresh blood to flow. She was in extreme pain but suggested a complex presence now, her eyes returning mild light to objects and forms. The lower part of her face was smeared with blood. She spat out loops of thread. Blood in starry drops fell to her breasts and thighs. With a last passionate grimace she freed her mouth of every lash of thread and cried through blood and teeth a single word.

"Pythagoras."

They waited for more, connected by a skein of utter dumb futility. But this was all she'd come to say. Mainwaring and Wu helped the woman to her feet, put the sheet around her and took her to the first-aid unit. With her thumb and index finger Edna Lown picked a speck of tobacco off the end of her tongue. She studied it a while, then went to her quarters. Bolin put the radio on Softly's desk and turned it on.

"I guess if we're going to find out for sure, this is the way to do it," Lester said. "Things have been going the wrong way lately. We're due for some good luck, Bobby."

Billy looked at his long-time friend and mentor.

"Just a rumor," Softly said.

Within the limitless range of intersecting static, an announcer could be heard.

"Greenwich mean time," he said. "At the tone: fourteen, twenty-eight, fifty-seven."

System interbreak: eclipse track Asia: children being sold in Madhya Pradesh, eating rats to live, baring trees of bark and leaves to live, external reality, flies on whitewashed walls, old men in loincloths collecting the dust of a cycle rickshaw, oblivious mud bodies, mouths edged with coated sputum, rows of sandals set around the borders of a temple courtyard, women in saris drifting through the shops wearing muslin, bone, plastic and glass, saris of handspun cotton (in bare rooms), women spaced across the upland slush of rice fields, tending dung fires, gliding past the stalls in anklet bells and bangles, a mass of pondering voices (in bare rooms reserved for menstruation), black disk abstracting the edge of the nurturing sun. People surround the outdoor kitchens waiting for their gruel and milk, eating grass to live, bodies of the starved abandoned on tiled verandas, human experience, electric fan moving air across a room adorned with flapping pictures of the gods. Monkeys vanish from a window, reacting to the soft beginnings of eclipse, the lunar shadow moving in a northeast arc, its path of totality a fairly standard band in length and width, its rate of speed routine, its time span roughly average. The eclipse is notable solely for its un-expectedness, the year's only scheduled solar eclipse (total) having al-ready taken place (northwest U.S. and Canada), an image projected on a cardboard screen (two point seven minutes). As hypothetical ARS extant (transferred, by whatever means, from your nonquantum state Outside), you have the benefit of an omnidirectional viewpoint and are able to observe, regarding this event, that the earth along the eclipse path and its outer borders of partial darkness resembles a charred im-mensity, children with begging bowls, men surrendered to meditation. You enter a cell in an ashram, several monks in ochre robes, one of whom (bald, sleepy, smelling of hemp) tells his fellows about the hand-clapping Africans seized by the spirit of eclipse who beat on drums to make the sun return, who hide in their palm leaf huts, who fall into convulsions; about the medicine man who chews on bitter leaves and spits the curative pieces at assembled villagers; about the natives who cover their bodies with white clay to counter the darkness, whole villages white in this way, weepings and seizures, dancing mania, morbid homage to their lord. His fellow sadhus are amused, nodding in unison, the empirical source, children immobilized by gastroenteritis, scaveng-ing to live, to know what passes above, this nearly sunset occurrence, shadow moving toward the eastmost Ganges, choleroid feces, choleroid dehydration, choleroid vomit, girls with finger-cymbals laughing in a mango grove, the cowrie, the owl of good fortune. It is as everywhere, the soul of one experience passing untouched through the soul of an-other, men with the white marks of Shiva, oxen on sparse farms. To re-direct yourself from the Outside, as you're able to do (having learned to count to n), is the equivalent of entering once more your outgrown frame of logic and language. Having dismantled the handiwork of your own perceptions in order to solve reality, you know it now as a micron flash of light-scattering matter in a structure otherwise composed of purely mathematical coordinates. The blind stand begging in places that are the same, hanging wash, some goats, as places everywhere, toy stores, colored glass, the squalor that customarily surrounds the working of miracles. To breathe but not to speak, to sleep in the earth, to live in self-inflicted pain, to aspire to blindness by the sun, to speak but not to move. Children play a shadow game in last light, small birds picking insects out of human excrement, the players safe when they make their shadows disappear. There is evening raga in a music room, girls in bare feet who hide in the shadow of a water tank, the arguments of crosslegged men all fiercely disposed to the notion of suffering as macrocosmic sport, this girl and that in obliterated twilight, cries of their pursuers. You perceive completely. Women with twig brooms. Children dead in darkened archways. The girls slowly rise from their enfolding shadow, aware the game has been absorbed, all shadows subtotaled in this nightstreaming dye. A woman touching a mote of vermilion to her forehead. The insistent density of hand drums, tamboura and sarod. You see the itinerant mystic's dinner plate with its orderly dole of almonds, the real world, this man of sect marks and open sores. A student sits on a pallet repeating phrases from a textbook, his voice half prayerful with drowsiness, as everywhere, mathematics coinciding with the will to live. In cities built, the T-squared temporary cantonment, the practical means to survive, in oceans crossed (he reads) it is mathematics that makes the way for the whittler's sleight, gives directional reference to the man at the bridge rail adjusting a small-boned instrument of navigation. At the contact line of nature and mathematical thought is where things make sense, things accede to our view of them, things return to us a propagating wave of reason. On his pallet, drowsily, on pocked floorboards beneath a shuttered window, the young man mutters back to his book, a printed seed of the race no less than some Vedantic text, India (from the Sanskrit for "river") being the source of positional notation for the decimal system and of the symbols for the numbers one to nine, cane baskets on women's heads, lifelong celibates grinning out of broken teeth, children begging for a cracked fragment of biscuit, the physical universe, eating crumbs to live. Then northward here, vultures hunched in trees, the shadow curves on eventful waters, fishing boats, bamboo rafts that carry bodies dappled with jasmine and rose petals, these being children spared the pyre, and there is sandalwood afloat. What is the universe as it exists beyond the human brain? The sadhu stands naked in his cell, body lacking hair at every point. Mathematics is what the world is when we subtract our own perceptions. In your earthly study of the subject, you went beyond its natural association with the will to live and found that it contained a painless "nonexistence," the theoretical ideal of n-space. And so you beamed into the heavens a clue to the limitations not only of (y) our science but of human identity as well, that very possession this naked monk seeks to dissolve in his methodical swallowing of the world's offal and mold. You hear the temple priests and vendors, the mendicants in wooden beads, the will to live (he reads) being an attitude embedded in the prolongation of order, a condition defined by mathematics. As everywhere, the ghosts of these experiences pass through each other, the beating of clothes on stone, sex inside mosquito nets. The shadow crosses into Bangladesh, thousands waiting on line and for each at best some pebbles of unleavened bread, control maintained by men with sticks. You read the grieving man's belief in the everydayness of the absolute. Families set down their mats and prepare to sleep on pavement, the empirical source, children stealing to live. To be Outside is to know an environment infinitely less complex than the one you left. Far from wishing to revisit misery, you are nonetheless able to experience once again some of the richness of inborn limits. You see our rapt entanglement in all around us, the press to measure and delve. There, see, in annotated ivory tools, lengths of notched wood, in the wave-guide manipulation of light and our nosings into the choreography of protons, we implicate ourselves in endless uncertainty. This is the ethic you've rejected. Inside our desolation, however, you come upon the reinforcing grid of works and minds that extend themselves against whatever lonely spaces account for our hollow moods, the woe incoming. Why are you here? To unsnarl us from our delimiting senses? To offer protective cladding against our cruelty and fear? The pain, the life-cry speak our most candid wonders. To out-premise these, by whatever tektite whirl you've mastered, would be to make us hypothetical, a creature of our own pretending, as are you. Geometric space of any number of dimensions. Awareness of not being self-aware. The metaphysical release at the center of the value-dark dimension. Intones the bony old man *sannyasa* in his scrambled loincloth *sannyasa* mud body oblivious to the vast ashen inevitability of all things that pertain to his particular snag of earth. With burial grounds full, people deposit bodies in shallow graves long bared by local dogs. Tourists photograph the corpses, human experience, scheduled collections made of bodies in the street. The shadow passes into the state of Assam, leaving behind these trophy bones of epic death, families sitting in the dust outside a feeding center, external reality, their eyes suspended forever in this medium of exaggerated nutrient humanity, surrounded as they wait by clamor, lamentation, audible drone of sacred names, as everywhere, all the plain-weave variations of supplicating noise, shadow moving swiftly into map-blue China, system of hushed assumptions.

Robert Hopper Softly in a natty black suit stood in a patch of bedazzling grass, briefcase in hand, a modernistic pair of dark glasses covering much of his face. Finally the somber prow of a limousine appeared at the top of the ramp that coiled on down to the main garage beneath the cycloid structure. As the Cadillac leveled out and moved slowly toward him, Softly found himself straightening up a bit, as though trying to occupy more fully some spectral frame of authoritarian ethics.

Something here made no sense. If, as the youngest of his colleagues had very recently stated, the lunar shadow first touched the earth at the universal (or Greenwich mean) time announced on the radio, and if only half an hour had passed from that moment to this, and if it was therefore midafternoon at the prime meridian, why, considering his (Softly's) position in terms of longitude east of Greenwich, wasn't it nighttime here? Not the deviant night of total solar eclipse but simple ordinary everyday night, the interval of darkness that accounts for an important part of every twenty-four hour period during which the earth completes a single rotation on its axis. Noncognate celestial anomaly living up to its name. Even if it wasn't getting on to night, it was definitely getting on to eclipse. Yes he sensed the shadow speeding toward him.

The driver brought the car to a complete stop. The man next to the driver leaned out the window toward Softly.

"I don't know about doing this."

"Open the door and let me in."

"You're not on the docket," the driver said.

"I don't have time to argue."

"We have a pickup to make in the other direction with delivery here."

"I want to go east."

"That's just it," the other man said.

"I'm anxious to get going."

"In the other direction there'd be no problem taking you," the driver said. "Being that's the way we're headed."

"Open the door," Softly said.

"If you were on the docket, we'd try to work things out."

"I'm suffering."

"In what sense suffering?"

"In the sense that I feel enmeshed in extreme unpleasantness."

The man nearest Softly turned toward the driver.

"He said he's suffering. Then he defined it."

"I heard."

"It's out of our way, where he wants to go. It's in completely the wrong direction."

"How far in miles?"

The man turned toward Softly.

"How far is it where you want to go in completely the wrong direction in miles?"

He stood in the dim light at the top of the elevator shaft and watched the guano buckets rising diagonally on aerial tramways, each container about the size of a living room, brimming with product.

"Get ready to jump out."

434

"When?"

"When we get there."

"Aren't you being premature?"

"Because I'm barely stopping."

Softly in the middle of the back seat looked straight ahead, fearful that even a brief glance out the side window might reveal an early trace of shadow. He was trying not to think clearly. This was a self-protective maneuver he used whenever confronted with the kind of dismal insight that caused twinges of professional shame. It was deplorably obvious, the matter he was trying not to think about. The eclipse, in a strictly logical sense, was no cause for fear, alarm, anxiety or dread, despite its unscheduled nature. Logically there is no connection between events. To believe otherwise is to fix oneself to a mystical intuition. An unforeseen eclipse is no more startling, logically, than an eclipse predicted decades or centuries earlier. That the latter event will take place is sheer conjecture. He knew this as surely as the fact that he was in distress. The mohole totality itself in no way contradicted the postulates of logical thought.

How, knowing this so surely, did I manage to forget it?

It wasn't forgetfulness, he realized, but a deeper than logical fear that drove him into flight. Fear (perhaps) of eclipse per se. A wish to bang on hollow objects. A need to chew the fleshy leaves of aloe plants. An impulse to hide oneself more fundamentally than was possible in the antrum. It wasn't his logic that had broken apart, or the world itself, but something more essential to the spiritual fact that bracketed his existence. He had never been in the path of a total eclipse. He had read about but never experienced the chill in the air, the cunning onset of dark, the sight of white villages, of animals seeking their nighttime roosts or holes, of nocturnal creatures stirring in the fugitive gloom, the general motivating tendency being one of rapid physical adaptation to a mistimed event. Was it possible that nothing more than his body had been deceived? If so, did it not follow that the phrase "nothing more than" referred, in successive reflections, only to itself? Of course, he thought, we continue to lack basic evidence that an eclipse is indeed taking place. With no simple rigid structure of judgmental data, we can't be sure it won't turn out in the end to be nothing more than rumor.

Keep believing it, shit-for-brains.

He took off the dark glasses, put them in the breast pocket of his suit coat and got down on hands and knees. The wind seemed to be subsiding. It was still light, still light. Some forewarning mechanism made him begin to crawl, knowing, everywhere, feeling it, a sense of violated space, the air itself infused with this infrared surprise. Experimentally he made some sounds. Huge cylinders full of guano moved diagonally through the dimness, powder rising in clouds. He climbed into the Cadillac.

He sat in the middle of the back seat, sweating incandescently, feeling as though his body were covered with pond scum. He lifted the briefcase onto his lap and felt around inside for the old glue bottle that contained his most extreme deliriant, a sudsy composite of lighter fluid, paint thinner, airplane glue, nail polish remover and several types of aerosol propellant. With some effort he removed the old-fashioned rubber cap (with brush attached). Then he held the sticky rim of the bottle right under his nose. He inhaled deeply several times, sitting primly in the geographic center of the back seat, his lids descending slowly behind the glasses.

"I think I see it," the driver said.

"In what sense do you mean that?" the other man said.

Softly nodding briefly into history pondered unopposed (by his own precedent) the mock battles that were fought in old Egypt and Mesopotamia to accompany the conflict suggested by various celestial events. In this way the crisis of time (of light that fades and season that ends) was made specific and personal, detached from abstraction. People translated the event into the sweating arcs of their own bodies, perhaps trying to act beyond their fear, inventing games to fill this crevice in the heavens. The briefcase was between his feet. He tapped his fingers on his knees. Fumes, nausea, salty moisture. Deciding to address the driver he opened his mouth slowly, half expecting to see a bubble emerge.

" 'We' 'are' 'here.' "

"Repeat," the driver said.

" 'It' 'is' 'time' 'for' 'me' 'to' 'get' 'out.' "

"I don't think my ears are hearing."

" 'Stop' 'the' 'car.' "

The wind was fairly strong. He handed his briefcase through the open window to the man at the passenger's end of the front seat. He stood for a moment a few feet from the car. He heard it start, turn and move off. Then he walked across the grass, still some light, and realized he was lurching even more than usual. He kept his head down. When he got to the edge of the hole he paused, syllogist of dire night.

"My ears hear."

The hole was roughly rectangular in shape. One side was less steep than the others and he chose this surface for his descent. He entered the hole more or less sitting down, his feet before him performing braking maneuvers, his hands employed to balance. At the bottom he stood up and brushed off the seat of his pants. He took off the dark glasses, put them in the breast pocket of his suit coat and got down on hands and knees. The wind seemed to be subsiding. It was still light, still light. Some forewarning mechanism made him begin to crawl, knowing, everywhere, feeling it, a sense of violated space, the air itself infused with this infrared surprise. Experimentally he made some sounds. He crawled the full length of the hole and entered the hole's hole. The tunnel began to slant downward as he moved into extreme darkness. The hole was low and narrow. He began to crawl faster. The rate of inclination gradually increased. His fingers scratched at the hard dirt. He made more sounds. There were sectors so narrow he had to chop and claw at the dirt walls to give himself room to move forward. The darkness was total now. His hand touched something cold and hard and he picked it up, a length of barely pliable metallic wire, twisted at one end, curved sharply at the other as if to fit over a hook or rod. He used it to clear the dirt in narrow areas, crawling faster now, the slope angling ever down. His hands felt scraps of clothlike material, thin strands of it, littered here and there along the floor of the hole. He moved forward into a large and slyly constructed object, human (it would seem) and covered (his hand determined) by whole cities of vermiculate life. Softly did not pause further to investigate for signs of pulse, heartbeat, so on. He crawled directly over the human object and straight into a solid mass of dirt. Again he did not pause. Using both hands he gouged out chunks of heavy earth. He made noises and sounds. His fingers scratched and clawed to clear a passage. He used the curved metallic object on areas where the dirt was firmest. The angle of descent was very severe. He continued to dig the hole's hole. The sounds he uttered became by degrees more rudimentary and crude. He crawled, knowing, he scratched at dirt, he clawed the hard earth, everywhere, feeling it, a sense of interlocking opposites, the paradox, the comedy, the fool's rule of total radiance.

Zorgasm.

On the surface another figure moved, this one on a white tricycle, heading the same way the Cadillac had come, madly pedaling, a boy a bit too large for his chosen means of transportation, knees bowed outward, elbows high and wide, head drawn into torso, his thumb on the small bell attached to the handlebar. He wore a jacket and tie. A measured length of darkness passed over him as he neared the hole and then he found himself pedaling in a white area between the shadow bands that precede total solar eclipse. This interval of whiteness, suggestive of the space between perfectly ruled lines, prompted him to ring the metal bell. It made no sound, or none that he could hear, laughing as he was, alternately blank and shadow-banded, producing as he was this noise resembling laughter, expressing vocally what appeared to be a compelling emotion, crying out as he was, gasping into the stillness, emitting as he was this series of involuntary shrieks, particles bouncing in the air around him, the reproductive dust of existence.